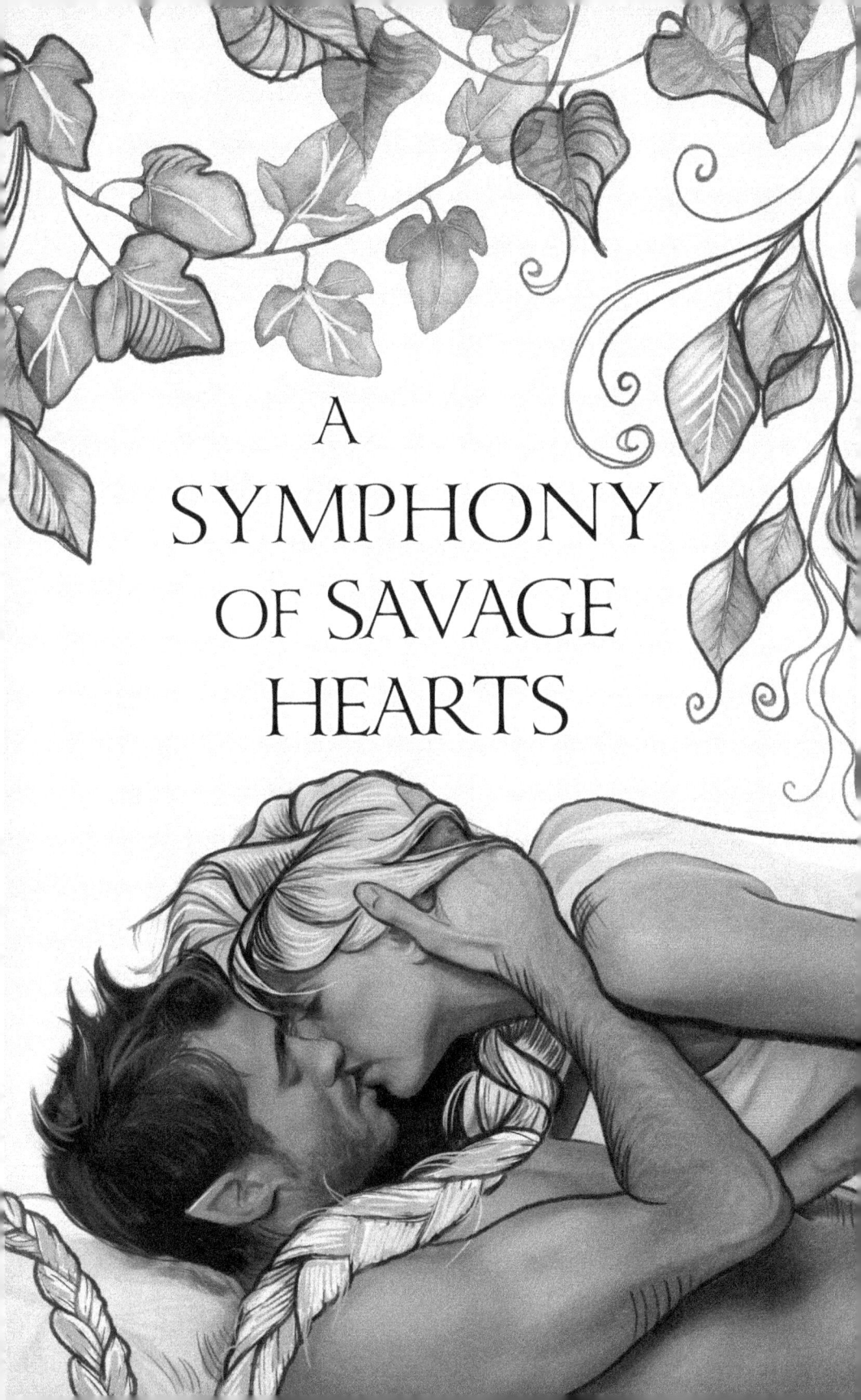

# A SYMPHONY OF SAVAGE HEARTS

A FAE GUARDIANS NOVEL

**LANA PECHERCZYK**

Copyright © 2022 Lana Pecherczyk
All rights reserved.

A Symphony of Savage Hearts
ISBN: 978-0-6450884-6-5

This is a work of fiction. Names, characters, businesses, places, events and incidents are either the products of the author's imagination or used in a fictitious manner. Any resemblance to actual persons, living or dead, or actual events is purely coincidental.

Text copyright © Lana Pecherczyk 2022
Cover design © Lana Pecherczyk 2022
Structural Editor: Ann Harth

www.lanapecherczyk.com

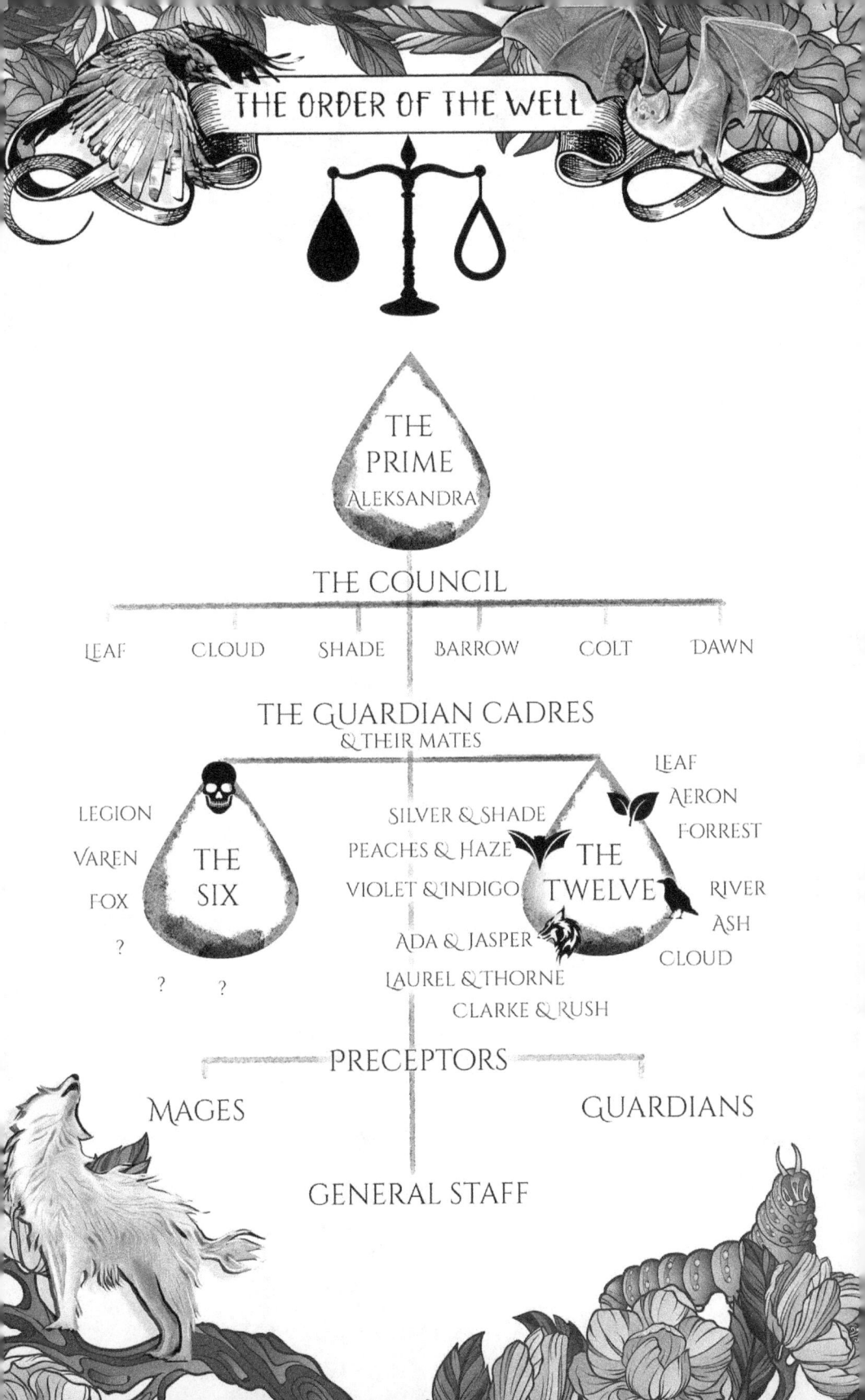

# PROLOGUE

Rory's boots clicked across chipped tiles in the Sky Tower greenhouse. It stank like moss rot and the air was thick, despite being hundreds of feet above sea level. Rusted iron frames barely held the windows and dome ceiling together. Howling wind battered the two stories of glass. Any minute, she expected the panes to crash down, but they held. Always had.

Plant specimens of all kinds filled spaces between pipes, cluttered tables, and spiral staircases. Between ferns, vines and palm leaves, taxidermy fae creatures watched with dead eyes. Bull horns and ivory tusks dangled from cages. Clockwork gadgets whirred. Copper boilers puffed steam to humidify the air. *Pip pip,* went the valve release ever so softly between ticking and chiming.

Rory patted a stuffed antlered rabbit as she cast her gaze about, searching for her father. She expected to see him by the table strewn with maps and cartography equipment, his impeccable suit pressed to a crisp and his shrewd gaze calculating. But he wasn't there.

Biting her lip, she held onto her tension a little longer and wiped her hand through condensation on a window to look outside. This lone tower existed at the epicenter of the grimy, crowded and diesel-stinking metropolis known as Crystal City to the outsiders. To her, it was simply home. It was all she'd known her entire life.

Down in the city, plumes of black smoke billowed and mixed with low-lying clouds frigid with cold weather. This tower had been here long before she played in the shadow of greenhouse palms as a child, and long before her father had wrested control from the previous inhabitant and married her mother—the daughter of the last leader, or so she'd been told. History books weren't kept. The unforgiving razor wire mesh soaring from the tower to the citadel walls was all her father's doing. It allowed daring—or stupid—winged creatures to drop in, but also ensured they never escaped.

She remembered the day it went up, but not why—what triggered the sudden defense tactic? For a moment, she imagined someone plucking glossy black feathers one by one. The room's ticking clocks and *pipping* steam became a teenager's scream. But that was all she could grasp from her rambling memory before clouds took it away. And then her father's commanding steps echoed in the room.

"There you are," he grumbled, as though he'd been searching for her.

She pursed her lips. "You asked me to meet you here. Where else would I be?"

His scowl caused the wrinkles to deepen across his pale skin. She didn't remember the distinguished gray hair at his temples being there. But maybe more time had passed than she realized. She often lost herself in her work—training Reapers for field missions, even though she wasn't allowed on them herself.

Often she was too busy to speak to her father for weeks. Months.

When had her father's right-hand man, Bones, left for the Seelie city? When had he been captured? Was that a week ago... more? She shook her head to disperse the brain fog that clung to her memory more with each passing day. *Didn't matter.*

Nero was her father. The leader of the free people. And the future savior of their kind. Before he'd come along, the human population was dwindling and bowing beneath the pressure of fae rules imposed on them. Under his leadership, humans had clawed their way back from the brink of extinction. But resources were dwindling again. There was only so much recycling and repurposing they could do.

Humans would not go quietly. They were on this planet first. They had rights as much as any other. It was time to up their offensive. From the dark intent in her father's close-set eyes, he thought the same thing.

"It's time," he said. "There is no room for failure. Send out a small group, including your most ruthless, heartless son-of-a-bitch."

"That would be me." Rory lifted her chin, then added for propriety, "Sir."

He clicked his tongue in disapproval. "One never reveals the ace up their sleeve until the last moment. No—send another Reaper."

She clenched her jaw, bristling at being caged again. She made one mistake when she was a teenager, and her father had never let her forget it. But her time would come, and when it did, pity the poor fool standing in her way.

"Fine," she said. He wanted their most heartless son-of-a-bitch? "I know just the person."

## CHAPTER
# ONE

Sweat and oil stuck to Silver's skin as she lay on a trolley beneath a half-built airship. Diesel fumes choked the air, but her respirator kept the worst from her lungs. She tinkered on the undercarriage mechanics of a new cannon. This was the first prototype she'd been able to fit to the blimp-style aviation craft. With what they knew about the fae, and what technology she could remember from her time, it was shaping up as a solid military vehicle.

God, it felt good to get her hands dirty again. To put them to use doing what she did best—engineering weapons. She enjoyed working with metal, from the welding side to the mechanics. And she was done lying about it. She was done feeling guilty about it.

Six years ago, give or take, she'd thawed out after being frozen for two thousand years following a nuclear winter. At first, she'd been horrified to learn what had happened to her world—fae existed now, and they were the apex predators, not humans. It was humans who'd dropped the bombs around the world. While she'd never had a direct hand in the catastrophic event, she had still worked in the weapons industry. Her guilt had kept her away from Crystal City for over a year. If someone discovered her vocation, they might force her to do something despicable. But then she stumbled across humans spelled by fae to perform music until their fingers bled, and her blood had boiled. The more she learned about human oppression, the more she remembered why she'd joined the military in the first place.

So she'd helped the humans escape Cornucopia... and then followed them here.

To her people.

A tug of guilt caused the wrench to slip in her hands. The faces of two women she'd thawed out with came to mind. Peaches and Violet. Both were from the old world, like her. And both had the same culpability when it came to working in fields directly linked to the nuclear holocaust. Silver had encouraged them to pretend to be fae—to hide their true identities in case they were used to create more destruction. At the time, her motivation had been true. She wasn't on board with anyone *ever* building another nuclear weapon... but she'd never been against non-nuclear war.

Sometimes it was necessary.

The people of Crystal City were starving, and the fae cared nothing for it. Bitterness laced her tongue. No... *cared nothing* was poor word choice. The fae cared enough to laugh. They ridiculed. They said the fae deserved the lush lands because they followed the rules of the Well.

And apparently humans weren't worthy of the planet because they used metal and plastic.

*Pfft.*

What a crock of shit. As if they could boil the human condition down to that.

In the undercarriage's gloom, she glanced at the silver-plated vambrace on her forearm. Score lines marked her fae kills, starting with the vampires that had tried to capture her and drain her dry when she'd first awoken in this time. To be fair, most of those kills were Violet's, but Silver had taken down one. If it were up to the fae, she'd not be wearing the metal at all. But this was where it got tricky. If there was no metal on her body, she'd be vulnerable to what lived inside her.

Footsteps shuffled near where her feet stuck out from the undercarriage. She glanced down the length of her body to the light at the end. Two sets of worn leather boots stopped nearby.

"Get to work," a gruff male voice said. Sounded like Angus, the aviation dock foreman.

"Here? With her?" A smaller, shaky male voice. The smaller set of boots angled toward her.

"Got a problem with that?" said Angus.

"Well... I just... ah, I heard some things. That's all."

"Just keep to yourself. And don't look her in the eyes."

Silver snorted. She wasn't *that* bad.

"What happens if I look her in the eyes?"

"She bit the nose off the last person who did."

The resulting gulp was audible. "Okay, got it. Don't look her in the eyes."

"And whatever you do, don't ask her for a kiss..."

*Fucking Angus.* Silver anchored herself on pipework and propelled her trolley from the bowels of the airship. Once out and wincing in the glaring overcast light, she stood and undid the strap on her respirator, so it flopped to one side of her face. She glared at the two surprised faces. Angus was a big, surly man with hair over his face and body. The other was a kid—male teenager. Brown puppy-dog eyes and fluff on his upper lip. Both wore grease monkey coveralls, just like her.

"Silver," Angus sputtered. "Didn't realize you were under there."

Bullshit. She'd heard everything. He just never expected her to come out and call him on his crap. She smiled, tossed her wrench to her left hand, and then punched him in the nose with her right. It was a fast, powerful jab. Straight and to the point. The resounding crunch of cartilage was satisfying. Let's hope he learned his lesson.

Angus's eyes watered as he clutched his nose. "Fucking bitch."

"That's for spreading lies about me," she snapped and then pointed her wrench at the kid. "To be clear, it was an ear, not a nose. And it had nothing to do with looking me in the eyes and everything to do with him trying to take more than a kiss."

The dark memory of an earlobe unnaturally necrotizing beneath her lips surfaced, but she shook it off and tossed the wrench down. It clanked and rolled until it hit their feet. A filthy feeling curled her lip. She tightened the laces on her vambrace to the point of pain, controlling the feeling of slipping, of tilting into the darkness. If she could get to her under-bust corset through the coveralls without being obvious, she would tighten it too. But revealing any sign of weakness around here was as good as a death sentence. There were too many mouths to feed as it was. Losing one to a brawl was no skin off the Regulator's noses.

"Silver," clipped a female voice behind her.

Speaking of Regulators, the city's police, she tensed as a steady hand rested on her shoulder. She shook it off with a snarl and turned, half expecting to face one for her assault on Angus, but came face-to-face with the president's daughter and captain of the Reapers. Rory was tall, athletic, with gray eyes and caramel skin. She could pass as Silver's sister if it wasn't for the fact they were born two millennia apart.

Rory folded her arms and glanced at Angus's bleeding face. Copper clamps on her chin-length afro dreadlocks tinkled as she gave a concerning shake of the head. She tapped a restless finger on her arm, copper-plated knuckle rings glinting in the overcast light.

Silver couldn't help compare her own outfit and Rory's. Where Silver wore greased and crumpled overalls, Rory's tailored uniform was pressed. The shaved side of her head only accentuated her copper and gold jewelry. Rare metal accents were a sign of affluence in this city. Copper for the high-ranking officials, silver for the Reapers, gold for the president.

Silver flicked her unadorned, bleached braid and let the long length settle down her spine.

"He asked for it," she said. Not that she needed to explain herself. Her silver status far outranked someone like Angus and even the Regulators, whose only metal adornments were iron. The sad part was that she was still a grunt. Her rank gave her zero standing in Sky Tower. It was only pertaining to missions out in Elphyne that she had the power to make any decisions.

Rory's nostrils flared. Then she sighed. "Whatever. I'm not here for that. It's time."

"What?"

"Gather your team. I want you gone by dusk."

Team? A scoff burst from Silver's lips. She picked up the wrench, flipped it in her hand and walked away, shaking her head. *I can't believe this.* Silver hadn't had a team in over a year. "Too reckless" were the words Rory had used to describe Silver's behavior on her last mission, and now that she'd had some distance, she had to be thankful for the change in pace. Working with her hands, reconnecting with what she loved, had been good for the soul.

With purpose in her stride, Silver's legs made short work of the journey through the bustling riverside dock. Since the first airship prototype had passed a year ago, more ships were being built. A sky battle fleet to replace the derelict battleship wrecks they salvaged for parts. They would never have enough metal resources to make advanced vehicles like the old Apaches she used to work on. After the nuclear fallout, the quarantined humans spent centuries simply trying to survive in their underground bunkers while the weather and fae were mutating outside. Much knowledge was lost. Airships were a mix of old technology and new. *Better than nothing.*

Rory's boots pounded the pavement beside Silver as she made her way to the staff change rooms. The city's opaque crystal walls were on one side, the dock, its buildings, and the river on the other. They moved out of the aeronautics zone and into the nautical where fisherman hauled catches and raiders prepared for missions.

She'd gotten used to the smell of ill-drained sewage mixed with salty brine. She'd even gotten used to the trash in the streets. But she would never get used to the beggars and the malnourished sick who'd escaped the city gates for fresh air and scavenging.

They passed a stoop with a broken awning. A toothless, middle-aged woman in a moth hole riddled blanket reached out. A small blond girl with dreadlocks and probably lice clung to her legs. Rory kept walking, but Silver stopped.

The little girl's eyes widened when she saw Silver. "Aunty!"

Silver's heart tugged. She'd given the child an apple once, and apparently, now she was family. All she had in her pockets were tools today. No precious fruit. No dried meat. She gave the girl a fist bump instead.

"Hey Princess Polly," Silver smiled, then greeted her mother solemnly. "Carla."

The woman's confused eyes tried to focus on Silver, but they were too glazed to hold any sort of recognition. She stumbled into Silver. Gangrene fingers peeking from fingerless gloves plucked at Silver's greasy overalls. For what, Silver wasn't sure. The woman was too confused.

Rory twisted, saw Silver had stopped, and pursed her lips. "We need to get going."

"Why aren't you inside?" Silver asked Carla gently, gathering her disheveled blanket and tightening it to stop it from falling. Coming outside the city gates was perilous, especially with a child. Winged fae could attack without the protection of the barbed wire net overhead. She glanced down at Polly. "Where's Jimmy?"

Jimmy was Carla's fourteen-year-old son. When he wasn't working in the factories, he was scrounging and selling anything he could find to keep his mother and sister fed, warm, and alive.

"Jimmy?" Carla's eyes focused. Her voice sounded fluid and thick, as though she had a cold. "He's finding us food and medicine."

"Okay, well, don't you think it's better for Polly if you wait for him inside?"

Carla's eyes watered as she shook her head. "I'm their mother. I should provide for them."

Silver's throat closed. As much as she hated to admit it, Polly's and Carla's situation was a dime a dozen here in Crystal City. Too many people were without food, medicine, and clean living spaces. Silver beckoned to Rory.

"Give her a copper bead," she urged.

When no answer came, Silver glared. But the lieutenant's expression crossed from impassive to incredulous.

"I could give her all my copper and it would make no difference." Rory's hard eyes turned annoyed. "You know that."

Goddamn it, she did. The metal was precious because it was rare, but in terms of monetary value here on the streets, it was worthless. Crystal City had no currency. Everyone had a job, an expertise, and they were trained to do their part. In return, their welfare was looked after. But the problem was, these supplies were coming in short from the top. The elite living in Sky Tower stashed essentials for themselves. Silver had a fair idea of where to find the items, but even if she raided the stores, it didn't solve the bigger problem—humans needed to get out of this drab place. They needed virile land and sun. They needed what the fae hoarded.

Silver stared into the eyes of a woman she'd once thought her friend. But the past few years had changed Rory, and Silver couldn't put her finger on why. Rory used to be more welcoming, warmer, even laughed a few times. This war was changing all of them.

The sound of footsteps had them all bustling to the side as three fishermen ran toward an alley headed back riverside. Rory grabbed one's collar as he passed.

"What's happening?"

The fisherman's eyes widened when he realized who had stopped him.

"The p-p-president," he stuttered. Those wide eyes filled with awe. "Your f-father. He's giving a speech."

Rory grunted and shoved him away. She turned to Silver, probably to urge them to keep walking so she could explain exactly what it was Silver refused to do, but Silver wanted to hear what Nero had to say. If he was down at the docks, then there could be news. Maybe a raider ship had come in. Too many were disappearing on the water, or lost in Elphyne if they had to make an emergency exit through a portal.

Then again, Nero could be there to calm the growing unrest about supply shortages.

Silver followed the fisherman to where a small crowd had gathered around a man standing on a wooden crate. With the river and sky as his backdrop, Nero stood resplendent in his navy tailored suit, polished gold trim luminous in the dull light. Gray streaks at his temples, a Roman nose, and wrinkles around his eyes only added to the appearance of a man who knew what he was doing. She stood at the edge of the crowd and tuned in to his speech.

"... the fae didn't build the world. It was there before any of them. It was there before *us*." He paused for effect. "But we were here first. If anyone has a right to it, we do." Cheers rang out. Nero met the eyes of many, connecting with them as he continued with narrowed eyes and a hard voice. "*Of course* they don't want us to use metal, because it will help humans to rise above their oppression. *Of course* they refuse to trade with us. They're afraid their people will discover our value. And *of course* they humiliate and torture us because they're afraid of *us*."

Murmurs of agreement rolled around the crowd, and Silver couldn't help being one of them. How else could she explain the fae's unwillingness to negotiate, or even trade with them? They must be terrified the human way of life will infect theirs, and God forbid any of the fae having a choice.

"They want to destroy everything that makes us human. They want to erase *our history*," Nero continued. "They want to smother it as though we never existed. But humanity has survived for thousands of years. What makes them better than us? What makes their children better than ours? We were bred tough. We're not going to give up now. They might have magic, but we've got heroes who go out there with nothing but their skin and each other for backup to face the evil—" His eyes landed on Silver, and he pointed. "Heroes like her."

All eyes shifted to Silver. Time paused. Then a deafening roar of approval shook the wooden deck at her feet. Bile rose in her gullet, and her vambrace seemed to constrict on her forearm. They called her a hero, but she wasn't so sure.

Rory slanted a meaningful look at her, as if to say, *See? We need you.*

With a growl of frustration, Silver pivoted on her heels and headed toward the staff change room. She didn't stop until the swinging door closed behind her.

Long, low benches separated rows of lockers. Silver ignored Rory's entrance after her and found her spot. She pounded on her locker door with a fist until it swung open. She shoved her wrench and respirator inside. Tools were precious down here at the docks. You had to keep them secure.

After her items settled, Silver stayed staring at the shadows within. They seemed to reach out and take hold of her by the throat. *Heroes like her.* She itched to take the coveralls off and tighten the corset.

Rory's watchful eyes felt like an oven at her back.

"You said I didn't have to leave again," Silver whispered, refusing to face the woman standing behind her.

"Things change."

Silver's fists clenched.

Rory stepped closer. "You're the only one equipped for this mission. I wouldn't ask otherwise."

"No." Silver tugged on the vambrace laces.

"You haven't even heard what it is."

"I don't need to."

"People are starving."

"I know that."

"Every time we send a team into Elphyne, they don't come back. The fae are bolder with their retaliation. You saw the state of Alice's mind when she returned. You know Bones hasn't come back. Do this one thing and then that's it."

"That's what you said last time."

"Didn't peg you for a scaredy cat."

Silver whirled and hissed, "You know that's not the reason."

Unflinching, Rory faced Silver's fury. She might be the only person in Crystal City who stood a chance against Silver's fists. She'd trained Silver, after all. But she was also the only person who knew the truth if Silver let herself go. And that was why she was here. She squeezed her eyes shut as her memory slaughtered her.

"No," she cried and tried to hold the rapidly decaying body, but it crumbled beneath her touch. "No, no, no."

But nothing she did reversed it. The black poison poured from her heart and coated the man before her, infecting his every cell, turning it to *black ash, freezing his face in an eternal scream. The single rose in his hand, withering and dying.*

Rory's gray eyes dipped to the vambraces. "Take extra protection."

"I could be covered in metal, and it would make no difference if it was taken off."

They stared bleakly at each other, considering.

"I'll have something made for you," Rory offered.

At the idea of new armor, Silver almost capitulated.

Instead, she said, "Too risky."

Rory sighed and trailed her copper knuckles along a locker, clanking and knocking against the surface. Her eyes defocused as she spoke. "Every time we wake up, there is risk. Before I step outside my room, I think, will today be the day we run out of food?"

Silver pulled the scarf from her head. She tossed it into the locker. "You're laying it on thick, you know."

"I don't need to. You saw the state of Polly's mother. Building the airships will mean nothing if there are no people left to pilot them."

"In a city of almost a million, I doubt that." Silver slammed the locker door shut and faced her superior. But her words felt flat. They were the last ounce of defense against the guilt of her potential and past. She sighed and met Rory's eyes. "I don't have a choice, do I?"

"No."

"What is the mission?"

"A simple extraction."

"One of our own?"

"Sort of. The child of someone who used to be one of our own, or so my father tells me. I've not met her."

Silver's eyes narrowed. "Then how do you know this is true?"

"I don't question Nero, and neither should you. We need this child because she'll replace the psychic we lost. We need you because once you have the kid, no one will mess with you. You'll bring her safely home, unharmed."

Queasiness churned in Silver's gut. She'd never kidnapped before. This was next level shit. Her mind traveled to Polly and Nero's speech. *What makes them better than us? What makes fae children better than ours?*

"Fine," she said. "But make my armor a corset type breast plate. I need more support."

# CHAPTER
# TWO

A mile away from Crystal City, Shade lounged on the long bough of a tall, leafless tree. Small clumps of snow spilled as his leather clad leg dangled and swung restlessly while he watched the gate in the distance.

His eyes burned from holding a steady gaze, but he refused to remove his sight for an instant. It was bad enough he had to sleep during the day, but now that it was night, if he blinked and his mate emerged and somehow evaded him... a swell of something he could almost compare to panic rose within his chest and that was ridiculous.

Shade never panicked.

He planned. He waited. And what he wanted came to *him*.

He rubbed his chest. The ache was probably thirst. Every night for the past five months, he'd drunk the blood of rodents and other forest creatures stupid enough to wander nearby. Thanks to a choice taken from him, he now craved Well-blessed human blood.

Everything else tasted like cardboard. No matter how many creatures he supped on, the gnawing need remained.

*Not for long.*

Refocusing on steel gates between the opaque crystal walls a mile away, Shade pulled a pouch from his pocket and removed a lock of silver hair to count the strands. Only ten left. Violet and Peaches had donated the lock so he could cast a tracking spell and locate this fated woman. The hair belonged to their friend—another who'd thawed from a two-thousand-year sleep.

Shade had never trusted humans, but this woman's power was foretold by the Order's psychics to be strong. She would be a formidable partner for Shade, plus one feed from her would satisfy his insatiable cravings—this incessant dark whisper in his ear to claim and take and gorge on any creature he could sink his fangs into. One feed from her would sustain him for weeks.

Her name was Silver.

Just like her hair.

Just like the forbidden. Poison wrapped in a pretty package. Or so he'd been told.

He'd waited five months for her to emerge from the fortress, and nothing. Only two Guardians had ever been inside the city walls and come out alive. There was so much contraband in there, that access to the Well cut off, rendering any fae impotent where magic was concerned. Shade shuddered at the thought.

Rush, a wolf shifter in the Cadre of Twelve, wasn't much help in assisting Shade to get inside without being noticed. Rush had been cursed and invisible at the time he'd entered the city. Unless Shade wanted to court the inky side of the Well and risk the chaos a curse brought—including possible death—then he had to find another way to get in.

Shade's gift was walking through shadows. He could step through them to another place in Elphyne, almost like portaling. It relied on access to the Well. Any spell created to hide his identity and pointed ears and fangs would also be cut the moment he passed through the gates. He'd be vulnerable the moment he entered the city.

A rustle of wings announced the arrival of company. Metal, leather, and dirty male sweat told Shade they were Guardians straight from a mission. One landed on a branch to his left, and the other on Shade's bough, tipping his balance, creaking the wood, and spilling more snow.

Cloud, a tattooed crow shifter, crouched. Loose dark curls fell over his blue eyes as he judged the snow-covered swamp beneath them. He broke a twig off the thick branch and used it to scratch between his black, feathered wings. For someone who'd once been held prisoner and tortured in the city, the Guardian was remarkably calm.

"When was your last feed?" Indigo asked, drawing Shade's attention back to him.

Recently mated to a Well-blessed human, Indigo had never looked better. Color flushed his olive-toned cheeks. Mischief danced in his eyes. And he had the nerve to judge Shade for being in the same situation he was six months ago.

Shade hugged himself against the cold. Why were they here, anyway? Shade's mate was none of their business. Unless...

"Has Clarke had another vision?" he asked, hope lifting.

Indigo shook his head and returned a concerned look. "She's

been in a sleep-state for days. Rush thinks she's stuck in a psychic dream."

That couldn't be good.

Clarke was Rush's mate, and the first Well-blessed human to wake from the old world. Well, that's what they'd initially thought. It turned out others had been awake for years, hidden among the fae and humans. Prophecy said more would come. Some would join the fae, some would join the humans, and this coming battle over the last habitable land on earth would be the last.

Shade returned to watching the gate. "If you've come to take me back to the Order, you're wasting your time."

Cloud and Indigo shared a look that said they'd been talking about Shade. His lip curled, knowing exactly what they would have been saying. That Shade was on a fool's errand. That his mate might never leave Crystal City. That there were more pressing matters to attend to.

Unseelie High Queen Maebh had all but declared war on the Order, closing her borders to travelers. As if this looming war between humans and fae wasn't bad enough, the fae had to squabble amongst themselves.

Indigo packed a ball of snow in his hands. "Maebh still hasn't opened Unseelie borders. And there are reports of a new monster causing havoc in Elphyne. We think it's the one she created in her basement."

"You mean the one she denies exists?" Shade drawled. Since he'd left Maebh's employ decades ago, she'd spiraled into someone he failed to recognize. Once, Shade had considered being Maebh's royal consort. The power of such a position was everything he'd dreamed of, but when the position was within his grasp, he found he no longer wanted it and couldn't explain why. Maebh was raving mad.

"This beast is hunting all over Elphyne," Indigo said, still packing his ball.

"You'll handle it on your own."

Indigo and Cloud shared another loaded look.

"Spit it out," Shade clipped. "What aren't you telling me?"

If the Prime of the Order of the Well wanted Shade back, she could come here and ask him herself. After decades of service, she owed him this time. Besides, the Order needed Silver on their side.

Shade turned to Cloud, knowing he'd give a straight answer.

Cloud tossed the twig he'd been scratching with. Contempt twisted his features. "Before he was a monster, he was the human named Bones."

Shade tensed. He was sure Cloud had history with Bones. Something had happened between the two while Cloud was a prisoner in Crystal City over a century ago. The humans in charge had been perverting mana to keep themselves young. Who knew what other atrocities they committed behind those walls?

And Maebh had taken tips from Bones and experimented on him in her dungeons. Shade vaguely remembered the man had been chained and hung on a blood-stained wall, his body mutating and warping despicably. But at the time, Shade had been under the influence of Maebh's magic and unable to control his own functions. The queen and Shade had a long, convoluted history that went from a brothel to her bedroom as an amaro—as one of her harem.

Dismissing the memories, he studied Cloud. Power enhancing tattoos covered him from neck to toe, except the face. There was something else underlying Cloud's expression—something other than the usual permanent scowl. The unnamed emotion amplified every time Cloud stared at the city in the distance.

"Still don't see what this creature has to do with me," Shade said.

"Demogorgon. That's what she's called it," Indigo said. "And it's attacked your childhood home."

"What?" The brothel he'd grown up in? Surely it was a coincidence that Maebh's creature had attacked it. A flicker of doubt passed over him. Was Maebh still holding a grudge about his defection? Were the Rosebud Courtesans alright? "Are they okay?"

"No one is dead, but it can't be a coincidence it's your old home she's targeted."

"They're her own subjects," Shade gaped, wide-eyed.

"It doesn't seem this creature has a moral compass. It's picking through everyone. Hunting."

Shade shook his head with a frown. "It's probably just collateral damage. A coincidence."

"That's what we thought at first," Cloud said. "But then we realized some of the other attack sites were places you'd visited recently."

"*Fuck.*" This was just what Shade needed. He scrubbed his face.

"There's more," Indigo added. "We've yet to lay eyes on this creature, but we've seen the devastation it's caused. Witnesses are saying it's unstoppable."

"That's what they all say until a Guardian turns up."

Silence settled. Shade's gaze darkened on the city. Time was running out. He needed to find Silver and get back to work.

"Brother, I know you don't want to hear this... but it's time to come back to the Order," Indigo said.

"Nope."

"Shade—"

"I said, no." He shot daggers at Indigo, who only scowled in chagrin and tossed his snowball at Shade's head. Shade dodged and then shoved him off the bough. Indigo was adept at flying, but the ground was too close. He splashed into the snow littered mud.

Cloud snorted. Shade glared at the crow shifter, but he only stared at the city. Shade had the sense he waited to speak with Shade privately. Indigo caught the hint, brushed off the mud and flipped his middle finger up at Shade.

"Fine," Indigo clipped. "I'm going. But the next fae who comes won't ask nicely."

With that, Indigo flew away.

"You may as well join him," Shade said to Cloud. "I'm not leaving until I have her."

"No pussy is worth your life." Contempt skipped over Cloud's expression. "Believe me."

"Look at you," Shade drawled. "All worried about my life."

His knuckles whitened around the branch, pushing splinters into his skin. How could he explain his thoughts to a fae who saw things in black and white? Kill or be killed was Cloud's motto. Fuck commitment. Fuck ties to anyone but himself.

Shade expected the crow shifter to snap back at him, as he usually did, but there was one thing about this situation that Cloud understood.

"Once I claim her," Shade said. "I'll have power."

Cloud studied his tattooed knuckles. In the darkness, the ink gave off a greasy luminescence like an oil slick. When Cloud used his fists in battle, extra power imbued his strike. If there was anyone in the Cadre of Twelve who might understand Shade's need for power, it was this male beside him.

Cloud lifted his gaze and stared at the city for so long and hard that Shade wondered if a female was the cause of his hatred for the city. Why else make the proclamation he did? Maybe he'd been lured in when he was a young daring thief too naïve to recognize a bad egg.

Shade flicked snow at the crow. "If you know something that will help me get inside, say it."

Thunder rolled in Cloud's glare, but he said nothing.

"So, why are you here?"

"Fuck you too," Cloud snapped back.

Shade was getting nowhere with Cloud, so he tossed a single strand of Silver's hair into the air and summoned his mana to weave a tracking spell. He wasn't sure why he kept doing the spell. He knew she was in the city, but a part of him hoped she'd have the guts to leave and come toward Elphyne. It would make his life easier, and it would also mean his mate wasn't a push over.

He also worried she'd leave during the day when he wasn't watching, and the only way of knowing was to continuously check.

A blue glowing aura coated the strand as it floated from his hand, hovering for a moment before gliding toward the city. Shade stood on the leafless bough and stretched his aching wings. Then he took to the night and tracked the glowing hair's path across the dead forest, leaving Cloud behind.

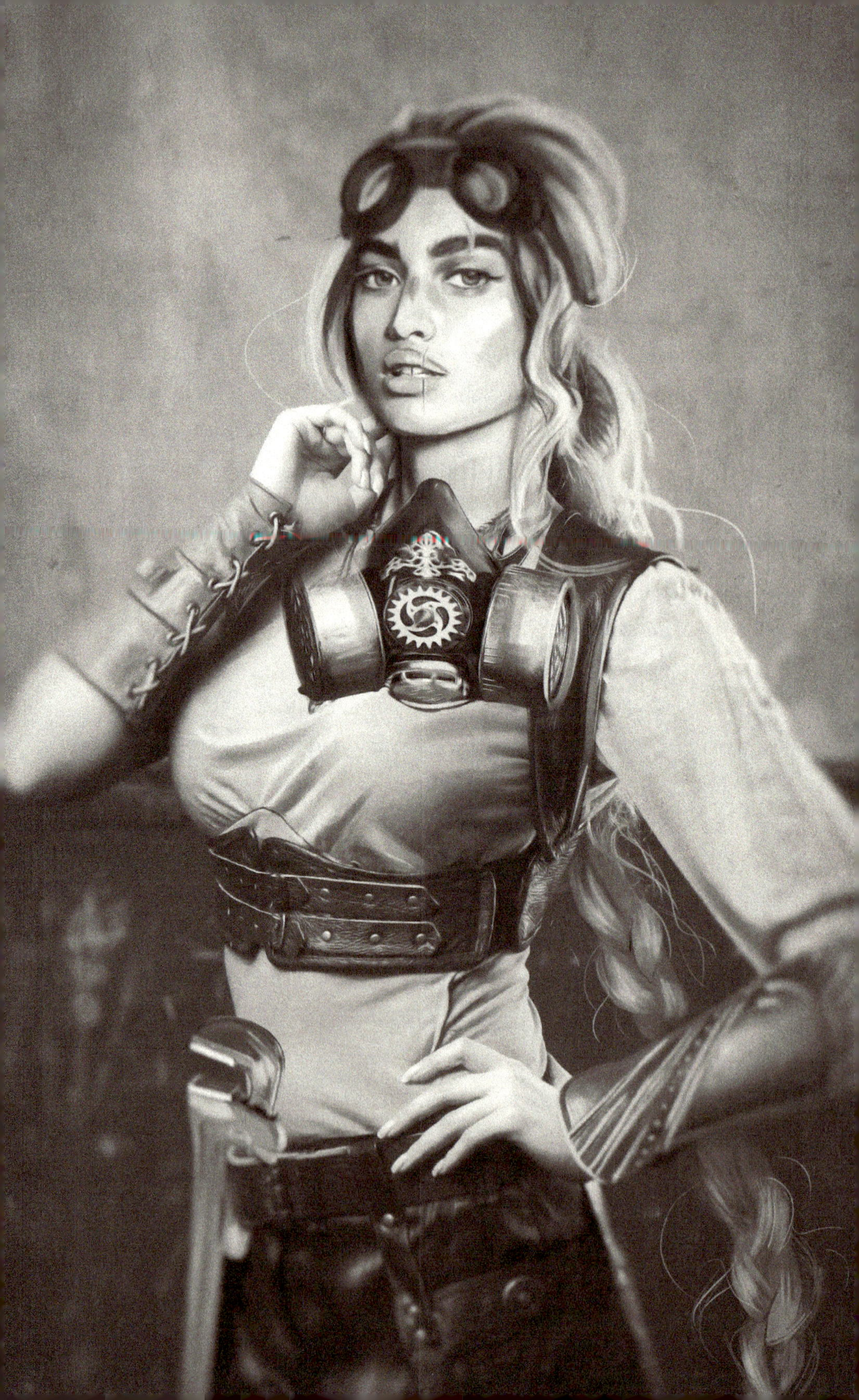

# CHAPTER THREE

Ignoring the icy wind, Silver hoisted her backpack over her wool-lined jacket and secured the strap around her new silver breastplate. True to request, Rory had commissioned armor that cinched like a corset, yet provided the added protection of metal against claws and other nasty attacks. It finished above her hips to allow movement and had easy access laces at the front in case she needed to release the dark power trapped inside her.

But she would be on death's door before that happened. The consequences were too dire otherwise. Unbidden, she remembered the frozen look of horror on the fae her power had killed. It knocked out her breath. She didn't think she'd ever forget that face. That mix of both helplessness and confusion. The fae had only wanted to give Silver a rose, but ended up ash for his troubles.

Silver briefly wondered if Peaches and Violet were also afflicted with a curse like hers, or if this special brand of punishment was made just for her.

Standing inside the city gates, she glanced at her three strong male companions. All Reapers. All special ops soldiers trained to kill—like her. None of them would stand a chance against Silver's black poison.

Martin was a dark-skinned man with a buzz cut. Roger had three scars running down his pale, freckled face. The same fae monster had wounded Silver, but where she'd escaped with a single narrow mark across her eyebrow and upper lip, Roger's scars had deformed him. He despised Silver.

The third man was someone Silver knew well—Sid, her ruggedly handsome and casual hookup with issues of his own. As he tied his caramel hair into a bun, his roaming gaze landed on her and then skated away. Like her, the man wasn't into love. He'd never asked questions about her vambrace or corset, even when she'd insisted on wearing them during sex. Probably thought it was a kink.

The entirety of their relationship consisted of turning up at each other's apartment when they needed relief. They banged in silence, and they never spoke about it again. As far as Silver knew, Sid had no personality, emotion, or political desire. He was a walking, killing, fucking machine. That was it.

Suited her fine.

She squinted at the moon peeking over the city's mined quartz walls. The temperature had dropped, but snowfall wasn't imminent. Just a cool, crisp night. *Time to go.*

Once certain they were packed and ready, she rubbed her gloved hands together and nodded to the gatekeeper. He pulled a lever and activated the portcullis. As the heavy grate lifted, the outer doors opened and fresh air gushed in.

The journey into the heart of Elphyne was through a muddy and bereft forest before trekking across an arctic tundra, over mountains, and through another forest. *Piece of cake.* It would take them around two weeks to get to their destination—the Order of the Well.

"*Get in,*" Rory had said. "*Get the kid, then get out and come home.*"

"Let's do this," Silver said to her team.

She patted her backpack and checked to see if the most important tool was still there. It looked like a pocket watch, but when opened, it turned into a clockwork transceiver. It even had a wind-up battery charger. The Crystal City Tinker and Silver had worked together on the prototype to ensure they had what they needed, when they needed it. She checked the weapons cached on her body. Two mechanical pistols in holsters, along with knives, a flash-bang, and a grenade. None of them were built to the standards in Silver's time, but they were better than swords and bows and arrows. Reassured, her gaze trained on the dead forest a mile away, and she walked forward.

Halfway to the forest, Silver stopped. Howling wind gusted, carrying the sound of running footsteps. The full moon allowed clear vision of the field they'd just crossed. Silver tensed and signaled for her team to be vigilant as they tracked the figure running toward them from the gate.

She almost thought she was imagining things when he came into focus. It was Jimmy, Polly's brother—Carla's teen son. He was decked out like he was going on a camping trip. Knives and a pistol holstered at his hip. Blond hair stuck up from the wind. Pimples around his nose. Backpack. Cold weather gear.

He stopped before them, eyes bright, chest heaving. "Take me with you."

*Did his voice just give a pubescent crack?*

Silver shot her team a look of surprise. Sid returned a blank face. Martin shrugged. Roger's scarred lip curled as if to say... *You're the leader. You deal with it.*

"Go back, Jimmy," she said. "Your sister needs you."

"That's why I'm here," he returned and tried to fist bump her. The action reminded her of Polly.

She pointed back to the city. "Turn back before you regret it."

His expression hardened. "I'm not scared of you. I want to learn from you. Rory said this might be your last mission, so I figured it was my last chance."

"Turn back now," she ground out. "Before I clock you and send you back unconscious."

"Then clock me." The stupid teen lifted his jaw. "But I want to help. Ma is sick because there ain't no medicine. Polly will be next. Rory said she'd get me some if I help you. I've got a good memory. I can be a runner for messages."

She had the radio transceiver for that, but couldn't say it. The true purpose of this mission was a secret only half of them were privy to. While Silver knew about the psychic kid, the rest thought they were there to commit a guerrilla attack on the Order. The fewer people that knew, the better.

This was the last thing Silver needed. Her fist curled, ready to discourage Jimmy. While she respected his drive, the fae wouldn't care. Jimmy was a human invading their territory. If they didn't kill him on sight, they'd entrap him in his own mind and force him to work for them.

"Little fucker," she muttered.

Roger snickered.

Martin started walking. "It's his choice."

His words triggered a memory, dragging her two thousand years into the past.

*"It's my choice!"* she said to her mother.

*"But who's going to look after me?"* her mother whined.

*"I've been looking after you since I was eight years old. You're the one who's supposed to look after me!"*

*"But, precious—"*

*"Cut it, Mom! Maybe stop looking for help down the end of a bottle and you'll be fine."*

Goddammit.

Irritated, Silver shook the reminder away. Thousands of years gone and still her mother had a way of weaseling into her thoughts.

She narrowed her gaze on Jimmy as he jogged away. She supposed she knew what he felt. He understood it was dangerous venturing into Elphyne. He would most likely get killed. But if he did survive, he'd return stronger.

That was the thing with humans and this brewing war. They wanted the right to choose. And if that choice was to accept metal and forgo the magic of the Well, then so be it. Humans had lived for millennia without magic; they could do it again. But the fae wanted their way or the highway. It wasn't right. People were different. They should be allowed to want different things.

And Jimmy was old enough to make this choice.

She sighed and walked on.

"Just what do you think we're doing here, Jimmy?" Silver asked as they arrived at the forest's edge and assessed the way forward.

Vines dangled from skeletal trees and swayed in the breeze. Wood creaked in the wind. Shadows loomed.

"I just want to learn to be like you guys."

"Why didn't you join the Reaper training crew, then?"

A guilty look flashed over his face. Shit.

"He didn't ask, did you, kid?" Roger nudged him with his fist.

"Rory has no idea you're here, does she?"

He shook his head sheepishly.

"You're going to get killed, you know that, right?" She roughhoused him by the collar. "Then who will look after Polly?"

"I'll be fine." But as the words came out of his mouth, his worried eyes darted to the woods. "I'll be fine."

"There's still a chance to go back," Silver urged. "Run straight back over that field and don't stop until you hit the gate."

Roger sent her a look that said she was a wimp for even suggesting it. She scowled back at him, daring him to test that theory.

Howling came from deep within the forest, reminding Silver she had no time to worry about a shadow following her. Nothing grew well in the woods, but magical twisted things had evolved to survive in the destitute landscape to make it their home. She supposed if Jimmy could get through this part, he would do okay in Elphyne. This would be a test.

Silver signaled for them to move onward.

Moonlight dimmed the further they penetrated the dead forest. Spindly, snow-capped trees blocked light until shadows amplified. Her team became watchful. Jimmy became twitchy. The higher, more civilized fae weren't often in this forest but word had gotten around Crystal City that some kind of winged creature hunted here. For a Reaper team, one fae should be no problem to handle, whether it was civilized or not.

They walked in silence for a few hundred feet until the twigs, overgrown roots, and tree trunks crowded them on all sides. Only their cloudy breaths, the crunch underfoot, and the occasional small animal's call made any sound.

"It's so dark," Jimmy whispered. He shivered. "And cold."

"Shh," Roger hissed.

"Aren't you scared?"

"Sing a song in your head," Silver suggested. Her go-to song was *Kokomo* by the Beach Boys. She felt like she was in a movie montage when she sang it, and for a while, life wasn't so scary.

"*Shh*," Martin added.

Silver glanced at Jimmy. He hunched over his pistol, eyes darting too fast to catch danger in the darkness. His jacket wasn't made for the elements. How he would last the trip was beyond her. First she gave him her gloves, then she tugged her rudimentary night-vision goggles from her head and handed them to him. They were nowhere near as advanced as the kind made in her time, but they did the job. She fitted them over his blond fluffy head and switched them on. A mechanical whirr ticked as electrons triggered the lens. His awe was worth the sacrifice.

Damn. She was getting soft.

This wasn't true darkness anyway. Not like what lived inside her. When that came... then she'd be afraid.

So much technology had been lost, but there were others like Silver who'd awoken from a deep freeze caused by the nuclear winter. Science couldn't explain how they'd survived. For a moment, a sliver of bitterness hit Silver as she thought about all the advancements the fae rules had cost humans. Those goggles allowed humans to see almost as well as nocturnal fae. Giving that advantage up so others could access this destructive and often chaotic magic seemed stupid.

*They want to destroy everything that makes us human*, Nero had said. *They want to erase our history.* She believed it.

It was all a matter of perspective.

Bad humans built the bomb that almost destroyed the world, but give the fae enough time and they would eventually find a way to use mana to do the same. They already were. Humans and fae weren't so different from each other. There were good ones. There were bad ones. And then there were ones like Silver, who existed somewhere in between.

A sound caught between a grunt and a gasp made her lift her pistol and aim into the thick of the forest. She strained through the shadow to count her men. Sid. Martin. But where was Roger? Heart thumping, she trained her weapon in a three-sixty, searching through the darker recesses between tree trunks and vines.

Silver caught Sid's eyes. His unreadable expression gave nothing back. She checked Martin—also calm and watchful.

"Where's Roger?" she mouthed silently.

*Thud.* Something landed behind her. Jimmy whimpered. She whirled to find Roger writhing on the ground, spluttering and clutching his throat as blood dribbled between his fingers. Not a gush. He'll live. Silver aimed her pistol into the branches.

"Vampire," she hissed and pulled out her windup torch to blind the fucker. Thankfully, she'd cranked it before leaving. She clicked it on and directed the beam into the branches.

"Oh God oh God." Jimmy crouched and checked on Roger.

"Bastard bit me," Roger grumbled.

*He's talking. He's fine.*

Roger stumbled to his feet and pulled out his pistol before cocking it and taking aim into the darkness.

Jimmy mimicked, but pulled the trigger, firing on air. The bullet cracked and echoed loudly through the forest.

"Stop!" Silver put her hand on his, lowering his firearm. It was bad enough she'd shone the torch, but the sound would carry and make them targets for anything else looking for a quick meal. There was a chance the winged creature hunting in these woods had nothing to do with the vampire.

Jimmy's hand trembled, shaking the pistol at his side. "We're gonna die."

"We're not going to die." She mentally kicked herself for letting him come and shoved him against a tree trunk. "Get down and wait."

She joined her team and quickly combed the area. Each Reaper stalked along, finger on the trigger. One bullet in the vampire was all they needed.

She could almost feel its eyes watching, studying.

"Did you see it?" Martin whispered to Roger.

Roger's jaw clenched. "Male. Winged. It took me up, bit me, then—" He frowned and stumbled, eyes drooping from the histamines in the vampire's bite. "Fucker spat out my blood and disappeared. *Poof.* Just like that. I dropped."

"Disappeared. Like, he teleported?" Silver asked, the hairs on the back of her neck prickling.

"Maybe. It happened too fast."

"If it can move like that, then it won't be an ordinary vampire." The threat level just scaled up. The vamp also didn't drink from Roger which was odd. If it wanted a full feed, it would have kept him longer. But it had spat Roger's blood and discarded him like an afterthought. Maybe it was playing with them.

A grunt to her right. Silver whirled, her heart leaping into her throat. Now Martin was missing. *Fuck.* Completely missing. Not in the trees. Not in the branches. Gone. Jimmy whimpered.

"Shh," she hissed, needing to hear better.

"We're gonna die. We're gonna die."

She would smack him if he didn't shut up soon. A vine rustled in the wind. She crept closer to the tree, silently thankful Jimmy had stopped talking.

Wait.

He'd stopped talking.

Dread dropped in her stomach. She turned back to Jimmy.

Gone.

What the fuck? Silver faced Sid just as black shadow exploded behind him. Ribbons of thick darkness enveloped him. Silver glimpsed a handsome man smirking from the heart of the shadow. Dark, styled hair. Pointed vampire ears. Arrogant amusement plastered on his face as he kissed the air in her direction. She fired her pistol. *Too late.* The bullet sailed straight through shadows he left behind and splintered bark.

Smoke curled from the barrel of her gun as her ears adjusted to silence again.

Sid was gone. Martin was gone. Jimmy was gone. The vampire had taken them into his shadow like a black hole vortex. Where was Roger? Silver located the man slumped against a tree trunk. Dead?

She put fingers on his neck, searching for a pulse. It beat strongly. Not dead, asleep. An overwhelming rush of panic welled inside her. The living darkness that scratched beneath her metal corset swelled against its cage. Gasping and suddenly breathless, she forced her vision to clear. To focus. To take control of the situation.

*Think about the tightness holding me together. I'm not afraid. I'm in control.*

Steeling her resolve, clenching her jaw, she hastily undid the buttons on her jacket to gain access to the laces at her front. But she wasn't near death yet. She gritted her teeth and squeezed until the laces cut through her palm. *Contain it.*

Gun fire in the distance had her running toward the sound, heedless of her lungs struggling against the constraints. She dodged low lying branches, pushed vines and hanging roots away. Leaves whipped her face. Her pulse roared in her ears as she kept her path straight and true toward the direction of the gunfire. Any minute.

Her crew sat on logs around a discarded campfire another Reaper party had left months ago. Even Roger, slumped and half asleep but still somehow chatting to Sid at his side. How did he get there so fast? Martin and Jimmy were on another log, and the vampire sat on a third log in the middle. He must have teleported back to collect Roger.

The vampire held his palms over the dead fire pit as though warming himself, as though this was an enjoyable game of charades she had stumbled into.

A perfectly trimmed dark beard accentuated a strong jaw. Soulful eyes surrounded by thick lashes pulled her in. Leather clad broad shoulders, tapered waist, and long legs. It was as though an artist had reached into Silver's deepest, darkest fantasies and crafted him especially for her. Must be a glamor. No one was *that* good looking.

The thought broke the spell he had on her, and she continued to assess the threat. Her finger tightened on the trigger. He wore a battle uniform with spiked pauldrons and straps holding knives. The hilt of a broadsword peeked out from over his shoulder. She must be hallucinating because the sword looked metal.

She gasped as the pieces came together. *Metal.* Black leather uniform. Shadow manipulation. She searched the handsome face and found the confirmation she needed. A small shimmering blue teardrop beneath his left eye. He was a Guardian. One of the rare, ruthless fae protectors who could use metal and access magic at the same time.

The deadliest to humans.

Sensuous lips curved on one side as he noticed her realization dawn.

Her aim had dropped, so she targeted between his eyes and checked her team. They smiled and chatted as though they cared nothing for the risk to their lives. What was wrong with them?

"Say hello to Silver," the vampire drawled to her team.

As though a puppeteer pulled their strings, they faced Silver, smiled, and waved.

"Hello to Silver!" they said in unison.

Silver fired. Her bullet carved a hole through the shadow the vampire left behind. He was there, and then he wasn't. Holding her breath, she pushed all her awareness into her senses and searched the darkness for long moments. Left, right, up, down. Her finger tightened on the trigger.

Sudden heat scorched her back. Something tugged her long braid.

"Now, now, darling," the deep, smooth voice said at her ear. "Save some excitement for later."

# CHAPTER
# FOUR

Shade shadow-walked moments before the bullet tore through the space his head vacated. He landed behind Silver and watched as she moved her pistol aim around, searching for him.

He breathed in her alluring scent and wanted to latch onto her vein and drink, to invite that life-saving juice into his mouth and swallow it down. His body cried out to claim her. The need pressed beneath his skin. But he was not a slave to his whims. Never had been. When the time was right, he'd taste her.

*If* she was the right woman. If this woman—this savage, fire breathing, lightning-eyed woman with grease beneath her fingernails—was meant for him.

His mate had tried to kill him. Twice. He wasn't sure if he was aroused or appalled. Maybe a little of both.

Holding the writhing shadows around him, he took his time

assessing her—his *mate*. This was surely her. The tracking spell had led him straight here, to a silver-haired vixen.

She wore silver armor, too. It couldn't be a coincidence. Names often bequeathed one with self-purpose or identity. His own name had been gifted upon emerging from the ceremonial lake, no longer a simple vampire, but a Guardian with a boosted capacity to hold mana within... and the special ability to manipulate shadow to a degree unheard of before.

By simply existing, he'd cast shade on those around him. Even the Unseelie High Queen herself had been so taken with him that she'd discarded her old amaros in favor of him. As her prized concubine, he took control of Maebh through her sexual appetite. In the latter part of their time together, he could get her to agree to anything between the sheets. Not only what stayed in that bedroom, but what happened without. The power balance shifted and for a while he lived for it.

He thought he had everything he'd ever wanted.

But he was never in love with Maebh. And his power was simply a reflection of hers. She asked him to be her consort, but he declined. He didn't like the view from the top with her and he couldn't explain why. He wanted someone who would push the sky down *with* him. Not *for* him. So, he left to learn who he was on his own. He found his way into the ceremonial lake.

If Silver truly was his mate, then she would be a strong woman. Stronger than a queen, and yet, his equal.

Mating instincts tugged from the moment he'd laid eyes on her. Still shrouded in his shadows, he walked around her, studying her from head to toe as she, in turn, scrutinized the surrounding darkness, never once breaking into a nervous sweat or trembling with hesitation. She couldn't see him, of course, hidden in the shadow as he was.

Two of her companions had pissed their pants when they'd first laid eyes on him, yet she'd jogged into that clearing and held her pistol grip firm. Confident. As though she'd fight until her dying breath for her convictions.

To be a part of her world... to share it. To be one of her convictions.

His skin buzzed with anticipation, and then his gaze snagged on the shiny garment she wore around her torso. A corset. *Interesting.* What secrets did she keep buried there? What put the scar on her pouty upper lip and eyebrow? Why the grease beneath her nails? Would she challenge him? Or eventually roll over and submit like all the others did?

A thrill rushed him at the thought of making her submit... but only for a little while, only if she did the same to him in her own way. This was why he struggled to meet his match. He wanted the best of both worlds, and that had never been possible.

His old mentor, Mistress Aravela, had called him her duplicitous devil. He smiled at the memory of being told to go home with nothing when he couldn't decide on what type of candied blood to get at a market stall. He'd ended up returning and taking it all. The vomiting that ensued was entirely his own fault. To be fair, he'd been twelve.

Shade zeroed in on the long, roped hair resting over Silver's backpack. The length ended mid thigh. Just the right amount to wrap his fist around as he fucked her from behind. Or to wrap around her throat if she displeased him. Or her wrists. He flicked the braid and watched her reaction, catalogued every detail from her trapped breath to her shoulders, tensing in awareness of his presence. Her trigger finger twitched.

"Now, now, darling," he drawled near her ear. "Save some excitement for later."

He felt pain in his gut before he realized she'd shoved an elbow back. A bark of laughter burst out of him. He couldn't remember the last time a female surprised him. He relieved her of her pistol, and then shadow-walked somewhere safe to discard it before returning empty handed.

He waggled his finger at her. *Naughty mate.* How many times would he allow her to attempt to kill him before teaching her a lesson about consequences?

Already with a knife in each hand, her face contorted with calm fury as she tracked him about the clearing. They circled each other warily, boots crunching on snow, each weighing the chances of an attack from the other.

Her body moved fluidly, except where it came to the corset containing her breath. With her jacket unbuttoned, he could see the silver panels cinched so tight that the mounds of her breasts pushed her shirt to its limit. His eyes narrowed on the laces down her front, and the matching vambrace on her forearm—over the jacket. Interesting choice of armor. The vambrace he understood, but the corseted breastplate? It was cumbersome and restrictive. Poor design.

Which made him wonder why his mate had chosen to wear it. Or had someone else picked it for her? The thought of her male companions regulating her slammed anger into his body. He wouldn't put it past the messed-up race.

"What have you done to them?" Silver asked, knives still pointed at him.

He said nothing, instead sniffed the air and tried to work out if she hid another pistol on her person. But the coppery, bitter scent was everywhere. It was impossible to tell. He couldn't shift into a bat and heal if metal was lodged inside his body. He preferred not to dig for shrapnel if he could avoid it.

"Answer me."

His eyebrow arched at her demand. "They're mesmerized."

"Let them go."

"Now, why would I do that?"

"Because otherwise I'll kill you." A mischievous glint in her eye was the only warning before she lunged and stabbed. He used his wings to propel him backward. She continued to stab at him, and he continued to dodge. Each time she lunged, she bared teeth and hissed like a little fee-lion pouncing on a mouse.

Shade couldn't help the delight that puffed out of his lips every time she came at him, a fact that infuriated her more with each failed strike. It only made his grin widen.

"Oh, darling. I'm sure you'll try," he said, after dodging her again. He wasn't even using the shadows.

Enraged and huffing, she flicked her wrist and sent a dagger shooting through the air toward him. He side-stepped, his wing snapping tight behind him. The blade barely missed. *Wait... was that a nick in his wing?* Right. Time to stop playing. He faced her with a hard stare, only to narrowly miss a second blade zooming past his face. A delayed sting surfaced on his cheek just as satisfaction bloomed in her gray eyes. His finger came away wet when he checked it.

"You made me bleed," he mumbled.

She barreled into his torso and took him down. He landed painfully hard. Air vaporized in his lungs. Water blurred his eyes. Without a second thought, he shifted his pinned wings away. Dirt exploded as air replaced the space the wings had occupied. She winced as debris hit her face. Shade grappled her and switched their positions. He flattened his larger body against hers. He pinioned her hands above her head.

"Enough," he snapped in her face.

Defeat was never a glimmer in her eyes. If anything, his demand incensed her further. Her knee found its way to his gut. He tapped it back down. Her now free hand worked at slapping him off her other hand. And like a merry-go-round they went. Every time he trapped her, she knocked herself free. Respect swelled in him. She knew how to escape, to survive.

How would she tussle in the bedroom?

"He's only a kid," she gritted out. "Let him go."

"And I'm only here for you, Silver."

"So let them all go. Or I'll kill them all. Better them die than be beholden to the fae."

But he wasn't thinking about the others under his thrall. He was looking at where he held her, at where their skin touched... no mating bond had triggered. *Disappointing.* Other Well-blessed unions had triggered upon touch—Rush and Clarke bonded the instant his curse broke. Thorne and Laurel were immediate, as were Jasper and Ada. Indigo and Violet—Shade's gaze snapped to the silver armor on Silver's body, and he bared his fangs at the contraband.

Metal had blocked Indigo's bond from first triggering, and

plastic had blocked Haze's bond from triggering with Peaches. Since a Well-blessed bond needed the flow of mana to work, it made sense theirs wouldn't with all that contraband on her body. So close to her, so *hungry*, he cared little for Silver's state of mind. Something so far beyond his usual demeanor that he didn't realize until too late. That, to her, what he was about to do looked unthinkable.

"That needs to come off," he snarled and dug his fingers into her corset, right at the gap between her breasts. Talons distended from his fingertips, ready to cut through the leather, but her eyes widened. Panic scorched her face, and she drove a knife into his stomach.

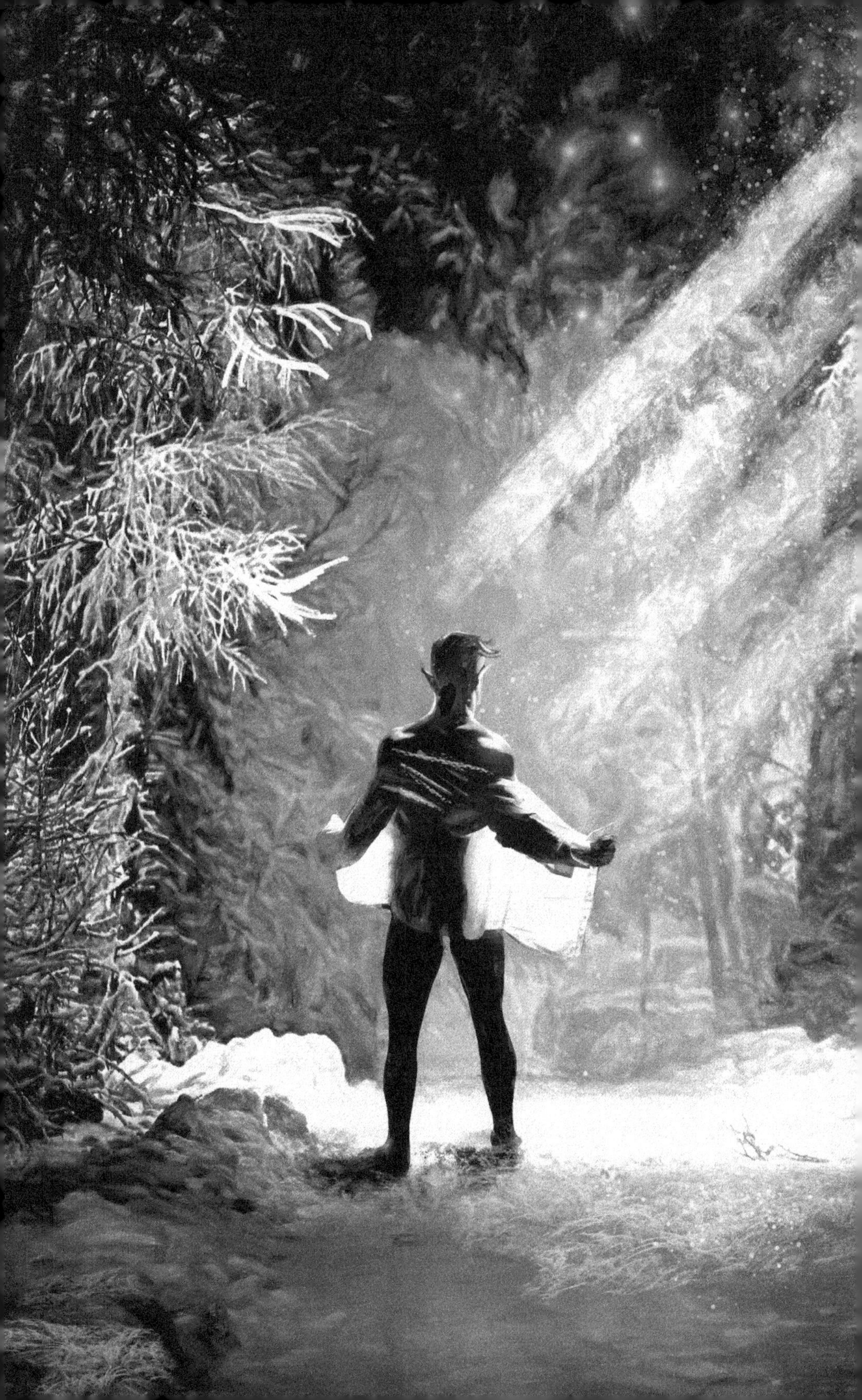

# CHAPTER
# FIVE

Silver's blade plunged into the vampire's body. Hot blood gushed over her knuckles. Steam rose as it hit the snow. Stabbing him had been easy. Seeing the betrayal in his eyes wasn't. And she couldn't understand why.

He looked at her like she'd just killed his puppy. But he was her enemy. He should expect to die.

*I'm only here for you,* he'd said.

Then this wasn't some chance meeting. He'd come here, perhaps even laid in wait until she emerged from the city. Had exploits of her previous fae kills prompted a bounty on her head? Or was this something else? She pulled the knife out of his stomach and readied to stab again, but a loud screech pierced the sky, jolting them both. A giant dark shadow burst through dead branches and hurtled at them like a missile. Silver glimpsed black eyes, reptilian legs, and wings made from tentacles.

Ribbons of shadow wrapped around her and wrenched her

through a rift in the world. They moved as though inside a water slide tunnel. Silver hadn't seen a water park since her time, but the ridiculous notion was all she could think of as shadows whizzed by and sounds muffled. When they cleared, a snow-capped evergreen glade appeared around her. Her stomach hadn't gotten the memo that they'd stopped. She lurched to the side and vomited.

*Can't breathe.*

She gasped and choked. Air wouldn't enter her lungs. Slowly, her vision crowded, darkening in the corners. She was suffocating herself but stubbornly refused to take off the corset or backpack. Not until she knew where she was—who she was with. Never again would she submit control. *Never.* Jimmy could still be near. The horizon tipped as she surveyed her environment. Her vision jumbled. She focused on the snowcapped fir trees glowing under the moon—a forest. Clear night sky. A lake in the distance. A cabin further up. And a tall, wingless and bleeding vampire scowling at her.

His hand was plastered to his stomach. Blood dribbled through his fingers, but he didn't seem to care about his injury. All he focused on was the leather ties laced at her front.

"Fucking pervert," she slurred—still dizzy from the travel. If he tried to molest her again, she'd finish him off this time.

He blinked at her, seemingly as dazed as she was. Fucker probably never heard the word no with that model-perfect face.

Well, life was full of lessons. Scrambling and forcing her mind to focus, Silver rolled and stood. She pushed effort into her legs, pumping them as hard as she could. *Breathe.* Just get away from him. Get to safety. *Then* fall apart.

Her eyes watered from the strain of forcing her woozy vision to focus. The tip of her nose froze. Her fingers hurt as she readjusted her backpack. Lungs were empty. Everything felt wrong. But she forced herself to keep running. She stumbled through shallow snow, continuing deeper into the woods, heedless of branches and twigs flying into her face, whipping her like a leather switch. Her lungs wouldn't cooperate. Taking a chance, she hid behind a tree trunk and caught her breath, watching clouds puff from her mouth.

She waited.

She listened.

He hadn't come after her.

No crunching footsteps.

A quick tug on the breastplate allowed her lungs room and blessed air wheezed in. Dizziness came over her with the sudden rush of oxygen. She half collapsed against the tree. It was still dark, but the moon was high, and the snow seemed to give off its own ethereal glow that turned the forest into a sparkling fairytale land. The vampire's shadow transportation ability must have taken them past the tundra. It was the only explanation.

That meant she was separated from her team. At least Jimmy was safe. She hoped.

Still leaning against the tree for support, she rolled her head back the way she'd come. *Damn it.* She hadn't run as far as she'd thought. The vampire was about thirty-or-so feet away, staring in her direction. Moonbeams landed on him through the glade. She ducked behind the tree again and waited, hoping that because she was in the dark recess of the forest, and he in the light, he'd not see her as clearly as she could see him.

*Stupid.*

He was a vampire. He could see in the dark. She should have

stayed hidden. But... if he'd seen her, he would have come running if he did. Right?

Maybe he was too injured. His blood had gushed. She bit her lip and braved a second look, only to gasp as he shifted into a bat. One minute he stood there, tall and imposing in his leather Guardian uniform, his ruffled hair moving in the wind. The next, air shimmered around him and he disappeared. *Poof!* His uniform, heavy sword, and weapons dropped with a thud. A tiny black winged creature flew and darted about, screeching.

*Oh shit.*

She couldn't outrun a bat! Her pistols were gone, so no bullets. Usually, the silver on her body protected her from any magical attack, but he was a Guardian. It didn't work on him. There weren't many other weapons in her backpack, and if they failed... all she had left was what lived inside her.

No.

She was better than this.

She would find a way to escape, complete the mission, and get back to Crystal City. She didn't care how many marks on her vambrace she needed to scratch.

Despite her concern, the vampire bat did not give chase. He shifted immediately into wingless fae form—probably an effort to make him seem more human. Silver's conviction to escape evaporated as her gaze locked onto the naked, brawny figure dressing. Her brows lifted. He certainly had a body to go with that face.

Probably another glamor designed to lure her in and forget he was a feral fae who wanted to drink her blood, humiliate her... and bed her. He took his time tugging on his leather breeches, taking special care to smooth his hand over his taut rear end, ensuring the worn leather fit snuggly. And it did, she realized. His ass was perfection, just like the rest of him—two globes of perfectly proportioned muscle—wait... she narrowed her eyes at his casual movements. He stretched languidly in a way that popped his biceps and defined every sinew. She gasped at the realization the bastard was putting on a show for her.

She leaned back to hide, to think, and to calm her racing heart, which may or may not have anything to do with the recent chase. *Goddammit*, he knew she was there. If she made a run for it, he would follow. But what choice did she have? He still had to put his weapons back on. She had time. *Fight or flee?* Her feet made the choice for her. She dashed deeper into the forest.

Silver used the percussion of her beating heart to keep pace. The slack she'd given her lungs by loosening the ties on her corset soon felt restrictive. Every footstep, every yard, made air feel like fire as she breathed it in. She must have jogged for an hour before the snow thinned. The ground slanted. She was headed downhill.

A haunting howl reminded her there were other dangers out here, just like that tentacled thing that had attacked them in the dead woods outside Crystal City. If the vampire hadn't transported them away, who knew what would have happened? The monster had seemingly attacked from nowhere. Tentacles. Scales. Facial pincers—or mandibles... whatever it was, she'd never seen or heard of any creature like it. But new, twisted things were being born all the time. This Well the fae revered also bred chaos. She put her palm to her chest. No one was immune.

*Jimmy!* Was he even alive? Or Sid? She was supposed to compartmentalize her feelings when out here in the wild, but it had been over a year since her last mission. She'd spent too long among the people of Crystal City, hearing their woes and building airships and weapons. Now all she could think of was how she would feel if she lost them? Something cracked open in her chest and a memory slipped free. It was of the woman who'd rescued Silver from a horde of vampires when she'd awoken in this time—Violet.

Hard as nails. Indestructible. Steady.

Jimmy's face flashed before her eyes, along with an ache in her chest. Dumb kid should have stayed in the city.

She had no idea where she was, only that she had to get away from the vampire intent on following her. Footsteps thudded behind her. She stuffed her emotions behind the metal armor strangling her lungs.

The vampire was catching up.

No time for feelings. If she could last until dawn, then he would tire and give up. A quick glance at the sky through the branches told her the sun was still a few hours away.

"You can't outrun me!" he shouted from behind her, almost happy in his pursuit.

Trees ended suddenly. Silver skidded down a rocky gully. Her hands grazed on giant boulders as she squeezed past. She bounded off a granite ledge and onto another without accurately assessing the distance. Her boots hit the flat surface and jarred her knees. She rolled with an *oof* as the wind was knocked out of her, but then recaptured her footing and continued down the rocks.

He landed behind her with a thud. Deep and smooth, his voice traveled. "I can go all night."

He didn't even sound puffed.

She cleared the boulders and propelled onto dirt. Snow was gone now. This journey had just become easier. Maybe it was self-inflated confidence, but she couldn't help tossing a cheeky remark over her shoulder, "All night, but not all day!"

A beat of silence as they ran. "Oh yes, darling. All day too."

Silver's footsteps faltered. All night *and* day? For a moment, her drive weakened, but then she realized something important. He was chasing her on foot. He, a fae who could bend the shadows and travel through them, yet he'd not used his gift since he brought them to this place. A smile spread across her lips. He'd run out of fuel, out of mana.

---

SILVER LOST track of time as she ran. She had no idea where she was, only that the sky was brightening, and her strength and lungs were failing. For hours, he failed to catch her. The notion struck her as odd right before her heavy feet slipped on pebbles and skidded—

"Watch out!" His voice boomed and echoed.

Echoed?

Too late, she saw the cliff, the chasm between her and the rest of the forest. Her arms windmilled. The toes of her boots slipped over the edge, raining dirt and rocks down to the cascading river fifty feet below. Like a scar, the gorge was a deadly drop that wounded the forest. And she was still going over. Her scream lodged in her throat as he jerked her backward by the backpack. She fell hard and rolled. The wind knocked out of her and she wheezed.

The vampire, also finding his feet, stood back a few steps. Contrary to her initial belief, he was out of breath. The chase had ruffled his previously perfect hair, and color blushed his cheeks, but the glimmer in his eyes was no longer playful. Silver barely had the strength to get to her feet. They eyed each other warily.

"That's enough," he clipped, his eyes dipping to her corset. "You're overextending yourself. You'll make yourself sick."

She wanted to say *Fuck you*, but she had no air. A fact that lifted the corner of his sensual lips in a way that made her want to smash him—or kiss him. Which was a damned stupid notion, considering she was running for her life. Screw him and his rumpled hair. How did he chase her through a forest for hours and still look so damned hot?

*Glamor.* It was all fake. There was no other reason for her to be thinking of him like this. Fae were dangerous. Vampires, some of the worst. They had ways and charms that lured unsuspecting humans in, then nipped off their heads like a praying mantis. He probably looked like a troll beneath the magic. She fought the feeling inside that told her to go to him. There was no place for it here.

She surveyed the cliff edge. *There.* Behind her, a fallen tree lay across the narrow gorge, its roots exposed but not completely upended. It was still alive and sprouting leaves. She could walk over it to the other side. If the vampire truly had no mana with which to shift his wings out, or use his shadow skill, then she could use the grenade in her bag to blow up the log and keep him on this side.

"Don't you dare," he warned, following her gaze and putting two and two together.

She darted for the tree and raced across, her boots balancing on the log like a gymnast. If she stopped to think about how incredibly stupid this was, she'd notice the rushing water below, or the wind, or—her foot slipped on the moss-covered bark. She landed hard lengthwise. Her forehead hit, blurring her eyes, but she gripped the log like a monkey. Wind gusted against her. Gravity yanked her heavy backpack. The horizon tipped as she rotated, falling. Hanging upside down, she locked her legs and arms and forced herself to slow her breathing, squeezing her eyes shut.

*Don't listen to the raging river below.* Don't think about how the heavy backpack would drag her under. Don't think—

"You'll always be trash," her mother shouted from her memory. "Wherever you go, you'll never escape your roots."

*She drunkenly stumbled to Silver as she stood by the door, suitcase in hand. She pointed in Silver's face.* "One of these days you'll see, you'll be a bigger disappointment than me."

"It's time to say goodbye, Mom," Silver said, her shoulders tensing.

"You fucking black-hearted bitch!"

"Hold on." The vampire's voice was almost lost in the wind.

Silver's eyes popped open. He stood at the edge of the log, removing his heavy weapons. Once divested, he placed a tentative boot on the log. It creaked.

Silver wanted to scream, but the damned corset was choking her at this angle. She glanced down at the river catching the dawn, sparkling like diamonds. Maybe this was how it should end for someone like her. Maybe her mother was right and what existed inside Silver was just a manifestation of her black heart. Poisonous.

"Stay away," she shouted to the vampire, her trembling voice betraying her fear, her doubt.

Damn it. She was stronger than this. The flip side of her memory hit her—her father standing on his front porch. He was dressed in his Pakistani military uniform, watching her struggle with her heavy suitcase to climb the steps. Not once did he reach out to help her. He didn't even step out of the way.

*"Aren't you going to help?"* she asked.

*He simply replied, "You've got it handled."*

Yeah, she had this handled too. Gritting her teeth, she shimmied along the log toward the other end.

"What are you doing?" the vampire said through clenched teeth. "Stay put."

His chase only spurred her on. Every time her fingers blindly felt something dislodge on the crevices of the log, she grasped and tossed it at his head. Twigs, pebbles, dirt. But she was making incredibly slow progress. Nothing deterred him. He caught up.

He gripped her ankles and bared his fangs. "There are far worse things than me to contend with in this forest."

She kicked him but lost her foothold on the log. Her knees slipped. Splinters sliced into her palms, and she made a horrible sound as her legs dangled to one side. She gulped in air.

He crawled closer, straddled the log, and gripped her by the elbows.

"What do you want with me?" she shouted, frustrated. He'd chased her for miles.

When he didn't answer, she glanced at him. Two eyes of molten chocolate looked back at her. No fear. No hate. Not even the usual hunger she was used to seeing in his kind. What stared back at her was... affection? His lips twitched as though he tried to contain a smile.

"What do I want with you?" he repeated, his gaze darkening. "There are too many things I want with you, little fee-lion. Now's not the time to list them."

"If you're going to give me the runaround, I'll take my chances with the river." She tried to pry herself from his grip.

His eyes flashed. All playfulness fled. He tightened his hold. "You have no idea what's good for you, do you?"

"And I suppose you do?" She kicked.

His hold slipped. She screamed and dropped an inch. *Shit.* He was really going to drop her. It was so far down! She squeezed her eyes shut, her stubborn pride dissipating in the face of her fear.

"You're my Well-blessed mate, Silver. *I'm* what's good for you."

Mate? As in that coupling the fae regarded so highly? It was more precious than marriage. More unifying to them than anything else. He was toying with her again. Steely determination pushed out her fear.

"You must be mad to think that would sway me." She tugged. Alarm flashed in his eyes. She tugged again until she slipped another inch. "We're mortal enemies. You're a blood-sucking monster. I'm human. There's only one way this will end."

A look came over him that drilled right into her bones. *Danger.* She knew not how or why. His expression gave away nothing. His eyes turned hard. She had the sense that if he'd had any power left, there would be no more conversation. He would end this and follow it up with long, torturous punishment. He would make her pay. A shiver skipped down her spine.

"My name is Shade," he ground out. "Not Blood-Sucking Monster."

She froze as he hoisted her up. The backpack slipped with every tug he made.

"Stop!" she shouted.

She couldn't lose her pack. Her mission was as good as dead without the transceiver.

But he cared little for her will. He continued to pull. She kicked and bucked. The one rule a Reaper learned was that the mission came first. Before the life of her team. Before her own life. She *needed* that pack.

But it slipped from her shoulders as he yanked, decreeing with each strident haul, "You will learn to address me as Shade." He pulled. "D'arn Shade." He lifted. "Or Mate." He snarled with effort, the tendons in his neck bulging as he slung her belly first over the log, right before where his powerful thighs straddled.

She dangled mercilessly, staring at the river, stunned that he'd had the strength to move her so effortlessly—even without access to his magic. Her legs on one side. Her arms on the other. Her ass pointed at the sky like a naughty child. Did she ever have a chance against him?

"I have a mind to spank you for your impudence," he grumbled.

She glanced at him as though he was insane, yet his furious eyes were locked on her bottom with crystal clarity.

*Oh my God. He's considering it.*

His palm came down with a *thwack!*

Pain lanced through her body, waking up all the cells numb from the cold or fear. Another thwack. And a third. Water leaked from her bulging eyes. Shocked. Completely stunned and motionless. She had no idea what was happening. She'd lost her backpack. Her weapons. Her mission was dead. And this fucking vampire—sorry, *D'arn Sha-ade*, she mocked in her head—was spanking her fifty feet above a rushing river... dangling from a goddamned log!

After his third spank, he caressed her bottom and cooed to her, "Good girl. You know, you were right. There is only one way this will end. The sooner you accept that, the better for us both."

"Your way?" she sneered.

*Thwack!*

She jolted.

"The way of the Well," he clarified. "Of life. Of death. Of balance and harmony. We exist only by the grace of the Well. The sooner you remove your contraband, the sooner our bond will trigger, and you'll see that I'm right."

*Wrong thing to say.*

Silver glared at him. He was all handsome smugness and cocky perfection. He truly believed he had the right to spank her. To force his beliefs on her. To touch her!

She locked onto her indignation to drown out her fear. She moved fast, with precision, and without remorse. She swung up onto the log. He thought it meant she'd capitulated.

It didn't.

She used her momentum to push him. He went over the side. Suddenly, their positions were reversed. He dangled from the log, feet kicking below, hard eyes glued to her face. She looked to where he gripped.

"Don't do it," he warned. "Little fee-lion, I can already see you're a female who enjoys courting trouble, and I like that. But do this and there will be consequences."

"Another spanking?" she teased. "What am I, five?"

"Of this we agree, a child, you are not."

"How do you do that?" She hit his knuckles with her fist. "How do you turn everything into something laced with seduction? Your words. The spanking. Your looks. I know what you're doing, and I don't buy into your glamor."

He laughed. The bastard laughed in the face of his death. So she hit him again, this time using her vambrace to crush his fingers grasping the log. He hissed in pain, his laughter dying.

"I'm not using a glamor, Silver," he confessed. "I rarely do."

"Liar."

"What you see—what you feel for me—is real. It's the bond trying to push through."

"*Liar.*"

She hit him again. He slipped and dangled from one arm. Panic reared its ugly head in her chest, hurtling against the cage she kept her heart in.

"How do you know my name?" she cried.

"Your friends Peaches and Violet told me."

She screamed her anguish and hammered her fist onto his final, gripping hand.

He slipped.

He fell.

Silently. Not a word. Not a cry. No goodbye.

The river swallowed his body, and she looked away, hating the feeling of something being ripped from her chest. She hit her breastbone and gave a strangled scream. *Guilt doesn't live here*, she told herself. There was no room for it.

He was nothing to her. A vampire. A stranger.

But the mission was dead.

*He knows Violet and Peaches.*

She forced her eyes open and scrambled back the way she'd come. Her fingers bled, her eyes stung, and her body ached, but she made it to where his weapons laid. She picked up a dagger and scored another mark on her vambrace.

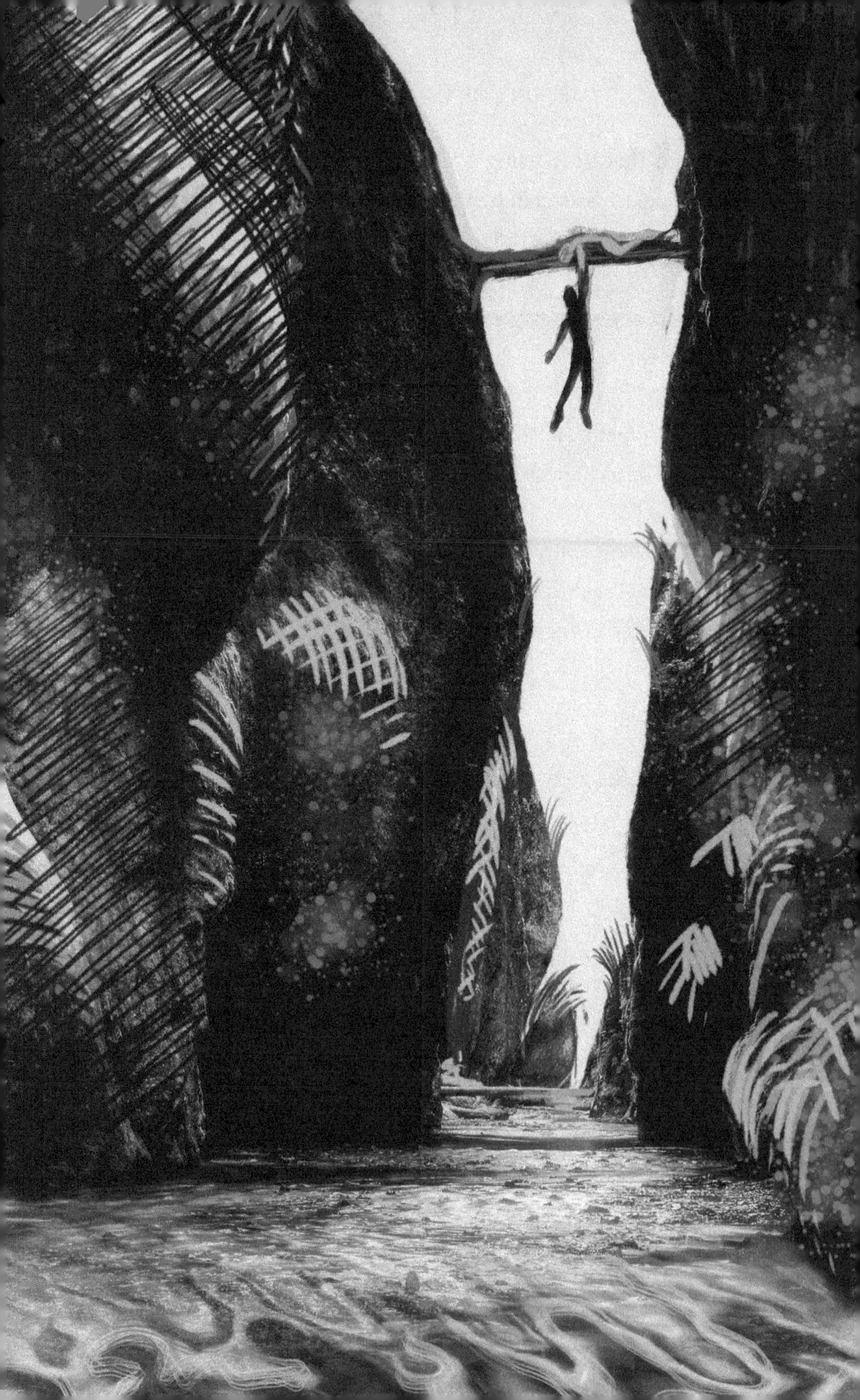

## CHAPTER SIX

Unseelie High Queen Maebh stared out her open window to the ocean kissing her wintery lands. Wind gusted in, brushing her face. Once, she would have used her mana to remove the ice from the air. But now, after creating her demogorgon pet, she had little to spare. And that was a dangerous position to be in for a queen.

Everything hinged on the appearance of power and the installation of fear. For her to remain in power, and to exact revenge on a cruel world, she needed three things. One, control of a monster so powerful it was unkillable. Two, the partnership of a formidable male. And, three—the nullification of her weaknesses. And then the entirety of Elphyne would be hers for the taking.

She squinted at the gray dawn sky. There, in the distance, a dark blob flew closer. Her hope soared.

Perhaps her sacrifice would be worth it after all. A shuffling sound drew her attention to the captain of her personal guard, Demeter. The loyal vampire stood tall and regal, waiting for his cue to leave or to please. He'd been a satisfactory replacement since her previous captain failed her. Before she'd made her pet, he'd also warmed her bed while she searched for the vampire who would become her consort—Shade.

Once one of her prized amaros, Shade—not his name back then—had given his body to Maebh, but apparently not his soul. He was the only subject who'd ever challenged and aroused her in a way that made her feel alive again. And he'd left her for greener pastures.

As the demogorgon flew closer, skipping through time like one of her old Sluagh, she couldn't help the cold notion that this was all she had left. This tentacled, bloodthirsty beast. This wintery land. An ache in her chest expanded at the memory of all she'd lost. Her eyes drifted down to her empty arms, to hands moving in a rocking formation she used so often to calm her newborn.

The ghost of a baby's cry filled her ears.

*"This is the only way, Maebh,"* Mithras said into her ear as she nursed her babe. *"Plant the memories of our people in her mind. Send her to them as a changeling. Have the memories unlock when she comes of age, and she'll take down the filthy human Untouched from the inside."*

Maebh remembered with a snarl. It was King Mithras who'd convinced her to give up her only child. It was he who'd stolen half of Elphyne from her, threatening to expose her failed attempt of subterfuge and subsequent needless sacrifice of her only heir. He'd pretended he had nothing to do with it. He'd made her fear that once the fae found out, they'd vilify her for handing over her own child to the enemy. And she, the weak queen that she was centuries ago, she'd believed him.

None of them truly understood how barren the human city was when it came to mana. Without it, the sleeping memories of her birthright never woke. Maebh's daughter never remembered her birthright and Maebh never saw her again. She probably died a human death, alone and never knowing the greatness she was made for.

The screech of the demogorgon filled the air. Maebh gestured to Demeter. He stepped forward and opened the bifold doors leading to the terrace. Frigid air swept in on the wake of her pet as he carried a limp male body in his hands.

To others, the creature was ugly—born of tainted mana from the inky side of the Well. But to her, he was magnificent. She saw not the deformity of species mutated together. Reptilian legs, tentacled wings sprouting from his back, a face only a mother could love with its split jaw and black, soulless eyes.

She'd used a human from the old world—one with a connection to the Well, although he'd never known it himself—and imbued him with power. Poetic justice, she'd thought. If the man had embraced his connection to the Well, he'd have out-powered her and escaped.

She'd also put a part of herself inside him, so she *was* his mother, in a way. And she already loved him more than she'd expected.

Especially because subservience to her was built into his makeup. He would never leave Maebh for greener pastures. He would always bow at her feet.

Her pet laid the body at Maebh's feet and lowered his head respectfully. Glossy writhing tentacles splayed out behind him.

"My sweet," she cooed and scratched him under the scaly chin. "You finally found him."

Her pet made a soft clicking sound in the base of his throat as he basked in her praise. But then Maebh looked down and her mood darkened. The body her pet had brought was dressed in black, yes. He was male, yes. His hair was dark and short, yes. But it was not Shade.

He wasn't even fae.

"What is the meaning of this?" Her soft touch under his chin turned tight and unforgiving.

Her pet glanced down at the human again, then back at her, confused. His tentacles wagged a little, like an eager Well Hound expecting a treat. She took a second look at the body. Fresh puncture marks on his neck oozed blood. Maebh cocked her head.

"Does it smell like him?" she asked.

Her pet nodded.

So Shade had fed from this human. She nudged him with her foot until he roused and lifted his face. Maebh's nose crinkled in disgust. The human's face was scarred and deformed. He saw her disapproval and snarled himself, hatred evident in his eyes.

He was not Shade, but he'd interacted with him.

Maebh gestured at his face but spoke to her pet. "Show me."

The demogorgon steadied his taloned hand over the human's head. The long, jelly like tentacles writhed out from behind his back and latched onto the man's head. The scream was slow in coming. It started out as shock. Perhaps he was paralyzed in pain, but when the horror of what was happening occurred to him, he opened his mouth and let out a sound no man would ever be proud of.

Demeter shuffled at Maebh's side, clearly disturbed at the

demogorgon entering the mind of the human and stealing his memories. Maebh held her palm out as a tentacle landed in the center. She grasped it and closed her eyes.

Behind her eyelids, as though hit with a manabee, she saw memories that weren't hers. A dark, dead forest—like the one near the human wasteland. Two tussling figures on the dirt, one Shade and the other a silver-haired woman. Then her pet burst into the scene. Shade threw himself on top of the woman—as if to shield her—and used his shadow gift to disappear.

Maebh let go of the tentacle and stared hard at the human, now twitching as his bowels released. Her lip curled and she threw her hand toward the prisoner.

"Take him," she said and walked out of the sitting room and into a hallway. The wet sounds of feeding followed as her pet had his meal.

Demeter scurried to keep up, hot on her heels. "What now?"

Her body trembled with fury, so she pushed into the only room that had ever given her calm—the old nursery covered in cobwebs. But this time, there was no calm in the memories of her daughter rocking in her arms. There was only emptiness and failure.

She picked up the rocking kuturi made from wood and hurled it across the room. The splintering did nothing to allay her mood, so she continued to lay destruction to everything she'd once held dear.

Maebh had seen that silver-haired woman once before. Almost a decade ago, Maebh's royal seer had foretold of three humans with the power to rebuild the weapon that had destroyed the old world. Two of which were now mated to Guardians. Shade protecting this human with his life meant only one thing.

Her love, her future Consort, was mated.

*Not yet.*

No... there had been no blue, glowing Well-blessed mating marks on either of them. Maebh still had time. Huffing with spent energy, she rounded and stormed back to her sitting room, where most of the human was now eaten. She gripped her pet by the split chin dripping in warm blood and forced his black eyes to hers.

"No more chances," she said. "Go. This time, don't come back until you've found him."

Her pet cooed and clicked in acknowledgement.

She'd had the woman in her hands once, and she'd slipped away. This same woman was now about to steal what rightfully belonged to Maebh. She wouldn't fail a second time. Her expression hardened.

"And kill the woman he's with."

# CHAPTER SEVEN

Shade mumbled curses as he carried a dead kelpie that had dared to attack him in the river. His sodden boots squelched across the riverbank. He dumped the horse-like carcass and then flicked water from his hands. He was soaked. Completely and disgustingly wet. He growled and tossed Silver's rescued backpack on the ground, wanting to stomp on it in his fury.

Damned, infernal woman.

*Thrice* she'd tried to kill him. Maybe more. Crimson, he was losing count. With the gun, then the knife, and then she pushed him off the log. He'd thought it fun to start with—a kind of courting—but now he was pissed. He forced his raging mind to calm and glanced warily at the idyllic sunbeams flickering through the surrounding green forest. He was so angry he'd not even noticed the lethargic pull of day.

His adrenaline still pumped from the recent battle against the kelpie, and then further back from the battle with his mate. As a

Guardian, he'd trained to work in all conditions, especially the natural sleepiness that overcame most vampires at sunup. He was a nocturnal creature of habit, but not immune to walking in the sun. This was something his mate would not know about him. She probably assumed, like most humans, that he would soon find a place to hunker down and sleep until the worst of the sun's heat was gone. It was an advantage he was well prepared to take.

He could just imagine the shock on her face when he eventually caught up to her. She thought the brief spanking he'd given her was offensive. She'd behaved incomprehensibly not once, but multiple times. And now she'd run into a fae forest minus her supplies. He glanced down at the backpack and shook his head. She had naught but the clothes on her back, and from what he remembered, no weapons to protect herself.

Was his mate mad? Insane?

His fingers twitched to reprimand her again, but he wasn't even sure if it would make a difference. Some people responded to a firm hand, others needed the guidance a more dominant partner could give. How he responded to Silver all depended on her needs, and sometimes those needs had to be coaxed from a dark, secret place they weren't even sure existed until faced with the truth.

He clearly remembered the night he'd learned that lesson. He might have been perhaps six years old. He'd been roaming the halls of the multi-level brothel that was his home. Usually, he'd had to keep to a particular floor where he wouldn't bump into anything a child shouldn't see, but on this day, he'd been feeling brave. His mother had abandoned him. He was angry, recalcitrant, and looking for attention. So, he'd crept up the stairs to see what was in the out-of-bounds area.

*His small, chubby hand opened the door a crack. Something was happening inside.*

*Gasps. Cut off cries. Whimpering. A man begging.*

*"Please, please..."*

*"Please, what, Marcus?"*

*"Please, Mistress."*

*"You were rude to me earlier. I don't know if I should."*

*"I'm sorry, I—"*

*The crack of a whip. A whimper... then a pleasure-filled moan.*

*"You what?"*

*"I..."*

*Another crack. Another moan.*

*"I wanted you to be mad at me."*

*"Why, Marcus?"*

*"Because I wanted to feel something."*

*"Good boy. For that confession, I will reward you. I will give you something to feel."*

*Drawn out groans and curious gasps increased with panting and—were they wrestling? What's happening? He pushed the door open another inch. The door creaked. He tried to angle himself to see more of the room without giving himself away. Perhaps he should shift into a bat and crawl in. No one would notice him—*

*The door swung open, and Mistress Aravela stared down at him with concern. She glanced over her shoulder at the male inside, then hugged her silk robe around her body and stepped into the hallway, shutting the door.*

*His little heart beat rapidly in his chest. His lips trembled. He was going to get in trouble—perhaps like the man inside.*

*Aravela knelt before him. He flinched, expecting punishment, but* her heavily made-up eyes softened with affection. "Darling, you know you're not supposed to be up here until you come of age."

"But..." He glanced at the door. "You're hurting him."

She touched his cheek. "My sweet little lion, always so curious. Pain is often confused with pleasure, my love. And he comes here because he trusts us."

"To hurt him?"

"No, sweet. He trusts us to allow him to become vulnerable. To get to the root of his desire or his hate. To give him something he needs when he doesn't realize himself what that is."

"What is it?"

She scowled. "First off, what have I told you about asking?"

"Um... Never ask. Ever. It reveals a weakness they can exploit."

"Good lad. Second," she sighed heavily, capitulating to his curiosity. "It's different for each individual, and only the best of us can uncover the truth. Sometimes one wants pain. Sometimes one craves domination. Sometimes it's the other way around. But one constant remains—when we uncover the truth of hidden desire, then freedom is attained. And let me tell you now"—she smiled wistfully—"this kind of freedom is the most liberating of all." She shrugged. "Besides, they pay us for the privilege of uncovering their most primal needs and then satisfying them."

Shade thought back to the sounds of the male inside, to how he often saw them downstairs as they left—with a satisfied and dreamy smile. Then he thought about what he deemed as a primal need—the love of a mother who'd left him and who'd hated him for being born.

"You mean needs like love?" he asked.

She cocked her head, studying him with sad eyes. "Like pain, love is easily confused with other emotions. To them, perhaps, yes, it is. To us...

*the truth-seekers... well, my dear. That is something we may never have the privilege of knowing."*

His eyes sparked with the answer, and he held up his index finger. "Only the best of you can uncover the truth."

She laughed and ushered him away. "One would hope. Now, quit dilly dallying. Idle hands are the Well Worm's playground. Back downstairs you go. If I catch you up here again, then I'll tell Madam Brindabella and you'll be cleaning chamber pots for a week."

The door closed on Shade's memory, and he frowned. His birth mother had been one of the most sought-after Rosebud Courtesans. She'd never wanted a child but hadn't yet taken the surgery to remove her womb. When he'd come along, she'd birthed him and tried to love him. Unfortunately, having a child severely impacted her trade and soon she became unwanted and used goods. Unable to look at Shade without blaming him for her misfortune, she disappeared and left him to the brothel.

She never came back.

But the courtesans cared for him in a way they thought was love. He looked up to them, and when he eventually came of age, he soon learned there were two things he could thank his mother for—his looks and the opportunity to use it to his advantage.

Contrary to everyone's belief about Shade, he wasn't a dominant male who enjoyed punishing lovers. Neither did he procure some sort of sick pleasure from their pain. He found no satisfaction when they squealed or begged, nor did he derive joy from their humiliation. He did what he did because he felt an intrinsic fulfillment—power, if you will—from taking care of another's needs, especially when they didn't know what they needed themselves.

He felt a rush when he protected and provided... and yes, sometimes that protection came at odds with the words coming out of their mouths. But their actions and their bodies never lied. He never pushed hard limits. He watched behavior carefully, from their heart rate to the sounds they made when he gave orders. He tested them. He perceptively assessed. He became the best truth seeker Elphyne had ever known.

His mate had no idea what she needed. Something else drove her motivation, and it had nothing to do with her wellbeing. The thought grated on him. If she kept going at this rate, she'd be dead before they had a chance to trigger their bond.

Her behavior was reckless, yet not careless. She'd told him to leave the boy he'd mesmerized. She had a heart somewhere behind that corset, and he was determined to find it.

While Shade drained his boots of water, his mind traveled to the minute behavioral details his mate had revealed. She'd panicked when he'd threatened to remove her metallic garment. That reaction had been immediate and absolute. He didn't believe it was from fear of being unprotected. She'd traveled with him through the shadows. She knew he could access mana despite the metal on her body and thus hurt her, despite her armor. The fear had another source.

She was attracted to him, naturally. He could see it in her eyes when she looked at him, especially when she'd delayed escaping to watch him dress. That had been fun. But she denied her attraction and blamed fae glamor. This both amused him and concerned him. The woman denied herself a great many things. The pleasure of another chief among them. She refused to allow herself to *feel*, to *breathe*, and in so doing was on a one-way path to becoming dead inside.

Unless she found a safe release.

To be vulnerable.

To trust.

To be free.

Maebh came to mind. When he'd graduated to her bed, she'd been cold and distant. He'd felt like he was making love to a corpse half the time, despite the snarky words that came out of her mouth, or the sometimes brutal and cruel techniques she employed. But Shade had seen it as an opportunity. He'd always felt something was missing in his soul, a companion for the shadow encasing his heart, and who better to share it with than the ice queen herself?

He'd listened, he'd learned, and he'd pleased his mistress until he'd turned the tables, discovered her truth and crumbled her walls of resistance. Hate and cruelty were often borne of vulnerability. Shade had learned Maebh's. But when he had, when he'd broken down the highest, most challenging fae he'd ever laid eyes on... and his shadowed heart was still aching and empty. His own walls had slammed up.

He lifted his shrewd gaze to the log he'd been *pushed* from. The climb back up the gorge would be laborious, but he could not use his limited stores of mana. He needed to conserve every ounce, for when he found Silver, he was pulling no punches. That metal was coming off. He was going to discover her truth, even if she denied it.

Hunger gnawed at his insides. A fresh meal lay at his feet, but he craved his mate's blood and since he'd scented it during their quarrels, he wanted nothing less. He glanced up at the rocky cliffs baking in the morning sun and cringed. Once up top, it wouldn't take long to track down his mate.

*Quit dilly dallying. Idle hands are the Well Worm's playground.*

He shrugged off his jacket and squeezed out water before putting it back on. Damned leather would chafe now. He set himself to climb the rocky facade.

When he finally breached the top, he shouted a new string of virulent curses at the trees. She'd taken his weapons—she'd damned well crawled back over the log *specifically* to steal his weapons before heading back to the other side and continuing her journey. He gave a feral grin as he wiped sweat from his brow. The hunt just got even more enticing. It was one thing to try to kill him, but another to take a Guardian's sworn weapon.

*Patience*. He could scent her trail. She would not see him coming in the daylight.

## CHAPTER
# EIGHT

It took Shade an hour to find her. In the end, after scenting her trail, his hunger flipped a switch inside him. He accessed the little mana he'd slowly regenerated, and stepped through the shadows to reach her.

The shadows were cooler than the sun, and when he arrived by a small lagoon in a grotto, he stayed hidden out of instinct. But when his eyes landed on her, he stayed hidden out of necessity. The urge to uncover her truth was more severe than the desire to confront.

He lowered the backpack and lounged against a birch tree. He watched as she bathed—still wearing her shirt, metal corset, and vambrace against her bare skin, not over the jacket. Odd that she kept the armor on while wading in, as if she was too afraid to spend a moment without it. The glimmer of skin beneath the water revealed she'd removed her pants.

Unwilling to underestimate her a fourth time, he surveyed her campsite and located two of his daggers. His broadsword *Mercy* wasn't there. Neither was her wool-lined jacket. The campfire smoldered with the remnants of a small animal carcass picked free of meat. She'd hunted and fed herself. She'd have had little time for sleep.

Movement back at the lagoon caught his eye. She plucked at the corset laces down her front, wincing with each movement. When she peeled the metal panels from her skin, alarm prickled his skin. Bloody patches had soaked through her linen shirt. When she removed that, too, she revealed welts in the shape of the metal panels. The metal had been cinched so tight on her skin, it would have pinched and cut every time she moved. Even through her shirt.

*Why torture herself?*

His brows lifted in the middle to see her in pain as she lowered agonizingly slow into the water. Tears glistened at the edges of her closed eyes, and for a privileged moment, he glimpsed her vulnerability before she covered it with a mask of indifference. She didn't indulge for long. She dunked her head and then waded back to shore.

He could have rushed her then—could have been at her side in an instant with only one last piece of metal on her arm blocking their bond from triggering, but as he watched her wince and flinch while she doggedly refitted her armor, he wondered who was she trying to protect? Herself, or others from her?

She didn't move to the campsite as he'd thought, but instead turned in the opposite direction and bent into some brush by a fallen tree, some twenty feet away. She tugged out dry clothes from within the shelter and redressed. When she gave her surroundings a scrutinizing once over before disappearing herself into the brush, he realized it was her sleeping spot. Clever to make it different to the campsite. If anyone stumbled across, or was lured by the vestiges of a meal, they wouldn't find her exposed.

He wondered the best way to proceed. A part of him was dying to know why she tortured herself. Another part didn't give a flying fuck and was ravenous. His fangs ached in his gums. When he finally forced himself to follow her into the brush, he found her sleeping on her jacket in a burrow she'd dug out. It struck him that he could feed from her while she slept.

The thought both equally disgusted and allured him. On one hand, sleep feeding was a task reserved for the weakest of vampires. He'd never in his life fed from sleepers, especially not from one intended as his mate. It made him feel sick to contemplate. On the other hand, drinking from her would bring her memories. He would get a one-way ticket to the inner mysteries of her mind.

Premature histamines dripped from his fangs, coating his tongue in sweet syrup. She could very well remain asleep and wake none the wiser to his feed. Or she could wake and try to kill him again. His shadows curled over her sleeping form as though visiting a friend. She'd fallen asleep so fast. Attempting to kill your mate must be exhausting work.

He held branches away from her alluring face, then nudged her long braid from her neck, exposing the vein pulsing with her lifeblood. His stomach clenched.

*This is wrong.*

But she'd set the precedent. And he was tired of denying the part of him that wanted Well-blessed blood. Everything else was cardboard, and here she was—nectar of the goddess incarnate—sleeping soundly. Shade's eyes tracked down her body. The swell of her breasts spilled out of the corset. He wanted to take it all off and lick her wounds until his saliva both numbed and healed her. He wanted their bond to trigger.

His craving won the war between head and heart. He eased her backpack from his arms, careful not to make a sound, and then lowered to her neck. A long, torturous inhale brought in her undeniably feminine scent. His lashes fluttered as possessive need cascaded through him.

He licked gently along her vein, numbing the flesh. She didn't stir.

*Stop.*

He was not weak. He was not a sleep-feeder. His heart rebelled against his cravings, even as his mouth lowered and sealed around her flesh. But he couldn't take the final step.

His gaze flickered to the other bite marks on her skin. Old scars put there by vampires. He remembered how hateful Violet had been against his kind at first, and the story she'd told of Maebh's soldiers taking her prisoner the moment she'd awoken in this time. Her... and Peaches and Silver.

Without a single drop taken, he disengaged and sat back on his haunches. Silver's breath puffed gently against a stray strand of hair. He cocked his head. She was so fragile and peaceful when she slept, so completely at odds with the vixen she was when awake.

He imagined what a life with her would be like—challenging during their waking hours, tangling like enemies in the sheets, and then languid and warm together when asleep. A desire much stronger than hunger took hold of him and he pushed away from her. Then he took his weapons, her backpack, and left.

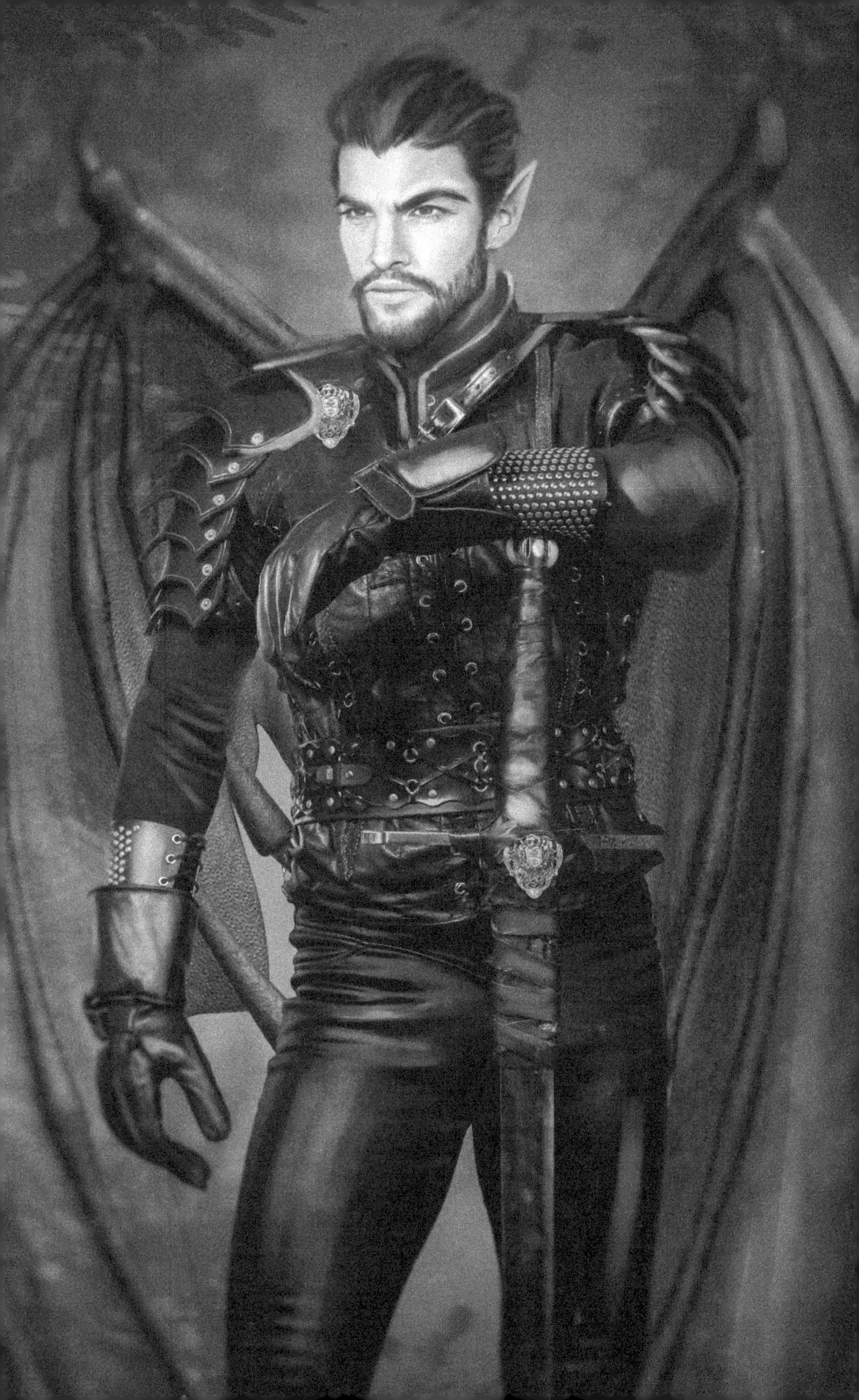

## CHAPTER NINE

Silver dreamed fitfully. It was the same scene that always played in her head. The day she left her drunk mother behind. For good. Only this time it wasn't her mother. It was the two humans she'd met when she'd awoken in this time.

"You'll always be trailer trash," Violet shouted from her place in a locked cage. "Wherever you go, you'll never escape where you came from."

A storm brewed overhead. Cold wind whipped at Silver's face as she stood outside the cage, lock key in hand.

"It's time to say goodbye," Silver said, her shoulders tensing.

"No!" Peaches cried. She gripped the bars and pressed her face against them. Tears ran streaks down her face. "Don't leave us. We need you."

Silver's throat closed. She should stay with them, like she'd promised. But they'd only hold her back. They'd keep her from joining her people. Three of them in one place was too much.

"Don't leave us. Don't—" Peaches sobbed.

*Enough!*

*Silver's knuckles whitened on the key.* She scowled at the caged women and the lie dripped easily from her tongue. "We have to separate because we're dangerous together. We can't go to the humans. We must assimilate with the fae. It's the only way."

*The only way to stop another holocaust.*

*Coldness spread out from Silver's chest. When she looked down, a black stain oozed from her heart. Horror filled Silver as powder black tendrils reached for the women. She tried to batt the smoke away, but it only avoided her touch and then rejoined in the middle before continuing its deathly trajectory.*

Violet battered the cage. "We always knew you were a black-hearted bitch!"

"No!" Silver cried, and tried to gather the smoke back into her body, but it had already started to infect the rest of her—any time she touched it, she blackened herself. Alarmed, she looked at the women as black smoke infected them too. They turned to ash, their faces immortalized in horror, and then they crumbled at her feet. "Nooo!"

Silver woke with her scream echoing in her ears. Her heart rammed against her ribcage, just like Violet had rammed her cage.

*It's just a dream.*

It was just an amalgamation of her past—her mother, her first kill from her gift, and the guilt over lying to women who'd only been kind to her. At least, that's all she hoped it was. The past.

Silver stared at the wind blasting the leaves of the brush overhead. Dim sunlight cast shadows across her face. Almost sunset. She'd slept longer than she'd planned.

*Better get up.*

Every muscle in her body ached, especially the parts down her torso the corset had captured. At least she hadn't worn the contraption against her bare skin like she'd originally considered. Lifting herself up with a stifled groan, she scrutinized her surroundings with all senses. Sound—just the wind. Smell—nothing untoward. Sight—seemed exactly like it was when she left it... except for that object on the floor.

She picked up the small, round tin. Her transceiver. Alarm jolted through her. The last time she'd seen it was in her backpack. Her eyes widened when she realized something else was missing—the vampire's weapons.

*Shit.*

He wasn't dead. She breathed calmly and waited for the disappointment or fear to hit, but it never came. Instead, she felt a little flip in her belly. Relief. *No.* She shook her head. *Don't be stupid.* Why would she be relieved that a vampire had survived?

*Because he said you're his mate.*

Because maybe the idea of belonging was something she'd dreamed of her whole life. Of unconditional acceptance. But she got that with Rory and the humans of Crystal City. What they gave her might not be romantic, but it was belonging. It was good enough, and it was virtuous. It was more damned virtuous than these fae. Even if Violet and Peaches had defected to them.

But Silver had told them to do that. It was her fault they were here.

So why did she feel so guilty about the lie? They were happy now... right? Shade had mentioned them giving him her name. Unless they were tortured into it.

The truth was, she would never know unless she spoke with

them. Her guilt would always be rearing its ugly head until then. Silver turned the transceiver in her fingers.

Why hadn't he killed her? He'd had ample opportunity while she slept. He could have fed from her, molested her, and she wouldn't even have known it while blacked out and under the influence of his sleep magic.

Could his claim be trusted? Did it matter? And where was he?

She grabbed her jacket and crawled out from the brush only to freeze upon seeing said vampire lounging against a tree nearby the used campsite. The fire had long since gone out. One hand rested on the hilt of his long broadsword in the dirt. The blue Guardian teardrop twinkled beneath his closed eye. His head rested back, exposing a masculine neck and pronounced Adam's apple. His knees were bent, and one wrist rested on a knee. Wind ruffled his hair. *Asleep?*

Sexy, masculine, and so casually so. He belonged on a runway in Milan, not covered in leather, dirt, and scratches in Elphyne. He was the kind of male who caused mouth paralysis if he came near and then smirked knowingly while you tried to untie your tongue. The glamor he'd cast on himself was at the heart of every woman's fantasy.

A fantasy, she had to remind herself. No. The dream she'd just had was more of a nightmare, but it awakened her to the truth. Vampires were the evil shits who'd locked her in a cage.

For all Silver knew, this vampire wanted Silver to be his own personal blood slave.

She slipped on her jacket and put the transceiver in her pocket. There were no other weapons on her body. He'd taken them all. She eyed them at his side and took a cautious step closer.

Long lashes flipped up as his eyes opened. She stilled. He zeroed in on her and straightened.

"Trying for the lucky final time?" Amusement twinkled in his eyes.

"You should be dead," she noted rather dumbly.

"Should I be?"

He made no move. And she wasn't sure what was happening.

His expression darkened suddenly, and then he kicked something near the dead fire. Another carcass, but not the rabbit she'd hunted and cooked. This one was a cross between a boar and an armadillo—she thought maybe it was called a warada. He refocused his judgmental gaze on her. "You should *never* have come into fae territory so ill prepared. That prickly bastard tried to eat you in your sleep."

"But not you," she blurted.

"No, not me." He grinned. "I prefer my females awake when I feast on them."

Her cheeks heated at his velvet voice. What was happening? Who was this guy? He tossed innuendo, and it looked good on him. Shade was his name... but *who* was he? Were all Guardians as seductive as him? A million thoughts ran through her head.

Shade slowly straightened to his six-foot-something height. He moved slowly, as if afraid to startle her. The notion sent her lungs into hyper-drive. She felt lightheaded.

"Why didn't you kill me... or bite me?" she asked.

His gaze darkened, but he didn't answer. Instead, he took a step closer, leaving his weapons on the floor.

"I have your bag," he offered as he scooped it up.

"Did you open it?"

He gave a half shrug. "It's a bunch of contraband. I should destroy it."

"But you haven't. Why not?"

His long lashed, soulful gaze leveled her. "You need it. And I need you. I'm willing to trade."

His voice had deepened with every word until she had no choice but to imagine the intimation. Trade? She shouldn't shiver at his words. She shouldn't feel them trail down her skin like a lover's caress, waking every nerve in her body. She shouldn't crave more.

He walked over and stopped toe-to-toe with her. He glanced down. A lock of rich brown hair dropped over his eyes. He smelled like the essence of the forest—pine, dirt, and danger. She went for her bag, but he held it back, teasing. She grasped his forearm and pulled. He hid the bag further behind his back, a crooked smile gracing his lips. He twisted away, pulling her against his chest. The corset pressed against her breasts. Sensation exploded in her affection-starved body and she coughed to cover her gasp. All she wanted to do was fall into those eyes. From the moment she'd laid eyes on him, his existence was holy light to her shadow.

"Stop it," she breathed, knuckles blanching on his forearm.

He lowered until his lips hovered near hers. "Stop what?"

She shivered.

She quaked.

"Stop trying to seduce me with your glamor."

His upper lip lifted, flashing fang. He chased her lips with his. She darted back.

"Darling," he murmured intently. "I don't have to use glamor. You'll beg for my bite just the way I am."

Her legs weakened. God, she was frozen. Face-to-face with him.

Nipples hard and aching. Desire pooling between her legs. Her will was locked in a war of instinct versus logic. Kiss him versus—

"Glamor has nothing to do with it," he promised. "This is the real me. Explore me if you don't believe it."

A flash of his muscled, naked body came to mind. "As in, touch you?"

"A glamor is an illusion. It won't change the physical state. So, touch me. See what's real. Anywhere you want."

Should she?

"I said, touch me, Silver." His voice deepened with authority and all she wanted to do was comply. "You need this."

Her free hand stayed stubbornly at her side, and the other remained frozen on his arm holding the bag. What if this, too, was a trick?

His eyes flashed. "Touch my face, little fee-lion, and I will reward you."

She raised a single brow. "With a kiss?"

"No. But I like where your mind went." His eyes crinkled. "I'll give you the bag, darling. The bag."

Right. The bag. Right, right.

The instant her fingers made contact with his cheek, they both made some kind of embarrassing sound of need. Air rushed out of their mouths. An ache filled her with the urge to step into him, to somehow become a part of him. How could this be real?

"Keep going," he muttered.

He studied her as she traced the contours of his face. Sharp cheekbones. Thick scruff, surprisingly soft and welcoming. Smooth skin. Long lashes. Strong brows. Velvety lips... Perfect, sexy symmetry. Everywhere she explored, her eyes reconciled with the touch, and her body wanted more. He was real. No glamor.

"You can touch anywhere," he reminded. "I won't bite. Yet."

Her eyes snapped up, and she stepped back. "I'm good."

She held out her tingling palm. He studied her some more and then reluctantly handed her the pack before retrieving his sword and strapping it between his shoulder blades. He picked up the dead warada.

"I'll skin it so you can eat," he offered.

"I don't need you to feed me."

"Too bad."

"Shade—"

"I like it when you say my name." He flashed her a heart-stopping grin before returning to the warada and stabbing its soft belly with a dagger. "Keep talking."

Her jaw dropped. "I don't want your food."

The rumble in her stomach said otherwise. She couldn't deny that eating this meal would make her mission go faster. But if she let him think he was providing for her, then he would believe they were friends... or worse, that she'd accepted his claim they were mates. That couldn't happen. Whatever this small truce had been, it was over. He must have sensed her thoughts because the moment she stepped in the opposite direction, he left the warada and rushed to block her way into the forest.

She sidestepped him. He allowed her a few paces before jogging after her and getting in her way. Fire and defiance flashed in his eyes as he wordlessly faced her down. She hardened her jaw and side-stepped again. He did the same. She met his infuriating eyes and called his bluff.

"You clearly have no fuel left in your tank, otherwise you'd just do your shadow teleport thing. So that means you can't shift. Either you leave me alone, or we're back to me stabbing you."

"You're out of weapons," he pointed out.

"That's what you think."

She jabbed her fist at him. It glanced off his jaw but split his lip. A thin rivulet of blood ran down his bearded chin. When he snapped his gaze to her, none of his determination had diminished. Out darted a pointed, pink vampire tongue and licked the edge of his lip.

*Son-of-a-bitch.*

She cracked her knuckles and raised her brows, waiting for his reply. She would fight him if necessary. Until one of them was dead. Doubt flickered on his face. Clearly, the vampire was not used to people walking away from him.

A screeching sound had them both looking up. Through branches, a blurry dark shape descended at an alarming rate, coming straight for them. Shade pushed her aside and took the brunt of the attack.

Silver hit the ground. The backpack dislodged from her shoulders. She rolled out of the straps so she could fight unrestrained. Darting her gaze about, she assessed the situation. Shade was right. She had no weapon. Maybe a grenade in the pack. Fists would not hinder this beast—it was the same one that had attacked before.

Shade grappled the monster with reptilian legs. Taloned hands tried to grasp him. Those great tentacled wings fanned out and flapped, throwing up dirt and twigs like an octopus out of water. It tried to take him with it as it flew and flickered in the air, but Shade slipped out of its hold, fluidly rolled, and got to his feet in a fighting stance, broadsword already in his hands. He drew it so fast she'd not even seen it.

*Get your own weapon.*

Silver checked the warada and located Shade's bloody dagger. She dashed to pick it up and faced them just as Shade took a powerful swing at the monster, his neck tendons contorting with strain. The sword passed right through it like smoke. No... not smoke. The monster's body *moved* to avoid the metal like oil separated from water. Then it rejoined in the same form as before. Shade thrust and the same thing happened. The metal sword repelled flesh and bone.

Silver glanced at the dagger. It was futile against this creature. What use was metal against fae if you couldn't pierce the flesh? Horror dawned as she faced the truth—they were going to die.

## CHAPTER TEN

Shade was a vampire who knew the way of the world. Since his birth, nothing had been sugar-coated. The courtesans who'd raised him never kept the truth from him for long. He'd prided himself on being one of those fae who knew everything from the inner workings of a queen's mind to the machinations of politics, to what made a *ponaturi* tick.

But this creature before him... he'd never seen the likes of it before. Not just its appearance, but the way it behaved, the way it moved and bent around his sword as though it were made of liquid. It defied the laws of nature, even the laws of the Well.

This was a perversion. It felt wrong, but familiar, like Queen Maebh, Bones, and a Sluagh all rolling in the inkiest, rottenest depths of the Well. The worst part was he didn't think they'd begun to scratch the surface of what this creature was capable of.

A Guardian with an ineffective sword—or mana—was a lesser

fae. Shade had no weapon against this creature. How would he protect his mate?

The demogorgon dug its talons into Shade's shoulders with a screech that sprayed spittle. Shade's vision blurred as it lifted him off the ground. With his shoulders pierced, he lost control of his arms. He dropped the sword. It was useless anyway.

But there was one weapon a vampire never lost. Baring his fangs, he bit into the first reptilian arm. The blood tasted like bile. Unlike the metal sword, the arm did not bend around his fangs. Its aversion to metal was a weapon against the humans and Guardians in one. It couldn't be a coincidence Maebh had created it so soon after Jasper had proven her Sluagh were fallible against his gift.

Shade tasted memories in the blood. It definitely used to be the human called Bones, but was now warped and demented beyond recognition. Shade saw the screams of the man as he hung on hooks in the queen's dungeon as she experimented on him. He clamped down harder until the creature screamed and pried him away. They both hit the ground hard. Wind knocked out of Shade. He rolled, and went for the second arm, but a tentacle whipped around from the back of the beast's body and hit Shade clean across the cheek. *Stars.* He went flying and ricocheted off a tree, hit his head, and lost sight altogether.

Slimy strong tentacles pinned him. The demogorgon screamed as though frustrated at Shade. As Shade's blurred vision slowly came back, he came face to face with a split maw opened like an insect's mandible.

But it wasn't going for the kill shot. Why?

Silver vaulted onto the creature's back, her expression stony as she pried tentacles from Shade. He shook his head to clear his vision. Surely he wasn't seeing that. Because if he was, then his mate was putting herself in harm's way to help him. His mate, who claimed to want nothing to do with him.

"What are you doing?" he bellowed, his voice almost drowning in the beast's angry roar.

"If we work together," she bit out. "We might win."

He punched the creature in the eye. "Run! Get to safety."

She slid arms around the thick scaled neck and choked as she locked eyes with Shade. "And let you have all the fun?"

He fell in love in that moment.

The beast roared and twisted to pluck Silver from his body, but she was in its blind spot. It bucked like a bull, whipped her with its tentacles, and threw her back into Shade. He caught Silver as she collided with him. His head hit the tree again and pain slammed in. In a daze, Shade slid down. Nausea rolled. Ringing in his ears. Somewhere ahead, he vaguely saw Silver get to her feet.

"Wake up." Urgency filled her tone as she patted his face. "Jesus, Shade. Wake up!"

*I'm getting up.*

But his mind wouldn't connect with his body. Silver repetitively cursed. He blinked, trying to clear his vision. She pointed a dagger at her chest. *What the fuck?*

Thinking the worst, panic and adrenaline surged through him, but the blade sliced her laces. In one swift stroke, she cut the corset armor from her body. Before it hit the ground, she cut the laces on the vambrace. She glared at the snarling demogorgon creeping forward, his voice rattling the air. Tentacles writhed in vexation, and then Silver dropped the dagger.

It was the strike to a match.

Black smoke burst from her chest. She gave an agonizing scream as night drowned out the light. Her scream died, only to have another's fill the air. Somewhere beyond the darkness, the demogorgon was in pain. With wild eyes, Silver glanced at him from over her shoulder.

"Now would be a good time to use that teleporting skill of yours."

But he'd run out of mana.

She must have seen the bleak look on his face and asked, "You truly have no fuel left?"

He shoved aside the fact his mate had elemental chaos pouring from her soul, or that she'd tried to lock it away behind a wall of agonizing metal, and then clarity hit him. She was free from metal, free from blockages to the Well. He took hold of her hand and said, "I do now."

The moment they connected, blue light ripped up their joined hands, carving organic patterns into their flesh, weaving and eddying along their skin until it hit their necks and then faded away. Triumph surged through Shade. The Well-blessed bond had triggered. Euphoric power licked his skin—and it came from inside her. He drew it into his body, borrowing what he needed to refill his reservoir, and then he stole her through the shadows.

⚖

They tumbled into powdery white snow. It was the same forest he'd taken her before and wasn't far from Rush's vacant cabin. He'd hoped it would provide a sanctuary. The howl of wolves greeted their arrival and Silver scrambled to get to her feet. There was a pack of wolves under Rush's command in these woods. They knew to trust a Guardian in uniform.

Blackness still leaked from Silver's chest, but at a slower rate. He sensed her fear and panic down their bond like it was his own emotion. She'd hidden so much during the battle. Even now, she put on a stoic front.

He stared in awe at his hand. The blue twinkling light of their union disappeared under the cuff of his jacket sleeve. If it was anything like the other mated pairs, it would cover his entire arm. If he wasn't concerned about Silver's wellbeing, he'd let his victory show.

But she was spiraling.

He reached for her.

She flinched away. "If you value your life, don't touch me."

"What are you talking about?"

"This black stuff kills on contact. Everything it touches goes necrotic." She backed away, dismay in her eyes and hurtling down their bond. "I can't control it. I need my corset."

"I don't have it."

"Then any metal. *Anything!*"

He calmly held out his palm, but her panic battered his defenses, trying to infect him as surely as if it was his own. But the Well would not pair them together if she was harmful to him. If there was one thing he trusted more than his instincts, it was that the Well had a plan.

"Silver, I can help you."

"No one can help me."

"I'm your mate." Of course he could. He held up his blue patterned hand. "Listen to the bond and know I'm telling you the truth."

Her eyes widened at the blue glowing marks on her hand as if she'd just registered what had happened. She'd lived with the fae for a time, he was sure of it. When he'd mentioned her being his mate, she appeared to understand. But she shook her head and backed away. "This changes nothing."

"I can help you, Silver. I can train you to control your gift."

Incredulous eyes speared him, and she spoke with disgust. "Gift? This isn't a gift. It's a curse. And you can't control this. It controls you."

She turned and ran. Darkness streamed behind her like a twisted bridal veil. She disappeared through the trees. He should chase her, but it was clear she wasn't ready for the truth. Some people never were. There was a reason people went to the Rosebuds. They wanted someone else to blame for their desires.

Perhaps Silver needed a moment alone with her thoughts. It was one thing for her to deny their union when she'd convinced herself she was wholly human, but this bond had blurred the lines. And her gift was something he'd never seen.

The demogorgon's scream had been laced with pain as her dark power engulfed it.

Had she killed it?

She'd said her gift killed anything it touched, but this creature was a friend of the darkness. He doubted it would be down for long, but it wouldn't find them so easily here. At least not right now.

No wonder Silver was driven by fear. No wonder she needed

metal in her world. She'd tried to smother the part of her she thought was evil.

And now, because of him, it was breaking through.

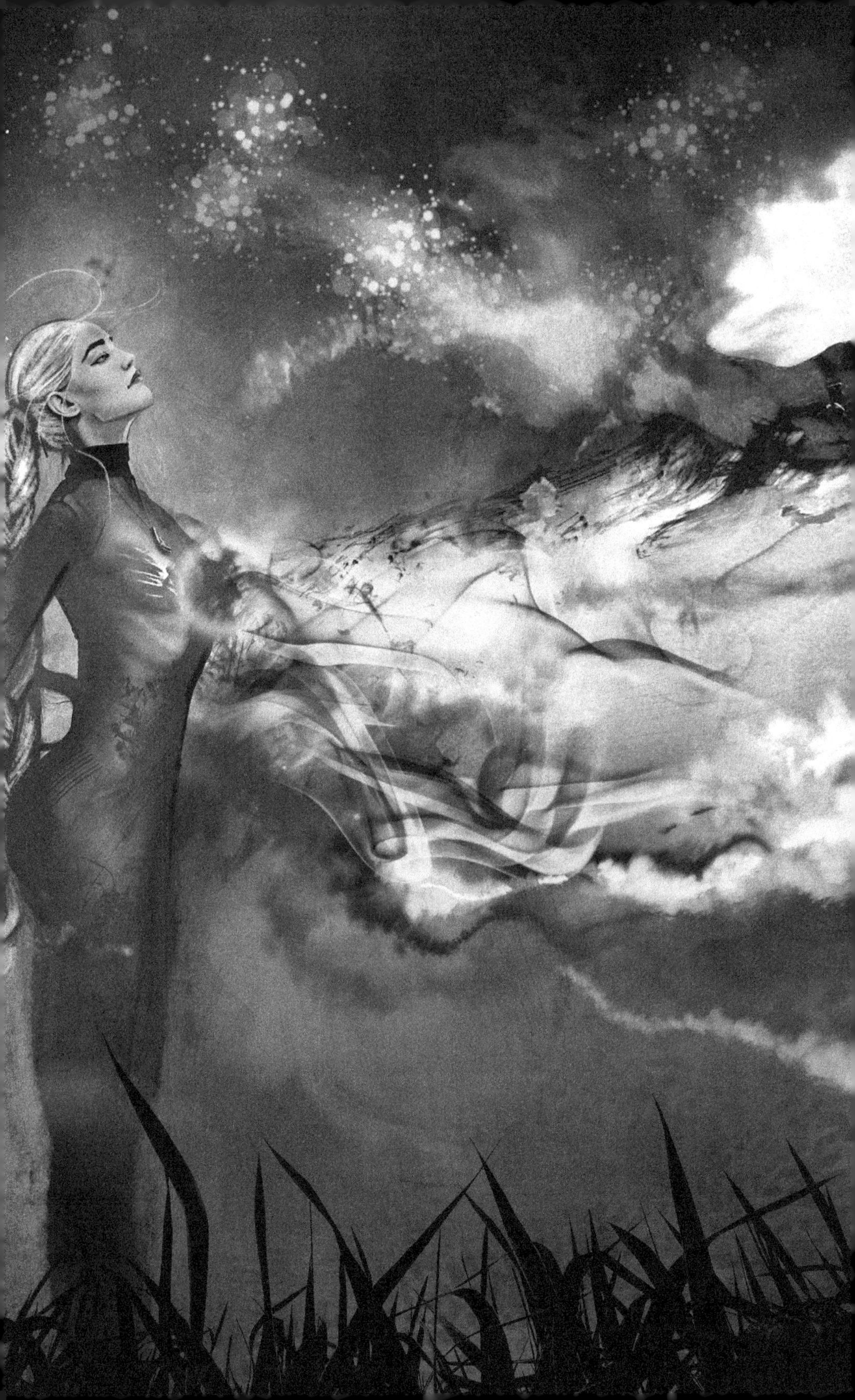

# CHAPTER ELEVEN

Silver ran as fast as she could. She had no idea where she was going, only that she needed to get away from Shade and any living thing. She needed metal. She needed her vambrace and corset. Nothing else would contain the darkness inside.

It was one thing for her to stab or slice the throat of the enemy, but it was something else to have her choice taken from her. When she killed, she did it with purpose and with agency. She did it for the survival of humanity. Her reputation for never hesitating was because she didn't want to be in this position. And it had worked. She'd kept ahead of the curve until now. Until she couldn't just let that monster take the insufferable stalker vampire.

What was wrong with her?

Crunching through the snow, she shivered. White clouds puffed from her mouth. The arctic temperature drilled through her clothes and froze her bones. With her connection to the Well rushing in, every sense in her body amplified. The gray sky became luminous. Evergreen trees grew saturated. The heady smell of wild, frost hardy roses and crisp ice made her feel dizzy. Out of breath and gasping, she came to a stop.

With trepidation, she dropped her gaze and almost vomited at the sight of the black smoke still pouring free from her chest.

"Stop." She batted it away, but the smoke only swirled around her hands and then reformed—kind of like the monster's flesh had done when repelled by metal. Was she any better than it? She tried to scoop the blackness and shove it inside her chest, but it was a fool's errand. Tears burned her eyes and her throat closed.

She hadn't felt this helpless since she'd come to the human city in pieces. Rory had taken one look at Silver's destitute eyes and then gave her the vambrace to stifle the curse. No one would help her out here. She'd run from the only person who seemed to want to help her. Now she was alone.

*Wherever you go, you'll never escape your roots.* Her mother's drunken cackle filled her ears.

Silver started running.

*You'll never escape your roots.*

She stumbled, and then a hard projectile hit her in the torso, taking her to the snow.

"Oof."

Strong hands rolled her to face the sky. Shade loomed over her, his expression fierce as he pinned her arms and flattened his body against hers. Ice seeped into her back as the snow made a home in her jacket. Intense brown eyes settled on her and held. She bucked, but he was as immovable as a mountain.

"You clearly have a death wish," she blurted.

"Stop struggling."

Maybe the fight left her. Maybe her mother was right, and it was time to accept her rotten soul. Maybe this was her giving up, because she stopped struggling.

"Good girl," he praised.

She didn't even have the energy to snap back.

"Silver," he said calmly. "Look."

Only then she realized her eyes were shut, and she'd turned away.

"Look at us," he growled. "*Look between us.*"

Frowning, she lifted her lashes. As always, his eyes were arresting. Breathtaking. Why did they feel warm and safe, as though she could crawl in there and make it a home away from her troubles and fears? The thought unsettled her, but it felt right. It *hurt* that it felt right, as though her distrust was ice breaking for a ship. She tried to shove the feelings out of her head, but it was impossible with him on her. Male spice, sweat and heat was everywhere. The pressure of his weight felt remarkably soothing, like her corset.

"Look," he repeated and pushed himself up a little.

She glanced between their bodies, to where her black smoke should be eating him alive, but it oozed from her chest and curled around his own shadows. Smoky ribbons twirled together until it was impossible to see whose was whose. He was not necrotic. He was not dying. He looked at her with the same wonder she felt.

"How can that be?" she gasped.

His lips lowered to her ears. "My darkness dances with yours."

"But…"

He nipped her jaw playfully, and she shivered.

"Can't you *feel* us?" he rasped against her skin.

She squirmed and wished she hadn't. Without her corset, every ridge and line of his jacket electrified her body. Aching torso welts blended with pleasure as her nipples peaked and rubbed, shooting liquid fire to pool between her thighs. The cold stopped existing. Unable to help herself, she arched into him, needing more.

A groan of need slipped out of him. His hips rocked against hers and he nuzzled her neck, inhaling deeply, muttering almost too quietly for her to hear, "Silver, my mate. I've caught you."

"Get off." Her words sounded hollow as she shoved him. He grappled her again.

"You don't want that," he said, baring fangs.

"How on earth would you know what I want?"

"Because I feel your emotions, just as you feel mine."

She refused to acknowledge what she knew in her gut to be true. This link between them went both ways, and it was unbreakable. She shoved him again. "I said get off."

"Not until you accept this bond."

"I accept nothing."

She rammed the heel of her palm into his nose. His head snapped back. Silver covered her mouth, shocked. *She'd just hit him.* She'd hit him before, but somehow this felt different. Something had shifted inside her at seeing their darkness dance together. Her body had responded to his touch. That little girl who'd spent her childhood caring for a mother who never cared back was screaming for Silver to give in to him.

Shade's eyes slowly came back to Silver, but instead of getting angry, his lips curved on one side. His smile wasn't wicked or cruel, or the promise of retaliation. It was a smile she'd seen on Polly wrestling with her brother, alight with playful competition. *Oh, shit.*

"You want to fight?" His brows winged up, and he wiped his nose. "Then let's fight. But I'm not running away. You don't scare me, so show me your best."

She shoved him as hard as she could, but it was only to distract him from her feet trapping his own. She rolled them. He landed hard on his back, and she was on top—now pinning him with her thighs and hands. She went for his face, but he caught her wrists and yanked them out and down. Her body slammed into his. Her forehead hit the snow behind his head. Pain exploded, but that wasn't the worst part. The bastard had a face full of her breasts, an outcome he clearly delighted in.

Outraged, she kicked off and rolled again, but he was with her every step of the way. She attacked again, and again. Their grunts drowned out the tweeting birds until somehow, she was back on top, but reversed, her back against his front. His arms banded about her middle, his legs snaked around hers, trapping her as they laid there.

"Done yet?" he growled. When she didn't reply, he tightened his steel embrace and added, "*Listen.*"

Panting and frustrated, she stilled. What else could she do with his arms and legs wrapped around her like a monkey? She glared at the snowcapped trees around them. Wind blew gently, calmly. Birds chirped as they flew from tree to tree. One landed on a bough and then took off, dislodging snow with a thud.

"Listen to *us*," he corrected, still holding her firmly.

Her focus narrowed to the sounds between them. His heart, her heart, beating like the staccato rhythm of a symphony. Their breaths were in sync, adding to the music of nature. The fight left Silver, and she dropped her head back to land on his shoulder.

He angled his head to hers. When he inhaled her scent, his soft groan rattled through her back. Pleasure purred into her body. She writhed, instinctively seeking out the sensations their connection elicited.

"Yes," he said. "Do you feel it?"

"I'm on top of you," she breathed. "Of course I feel you."

"Not me, darling. *Us*."

"What?" She had no idea what he meant. All she could concentrate on was the electric places they touched. Scorching awareness at her head, along her back, buttocks, and legs.

"We are joining, becoming one." Another groan. A nuzzle with his nose at her ear. A lick along her skin. Shivers down her spine. "That urge I sense in you, that *need* to be together, is the Well's approval. Our bond is sacred, Silver. Don't ignore it."

She let him scent and burrow into her like lovers do because she needed it. Her whole life, she'd needed it. Her hand arced back to thread in his hair, sweaty and damp from their exertion. Now that she'd stopped fighting, she started feeling. Overwhelming emotions swirled and eddied inside.

"What's happening?" she gasped.

"We can share mana and emotion. There is nothing between us now but our desire entwining."

Silver wriggled around until she faced him. Serious eyes studied her as he repositioned his hands to settle on her ass... and she let him. His hands felt like they belonged there, just like the emotions and magic flushing between them. Was that why her black heart didn't affect him? Their souls were one?

Through their bond she felt his eagerness clash with concern at her confusion.

Maybe that's why she dropped her lips to his and kissed him, and when he opened to her, inviting her in, maybe that's why she penetrated deeper. The taste of him was pure, heady and male. Their tongues danced just as their darkness had. It started slow and languid, a means to test each other and learn the steps. She traced his fangs, his lips, his pointed tongue. Then, with the increasing beat of their hearts, the dance steps turned wicked and obscene as they clashed and clutched each other, writhing and thrusting, humping over their clothes.

He was the enemy, despite this new bond that stole her sense and made everything heightened. Somewhere far away, she knew this was wrong. Her mission would accept nothing less. But it felt good to forget, just for a moment. It felt good to lose herself in his kiss, to slide her tongue along his velvet lips. That comforting place deep in his eyes became real, not fantasy.

They came apart, equally dazed, and stared at each other.

Did that just happen?

Her mouth opened and then closed. He did the same. They were speechless. Still with her palms on his chest, her braid draped beside his head, her mother's words came flinging back. *Black-hearted bitch.*

She scrambled off him, panting.

"What are you afraid of?" he asked, feverish eyes searching hers as he stood. "You need to stop seeing me as the enemy."

*Enemy.* Her wits came tunneling back. *The mission comes first.* She mustn't forget her purpose, despite the pretty package he presented. She shut her jacket tight. How on earth was she going to avoid him now?

This need between them was a luxury she couldn't afford. Better to cut it off now than for it to bloom and fester into something dangerous.

"I need my corset and vambrace," she demanded, her voice trembling. Her gaze dipped to the backpack at his feet. At least he'd had the sense to bring it. "And that."

He tossed it to her. "This, I'll allow."

She scoffed and put the pack on, slamming up her snark as a shield. Maybe if he hated her, he'd back off. Because she sure as shit had trouble walking away. She flipped her hood up to shield her ears from the cold. "Allow? One kiss and you think you own me."

"One kiss is the least of what I'll give you. You're mine to protect, mine to hold, and mine to bring to insurmountable pleasure."

Silver sighed and rubbed her temples. He was impossible.

"Shade," she warned. "I'm death. Maybe not to you, but surely to the people around you. Trust me, you don't want that."

"You're the only one that matters to me."

"You say that now. But what if that truce our darkness has for each other fails? What then?"

"You tried to kill me multiple times, and yet here I am." He held his hands wide to prove his point, but all it did was gift her with the perfect view of his masculine physique. *Goddammit* that leather looked sprayed on. And she'd been all pressed up against it, writhing and moaning like an alley cat in heat.

She hardened her expression. "It's when I stop trying that you need to worry about."

Something like pride swelled down their bond, and she scowled. Of all the things for him to be proud of, it was her savagery.

A sparkle entered his eyes, and he grinned. "So... if not one kiss, then how many?"

Her mind blanked for a moment, then she put two and two together. How many kisses to own her? He was joking, but what had passed between them should never have happened.

"If you refuse to take me to my armor, then I'll find it myself."

"Avoid me all you want, but I know what you're feeling. There are no secrets down our bond. You want me. It's too late to deny that now."

No secrets? Then, being with him was even more dangerous. "The kiss meant nothing. Take me back to my campsite."

Something like hurt flashed in his eyes before it was gone. He pointed in the direction she presumed the old campsite was.

"Go back there and you're courting danger," he warned, all joking aside. "The demogorgon won't be dead. It's too powerful and you're not ready."

"That's what it's called, a demogorgon?" She raised her brows and used the monster to distance herself from what had happened between them. "He looked eerily like someone I knew called Bones. And that can't be a coincidence. If you fae have turned him into a monster, then he's nothing but a mutant, like you. I can take him on."

Ice ran fingers down her spine, and it had nothing to do with the frigid temperature making her nose run. Shade's stare became lethal, and his shadows peeled away from his body like black steam.

"You won't be able to take anyone, or anything, until you learn to harness your mana," he said. "I can show you how. Let me teach you."

"By route of kissing?"

"If that's what it takes," he smirked.

"I'll pass."

She checked the sky and her surroundings. This forest looked remarkably like the one he'd taken her to the first time. The same herbs and flowers struggled to grow at the base of the trees.

"You'll be back." He reached down and plucked a wild rosebud from a bush, then leaned his shoulder against a tree and twirled it in his fingers like he had all the time in the world.

"I don't need you to look after me."

"You're a kitten, a little fee-lion, and at the first taste of the pleasure I offered, you rolled over and showed me your belly."

She flipped up her middle finger at him and walked away. His deep chuckle stayed in her mind well after the sound had passed.

## CHAPTER TWELVE

There was no room in Silver's plan for Shade. He might not have tried to kill her, he might have given her the best damned kiss she'd had in her life, and she might be his mate, but none of that mattered when an entire race of people was on the brink of extinction.

Stewing in her discontent, she crunched through snow, heading back down the mountain toward where her campsite had been. The journey felt lighter without her corset. At least, that was her excuse. It certainly wasn't the brief tryst she'd had with a vampire whose shadows danced with hers. She glanced down the length of her body. Darkness oozed from her jacket sleeves and at the hem near her thighs. If she glanced behind her, she would probably find dying plants in her wake.

But she didn't look back.

She doggedly walked until she made it to the rooted tree that had fallen across the gorge and raging river, its green leaves blowing in the wind. She barely gave it a glance and continued to cross.

*Keep going.* Don't think about the fall. *Don't think about how I pushed Shade off.* How he could have died... because of her. *Don't think about the uncomfortable feeling in my stomach when I think of that.* Silver's footing slipped on moss, and she fell to the log hard. A short, sharp cry ripped out of her, and she bit her lip until she tasted blood.

*Breathe.*

*Sing some Beach Boys.*

*Calm down.*

Why was he so infernally incorrigible? The vampire was confusing the hell out of her. She couldn't believe she'd laid with him in the snow and... and kissed him like her life depended on it. She ripped leaves from the log in her frustration. The dazed look he'd given her after their kiss was as though he'd been stunned into silence at how good it was. Or like he'd never had someone kiss him that way.

"Why are you even thinking about him?" she grumbled aloud.

She swallowed hard and forced herself to crawl across at a snail's pace, ignoring the way her heart pounded. She was going swimmingly... until the smoke from her chest started to eat at the wood beneath her fingertips. First, the color leeched from the tree, then wood blackened and splintered off in crumbling chunks, as though remnants of a fire. She wasn't wearing her Well-blocking garments. *Shit.*

There would be something in her backpack, but if she reached around and opened her bag, she might fall anyway. She glanced down at the raging river. Shade had survived. She could, too. Right?

*Keep going. Hurry.* People depended on her. An image of Carla's gangrene fingers hit her squarely behind the eyes. Jimmy, and the medicine he needed for her. Polly and her malnourished eyes. Silver had to keep going. There was a reason Rory picked her for this mission. Silver had no ties, no family, and no friends. It wasn't as if she was going to kill a child. No, she was going to take her to a better place. She was going to save humanity. Nothing would get in Silver's way.

Except Shade.

And not only because of his effect on her, but because of the place she was headed... he was probably headed too. She needed to get into the Order of the Well undetected, not chased by a seductive, incorrigible vampire.

Almost at the end, she increased her pace until she made it to the other side and collapsed onto her face. The sounds of the tree falling apart behind haunted her. It crumbled and dislodged with a sense of foreboding. That could have been her. All these years, all that the tree had suffered, and it still managed to grow as it laid across that river gorge... until she came along and undid everything in a matter of seconds. *That* was why she needed her armor. Screw Shade and his training. There was no controlling her curse by manner of will. She shut her eyes, silently flabbergasted at everything that had happened. Of all the obstacles she'd planned for, being mated to a fae had never entered her mind.

She got to her feet and continued to walk. She didn't stop until she made it to the campsite. Warily, she approached with her senses blaring, ready to pick up any hint of danger. If the demogorgon was here, she'd stay back. Keeping her footfall light, she crept closer to the site and surveyed the area. No demogorgon carcass, which meant Shade had been right, and it lived.

It was probably out there hunting them. Attacking twice wasn't a coincidence. Something, or someone, had sent that beast. Casting her mind back to both attacks, she replayed the scenes. In both instances, the demogorgon had tried to fly away with Shade, but not kill him. With her, it had gone for the throat. So, it must be him the creature was after, and Shade was too wrapped up in claiming Silver as his mate. He probably had no idea he was being hunted. Or didn't care.

Again. Not her problem. She straightened her shoulders and stepped into the clearing. It had been half a day since she'd been here. The dirt was still turned from their battle. The fire pit, long since dead. And there was no sign of her armor anywhere. How could that be?

Frantically, she walked around the clearing, searching. Maybe she'd left it in the brush she'd slept in, but after a quick check, she found it empty. She put her hands on her hips, eyes sweeping the place one last time.

She found no glint of silver, but a flash of scarlet lay near the edge of the brush. She moved closer but didn't touch. A wild rose... the kind Shade had been toying with as she'd left him. None grew nearby.

*Son-of-a-bitch.* He'd been here, and he'd taken her armor. Frustration burned through her veins. She raised her face to the sky and screamed, uncaring if she was a beacon to any predator nearby. Her fury would not be tamed. She would *kill* him this time.

She dropped her backpack and opened it, just to make sure he'd not stolen other items. Her eyes landed on the metal clockwork transceiver, and she mentally kicked herself. She should have held it the moment she left Shade. He was ruining everything. It might be hard to continuously hold, but it was better than nothing. She pocketed it and checked her darkness. It stopped. Having the item in her pocket must be close enough to block the Well. For now. She then rifled through and found a small hunting knife—her head snapped up at the sound of rustling.

She gripped the hunting knife. A tall, gangly teen with blond hair burst into the clearing, followed by Sid and Martin. All three were a little worse for wear. Blood and scratches covered half of their bodies. But they were alive. Relief poured through her along with a tightness across her chest. She wasn't supposed to think about them like that. This Reaper business was lonely. The mission came first, but she was glad they'd escaped unharmed.

Sid lifted his chin in a silent greeting. Martin checked the campsite, his pistol out and cocked. Jimmy almost wept at the sight of her. "You're okay!"

He bowled into her and hugged fiercely. Fucker was stronger than he looked. She allowed a guilty moment of reconnection before shoving him away in case her curse infected him. Then something else occurred to her. The Well-blessed mating marks. Were they hidden now too? A quick glance down at her hand showed all traces of blue glow still there. She shoved her hands in her pockets, hoping the part near her neck was hidden by the woolen hood.

She gave Jimmy the once-over as he stepped back. Unharmed for the most part, despite Shade's mesmerizing of them. It must have worn off, and the demogorgon must have—wait... where was Roger?

She lifted her gaze to Sid. He gave a bleak shake of the head.

Roger hadn't made it. She'd never gotten along with him, but the loss of a team member still hurt. He'd saved her life on more than one occasion, and she'd had his back, too. This mission, and her purpose, just got more real.

"What happened after I left?" Silver asked. Roger's bite mark had only been shallow, not enough to kill him.

"Roger was gone when we woke sitting on this log in the middle of nowhere," Martin explained. "We have vague memories of a vampire."

"He mesmerized you."

Sid spat his disgust on the dirt.

"Is that what happened to you too?" Jimmy asked, then scowled. "If it hurt you, I'll track it down and kill it."

All Silver could see was Shade's heavy-lidded gaze as she kissed him. Guilt peppered her heart, and she swallowed hard. "No. I wasn't mesmerized or hurt."

Martin lowered his pistol. "What happened then?"

A million replies hurtled through Silver's mind. She scrubbed her face, trying to think of a good answer. A rush of conflicting emotions whirled through her.

"What the fuck is that?" Martin asked abruptly.

Silver had wiped her face. The blue glowing evidence of her mating bond glittered brightly on the back of her hand. She quickly hid her hand, but it was too late. They'd seen the glow. They knew it wasn't natural.

Jimmy stepped back, hurt in his eyes. "You're one of them?"

Martin pointed his pistol at her. Sid narrowed his eyes but remained calm. Silver raised her palms, including the one holding the knife.

"I'm on your side," she reminded them. "Trust me."

"Then what is that?" Martin asked, nodding to her marks.

"That is... something I can't control." She glanced at Sid. His firm gaze gave her the courage to come clean. "It's a Well-blessed mating bond."

"What does that mean?" Martin asked as he circled her.

"It means she's got some kind of connection to the fae magic source," Sid answered for her. "Right?"

She nodded. "I've had it since I awoke in this time. I tried to smother it with metal, but since coming out here, it's finding a way to come out."

They all looked at her warily.

"I'm still one of you," she insisted.

"What is it?" Martin asked, still pointing the gun at her. "Your fae magic? What does it do?"

"It's nothing good."

"That doesn't answer my question."

She sighed. "You really want to know? It's death. Black stuff leaks out of me and kills anything it touches like poison. I found out the hard way after some guy kissed me. The stuff came out, touched his ear, and his flesh decayed."

Knowledge dawned on Martin's face. "The rumor of you biting off that ear."

She nodded. "I bit it to hide the evidence, and to stop the rest of him from dying."

"Who else knows about this?" he asked.

"Rory knows, doesn't she?" Sid stepped forward. He'd never judged her. Never really cared about much between them except the occasional dance between the sheets, but she couldn't help feeling bad at the kernel of disappointment in his eyes. "She's the one who made that armor for you."

"Yes."

His jaw clenched. He gave her his back and ran his hand over his head. Silver looked at the sky. If there was one thing that tied this team together, it was a unified "Us versus them." And now that was gone.

"I'm still dedicated to this mission," she said.

"How do we know that?" Martin steadied his aim at her face.

"I'm here, aren't I?" She threw her hands in the air. "I tried to kill him. I left him behind and I'm here."

Sid came at her, all imposing alpha and broad chest. She lifted her chin and met him eye to eye. "You want to kill me, then do it. If not, we're wasting time."

He drew his fist back, eyes blazing, and she understood. He needed to take out his feelings of betrayal on her. Their relationship was supposed to be easy, but she'd gone and made it anything but. She'd never seen so much emotion play out over his features and could clearly see he felt something for her, as small as it might be. She braced herself to take the hit. She deserved it.

*You're the only one that matters to me.*

Sid's fist never connected. The shadows darkened. Black incorporeal ribbons exploded, and the epitome of the night burst into being in front of her. Silver glimpsed the breadth of Shade's leather clad shoulders, the back of his head, and then his hand snapped up to catch Sid's fist. A crack of bone, and then a cry of pain no man should make. Sid crumpled to the ground, clutching his mangled hand.

Shade disappeared in the shadows. He appeared before Martin

and grabbed the big man by the scruff of the neck, looked into his eyes and commanded, "Sit on your ass and twiddle your thumbs."

As Shade stalked Jimmy, Silver recovered enough of her wits to get in the way. She held the hunting knife to Shade's neck as he reached for the teen.

"Touch him and you die," she warned.

Incredulous eyes slid to hers. His voice was a snarl ripped from his lungs. "*They* die for touching *you*."

She'd never seen Shade so wild and rumpled. Madness existed in his expression. For a moment, she truly feared he would obliterate everyone, just like his shadow had obliterated the sun.

"I deserved it," she blurted. "I lied to them all."

"No one deserves to be beaten. Especially not my mate." His voice was not his own, but beastly and gravelly. There was no hiding his fae roots.

"*He's* your mate?" Sid choked out. "A mother-fucking Guardian?"

"I'll kill you where you stand." Shade glared at him.

This was going from bad to worse. Silver pointed the knife back at Shade. "You need to leave."

He looked at the knife as if it was a feather. "I'm not leaving without you."

"Well, I'm not coming."

"Darling." His voice softened to a velvet chastise, as though she were a child. Or what was that he'd been calling her? Kitten? Feelion?

Heat flamed Silver's cheeks. "Fuck off. Last warning."

He seemed to think about it, then let go of Jimmy and stepped back with his palms in the air. "I'm still not leaving without you. No more games."

On the floor, Martin twiddled his thumbs. Jimmy scrambled back to get away from Shade as far as he could.

"I'm sorry," Silver whispered to Sid as she crouched before him. "This is a complication none of us could predict. Not without... well, not since the president lost his psychic."

Because of this, for the past few years, human military tactics had been hit and miss. They used to know what was coming. Nero's psychic had helped him figure out where humans from Silver's time awoke and thawed. But then the psychic had died, and Nero failed to find a new one.

Sid's pained eyes met hers. "He's a Guardian, Silver."

"I know, dammit. It's not like I signed up for it. It just happened."

She tried to help him with his wrist, but Shade snarled from his spot, fangs glinting in the dying sunlight. She glared back, unsure if he snarled at her for approaching Sid, or at Sid for existing. Didn't matter. She checked his hand. It was definitely broken. He'd need to return to Crystal City for medical attention. But knowing Sid, he would probably set the bones himself and carry on until he died.

That's what Reapers did.

"I don't think you understand," Sid murmured under his breath. "He lives at the Order."

Their eyes met briefly before she went back to his injury. Shade was a Guardian. Her mission ended at the Order. She'd been so caught up with denying his claim that she'd failed to see their bond would garner trust. No, she'd not failed to see it. She knew. But part of her was afraid that if she surrendered to him, she'd mess up. She already knew she had trouble walking away from the vampire. If she walked willingly into his arms for this, then what chance did she have of resisting and completing her mission?

She busied herself with making a splint for Sid's wrist and secured it while turning over the idea in her head.

If she went with Shade willingly, she'd have to play along with what he wanted. No, not play. *Be.* She had to *be* mated to him. With the bond sharing their emotions, she had to actually submit to everything, or else he'd sniff out the lie. Her stomach did a little traitorous flip at the thought of what that submission would entail. Spending time with him would be easy. A little too easy. She never thought she'd think about a vampire that way, especially considering she had bite scars over her body to remind her of their viciousness.

The hard part would come when she had to betray Shade and complete her mission. She was only human, after all. She had feelings, even if she was good at shoving them aside for the mission. Sid seemed to think she could do it. His earlier rare display of emotion was because he cared for Silver. He'd believed in her. He still trusted her. He knew that sometimes they had to use every weapon in their arsenal to win this fight. And she had the black heart to prove he was right.

"Fine," she said to Shade as she finished securing the bandage around Sid's hand. "I'll go with you on one condition."

Shade's brow arched as though he'd expected nothing less.

"I want you to take them back to Crystal City and leave them unharmed at the gates."

Shade darted a glance between the humans and her. "Or I could kill them now and save some trouble."

His pointed vampire ears probably heard her pulse escalating, but she could use this. The truth was, she did fear for their lives. She'd spent too much time working among the people of Crystal City. She'd become attached, and that was something a Reaper should never do.

"What do you want?" she asked Shade.

"I want you to drop the knife and to come with me. Leave your bag behind."

"Fine." She collected her backpack and handed it to Sid. Then she turned the hunting knife hilt first and handed it to Jimmy.

Somehow, the transceiver in her pocket wasn't enough to block her connection to the Well this time. It rushed back with the force of a tidal wave. Her eyes fluttered at the rush, at existence amplifying, and she almost swooned. The glowing marks on her arm flared brighter. And the blackness started leaking out. She stepped away to avoid any of it getting on her team.

"You'll teach me to control this?" She gestured down her front.

Shade gave a curt nod.

"Then I'll go with you. I agree to your terms."

"We'll strike a fae bargain." Shade gripped her forearm, squeezing it like her vambrace. He looked deeply into her eyes. That she couldn't see intention behind his shuttered expression worried her. No telling emotions filtered down their new bond, either. But she held her spine straight and unwavering.

Shade reiterated their earlier words. "You will remain in my care until I teach you control. I will return your companions unharmed to your city gates immediately."

"Deal."

Lightning snapped through her arm and zipped up her spine as

Shade enforced the bargain through their mana. The shock of it caused her to gasp, and she knew, without a doubt, that if either of them tried to get out of their bargain, there would be dire consequences.

Shade walked over to Jimmy, grabbed him by the collar, and then the night exploded. They disappeared in a blast of shadow. A few seconds later, he returned to take Martin. Silver had no time to speak privately with Sid before Shade spirited him away, but she did manage to pull the transceiver out of her pocket and show Sid.

The mission was still on.

# CHAPTER THIRTEEN

Shade took Silver to Rush's old log cabin by the lake. Decades ago, Rush had been cursed as punishment for unsanctioned breeding under Seelie law. He'd been exiled. This was his hideaway and home. But that isolation ended a few years ago when he met his mate Clarke—a Well-blessed human awoken from the old world like Silver. For the past few years since Rush's curse had been lifted, the cabin had served as a sort of getaway, or an unofficial outpost for Guardians as it was the closest settlement to the human city. It would serve well now for Silver's training.

He explained this history to Silver as they stepped out of his shadows and onto snow littered sand. While Silver gathered her breath and equilibrium, he surveyed the area for danger. They were bracketed by a lake on one side, and a forest of fir trees on the other. The demogorgon had attacked Shade twice now. Indigo had said it also attacked Shade's childhood home. It couldn't be a coincidence. Maebh wanted Shade back. He'd thought she'd given up when he joined the Order, but it looked like she'd only bided her time until she amassed more power. Sooner or later, Maebh would eventually get to him.

He only hoped he could prepare Silver before then.

Silver flipped her long braid over her shoulder as she straightened.

"I thought you'd take me to the Order," she said.

He almost laughed. "Your darkness might play well with mine, darling, but it won't with others."

She looked disappointed. He supposed she'd be eager to reunite with her fellow humans Peaches and Violet, but in no world would Shade allow Silver to be in the same room with another male until his protective mating urges were over.

Shade filled with anger as he remembered how the Untouched human trash had tried to hit his mate. He forced a deep breath to gather composure, but his anger rose like a viper when he remembered how she'd *cared* for the human. Shade wanted to hurt the man all over again.

*How dare he touch her?* How dare he look at her like... like... Shade tried to recall the way that bastard had looked at Silver. At first, he'd looked at her with agony—the kind of bitter pain one felt when betrayed by someone they cared for. Shade's gaze had darted between the pair and when she'd touched him with familiar care, he knew in his gut that they'd been intimate before. Perhaps their relationship still existed.

Vicious jealousy rode him. The beast roamed his soul with grimy, sneaky claws that curled around his heart and made him want to lock Silver away with him.

Shade, who had females chewing their own fingers off to have a quiet moment with him. He who walked into a room and females melted with desire. He who commanded any beneath his fingertips and fangs. He who could not convince his mate to be his.

Talons pressed beneath his fingertips, begging to release and slash Silver's human across his face—to ruin him for her, or anyone else. But he'd taken the man back to Crystal City as bargained. Shade had dumped him before the gates and rushed back to his mate before he did something stupid.

He'd tasted not one drop of her blood, yet already she had power over him.

She'd agreed to let him train her while in his care. That was what mattered for now. Not this resistance between them. Not the other man. Not the queen and her beast. Silver was here with him, smelling like the moon goddess herself. Anything was possible.

A tendril of smoke curled from the cabin's chimney. The resident fire sprites were keeping the place warm. He'd visited a few times over the past week to stock firewood, but knowing how those little miscreants liked to play catch with embers, they were probably out by now. Rush allowed the sprites to live in the cabin if they didn't burn it down, and they kept it warm for travelers, so Shade had to put up with them.

As they walked through the light snow, Silver shivered beside him, hugging herself against the cold. The sun had set, but he was no more energized than he had been in the morning. Lack of sleep dragged him down, and lack of proper nutrition weakened him. If he didn't feed from her soon, he would waste away.

But if he tried anything now, he wouldn't be able to restrain himself. He might hurt her in his eagerness. Better that he trained her first, built some trust, and then made it so she was the one who asked him. He didn't ask. He *was* asked. His stubborn pride might be the end of him, but he did promise her she'd beg for his bite, and he was already conceding too much to the woman.

When they'd kissed, his mind had emptied of all but her taste. He'd forgotten every lesson he'd learned in seduction.

Shade stomped toward the cabin, yanked open the door and gave the inside a sweeping check. One room. A corner plant had grown into the cabin and spread its leaves in a canopy over the bed. It smelled like the forest in here. A modest kitchenette counter was in a corner, and a stone fireplace was at another. A single wooden chair sat before a fire that was almost out. Demanding squeaks came from the fireplace.

The male fire sprite jumped on the charred log and pointed voraciously at the dwindled pile of wood near the hearth. They'd impatiently jumped the hearth and in doing so, could have burned the whole place down.

"Spoiled little ingrates," Shade grumbled and picked up the ax before heading back to the door.

Silver sidestepped to get out of his way. "You're just... wait. Are we going to talk about this?"

Shade faced her. She still hugged herself from the cold. He let his eyes rake down her figure. They'd spent the past few days playing a game of fee-lion and mouse, and she was filthy, just like him. Probably starving too.

His protective instincts surged to the surface and drowned out everything else. He walked up to her until they were toe to toe. To her credit, she didn't wilt. He wondered what it would take to finally have this strong-willed woman melt for him, to beg for his lips on her breast? On her mouth? Between her legs, ravishing and feasting on her until she pulsed against his tongue? For a moment, his head clouded with the fantasy image until her voice brought him back to reality.

"Shade?" She arched a brow. "What's—"

"I have questions," he clipped.

Chagrin flittered over her expression, but she gave a curt nod, so he continued.

"What do you like to eat?"

She was visibly taken aback. "What?"

"Your food preference. I need to know so I can procure it."

"I told you, I can hunt my own meal."

"I never said you couldn't, but you are in my care now, as per our bargain." He slowly twined the length of her braid around his fist, all the while holding her gaze steady. "What do you like to eat, Silver?"

Her cheeks flushed with a pretty glow. Exasperation and something else—a flare of desire—sparked down their bond. From the way her gaze skated over his hold on her hair, he thought she was thinking of their time in the forest fondly. He was sure he'd grabbed it in his daze at some point during their kiss. She folded her arms.

"I'm not fussy. I'll eat anything."

Anything. As he continued to wrap her braid around his palm, his mind went to dark, sensual places that had no business in the conversation. Her braid looked like rope. It was strong, too. There were so many ways he could use this during love play. She narrowed her eyes at him, no doubt sensing his lust clawing for control. He unwound her braid and stepped back.

He had to get out of there before he ruined the minuscule amount of trust they'd built. He had a million questions, but not now. Change of plans. He pointed at the carved wooden trunk at the end of the bed.

"Clothes." He shifted his finger to a bowl near the counter. "Wash bowl. I'll find food and wood."

She smirked wryly. "You Tarzan, me Jane, huh?"

Whatever that meant. He glowered and replied, "Don't go anywhere."

"Or what?"

"Or I'll teach you what happens to little fee-lions who misbehave."

He didn't give her a chance to answer and walked outside, shutting the door firmly behind him.

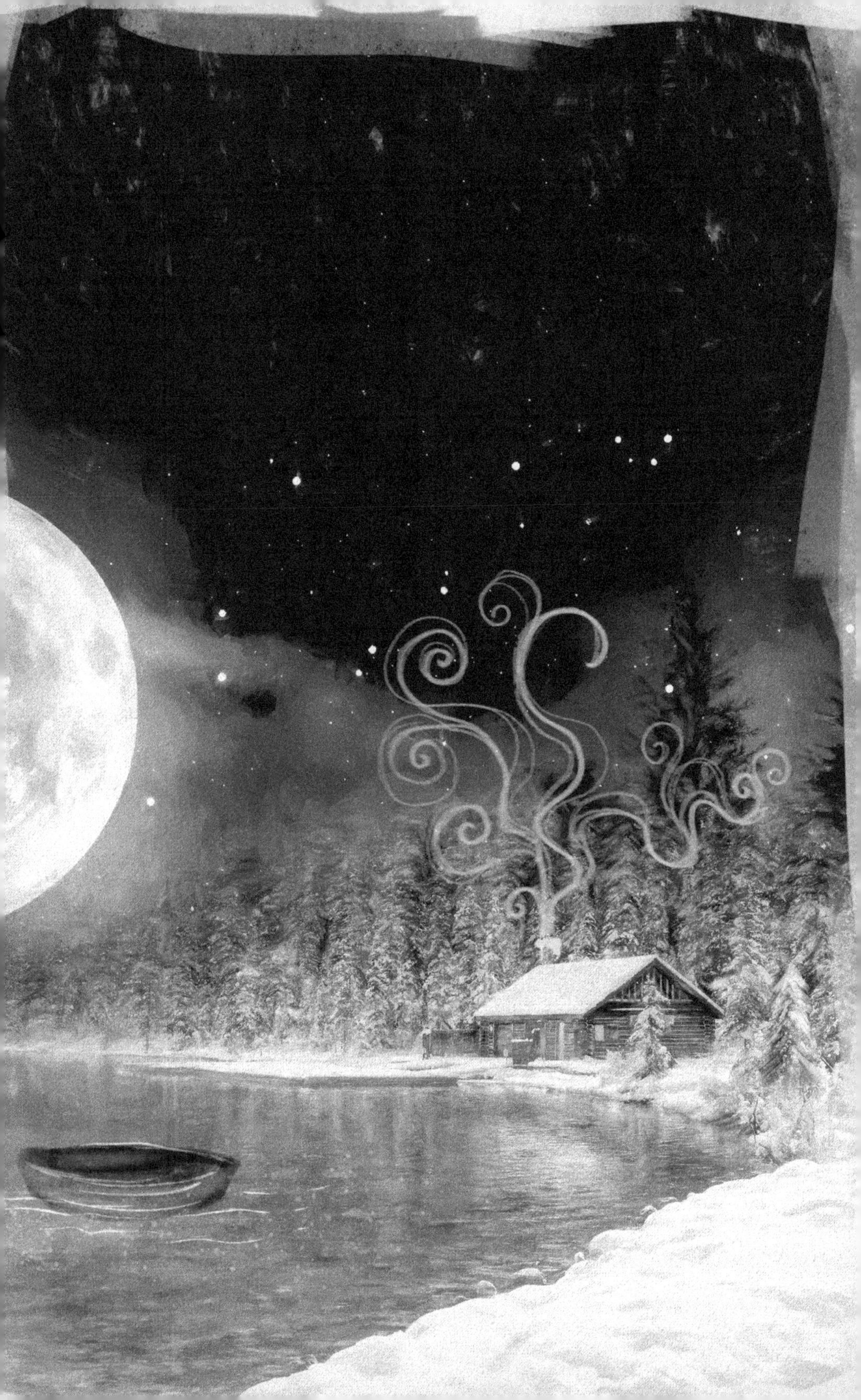

# CHAPTER
# FOURTEEN

Silver gaped at the door. Somehow, she couldn't get his words out of her mind. He would *teach* her what happened when fee-lions misbehaved? *What was she, five?* She rummaged through the cabin for a weapon, all the while cursing at his attitude and daring him silently to even try to lay his hands on her butt like that again.

She pulled out a small drawer beneath the counter and found ceramic knives and a serrated bone knife that looked good for filleting. She placed one under the pillow. Shade could sleep on the floor for all she cared. Then she sat down on the bed and stared at the fireplace.

Three little people made of flames stared back at her.

"What are you looking at?" she snapped.

They squeaked and hid behind the charred log. The darkness leaking from her heart intensified, as if to punctuate her guilt and regret. She reached into her jacket pocket and clutched the transceiver until her darkness ebbed. This was not a solution. She couldn't very well have Shade see her clutch something in her pocket every time she wanted to block her poison.

Or maybe... just maybe she should throw herself into trusting this vampire and learning to control her mana. If such a thing was possible. Every instinct in her body rebelled at trusting him. She would die when it came time to finish what she was sent here to do. Goddamn Rory and her insistence that this had to be Silver's mission. She was happy enough building cannons and tinkering with weapons.

She fell back on the bed and stared at the canopy of leaves. They were beautiful. Arrestingly so. Green and full of life.

Shade's emotions filtered down through their bond in little waves that made her think he was trying to hold them back but failing. Sometimes she'd get a burst of lust, of longing. Then she'd be hit with a surge of anger and annoyance, as if he'd chastised himself for having such feelings. She knew that reaction well. Other times she felt his need so intensely that it put her in defensive mode, despite knowing he wouldn't hurt her.

He couldn't.

Despite her attempts at killing him, he'd not once lifted a hand in violence to her... not the way Sid had. Shade's spanking on the log was nothing but a show of dominance and desperation that failed to stick. It was his belief she wasn't an equal. It was disrespect.

But then there was the kiss that dazed them both.

There had been no treating her like a child then. Her slow, then passionate kiss had surprised him, almost as if he wasn't used to that kind of tenderness before the heat. Maybe his past relationships had been like Silver's, sharp and to the point. Maybe they were more suited than she realized.

She stabbed the bed sheet with her knife and then ripped a strip off. The loud, repetitive chopping outside provided a motivational soundtrack. Every time he chopped, she ripped. His sounds soon fell in time with her pulse. Shade cut wood, and she cut the hopes and dreams daring to show their face in her heart.

*My darkness dances with yours.*

Impossible. There was no such thing.

She removed her shirt and jacket, then hastily wrapped bandages around her middle, making sure to simulate a corset's restraint. The bindings felt good, like control. It wouldn't physically stop the darkness leaking out, but it would be a reminder to stay vigilant. She hoped.

Shade's chopping took on a frantic, demolishing pace. Silver tied off her bandages and put her jacket back on before peeking out the window. Outside, amongst the snowy twilight, Shade stood with his fist around the handle of an ax. His jacket was slung over a log, which left him dressed only in leather breeches and a clinging undershirt. The last rays of light bounced off his skin. Sweat glistened, accentuating every slick slab of muscle and sinew. Now that she could see more of him, he looked a little dehydrated. Was that because he'd spent too much time chasing her?

Silver tugged at the bindings over her chest. *Too tight.*

Chop after chop, she watched him. He pulverized wood—not even caring to make some for the fireplace. Angry strokes and feverish frustration echoed down their bond. He'd been hiding that from her. Her own irritation poked back and before she knew what she was doing, she pushed outside and stomped down the steps.

Broad chest heaving, he stopped and glared at her. "What?"

"Don't *what* me," she snapped and prodded him. *Mistake.* He was hot and sweaty, and it plucked at her feminine instincts. She wanted to explore his body more, but instead fisted her hand at her side. The bindings made her next words came out breathless. "It wasn't my idea to come here. It was yours, so I don't want any of that anger targeted at me."

"It's not."

"Wait... it's not?"

"No." He stepped closer, cutting into her personal space, inspecting her far too perceptively for comfort. A lock of brown hair dropped over his forehead as he looked down at her. "It's directed at me."

"Oh."

"Silver," he said. "Why are you out of breath?"

His fingers went to the hem of her buttoned jacket, faster than she could blink. He ripped her jacket open, breaking the buttons, baring her bindings with a scowl. She'd not put her shirt back on in her haste to look out the window.

He snarled, digging his finger into the gap between her breasts.

"Fuck off." She slapped him away.

"I will be your restraint. Do you understand? I will take care of you."

Damned alpha son-of-a-bitch.

He growled at her, unamused, and then scrunched up his face as though trying to contain his patience.

"Go inside," he ordered through gritted teeth, and pointed at the cabin with his ax. "Remain inside until I say so. Next time you leave, you'll be punished."

She scoffed and rolled her eyes. He didn't seem to care. He dropped the ax, picked up a pile of kindling that was too pulverized and then planted his palm between her shoulder blades. As they got to the door, he gave a shrill whistle.

A shaggy gray wolf emerged from the forest and bounded over. Shade scratched it under the furry chin and then pointed at Silver inside the cabin.

"Don't let her go anywhere," he said to the wolf.

The wolf plopped down on its hind legs and stared at Silver with steady, hard eyes and a low growl.

"You've got to be kidding me," she groaned. "A babysitter."

Shade dropped the wood by the fireplace and then went back outside to collect his jacket. Silver wasn't sure which came first, the night or his shadow, but by the time true darkness dropped on the landscape, Shade was gone.

She was left thinking she needed to start dropping her guard. Her stubborn pride was pushing him away. If she ever hoped to get invited to the Order, she had to convince him they were on the same side.

# CHAPTER
# FIFTEEN

Shade returned to the cabin in the middle of the night. Gray kept watch outside on the porch like he'd asked. The wolf gave him a tired look and then trotted away with a huff, bumping into Shade's legs as he went by. Shade had the feeling he had just been scolded for being late. Gray probably wouldn't come again. Shade was lucky he'd come at all, let alone listened to him, a non-wolf shifter.

Exhausted and starving, Shade eased himself into the cabin as quietly as he could. He'd shadow-walked to the nearest village—Crescent Hollow—and procured human food for Silver. The journey was a few days on foot, and it was the longest Shade had ever attempted to travel by shadow in one hit. But since his bond had triggered with Silver, he felt stronger.

The tavern had been abuzz with talk of the demogorgon terrorizing villagers. They'd taken one look at Shade's Guardian uniform, and instead of their usual grumbling about being taxed coin for hunting monsters, he was welcomed. Sought after, even. The change in heart had filled him with dread.

Word got around to High Lady Kyra Nightstalk—Rush's sister and alpha of the village—and she cornered him while he waited at the tavern for the meal. She asked him to stick around town in case the demogorgon came back. He'd listened, but then made excuses, took his meal order, and quickly left.

He'd neglected Guardian duties during the months he'd searched for Silver. It was surprising the Prime hadn't come running to reprimand him, or Leaf, the Cadre of Twelve's team leader. But the Order was desperate to include all the Well-blessed humans in their stable of warriors, he assumed this was why his leash had been loosened.

Guilt followed him.

The monster was after him specifically at Maebh's behest. This meant the death left in its wake was Shade's fault. For Silver's own protection, it was better he trained her sooner rather than later. Trouble was on the horizon.

The fire crackled as the sprites snoozed on the log, basking in flames. Shade put the food package on the small counter and then eased himself onto the fireside chair. Silver had sprawled across the bed in a way that suggested she usually slept alone. That would change. Soon she would be wrapped by his body every single time they retired. Her long braid dangled off the edge. He tucked it by her side. Closer now, he noticed her shallow breathing. Upon investigating, he found she still wore the bindings around her middle. She'd also wrapped her forearms and knuckles as though expecting a fight.

*She tried to protect herself, even in sleep.*

Dark ribbons seeped between the bindings over her breasts. A thought occurred to him, and he hovered his palm over her chest before letting his shadows out. They dropped from his palm and flowed over her darkness like an umbrella. It seemed even that instinctive part of him wanted to keep her safe.

Silver murmured in her sleep and frowned. She clutched the bindings at her chest and gulped air. He should slice them from her body, but moments after she stirred, she settled. He drew his shadows back into himself and wondered if she'd ever been vulnerable, or was the moment they'd shared in the forest the first time she'd let her guard drop. He couldn't imagine her as a child hiding behind her mother's dress, or her ever asking for help.

That kiss they'd shared had been a first for him. It was tender, emotive, and passionate all rolled into one. It felt as though she'd kissed him not because of his looks, or what he could offer with his body, but because she'd looked deep into his eyes and saw his true self... and that was all she needed.

So why had she pulled away?

For the first time since meeting her, suspicion hit him. She was in Elphyne for a reason, and it had nothing to do with her training. Or him. Usually, he was sharper than this. Usually, he was the one controlling the narrative. But she had a way of undoing him without him knowing.

*Tomorrow.*

He'd solve the world's problems tomorrow. Tonight, he would sleep and pretend that hunger wasn't gnawing at his insides, or that her alluring scent wasn't a bouquet picked just for him.

Shade sat in the chair and only rested his eyes for a moment, but it felt like he blinked the night away and soft light illuminated the window. Sitting on her bed cross legged, Silver ravenously ate the food he'd left, and stared at him in much the same way he'd stared at her.

A quick glance at the door showed his sword and weapons untouched. He also checked down his body, half expecting the hilt of a knife to protrude from his belly. Nothing. Could it be she was finally trusting him?

With a long stretch to loosen his stiff back, he came back to himself. Barely. The sun's drag coaxed him to return to sleep until twilight, but he forced himself to his feet and checked its position through the window. Midday. Partly overcast. Looked like rain on the horizon. If it fell on the snow and froze, training out there would be tricky. Shade scanned the lake and found a small dinghy moored. An idea came to him for her education, but first, he needed to feed. Hunger stabbed him and his mind swirled. His palm hit the window to steady himself. Even though he'd fed in the village, nutrition from regular donors was not satisfying. His throat was sandpaper. His fangs ached for the woman behind him, staring at him with wary eyes.

"You okay?" Silver asked.

"I'm fine."

"You don't look fine."

He may have growled. To be honest, at that point, his mind wasn't his own. He was still half asleep, still a slave to his instincts, and there was no more wood to take it out on. A dip in the lake was looking like a good distraction. Maybe he should go straight back to sleep. He stumbled toward the bed.

"What are you doing?" She stiffened.

"Sleeping."

She stood as he flopped. Her scent surrounded him. *Big mistake.* Now he wanted her more. He bit the blanket, squeezed his eyes shut and prayed for sleep to take him, but the bastard wouldn't listen. The sound of Silver's bowl being placed on the counter filtered back to him. Then her footsteps and scent grew closer. He held his breath.

*Go away unless you mean to be my next meal.*

"You mean drink my blood, right?"

He opened a single, cautious eye. Did she just read his mind... or had he said that out loud?

"Shade," she said, none too pleased. "If this is going to work, we need to trust each other. You can't train me if you're hungry. And, frankly, I don't think it's fair that you're hiding your hunger while you gallivant around insisting *you* find *me* food—"

"I do *not* gallivant."

"And while I can't exactly *feel* you're hungry down our bond, I know you're longing for something. Yearning for it. And I can see your eyes dip to my neck every few minutes. I see you swallow. Be straight. Tell me what you want."

As Shade slowly sat, his insides wrenched with delicious yearning. She was right. His gaze did often dip to her neck. His mouth watered like a tap. His fangs ached with a burning need. She had no clue what she courted with those words.

"What I want," he said. It was on the tip of his tongue to confess everything, but this wasn't how he worked. He didn't *ask*. "What I want is for you to stop talking so I can go back to sleep."

"Fine," she clipped. "Let's go back to sleep."

She lifted the blanket he laid on, exposing the sheets. She tugged the cover rudely to make room.

"Darling," he warned, halting her. "If you get into this bed, I'll sink more than my fangs into you."

She paused, considered, then called his bluff. "No, you won't."

He watched dumbstruck as she nudged him to the edge of the bed and then climbed in.

She yawned and snuggled into her pillow, giving him her back. Her next words were muffled. "By the way, I would have let you. If you'd asked."

In the deafening silence that followed, Shade stared at the canopy of leaves and tapped his fingers on his leather covered chest. Every instinct wanted to wait to feed, despite the pain it caused him. To make her beg for his bite, like he'd promised. But there she was, lying next to him, a little temptress taunting him with her consent. The curve of her rear was only an inch from his thigh. He swore he could feel the heat of her body glazing his skin like the sun.

This was *not* how he fed. He did not ask. He *was* asked. Always.

He stared some more.

He strummed his fingers.

*Fuck.*

This woman was turning his world upside down.

*It's just a question. Say it—May I feed from you?*

He mimed the words to practice.

*Say it.*

Shade cleared his throat. But the words of his old mentor, Mistress Aravela, came back to haunt him. *Never ask. Ever. It reveals a weakness they can exploit.* He clamped his lips shut as his schooling came back to him. Having needs met without asking was a sign of power. Having desires anticipated was everything. Not only did you get what you wanted, but your enemies didn't know why. In the bedroom, every desire was commerce, and every customer was a potential enemy. Let the wrong person know your secrets and then what did you have left?

Nothing.

Not allowed to join the business until he was eighteen, Shade had done what he could to help. He'd gone to the markets, cleaned, mucked out the stables, served refreshments, even helped with the bookkeeping. He eventually learned the trade and became the Rosebuds' protector as well as their family.

"Shade?" Silver said, still with her back to him.

"Yes?"

"Why is a demogorgon after you? And why does it look like Bones?"

He inhaled, held his breath, then let it out. "Queen Maebh did something to him."

She rolled to face him. "So, you admit it. He *is* Bones."

"I never denied it."

Anger tightened her voice. "How can your people do that to mine and be so glib about it?"

"Maebh is not, and will never be, my people," he snapped.

Her eyes darted over him.

"What am I supposed to say to that? Bones was one of our own—"

"Who tortured at your leader's behest?"

"So do you, I imagine."

The Order had Bones in custody months ago. Cloud had taken the lead in the interrogation, but Shade also had a turn. None of their methods worked. Bones revealed nothing about the plans of the human city. Maebh suggested she would find a way to get through to Bones. And for all intents and purposes, she did. She used her Sluagh to rape his mind, but then she claimed the human had died. As it turned out, some of the secrets she'd stolen were about perverting mana for personal gain—something the humans were good at. Maebh made the demogorgon shortly after.

It occurred to Shade how truly opposite he and Silver were. She'd been saying they were enemies all this time, but he'd not fully comprehended it. He'd always thought the Well wanted them to be together, and so they would. End of story. But the wall between their peoples was high, and he had to somehow convince Silver to betray hers and join his.

"How is this supposed to work?" she asked, as if reading his mind.

He faced her. "It will."

"I mean, what happens from here? You train me, then what?"

"Then you live with me at the Order."

Her dark brow arched. "And simply swap sides? Defect and forget about my people?"

"They're not your people anymore."

"They are always my people."

"I'm your people now and you're mine."

"Those are just words you keep saying, Shade. Sometimes I think you're saying them to convince yourself too."

A cocktail of anger, hurt, and regret simmered between them. He wasn't sure who was projecting what.

"I don't even like you," she teased. "What makes you think I'll live at the Order with you?"

He gave a half shrug. "I don't care where we live as long as it's in Elphyne."

"And not Crystal City."

"Silver," he chided. "Do you really want to live there after coming here?"

He gestured at the leaves overhead to make his point. How could anyone want to live on desecrated, forsaken land? It defied nature. Storm clouds passed over her expression, and she huffed and stared into space. "I don't see why we can't all share this planet."

"Because your people messed it up."

The look she shot him could have cut steel.

"In case you missed it, *mate*," she clipped, "they were your people once too. You evolved from us. You keep saying we're not enemies, but you're the one separating my people from yours. You're the one with a different set of rules than me."

His jaw clicked shut. She had him there. Fae had mutated from old-world humans through the grace of the Well. And he did have a different set of rules for himself, but that was because it was his job to protect her and to protect Elphyne. They could argue about their differences for eternity, but his stomach rumbled.

"You're hungry," she accused, and he lost all sense of composure with his response.

"I'm always hungry around you." He flung his hand in her direction. "You were made for me. The Well turned you into something so enticing that every time I look at you, I want to tie you down, lick you up and down, and feast on you in every imaginable way. But I can't."

She spoke through a held breath. "Because you'll get drunk on my blood?"

That was half the truth. She didn't need to know the rest—that if he gave himself over to the mating hormones triggered after he fed from his mate, he was afraid of what he might feel. What vulnerabilities he might share. So, he warned her. "You'll be locked in here for days, a slave to my carnal whims, and you'll hate me for it before you've even had a chance to get to know me. You'll permanently put me in the enemy zone, and I can't have that."

She snorted. "You certainly think highly of yourself."

"Excuse me?" He propped himself on his elbow to give her an incredulous look. "It's the truth."

"Yeah, yeah." She waved her hand down at him. "You're an Adonis. Ladies drool over you. Blah blah, fae can't lie, so it must be true."

He tugged on her braid. "Is that a challenge?"

She bared her neck and glared at him in defiance. Her fierce beauty in that moment struck him. It sent a bolt of heat right down his spine. His cock hardened. Was this what Maebh always felt when he challenged her? Was this why she wanted Shade so badly? Silver surprised him at every corner, and it was... refreshing.

"Whatever floats your boat," she goaded.

He bared his fangs, but she didn't balk. She boldly held his stare and said, "Feed."

A demand, not a request. And, fuck, he wanted to comply. Every cell in his body was thirsty. This was the moment he'd been waiting for, but he wasn't stupid. Silver had only agreed to come with him to save her team. Since they'd been together, he'd sensed trepidation from her and something else he couldn't name. If he fed, he put his life in her hands, and she had a habit of trying to kill him.

"Not on the bed," he conceded, and planted his feet on the floor. If they were going to do this, then he would only take a few sips. Just enough to take the edge off. He searched the cabin for a prime position. The chair, with her kneeling at his feet? The kitchen counter, with her hands on the surface so she couldn't touch him? He could feed from behind and not even look her in the eye. Or, perhaps, just standing on neutral territory.

None of it felt right.

"You're overthinking this," she said and did her best to look bored, but he knew it was a defense mechanism. Her fingers twitched nervously.

He shucked off his jacket and pulled off his boots. May as well get comfortable. He sat on the chair and pointed at the floor.

"On your knees. Hands behind your back. Neck tilted to the side."

"No." She looked down at him and held out her wrist. "This works."

If she was anyone else, he would have forgone the feed until his donor learned some manners. His abstinence would be their punishment. He would play the game and come out on top. But Silver unraveled his resolve. She pushed him past comfort and into mindless need. Every single time.

He took her wrist but didn't bring it to his lips. Not yet. First, he tugged her onto his lap. With a surprised gasp she latched onto him while he made her straddle him, face to face.

"You want to play power games?" He tossed her long, ropey

braid back from her neck and then ran his thumb down her vein. "Fine. We'll play."

He moved her hands behind her back.

"What are you doing?" she said, eyes widening in alarm.

"I don't allow touch while I feed, especially from you."

Offense flashed over her expression. She frowned as if she wanted to push the subject but didn't contest. *Curious.* He expected more pushback. His cunning little fee-lion wasn't one to acquiesce without gain. She pestered, poked, and defied. He'd spanked her and she'd attempted to kill him. So why was she now looking at him with expectant eyes with a simmer of anticipation down their bond? *Let's see where this is going.*

"Now..." He twirled her braid. "Be a good girl and keep your hands there, or will I need to tie them?"

"I'm sure I can resist you long enough."

He lowered his mouth to her ear and whispered, "That's what they all say."

Goosebumps erupted over her neck. Satisfaction flittered over his smile. He pressed the tip of his tongue to the plump vein pulsing with life between her jaw and shoulder. She shivered. Hunger flared, urging him to bite down. One thought pierced the craving. *Level the playing field.* If he was about to lay out his vulnerabilities, then so should she. A drop of his blood would be like a drug for her. He pressed his tongue to a fang until blood welled and licked the spot he would bite. Then he sank in.

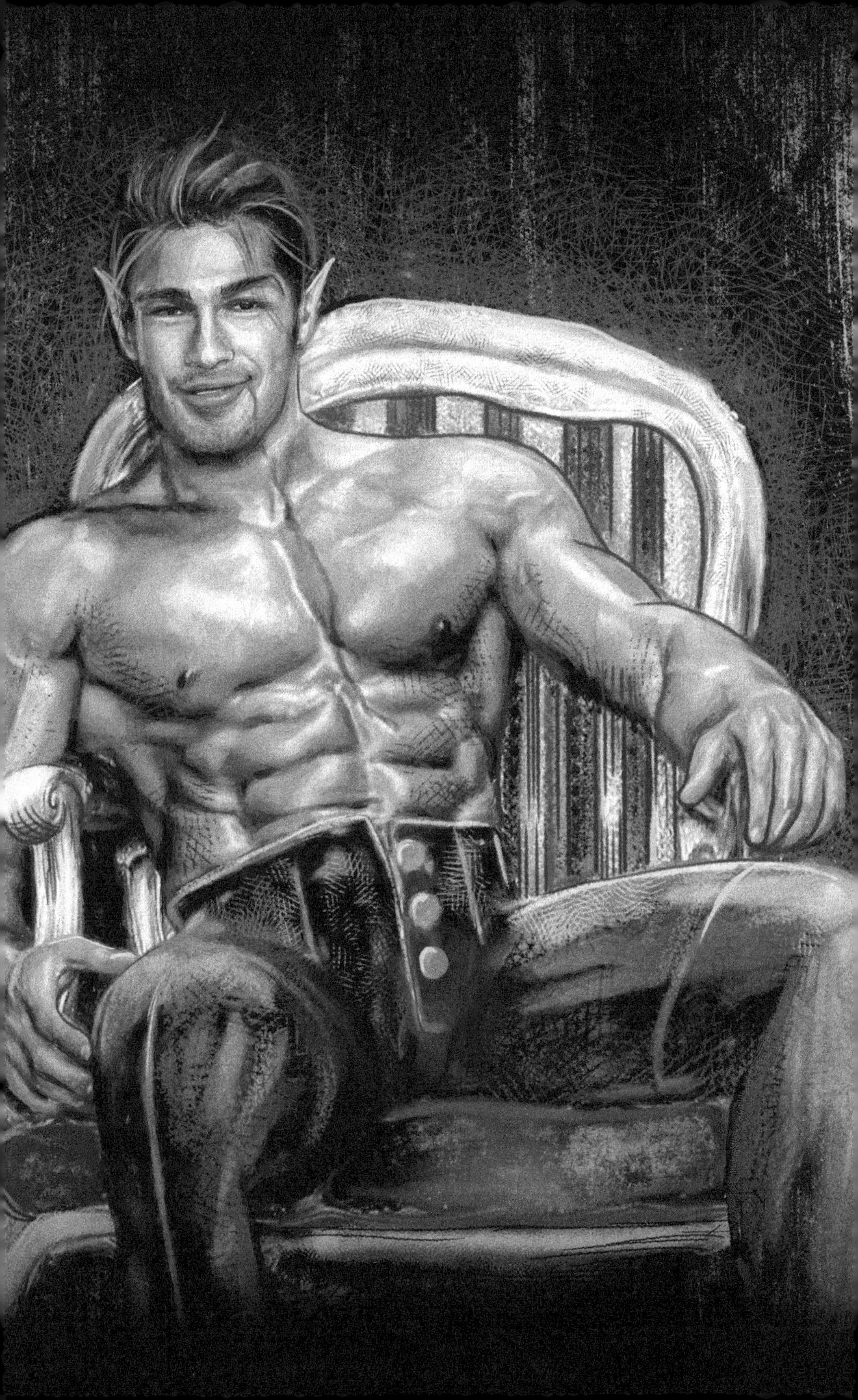

# CHAPTER SIXTEEN

Silver thought she was prepared for Shade's bite, but the moment his fangs pierced her flesh, her grand plans of controlling the situation evaporated. She'd thought if she instigated the feed, she could throw him off guard, get him drunk, and then decide what to do afterward. He'd be putty in her hands.

But his fangs sank in and liquid fire shot through her body. Her nerves zinged. Her nipples hardened against their bindings. Her sex grew heavy with need, and she gasped, arching into him, rocking wantonly, feeling her composure unravel. What had he done to her?

None of the other bites had felt like this. Those had been painful.

This... multiple sensations warred with each other. She tingled and sparked. He licked and laved. She couldn't breathe. The walls tilted and her eyes rolled in euphoria. She tried to hold on to him, but he captured her hands before she knew they'd moved. He looped her long braid around her wrists and secured her. How he had any sense of logic in this state was beyond her, but he bracketed her throat with his fingers—holding her steady for him.

"I have you," he murmured. "I won't let you fall."

His words cost him. Warm blood trickled down her neck. He darted down to catch the errant rivulet, but the moment he tugged at her bindings to make room for his pointed tongue, she was gone. An embarrassing sound of need slipped out of her.

He was sex incarnate. He obliterated logic.

She cared nothing for her mission or her people. She only wanted to please him so he would continue to use her. Her attention zeroed in on the gentle lave of his tongue as it traveled back up her decolletage. God, what would that feel like between her legs?

*Every time I look at you...*

Chocolate eyes locked with hers as he fed.

*I want to tie you down...*

His gaze turned molten.

*Lick you up and down...*

He pressed his erection into her wet, sensitive core.

*And feast on you in every imaginable way...*

Silver's mind clouded as she struggled to breathe. Too tight. She'd bound herself too tight. She panted, hungry for air, hungry for more of... *him*. His licks grew faster. His breath grew ragged. The heat of the moment amplified within their bond. She felt his every desire like a hurricane, and he felt hers. He made contented grunts from the base of his throat. Silver wasn't sure if it was the blood loss, the bindings, or the histamines, but she melted into him completely. Her braid unraveled around her wrists, freeing her arms. She plunged fingers into his hair and held him to her neck, needing, wanting this to never end.

He gripped her hips so painfully that she cried out. Shade suddenly threw his head back to expose a thick, corded neck. His pointed ears twitched. Agony tightened his handsome expression as he snarled skyward. The change came over him like a tangible thing. Tension bled from his shoulders. A wistful smile stole his snarls. He relaxed beneath her.

He was done.

Over.

And she couldn't help feeling left wanting, but it was good it never went further. Her hands trailed down his neck, rasped over the shirt at his ridged stomach to a... wet spot on his breeches? Right at the tip of his erection.

"Is that what I think it is?"

He glanced down, gave a lazy shrug and a smug smile. "I'm not even sorry."

"What?"

He licked his fangs. "How did you expect me to react the first time my mate feeds me? I told you not to touch me."

As if that explained why he'd come in his pants, just from drinking her blood. To be honest, she'd been close herself. And if she'd let things continue at the forest, she'd be right where he was. Still catching her breath, she wondered how this pull between them was ever going to fade. How was she supposed to walk away from it?

"I thought you could go all night," she teased.

"I can." His smile dropped as his heavy-lidded gaze landed on her neck. He frowned, reached behind his neck, and pulled his shirt over his head. He scrunched it and pressed it to her bite wound.

"Hold that," he grumbled. "Your blood is tasty. I drank too

much. You're lucky that happened, or I'd have you on the bed right now."

Too long, she stared at his rumpled shirt in his hand, and she wasn't even sure why. Maybe it was the glistening abs behind it. Maybe it was that lopsided smile of content on his face.

"Or I could lick your wound to heal it," he offered.

She accepted his shirt, and he reclined backward, holding her gaze with a shadow of his smug smile still dancing on his lips. His thumbs traced lazy circles on her hips as though he truly contemplated his words. He looked so goddamned erotic with his rumpled hair, bedroom eyes, and flushed cheeks. She should get off his lap. He tightened his grip, halting her. Sleep circled her mind, making everything feel slow.

"Considering what just happened, I shouldn't tell you this," he slurred. His posture slouched. "That was the best I've had in my life. I would sell my soul to a Sluagh to have more of that." He whispered, like he was telling her a secret, "The thought of being inside you next time makes me hard again."

He was drunk. She was sleepy. There were a million responses her brain should fire back at him, but all she could muster was, "Why shouldn't you tell me?"

His lashes lowered, shuttering his eyes. His smile abandoned his face. "Where I come from, admitting desire is weakness... it's death."

"Who taught you that, your mother?" God knew Silver's mother had taught her a few unforgiving lessons. She pulled the shirt from her neck. The bleeding had stopped.

"No." Shade sighed and dragged his palms up her waist. He scowled. "My mother abandoned me. Apart from her turning up once she learned I was with the queen, I never heard from her again. I learned that lesson from the whores who took me in."

An ache pierced Silver's chest so suddenly that, for a split second, she thought her black heart was pouring out poison. But when she looked down, there was nothing. Shade placed a palm over her heart as if he sensed her pain. His eyes were still closed, but his brows furrowed. His next words were almost inaudible.

"Please let me keep you."

His palm slid down drunkenly as sleep came over him. Before it claimed her too, she roused him enough to get him moving from the chair to the bed. She helped him under the blanket.

"Are you tucking me in?" he mumbled.

"Nope," she replied, and collapsed next to him.

He instantly tossed his arm over her, trapping her to his side. "I'm not cuddling you."

He found her bite and licked it a few times, mumbling something about faster healing, and then went silent. A dead weight. Silver waited until she was sure he was asleep, then loosened the bindings on her body.

He was unlike any vampire she'd come across.

She didn't like it.

And she most definitely *did not* just tuck him in.

## CHAPTER SEVENTEEN

"My mate is lying to me," Shade said as he stepped out of the shadows and into the brothel that was his childhood home.

Madam Aravela turned from where she sat drinking blood from a rose patterned teacup. An artful arrangement held her long silken black hair together with two tasseled pins. The vampire was ageless as the day he'd arrived. Aravela had taken over as Madam sometime after Shade had joined the Order. While she'd never be mistaken as classically beautiful with her hook nose and masculine jaw, she nonetheless commanded the room and had a waitlist a mile long.

She was an artist, a leader, and Shade's family.

He came here to check in on them, but the moment he'd seen his mentor, he'd blurted out his fear.

Her violet eyes held a note of humor as she raked her gaze from his top to bottom, lingering on the blue markings glowing down one arm. Before coming here, he'd washed in the lake and redressed in casual clothes. Silver had been fast asleep.

"D'arn Shade," Aravela greeted, a wry smile on her red lips. She placed her cup down on the saucer. "How lovely to see you, my son."

"I've been rude," he confessed and lowered himself to a knee and begged her forgiveness. He took her hand and kissed the ageless back.

Aravela placed a palm on his head then tapped him like a recalcitrant pup. "Up."

She pointed to the adjacent seat and pursed her lips. "You know better than to come in here, head down, horns up like a raging muskox."

Heat flushed his cheeks as he sat. No other female in Elphyne could make him feel shame like this. He felt five years old again. And she was right. Entering the chambers of a Rosebud Courtesan unannounced was courting danger.

He rubbed his fist over his heart in the fae hand-sign for an apology.

She waved him down. "Now, do you want to try that entrance again?"

"Are you well?" he inquired. "There was word of an attack."

She raised a brow. "Come now. We both know you're not here for concern over our safety. Especially when you've not visited in half a decade."

"It's been that long?"

She nodded, her eyes narrowing. "And much has changed for both of us."

When Aravela collected her teacup, he caught the fresh scars on her knuckles and halted her. He gently gathered her hand and inspected it. Unease prickled in his stomach. There was one client of hers who took more than Aravela should give. And, although Aravela had been the one to teach Shade to respect his own limits, she never seemed to take her own advice. She twisted their hold, so it was she looking at his marked hand, not the other way around.

He looked into his mentor's eyes and realized she was why he'd always strived for more. He saw the same desire in everything she did. The same fear inside that this was all she was worth.

"So my beautiful darling has been blessed by the Well," she said. "Can't say I'm surprised."

"Why?"

"When someone holds as much love and chaos in their heart as you, it's impossible for the Well to ignore them."

"It's not love," he sneered and took his hand back. Chaos, he'd agree with, but not love. "I doubt that will ever be something we share."

Her eyes narrowed perceptively. "Though not from want on your side. Who is she?"

"A human," he confessed. "From Crystal City."

"How is that possible?"

"She's from the old world, like the others, but where Indigo's and Haze's mates were living in Elphyne since they thawed, becoming accustomed to our ways, this one was in bed with the enemy, helping them stoke the flames of dissent." He sighed and rubbed his temples. "I fed from her for the first time last night."

"What did you see?"

"She has a heart of stone."

"Stone is not a bad thing. It is strong."

"It's unforgiving."

"It can be weathered."

"Over time I do not have."

Aravela took a sip of her cup, flashed fang as she licked her lips demurely, and then put the cup down. When she pondered like that, Shade was reminded of how she used to be with him every time he came running to her with a new problem to be solved. Nothing was done in a hurry.

"Humans," she scoffed. "They lie like they take breath. What has she lied about?"

"She is only humoring me with our bond. There is something beneath the surface of her actions I can't quite place. When I fed from her, I saw her working with the humans to build war machines. There is only one reason they require those."

"Shade," Aravela scolded him. "You know I'm not the person you should be talking to about matters of the Order."

He clamped his mouth shut.

"Why did you really come here?" she asked. "If it were to check on our welfare, you would have come immediately after the demogorgon's attack. And besides, we can't really call what it did as an attack. It was searching for something."

For him. And he'd been hunting Silver, stalking her, waiting for her to emerge from the Crystal City gates.

He wanted to ask a thousand questions. Was it possible for Silver to love Shade? Would their bond transcend their beliefs? Could he get her to trust him enough to betray her people? Should he?

In Silver's blood, Shade had also seen much of the sadness Silver claimed existed in the city. Hungry people. Cold, dank, streets. His enemy was no longer faceless and nameless. They were suffering, and now that he was closer to it, it was harder to lack empathy. Knowing this disturbed him more than he wanted to admit.

But he revealed none of his concerns. Instead, he stood and pointed at the door. "Is the wardrobe still in the same place?"

She inclined her head.

He touched two fingers to his lips and pushed his hand down and out in gratitude. "And one more thing."

"You know we're always here for you."

"I need to suppress my mating urges."

Aravela frowned. "Nothing good comes from denying the Well, or one's natural urges. We've built our business on this truth."

Shade wanted to laugh. "While that might be true for a vampire of my caliber and experience, she's not ready for a multiple day mating frenzy."

She stared at him long and hard. He thought for a moment she was going to withhold her secret methods to suppress libido. The rumors were rife when he used to live here. If they had a particular client with a history of misbehavior, Aravela would dose them with something to dull their vigor. The Rosebuds would get paid, and the clients would walk away thinking they were at fault for the mishap.

She smiled tightly. "You always were a maestro of the heart's desires, but think carefully before messing with your mate in this way. Once broken, trust is hard to rebuild."

"It's not for her."

"Then I suggest you see Mistress Larelle. She has what you need, but Shade..."

"Yes?"

"I know this might come as a shock to you, but perhaps try to connect with her on a personal level first."

The memory of her tender kiss came to mind, and how it had shocked him.

"I don't do personal." He didn't do vulnerable. Last night with the feeding was the closest he'd ever been, and he couldn't remember much of what he'd said under the influence of her blood. That's what concerned him the most.

Aravela clicked her tongue in disapproval and admonished, "Have you forgotten vulnerability is a vital ingredient to seduction, or is your hesitance because of something else?"

"Like what?" he snapped, his ears burning.

"Like the fact she's the one your heart has been searching for all these years and, perhaps, my son, you're afraid she'll see you stripped bare and still walk away."

He stared at his mentor—his adoptive mother—for a long, hard moment. She'd seen him at his worst. She'd seen him cry and beg and shout at the moon goddess over his abandonment, but he had been a child then. He'd grown up.

"You know what you need to do to get her on your side," Aravela continued.

He hand-signed his thanks, dismissing her train of thought. Drinking Silver's blood had reminded him to remain cautious. She could have killed him after he'd passed out from the effects of her blood. Instead, she'd tucked him in and he had no idea if it was a game. Until he knew, he had to take things slowly.

"Are you sure no one was hurt in the attack?"

"A few rooms damaged. Nothing we couldn't handle."

He paused with his palm on the doorframe and glanced back at her from over his shoulder. "The creature was only here because of me."

"I know." She smiled fondly at him. "It's nothing you can't handle."

## CHAPTER
# EIGHTEEN

When Silver woke, Shade was gone. Night had well and truly fallen. The cabin, once warm and homely, felt bare. The sprites weren't at the fireplace, but it smoldered enough to dry a pair of leather breeches and a Guardian jacket hanging on the chair. Another bowl of stew sat on the counter. This time, a cup of cider and soap sat next to it. Silver scrambled out of bed and made short work of eating and drinking. She wiped her mouth, did a little belch, and then trotted to the window.

She really needed to relieve herself. The cabin had no plumbing and no chamber pot. From what Shade had told her, another Guardian had lived here, so the bathroom was probably in the trees outside. It didn't bother her. She'd been in worse situations. When she put her hands on the cold glass window, a whiff of her body odor lifted. Yeah, she needed to bathe, too.

She quickly put her jacket and boots on, grabbed the soap Shade had left, then let herself outside. She would have to thank him for his attentiveness to her wellbeing.

The air was crisp and smelled sweet, as though recent rain had disturbed the plant life. She relieved herself in the woods behind the cabin and then made her way back, careful not to slip on the new slick ice. Steam on the lake caught her eye. Curious, she tested the temperature and found it warm and inviting. It smelled a little like sulfur, but that was to be expected in thermal water.

Shade had probably bathed there and left his wet uniform by the fire. Silver checked her surroundings. It was hard to see in the dark. Rain clouds still covered the moon. She didn't see anyone out there. Couldn't sense Shade through their bond, either. Or rather, he felt far away. Like his essence was behind a wall. She wasn't sure why that bothered her. It wasn't like she missed him.

She wasn't even sure if this bond was a hindrance or a blessing.

She quickly undressed, bindings and all. She even unbound her hair. It had been braided for so long that her scalp hurt. Using the soap Shade had left, she cleaned herself and her hair, then floated on her back, staring at the smudged sky. Further along in the lake, bioluminescent aquatic plants drifted lazily. The blue glow of her mating mark glittered at her side. She held her arm before her eyes and inspected the bond. It reminded her of contour lines on a map. It was still hard to wrap her head around entirely. A connection that linked her emotionally to another. That allowed them to share mana.

A blessing. Her?

A wolf's howl in the woods snapped Silver out of her daydreaming. She was reminded that she wasn't alone out here. It might belong to the gray wolf that had doggedly blocked her from leaving the cabin, or it could belong to another. The demogorgon could show up at any time. Anyone could. She dried and rebound herself before slipping on her old shirt and pants. Shivering, she went indoors to sit by the fire and dry her hair.

The sprites were back. The male sprite stood before his little family as though Silver was a danger to them. She supposed she was. What she wanted to bring into this world was forbidden for good reason. They were beings of elemental mana—pure magic. They might die if Silver had her way. She wasn't setting out on purpose to kill them, but the flow of mana would stop with too much metal around, just like it did at Crystal City.

She thought it would probably be like deforestation. Some animals would lose their home to make way for others. The notion didn't make her feel any better.

They must sense this about her, and that was why they were wary. She gave them a fresh, dry log. After inspecting it closely, the male sprite allowed his family onto it. They seemed a little more accepting of Silver after this and resumed playing.

After an hour and still no Shade, Silver searched the cabin. She told herself it was to find a comb for her tangled, unruly hair, but she just wanted an excuse to snoop. Shade had said the place acted as an outpost for his Guardian brethren, but she discovered odd little wooden carved figurines she didn't think big, burly warriors would keep around. Other odd signs hinted at this place belonging to a family. Scratch marks on the doorframe indicated growth. The highest mark went up to her hip.

So maybe a young family.

The corner plant had a ring of new leaves on the bottom. It was almost as if someone small had plucked off their predecessors recently. Crouching, she winced at the tight pull of the bandages around her middle and distracted herself with the childish drawings scratched onto the floor.

Math equations. Silver huffed a short laugh. It was exactly the sort of thing she used to get into trouble for as a child. She didn't draw stick figures or rude pictures. She doodled equations. It drove her mother nuts, not only because she'd made a mess but because her mother didn't understand. One time, when Silver had been only six or seven, she'd been drawing under the table and her drunk mother hadn't seen her. She tripped on her hand, broke her leg, and blamed Silver for years.

Still, the hate her mother gave her over it was not enough to destroy Silver's love for numbers. It's what drove her to become an engineer in the first place. Well, that and escape from her toxic mother.

Did fae even do math? Her smile faltered as she ran her fingers over the drawings.

Lost in thought, she didn't notice the black smoke sifting through her shirt and bindings until it was too late. A curl of death wrapped around the base of the plant. To her horror, decay formed on the stem, crunching as the blight turned a living thing to ash.

"No," she cried, and shoved her hand into her pants pocket. She'd put the transceiver in there earlier in case Shade found her jacket. Her darkness cut off at the chest. But it was too late. Necrosis spread. In a matter of minutes, the entire plant could be dead.

*Fuck.* Her bandages were useless. She should have insisted she go back for her vambrace and corset. The door burst open, and Shade jogged in, alarmed. She did a double take. He wasn't wearing his Guardian uniform. Just a tight sweater and khaki pants that hugged muscular legs. His hair was freshly styled. Beard freshly trimmed like some kind of cover model from her time. It unnerved her how familiar he felt, like she'd watched him on television for half her life.

"What's wrong?" he barked and dumped his bag onto the bed. "I sensed your panic."

The sound of glass tinkling followed him as he rushed to her. He had something in his pockets.

"Silver. What happened?"

"It was an accident," she blurted.

He scanned the space around her as though expecting the demogorgon to materialize, but quickly found the source of her regret. With a sigh, he gave her a comforting pat on the arm, kissed her on top of the head, and then crouched to place his palm on the plant. Ribbons of shadow sprung from his fingertips and enveloped the blackening parts. Somehow, he managed to keep the death from spreading. Silver gaped. Never in the past six years had she imagined finding a solution to her black heart here in Elphyne. So stupid, really. They were the experts on how to use magic, and her solution had been to suppress it. Not control it.

She'd been so ignorant.

A niggling thought plucked at her. Would it truly be possible to control her curse?

Shade scrutinized the necrosis. "In time, we might be able to teach you to reverse it. We should start now."

Reverse it?

Her mind went straight to the man whose ear she'd bitten off to stop the death from spreading. The blood drained from her face.

"But what did you do?" She pointed back to the plant. "To stop it. How did you do that with your shadow?"

His gaze darted to her and then away, as though he were uncertain of the answer. He emptied his pockets onto the counter. Glass vials full of liquid rolled.

"Shade?"

"I don't know," he replied curtly, shaking his head to himself as he sorted vials. "I think my gift is evolving now that I'm mated to you. It happened with Jasper. It's likely happening now."

"Evolving into what?"

He met her gaze. "Something that can help you. Just like your gift helped me when the demogorgon tried to take me. If you need any more reasons to see that we're made for each other, I don't know what else to tell you."

She didn't know what else to say either, so she joined him at the counter and picked up a vial, turning it to inspect it. It looked like an Elven elixir. Her eyes narrowed. Shade leaned into her and suddenly all she could smell was him. Sweet yet masculine. He seemed to be just as enamored by her smell. His nose hovered near her freshly washed hair and he inhaled deeply. Silver's eyes fluttered as her senses overwhelmed. This close, she could see improvements in his complexion. That dehydrated look he'd had before was gone. *From feeding on her.* Or someone else? He touched her by the ear, just a feather light amount to shift her hair, and then he tugged the vial from her fingers.

"It's not for you," he murmured.

"What is it?"

"Plan B."

"I don't understand."

"Let's hope you won't need to."

"You're being obtuse. Fine."

Shade walked to the door. She followed him for two steps before she stopped herself. His touch had been so brief, but now that he'd put distance between them, it was all she could think about. It seared into her memory like a brand. A reminder taunting her and teasing her, begging her to follow him. Not to train like he'd said, but to climb over him on the bed and—

"Silver?" He waited by the door.

Heat flooded her cheeks. "You disappear for half the night, and then just come back looking healthier than ever, without an explanation, and expect me to jump."

Shoving her emotions into a little box, she cleared her throat and straightened. She was about to say never mind, when his eyes dipped to the bandages wrapped around her middle.

"You're right," he said with an exhale. "I left without a word. And you stayed. No babysitter this time."

He let the gravity of those words settle between them. She hadn't tried to escape. Nervous tension tightened her shoulders. Could he see through her ruse?

"Well, I couldn't exactly flee. We have a bargain."

"Right." His lips twitched at the corner. "Well, I suppose the reason I left was for the first part of that bargain. I need to take care of you. And, no, Silver, I didn't feed from another. Only your blood nourishes me."

"Oh."

"Now we burn those bandages."

"I told you that's not happening." Her heart palpitated at the thought of removing them. Logically, she knew they were ineffective. But for the past half decade, she'd had that tightness around her middle telling her it was safe. Her black heart was contained.

But he wasn't listening. He went for the bag he'd dumped on the bed and opened it. One by one, he pulled out decadent feminine items. A comb. An embroidered silk blouse. Leather pants were beautifully embossed with a pattern down the side. A boned leather corset. Her eyes stuck on that last one and she tried to hold her elation in but couldn't. When he came back to her, he cupped her face and looked deeply into her eyes.

"I want you to feel safe."

She swallowed. "Where did you get it?"

"Some friends owed me."

He faced her away from him and toward the fire, flicked her loose hair over her shoulder, and lifted her shirt off to reveal her bindings. He plucked at the bandages down her spine. Ripping sounds filled the room. Her pulse elevated as the bandages dropped to the floor, leaving her naked from the waist up. A light, brief touch near her painful welts had her suck in a breath. His touch shifted to a bruise and lingered. Then to another under her ribs.

The fire crackled before her, but his presence scorched her back. A pause as long as a breath pushed at her senses. Rustling behind her, and then warm fingers lifted her arms over her head. She held her hands high and paused, waiting for him. The audible lick of his lips made her think he was going to say something, or kiss her, but then he tugged a silk blouse on her, careful not to graze injuries.

He didn't stop his ministrations there. Done with her shirt, he moved to her pants and tugged them down her hips, crouching as he went. A muffled thud sounded as her pants hit the floor. *The transceiver.* Silver quickly feigned loss of balance and fell into him, holding his shoulders as he kneeled.

"Step out," he said.

She swallowed and glanced down. He didn't seem to notice the transceiver, so she stepped out. He collected the new leather pants from the bed and lowered to hold them open for her.

"In," he said.

The lingering touches continued. Shade pulled up her pants, knuckles sliding along her naked legs before he buttoned them for her. She could have taken over at any time, but this seemed like something he needed to do. And she wasn't done watching him. To have someone so virile serving her was intoxicating. It was more than his actions. It was the smoldering looks, the raging need, and the reverence filtering down their bond in waves—as though he tried to suppress how much this pleased him. But most of all, it was the complete and utter way he seemed consumed by her. Every time he grazed her bare flesh, he would pause, his breath would hitch, and he'd get lost in their connection.

"Do you dress all your ladies?" she asked quietly.

Long lashes flicked up as he finished tying her boot laces. Amusement skipped in his eyes. When he stood, there was no space between them. His impact blanked her mind, and the bastard seemed to know exactly how he affected her, because his eyes twinkled.

Without replying, he collected the final piece from the bed. He'd been against her wearing the corset. She was surprised he now offered one.

"I've been watching you, Silver. And learning. You like the feeling of being in control," he noted quietly and methodically fitted the piece to her sternum. Laces at the back. With every tug as he tied, he spoke. "Your last contraption cut you and hindered your range of movement. It wounded you. As did those bindings. I recognize your need for something, and I want you able to use mana to defend yourself. So, this is a compromise."

"I moved fine before."

"You know that's not true. You almost passed out from lack of oxygen."

Sweat prickled the back of her neck. She hated that he was right, but she'd committed to this training. She needed to get into the Order.

"Okay." She faced him. "What's next?"

He held up the ornate comb. She went to take it, but he snatched it away with a lopsided grin that weakened her knees. He was so smug, and he enjoyed every minute of this. Was he toying with her? No. He ushered for her to sit at his feet while he settled on the chair by the fire.

"It's a tangled mess." She leaned against his knees. "You should let me do it."

A graze at her neck as he gathered her hair. "I like tangled messes."

To her surprise, Shade not only combed her very long hair, but braided it too. The light, expert touch sent periodic shivers through her body. By the time he finished, and she inspected the intricately entwined length, she was ready to jump out of her skin and... she didn't know what.

"Where did you learn to braid hair like this?" The moment the words came out, she knew. He'd made an offhand comment before he'd fallen asleep after he'd fed. It was either at a brothel, or from time spent with the queen. At the thought of other women, especially one so powerful, touching him and teaching him how to care for her, Silver got an icky feeling in her stomach.

She faced him and caught the unguarded affection in his eyes before he stamped it out and stared down at her.

"Do you really want to know?"

The less she knew about him, the easier her mission would be.

"Yes," she replied.

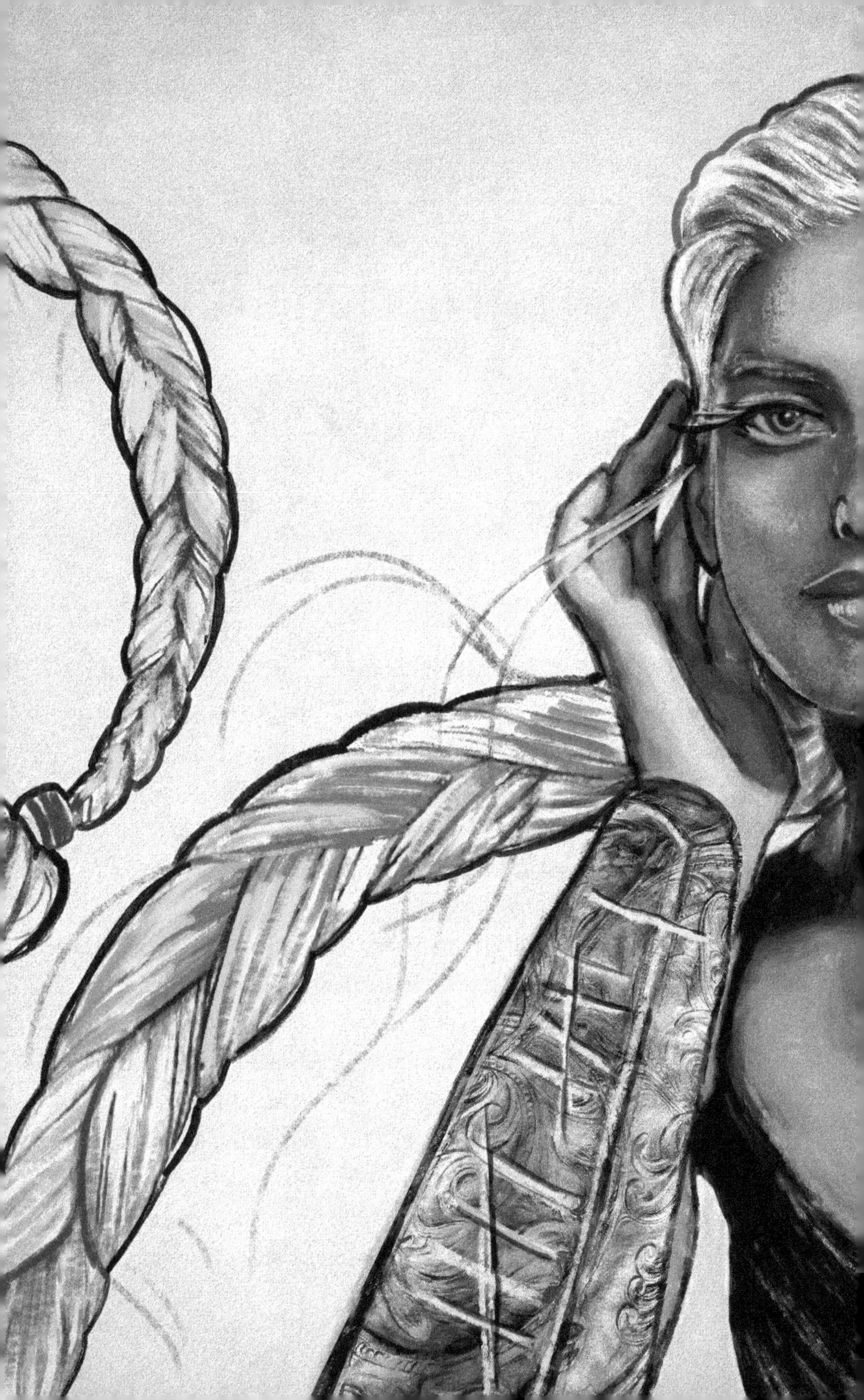

# CHAPTER NINETEEN

Shade coiled Silver's braid around his wrist. He liked how it looked against his skin. He liked the way the silken rope felt. He liked more that he'd tied it.

She wanted to know about his past, but he rarely spoke about it to anyone. Aravela had said if he opened up, Silver might trust him more. And he needed that.

She waited patiently at his feet.

He decided he liked her there too and supposed if he wanted their mating to be true, then she needed to know all about him. Including the dark yearnings of his heart.

"My mother was a highly sought-after Rosebud Courtesan."

Her brows puckered. "I thought they can't have children."

"That used to be a Seelie law. The Unseelie were never restricted from breeding. Although most courtesans had their wombs removed for ease of the trade, my mother was either too afraid, or thought the right elixir would keep her sterile. She was wrong. I was conceived, and after she gave birth, I represented everything wrong with her new life. Her rich clients shunned her, including whoever my father was."

"She blamed it on you." A sympathetic bitterness pinched Silver's face. "Believe me, I get it. My mother wasn't my biggest fan either."

"She left and I never heard of her again. The other courtesans raised me."

He cleared his throat and stood, guiding her up by the braid. That was enough sharing for now. More would come later.

"Time to start your training," he said, and motioned for her to go to the door.

"What will that involve?"

"If you were a novice at the Order, we'd test your elemental affinities and work out how to access each, but I've seen your power in action. It's like mine. I know how to help you."

"So... we'll be doing what?"

He smiled at her. "Learning how to not be afraid of the dark."

⚖

OUTSIDE, Shade kept his hand on Silver's elbow to stop her from slipping. They walked along the shore for a few feet until they came to the moored wooden dinghy.

"Get in," he said and kicked off his boots. He rolled his pants up to his calves and waded into the water.

She gave him an incredulous look. "I don't mean to be rude, but I'm not afraid of the dark. And this"—she looked up—"isn't dark."

The poor woman had no idea what she was in for. He would enjoy tearing down her barriers and helping her rebuild them.

"Darling, get in." Did he detect a hint of concern as she looked at the boat? "You're not afraid of water, are you?"

"No," she replied, but her tone was too animated.

A smile tickled his lips. "Can't swim?"

Her glare hit him. "I may have grown up in Nevada, but I was in the military. I know how to swim."

She yanked off her boots and grumbled that he'd made her put them on in the first place, then waded into the water and climbed into the boat. When it wobbled, her hands slapped on the rim and her face paled. Before she could change her mind, he pushed the dinghy forward off the sandbank and then climbed in himself.

The small space barely fit the two of them. Hopefully, lying down wouldn't be a problem, but for the exercise he had planned, they needed to have the sensation of floating.

He placed is hand in the warm water and created a current with his mana that pushed them to the center of the lake. The tip of the boat displaced mist. With each slow yard they progressed, her knuckles whitened further on the rim. There was no mistaking her unease. It flowed through their connection.

"I won't let you drown," he promised, halting the dinghy a hundred feet from shore. He wanted them far from the cabin, the woods, and anything in their vision when they looked up at the sky.

"I told you, it's not that."

"So, what is it?"

"I..." She peered over the edge and into the deep, fathomless water, a reflection of the black sky above. "Are there... Well Worms down there?"

*Ahh.* She was afraid of being judged. That made sense, considering what he thought blocked her from controlling her power. She didn't like the chaos she created, but pretended she could handle it by locking it behind a breathtaking corset.

"No," he answered. "Well Worms only live in the Ceremonial Lake. And while this lake does seem to be a source of power, there are no such beings living in the depths."

"Source of power?"

"When we bathe in it, our internal well refills at a rapid rate."

"Okay." Silver exhaled, and her tension eased. "Other predators?"

Shade shrugged at that. He had no idea.

"Great. You're real comforting."

"Aww." He leaned forward. "Is my little fee-lion afraid of monsters?"

"You know I'm not," she snapped. "It's just that I have no idea if my curse works in water, and I have no metal."

"Don't worry," he said, more seriously this time, and placed her palm over his chest as he made his oath. "On my life, I promise to keep you safe. Now, lie down."

He caught her eye roll as she reclined and wanted to press her buttons again. She must have sensed it, because she stared at him like a river pirate. "Don't you dare."

"Dare what?"

"That's the same look you gave me right before you spanked me."

He burst out laughing, much to her incredulous outrage.

"I'm serious!" she shouted. "I'm not a child."

Shade forced himself to sober, or he'd never get to their training.

She brought out feelings in him he'd not had in a long time. He touched her cheek fondly, before fitting his larger body next to her smaller one. There was a moment of wanting to stay on his side, facing her, so he could see her expressions as they spoke. Her thoughts animated her face, and he was fast learning she was better than a book or play. But he rolled to his back and looked at the cloudy night sky.

"Now what?" she asked.

"So impatient."

A huff to his left.

"When the gift comes out of you, what do you feel?" he queried.

"Firstly, it's not a gift, it's a curse. Secondly, I feel horror. What else would I feel?"

"You feel more than horror. Your *gift* is steeped in chaos. I sensed your conflicted emotions when you use it. You're full of panic, yet pride, dread, curiosity and a lot of denial. You need to know that's okay. It's *okay* to feel like everything is upside down. It's *okay* to not feel in control." He sighed with the thought. "What you're feeling is very normal. Chaos is a part of life. If you can't accept those emotions, then you'll never be able to harness it."

"You keep talking about chaos like I should know what it means."

"Chaos, Spirit, Earth, Air, Fire, and Water are the six elements that make up the Well. There is no Well without chaos. You have a place in this world, Silver. A valuable one. Don't fight it."

When she didn't answer, he raised his hand and enticed his shadows to swirl darkly in the sky, creating beautiful patterns for them. "Your darkness is a part of you, just as it's a part of me."

"I don't know what that has to do with being afraid of the dark."

"Can I tell you a story?"

"I'm sure you will, anyway."

*Crimson*, he wanted those mouthy lips on his cock. The mating urge welled up out of nowhere, but he squashed it down. This kind of violent desire was not what they needed in the moment, and certainly not what Aravela had reminded him about. But the awareness of Silver was prickling against his skin. He scrubbed his face to ground himself.

She craned her neck to look at him. "Why on earth my comment made you feel all *wanting* through our bond, I have no idea."

"Lie back down." He cleared his throat. "Unless you want to find out."

With a sigh, she did as she was told, and he readied himself to share more of his dark past.

"When Maebh added me to her menagerie of amaros—"

"*Queen* Maebh?" Her eyes narrowed perceptively. "That queen?"

"Unseelie High Queen Maebh, yes. And don't interrupt."

Another feminine huff, but then silence. Sharing was difficult enough for him, but she needed to hear this story before he took away her senses. He laced his fingers over his chest. The dinghy rocked a little, soothing his mood.

"When she took me—"

"You had no choice? Like she kidnapped you?"

"Silver," he gritted out. "If you speak again, I'm going to gag you."

She rubbed her fist over her heart in a half-hearted attempt at hand-signing her apology.

"Maebh never used to be as cruel and corrupt as she is now," he prefaced. "Back then, she was a harsh ruler with a ruthless ambition. She'd recently lost her only child, and all she wanted to do was —" Shade heard Silver's lips open and then her teeth clicked shut. His lashes fluttered shut with exasperation. "Fine. Ask your question."

"It's just that you said, back then. How far back? Exactly how old are you?"

"I don't know. A few hundred years."

"For real?" She sat up suddenly and rocked the boat. Her palm slapped on his chest for balance. Their eyes clashed and he lost his train of thought. What was he saying? Oh yes, the story. But all he could focus on were her two pools of darkness drawing him in. Her voice lowered as she spoke. "You look pretty good for that age."

"Your blood does me good," he admitted.

"No, I mean, for an old man." There was a hint of tease in her smile, and his mind emptied again. Something warm expanded within his chest.

"If I'm an old man, then you really are a child."

Then he realized what she was doing. Stalling. He took her hand from his chest and pushed her back down.

"Final warning," he ground out. "Interrupt me again, and I'll take this long braid of yours and tie it across your mouth."

"But you said I could ask!"

Chagrined, he went back to stare at the sky. "No more questions."

"Fine."

The story seemed stupid now. The moment had passed.

"Have you been to the Winter Court?" he asked anyway.

A pause. "Maybe once. Nowhere inside, though."

"The Autumn Court?"

Another pause. "To Rubrum City, yes, but again, not inside the palace."

"Maebh is an exhibitionist. A lot of Unseelie are. We like teasing and eliciting reactions from unsuspecting souls and displaying them for the world to see. We like pushing buttons and seeing what reaction we get."

"You don't seem that bad to me."

She hadn't seen anything yet. "There's a reason I was Maebh's most favored amaro."

"You mentioned that word before. I don't think I know what it means."

"Concubine."

"Oh."

"Now, here comes the story. If you interrupt, I'll turn you over, pull your pants down until the moon greets your pert little bottom, and then I'll bite it."

She probably didn't think he could see her eye roll in the dark, and it only made him want to make good on his promise.

He allowed more shadow to escape his body. One by one, the dark ribbons unfurled and rose into the air, darkening the sky to create his own little shadow puppet show to illustrate his words.

"Having recently come of age, I visited the palace with some Rosebud Courtesans, eager to test myself in the most debauched environment I could think of. I wasn't a courtesan myself. I did it for fun. I was good at it. It made me feel invincible. Then I caught Maebh's attention, and I thought, what bigger challenge could I find than the most powerful person in Elphyne."

His voice trailed off as fleeting memories tried to surface. Parties, drugging elixirs, orgies, gluttony. There was nothing he was afraid of doing. He pushed the limits on both himself and his sexual partners. The shame of it curled his stomach. And it wasn't shame because of what he did, but why he did it. He wanted approval from anyone.

Silver must have sensed his shame, because she touched him gently on the arm. The last thing he wanted to do was share this dark part of himself with her, but he had to. She needed to see what became of his own black heart.

Frowning, he reinforced his shadows and made moving shapes. The moon behind the clouds was a perfect backdrop for his shadow theater show. He took a deep breath and continued.

"Back then, the only shadow gift I had was being able to hide in it. So, I did. I spied around the palace. I searched, although I knew not what I searched for. Maybe my mother. I still held onto the hope that I would one day find her and confront her for what she did to me. I would ask her what was so wrong with me that she left. I think that was why I went to Maebh too. I wanted to show my mother that I was good enough to be with a queen, even if I didn't like the queen very much. Then one day, while I was on top of my game, standing by Maebh's right-hand side, my mother turned up at Court."

Silver gasped. "She's alive?"

He shrugged. "I don't know anymore. But she turned up, and she wasn't alone. She had a male on her arm, and they'd heard about my fortune. That's what they'd said, anyway. All I can remember is being furious that they thought I was with the queen through luck or handed down prosperity. But I worked my way into Maebh's amaros. I did things I never thought I'd do just to prove to her I was loyal. How *dare* they think I was handed my lot in life, and after what *she* did!"

Anger bubbled in his veins at the memory, and his shadows darkened as they formed the pictures of him standing by the queen, and two people at the foot of a dais.

"I couldn't stop thinking about it," he said. "And then my mother's true colors finally showed. She wanted in on what I had with Maebh. She thought that by association, she would gain affluence. It was then I understood why my mother left me, and it wasn't because I was lacking. She was. There was nothing wrong with me, and I couldn't see it on my own. That was the first moment I shadow walked."

Silver was looking at him now, not his shadow puppet show, so he stopped and turned to his mate. "I accepted myself, for all my twisted darkness. And the Well rewarded me. Do you understand?"

Her confusion still trickled through to him. He placed his palm over her heart. "Don't be afraid of the dark in here, darling. Learn to love yourself, for all your twisted darkness. I am."

⚖

Silence followed his story. For a moment, he thought he'd said too much. That he'd frightened Silver and she would want nothing to do with him. But she stayed silent.

Leaning in to her, he shifted out a wing and used it to create a cocoon over their heads, trapping the impenetrable darkness inside.

"What are you doing?" she blurted.

"True darkness," he explained, "is a mirror."

Her breathing quickened enough to rock the boat. He kept

himself as distant as possible. For this to work, she had to forget he was there. Shadow wrapped around his body, separating him from her. If he knew how to block his emotions, he would. But he was only learning how to control that part of himself.

"Darkness reflects the truth you don't want to acknowledge," he continued. "So, we're going to lie here surrounded in darkness, together but apart until you discover what this truth is that you don't want to acknowledge."

Then he shut himself off from her.

"Shade?" she whispered and reached out, but he'd become shadow itself. Her hand passed through him. *"Shade?"*

It killed him to hear the panic in her voice, but he kept his mouth shut.

# CHAPTER
# TWENTY

The son-of-a-bitch had left her. He'd left her surrounded by impenetrable and inescapable shadow with nothing but her thoughts.

Silver huffed and flexed her fists. She tried to sit up, but a barrier stopped her from going anywhere and she only succeeded in rocking the boat. *I'm still in the boat.* Laying back down, she calmed herself.

It was fine. It just felt like she was in a sensory deprivation tank. That was probably his point. Darkness is a mirror, he'd said. And she'd promised to follow through with his training. It was the only way to get to the Order.

Ugh. Fine. She stared into the black. The sooner she did this, the better. She wasn't sure exactly how staring at darkness would reveal why she was supposedly afraid of said darkness. If you had to ask her what her fears were, she would have said maybe Well Worms and monkeys. Those pesky jungle animals had rabies and stole your shit. Little fingers picking at your hair as they landed on your shoulders. Screeching into your ears with diseased teeth. She shuddered.

Come to think of it, Silver hadn't seen a monkey since she'd awoken in this time. A dash of sadness hit her. They were probably extinct. A lot of animals from her time were. Elephants. Rhinos. Lions. The entire Amazon jungle. *Shit*. Now she was thinking about all the things humans had ruined.

Cheeseburgers.

Rollercoasters.

The goddamned entire planet.

She took a deep breath and slowed her breathing, but her mind kept spiraling. She'd tried to ignore her culpability for the nuclear winter by focusing on all her troubles since awaking. Violet and Peaches had both accepted their part in the crisis from the moment they'd realized what had happened.

The memory of that time played out in the darkness. She'd been in a cage with Peaches, fed on by vampires addicted to their blood while they combed Elphyne hunting Violet. If it hadn't been for Violet's aggression and determination, their story would be very different for the past six years. They might have been the Unseelie High Queen's captives.

Silver's mind traveled from the past to the present, and then back again. She saw her drunk mother. She saw Sid's face as he learned what she'd kept from him. She saw Polly's little hand as she fist-bumped Silver. Then there was Angus as he spread lies about her and Nero's grandstanding by the docks.

Nero was a ruthless president. Before Silver had come along, he'd also tried to chase her and Violet and Peaches down. He could have made them build a nuclear bomb so he could take over Elphyne.

*"Whoever captures us captures power,"* Silver had said to the two women the day they escaped the vampires.

"We can't be together. Ever."

"Agreed."

Silver had advised the women to live in Elphyne and assimilate. She'd done the opposite. She'd failed them. She'd blamed her need to get back to the human city on her uncontrollable death power, to block it with metal, but the truth was, Silver *was* afraid. The darkness was where her cowardice lived. It was where her black heart oozed out from to infect everyone around her. Nero had taken one look at her and put her to use building weapons.

*You'll never escape your roots.*

But she'd tried. She'd been running from them her entire life. Two thousand years later and she was still a coward.

Once the word released, it was everywhere. She was a coward because she couldn't handle looking after her mother and so walked out on her. She was a coward because she'd built nuclear warheads despite knowing nothing good would ever come from them. Then she built cannons and warships because she made herself believe violence was the only solution to saving humanity. She did all that instead of accepting she had a part to play in their predicament in the first place.

And she was a coward for telling Peaches and Violet to stay in Elphyne so she could have the luxury of living in Crystal City without the guilt or fear of one day being forced to make another nuclear bomb. One year was all she could muster in Elphyne and then, at the first sign of her curse manifesting, she'd run away. She gave up. She was a quitter.

The truth slammed Silver in the face. She'd run from everything important in her life. And despite Shade being so incurably insistent with his pursuit of her, she would eventually run from him. Already had multiple times. She'd rather betray him now than risk falling in love and have *him* run away when she needed him the most.

And that made her the biggest coward of all.

She slammed her fists down on the boat and squeezed the burn from her eyes.

"What's the point of this?" she shouted. "How does hating myself help me control my power?"

"You don't mean that."

Shade's wing disappeared and the black void lightened. Clouds reappeared in the night sky.

"What did you see, Silver?" Shade asked.

"It was only a few minutes. I didn't see anything."

"It was a few hours," he corrected.

Hours? She'd stewed in her misery for *hours*?

"What did you see?" he repeated.

She clutched her chest. As if she'd tell him. "None of this makes sense."

"It probably won't."

"Then why do it?"

"You know why. Until you make peace with yourself, and the dark twisted chaos of your past, you'll never harness your gift."

"Make peace with my chaos?" With her cowardice and shameful behavior? "That goes against everything I know to be right in the world. Murderers shouldn't make peace with the death and pain they cause. That's just plain wrong."

"That's not what I'm saying." He sighed and stared at the sky. "No matter what you think, there is chaos in the world. There is suffering. And there is good. Sometimes there is no sense to it. It happens. The sooner you can accept that your past is a part of you, the quicker you will learn to find meaning in it, and you can understand how to draw on it, and to move forward."

"You sound like a shrink." She shook her head. "This is so stupid."

"Well, we'll be coming back here nightly until you share."

"Why are you even helping me? Really. And don't tell me it's because of this bond. Because the notion that suddenly you and I are some kind of dream couple just because of this"—she held up her marked arm—"is ridiculous. No, it's more than ridiculous. It's inconceivable. No one. And I mean no one can force falling in love. No one can force us to stay together."

"Why does the sun rise in the east? Why does the night sky hold an untold number of stars? Why—"

"Oh, my god, Confucius. I get it, alright? There are things we don't understand and accept them, anyway. Whatever. That still has nothing to do with my fears and why I can't control the death pouring out of me."

Shade was quiet beside her, in both sound and down their bond. Silver thought, for a moment, that she'd broken something between them. He threaded his fingers and rested them on his chest as he stared up at the sky.

"At first," he said, "I wanted you because you'll give me power."

Her heart stilled. "You wanted to exploit me."

"Yes," he admitted. "All my life I've wanted power. I thought it would somehow fill the void I was born with. I thought it would force respect, acceptance. First, the power I craved was over any female I encountered, then it was with the most powerful female I could imagine. Maebh might have thought she snapped me up to join her amaros, but the truth was, I had my eye on her for a long time. This darkness inside me is a void even Maebh couldn't fill."

"You have mommy issues. I get it. I do too."

He shot her a glare. "The power Maebh offered wasn't real. It was a reflection of hers. I realized that the day my mother turned up at Maebh's Court. So, I kept hunting. I joined the Order. I got into the Cadre of Twelve—the most elite of the Guardians. That still wasn't enough. I wanted the team leader role. I planned to go back there with you, my new power source, and claim the top position from Leaf. I planned to demand respect."

"Is that still your plan?" She couldn't say she was happy with it, but she could understand it. If she was in his position, she might be just as ruthless to get what she wanted. At least it felt like something other than failure.

"No," Shade replied.

"What? Why not?"

In the small boat, they were so close to each other, she could smell his unique masculine spice. He gave a small shrug.

"None of it feels relevant anymore."

"Why not?"

"Because all I want is you." It sounded like the confession surprised him.

"You don't even know me."

"Also irrelevant. The Well knows us both inside and out, and it found our union worthy. I can't explain it. No one can. It's chaos in its purest form. But I can't deny the way I feel about you every time you're near."

"Worthy?" She laughed cruelly. Tears stung her eyes, and she looked away from him, shaking her head softly. "How can you say that after the things I've done, and the lies I've told—" She bit her tongue to stop herself from saying any more.

"We'll make it work."

"But I want the choice to make that decision on my own."

"You want the choice to run away?"

The truth of his accusation hit her right in the heart. She didn't want to talk about this anymore. She wanted out. Silver slapped her hand on the edge of the boat and sat up, tipping the balance until they rocked side to side. They were in the middle of the lake. Where monsters and Well Worms could live. He'd said they didn't live here, but what if they did? What if they looked into her heart and saw the same things she did? *Coward.*

"I need off this boat," she blurted, her heart thudding in her chest. "Now."

"We'll resume tomorrow night."

He placed his palm into the water to do what he did last time to move the boat. Despite her new corset being looser than her old one, she struggled to take in air and grabbed him by the throat. Everything was unraveling.

"I don't think you understand," she wheezed. "I need off, *now.*"

# CHAPTER TWENTY-ONE

Shade felt Silver's panic as though it were his own. Without a second thought, he dragged them through the shadows to inside the cabin. When they landed, she wrenched from his grip and bent over, wheezing to catch a breath, tugging on her corset.

Panic attack.

He knew the training session would dredge up unwanted memories. And he knew she'd have no option but to experience them. It broke his heart at the same time as mended it. This was growth. And she wasn't the only one who'd had a revelation.

She was his sole purpose in life. He didn't give a shit about anything else, and he wasn't sorry about that. That was the darkness inside him. He was selfish and tended to go all in. He wanted someone to love, and she was it. The Well knew when it paired them together.

"What you're feeling right now," he said. "This panic. This fear. This chaos... remember it. See how your gift is activated?"

Agony pierced her expression as she met his gaze with a question in her eyes.

"Now shut it off. Any way you can. Stop feeling the way you're feeling. Whether it's a good memory, or something else that can switch the chaos to order, think of it."

She glanced down at her corset. A frown of concentration marred her forehead. "It's not working."

"Because, my darling," he said as he drew closer. "If that corset truly made you feel in control, you wouldn't gasp and feel out of breath the way you just did." He slotted his fingers in the gap between her breasts and tugged. "It's not tight, remember? So, think of something else. Something that gives you the sense that everything is right in the world, a sense that things are the way they should be."

Accusation in her eyes speared him. "Can we just stop with the training? I'm done. No more."

"Maybe what you need isn't containment... but freedom." He slid his hands up her waist and circled to the back laces. He tugged on the tie.

She slapped his hand away and stalked to the counter, refusing to show him her face. Her dark power was easing off, and at least the falling mist dissipated before it touched anything living.

"What were you afraid of, Silver?" he accused. "What did you see in the dark?"

She slammed her palm on the counter. "I don't want to talk about it."

"You'll have to at some point."

"Not tonight. Tonight, I just want to... I just want to forget about it." She picked up the glass vials he'd left on the counter and inspected them. "What are these? Elixirs? Will they get me drunk?"

He took them from her hands. "You don't want to know what they are."

She snatched one back and opened it. "I do."

Before she lifted it to her lips, he slapped it out of her hand. The glass broke on the floor. The elixir spilled.

"It's something to counteract my urges," he said, clenching his jaw. His next words came out huskier than intended, but he couldn't stop the truth from barreling out. It had been building for days. "You're my mate, Silver. I've tasted your blood. All I want to do is fuck you until my seed spills from your mouth or runs down your legs. I want it so badly that it hurts. We'll be mating like animals for days. You're not ready for that and I won't force it on you, so I need to force this on myself. I've already taken one dose."

She gaped at him. Then she glanced down to the erection straining his pants. It had been there since the boat.

"Clearly it's not working," she said with a wry smile.

"It's time for my next dose."

They looked at the remaining two vials on the counter.

"That's why you kept disappearing while I slept," she said. "You don't want to feel the way you do."

"I don't want you to feel obliged or uncomfortable, or—"

She smashed her fist down on the last two vials, cutting herself. His nostrils flared as the scent of her alluring blood filled the room. "Why did you do that?"

"Maybe you're right. A little chaos is what I need right now."

She kissed him. At first, Shade was shocked still. The touch of her lips was everything he'd craved and more. She'd come to him, not the other way around. But as he'd confessed to her in the boat, none of that power he'd so desperately wanted before mattered now.

She trembled against him, as though she knew this was the moment they couldn't return from. As though she knew what she offered was a lie. She wasn't doing this because she couldn't live without him. She was doing this as a distraction.

With all the courage he could muster, he pried her fingers from his face and pushed her away. It physically hurt to hold back his desire when the floodgates were already open.

"No," he ground out, breathing like a raging bull.

"No?" She blinked rapidly. "I've been taking a contraceptive for years, so I'm protected." Hurt and betrayal hurtled down their bond. Then something more insidious replaced it. She narrowed her eyes wickedly. "Are you afraid you won't last the night?"

His brows shot up. "What did you just say?"

She gestured at his crotch. "I mean, the last time you came in your pants, despite claiming you could last all night."

"I will *never* feel shame for how you affect me." She was *not* going there. Not with him. He advanced on her until he backed her against the counter and breathed down her face. "You're clutching at straws, little fee-lion, if you think those words would wound me."

Her palms flattened against his stomach, setting his senses alight. But she didn't do it to push him away. She did it to entice him further. To tease him. "So, prove me wrong."

He snarled. He'd always suspected that when they finally fucked, it would be epic. He was a fool to think his need for her eclipsed their personalities. He was a male who liked to dominate.

She was a female who needed containment to feel safe, but she tried to do it herself and she was failing. He could see it in her eyes, the panic, the need, the want, all warring with each other. And underneath it, through their bond, he felt the shame and denial she'd projected out on the boat.

Whatever she'd seen, whatever she refused to tell him, was felt so intrinsically deep in her being that she couldn't come out of it alone. Guilt. Shame. Cowardice. He'd felt a hurricane of self-deprecation come from her, and he didn't want it to continue for a moment longer.

All his good sense flew out the window as she swiped her bleeding thumb over his bottom lip. Her drug shot erotic bliss through his body, from his head to the tip of his painfully hard cock. He lifted her by the thighs and rested her on the counter. Impatiently parting her legs, he fit between them and thrust against her, giving her a taste of what was to come. A last warning. She gasped and clutched his shirt, her nails cutting through the fabric.

"You start this, darling, and I'll finish it."

"So finish it," she moaned, daring him with lust drenched eyes. "Just make it last."

# CHAPTER
# TWENTY-TWO

The glimpse of fang in Shade's feral smile sent shivers through Silver's body. For a split second, she thought she'd taken it too far. It was the smile of the wolf who'd caught his prey. What had she gotten herself into?

Didn't matter.

The black stuff still leaked from her chest, and he was the only one who could stop it. Being near him made her feel better. The truth of it was she didn't want to think about anything anymore. If she did, if she thought too hard about things, she'd see parts of herself she didn't like. And she'd also see that he denied himself to make her feel comfortable. She'd see he truly cared for her. And if he cared for her, then she was one step closer to realizing hurting him was a part of their future, whether she wanted it or not.

Walking out on him.

Failing him.

Betraying him.

*Coward.*

*Black-hearted bitch.*

"Fuck me," she demanded and grappled with his shirt, opening it down the middle. "Make me feel something."

He blinked and stepped back, leaving her on the counter. His hair was in disarray, shirt open, score marks already down his hard abdominals. He was everything she needed right now. Why did he stop?

"What did you say?"

"I said fuck me. Make me feel something." She was being crude, but this kind of direct talk had always worked for her before. She'd walked right up to Sid in a filthy dockside bar and said the same thing.

Shade cocked his head, looking at her as though he'd just figured her out. Gorgeous face pinched in concentration. He brushed his thumb across her cheek, leaving tingles in his wake.

"Oh, darling. You almost made me forget myself. Almost."

That sounded like he was going to ignore this between them. Anger fired through her at his rejection, and she lashed out.

"I thought you wanted me. I'm *all* you want. You said that."

"I did. And now you know what gets me off. You know my weakness." He trailed his thumb down her jaw, let it burn a path of need as he firmed his pressure around her nape, grasped her braid and forced her to meet his eyes. Tiny stings of pain in her scalp made her gasp, thrill, and need. That one grip, one movement, and he reminded her who was in charge. It was the look given to someone about to be claimed. To be owned. His passion and possession burned right through Silver until she let out a little shameful moan of need, and all he had done was hold her hair, and care for her.

"And now you know my weakness," she whispered.

He darted in as though about to kiss her, then pulled away with breathless words that undid her. "I've known since I tasted your blood and experienced your memories."

As if that wasn't confirmation enough, he laid it all out for her so she could never go back.

"You spent your life caring for someone else, but there is nothing you want more than to be cared for. At the first sign of affection, you do anything for them. You joined the military for your father. You tried to live in Elphyne for months for Peaches and Violet before you gave up and tried something else. You kill for the woman with copper in her hair, not for the president of your misguided people. You kill for the girl with the flower name and the boy who followed you." This time, he nipped her on the lip as he darted in. "But here's the thing, darling. Sometimes caring for someone means denying them what they want."

Dread pressed down on her, and she scrunched up her face in a pitiful display of disappointment. Did he know about her mission, too?

"You're not going to...?" Obliterate her pain? Give her unimaginable pleasure, like he'd promised?

His lips curved deliciously. He gave her a tender kiss before murmuring, "First we fix your hand."

He swiped the broken glass and tossed it into the wash bowl. Then he perched her back on the counter and gave her a reproachful look that made him even more handsome. His brows pinched together in concentration as he inspected her bloody palm.

"There's glass in there," he said and sealed his lips to the wound.

She hissed as the pain traveled up her arm. With two swirls of his tongue, and a strategically timed suck, he dislodged the shard embedded in her flesh. He spat it into the wash bowl and then went back to licking her palm. With each lave of his tongue, the pain ebbed as though he was drawing it into himself.

Her gaze trailed over his dark mass of his hair as he bent over her. Wide muscular shoulders, the slope of his back, and the heat of his body made her clench with delicious craving. He didn't know about the mission. If he did, he wouldn't be treating her like this. He hadn't seen it in her blood, but he still might and yet. She couldn't pull her hand away from the dart of his pink tongue, ensuring she clotted and healed.

Shade bustled about the room and found the sheet she'd ripped to make her bindings. He tore one more strip and used it to wind around her palm. When he was done, he put her on her feet and cupped possessively between her legs. She gasped at the sudden sensation.

"Now," he said, with wicked intention. "Let's see to that other ache of yours."

"Finally," she groaned.

He only returned her smirk with a wink. Something unsaid passed between them, and it had nothing to do with their shared emotions, or their unyielding battle of wills. It was a promise. This one night. She would see to his needs. He would see to hers. They would give each other this.

"Undress and get on the bed," he ordered.

She faced the bed and removed her pants and underwear, but when it came to the corset, she hesitated. It had always been on. She felt his presence before he shifted her hair out of the way and kissed her tenderly on the neck. His lips lingered in a way she thought the small taste of her blood was getting to him. With her skin buzzing with anticipation, he covered her hands with his and then directed them to her side. He squeezed them as if to say, *Hold them still. Don't move until I say so.*

Trusting a lover to take the lead was something she'd never done, at least not without the sensation of controlling herself through her bindings. She wondered what that meant for her future. Shade's gentle pluck of the laces at her back rocked her on her feet. Inch by inch, she could breathe again, and at the same time felt like she was drowning. But he did as he'd promised. He cared for her. He lifted her shirt over her head until she was completely naked, and then he surrounded her ribs with his hands and squeezed.

"Bend over," he whispered against her head.

When she hesitated, he guided her down until her hands landed on the bed. Open and vulnerable to him, her breasts heavy with desire, she waited for him to touch her. Exposed as she was, she felt the air tickle her wet entrance, and clenched, hoping he'd start there. He didn't. His palm landed on her spine and grazed downward.

"You're injured here too," he noted, gentling his touch around the welts the metal corset had given her. She tensed, not wanting him to see that, but he laved along those tender bits and showered them with attention.

His wet tongue rasped over her wounds, and it was the oddest, most surreal form of affection she'd ever experienced. It had her panting and aching, making little whimpers for more. He finished on her back, splayed his palm under her belly and supported her as he flipped her to lie on her back. He was back at work before she glimpsed his face, ravenously licking around her body, worshipping every inch.

"Shade," she begged, and speared his hair.

"Shh," he scolded.

"I need mor—"

He captured her lips in a demanding kiss, devouring deeply, promising he would give her more. Just not yet. He ignored her whine before resuming his exploration of her body. Done with her wounds, he set his attention to her breasts, full and aching for his touch.

"Yes," she hissed, arching into him as he pinched a puckered bud.

"Yes, what?" he mumbled, demanding as ever.

"Yes, Shade. D'arn Shade. *Mate*."

Eyes like burning coals locked with hers and crinkled, pleased.

"Ah," he said. "My little fee-lion has remembered her first lesson. That deserves a reward. A kiss, I think... but where? Here?" He sat back and pinched her other nipple, exploding sparks in her body. His dark gaze burned down her body and he swiped a finger through her slick folds, setting off fireworks. "Or here?"

Mindless with want, she bucked into him, chasing his touch.

"Good answer," he said and then spread her legs, lowered his head, and kissed her intimately between the legs.

His tongue swirled, probed, delved, and laved. Just like he'd worshipped her body, he now prayed to her sex. Every ravenous action stole her breath and had her begging for more. He used their bond to know exactly where to attend, what moves she liked, and when she liked it.

"Shade," she begged, holding him between her thighs, wanting that elusive euphoria that wouldn't break. She thrashed against the sheets, restless and desperate, until he pressed down on her lower abdomen, pinning her to make her still, containing her with one controlling push. She climaxed immediately with a scream, shuddering and pulsing around him as he finished his feast.

Still gasping and catching her breath, she watched the leaves shudder above her, as if they too had felt the earth move. Movement dropped her attention. Shade pulled his shirt over his head and tossed it to the floor. Firelight flickered, highlighting his musculature and making something so primal and powerful seem gentle and inviting. Holding her gaze, he undid his breeches and pulled his erection free. Her mouth watered at the sight of him. Hard like steel, and with a single vein running along the length. Moisture beading at the tip betrayed how close he was to the edge. He stroked his thumb over the crown and considered her, as if he had all the time in the world.

"I've waited for this moment for so long, and now I confess, I can't decide which fantasy to fulfill first. Here?" He widened her thighs, zeroed in on her swollen center, already greedy for more. Every muscle in his body hardened as he indulged. He pressed his tip against the heart of her heat and closed his eyes, savoring something he hadn't even begun to enjoy. It became too much. She squirmed. His eyes snapped open, and he pushed a large palm onto her abdomen.

"Be still," he said quietly. "I'm deciding."

But that feeling of his containment was her kryptonite. It triggered the safety net she needed to feel safe, to feel in control. She thrust up into him, sliding herself against his length, enjoying his composure unravel before her eyes.

"Vixen," he hissed through bared fangs.

"What will you do about it, spank me?"

"Oh, darling." The reproachful look he shot her almost had her reaching for him. "It's too late for that."

He tugged off his pants and then climbed up her body to straddle her chest, caging her arms with his muscled thighs. He loomed over her like a wild god, virile and entitled. His lips curved in a way that said they never asked for permission, only forgiveness.

"Open that smart little mouth, mate."

When Shade spoke to her like that, all confidence and velvet, it plucked a chord deep within her chest that resonated through her entire body, a siren's song enticing her to do anything he wanted. This was what she wanted. To be the source of that carnal joy in his eyes. Goddammit, she parted her lips.

"Stick out your sexy little tongue."

She did.

"Ah," he groaned. "Good girl."

He slid his cock between her teeth and then paused, locking eyes with a challenge in his own. Dark spiked lashes framed the sin within like brimstone. Did he think she'd run away? A coward? Maybe for some things, but never for this. She wanted to give him the same freedom he'd given her. And, strangely, she wanted to care for him as he'd cared for her. He'd been right. All her life, this was what she'd wanted. She gripped his taut ass, kneaded each muscular cheek, and then pushed herself forward until he hit the back of her throat.

"*Crimson.*" He slapped his palms on the wall behind her head. She had an eye full of rock-hard abs, clenching and shuddering in response to the sensations she'd given him. She grinned around him, feeling powerful, and pulled back and licked and laved along his length.

"Yes, darling." His voice was deep and guttural. It fell out of his mouth like a plea. "Lick me like I licked you."

She gave him what he asked for until he surrendered. She laved down the vein, around the tip, and then back down to his balls. She took one into her mouth and suckled. He tossed his head back, rocking softly against her while she tasted him. With a slow, teasing lick, she made her way back to the crown and drew him into her mouth. The tendons in his neck pulled taut. His abdomen rippled. His breath came in ragged and hard and when he started twitching around her, frowning and holding back, she came off him until they locked eyes.

"Use me," she decreed. "Make yourself feel good."

Something dark flashed in his eyes. Maybe doubt. Maybe hunger. Maybe fear that he'd frighten her away if he couldn't stop. But she steeled her expression and sent all the confidence she could gather down their bond until his composure broke. He wound her braid around his fist, and thrust into her mouth, using her to his whims. He pumped hard and fast, deep and greedy. He used the grip on her hair to direct her. She gave him everything he needed until he twitched, grunted, and shot his release into her mouth.

Breathing hard, he climbed back down her body to gain better access to her face. He wiped the corners of her watering eyes tenderly, and then did the same for her mouth with proud satisfaction in his eyes before holding her jaw firmly and kissing her like she was his world.

# CHAPTER
# TWENTY-THREE

"Unacceptable," Maebh shouted at the cowering monster at her feet. She picked up the old cradle she'd kept untouched for centuries and smashed it into the wall. "He cannot be mated. I don't accept it."

Since her pet had come in with his tentacles between his legs, feeding her his memories, she'd lost it. For the past fifteen minutes she'd let her rage out on the one room she'd always protected. On the daughter she'd lost.

Maebh had been in here, finally packing things up, getting it ready for her consort to move into when she received the news. Shade had a mate. A *Well-blessed* mate. And they'd both evaded her most powerful hunter. Maebh had put everything she had to give into this creature. She'd sacrificed her good standing with the Well. She'd started a war with the Order. She'd sacrificed her capacity to hold mana. She'd *aged*.

And here was her beast, telling her there was no point in taking that which was owed to her. She'd never get the love from him she deserved. She'd never replace the legacy she'd lost.

All her plans were unraveling before her eyes. Shade was supposed to come back to her after she let him discover himself. He was supposed to be the new companion in her miserable life. But now she saw it had never been about her. He was never going to come back on his own.

For thousands of years, she sacrificed for her people. She saved them from the humans. She gave her only daughter. Now there was nothing left.

She stared around the broken and battered room. Tears streamed down her face at what she'd done. She didn't even know she could still cry. She crawled to the broken cradle and sifted through the wreckage to find the soft woolen doll a loyal servant had knitted. She patted it gently. The old knit unraveled and an anguished wail wrenched from her soul. So much time had passed, there was nothing left. It decayed like the slow beating of her heart. Time was her enemy. Petty revenge and vengeance weren't beyond her, but she was tired. She didn't know what else to give.

Fond memories surfaced of Shade and her together on top of the palace roof, staring at the stars. They would point at each constellation and make up a story to go with the imagined shape. He'd use shadows to create puppet shows to go with the stories. She'd given him her hoarded, old world astronomy books, and they'd discussed their dreams like a game. It hadn't all been seduction between the sheets. He'd made her feel young again. He'd made her forget about her loss and believe there was something else out there for her. Maebh placed her palm over her stomach, then brought the tattered knitted doll to her arms and rocked it like she'd once rocked her baby before sending her to the human city as a changeling.

She'd always blamed King Mithras for convincing her to do it. But there was no one to blame but herself.

A tentative tentacle curled over her shoulder and slid against her face, trying to comfort her. Bones would never had done that. She'd tortured him, raped his mind, and turned him into something else. Something so frightening and fearful that she had been hesitant to unleash it fully on the world. That's why she gave it the name of the most feared monster from her old-world books. But he was new. He was terrifying. And he was hers.

Maebh got to her feet and tossed the doll down.

"One last try," she mumbled. "One last try before I stop caring and we burn the world with everyone in it."

The demogorgon clicked deep in his throat, cooing and approving of her new decree. His very existence hinged on devouring, and the world would seem like the ultimate feast. Maebh pointed at the window he'd flown in through.

"Go and get him," she said. "Bring him back to me at any cost. And kill his mate."

# CHAPTER TWENTY-FOUR

Shade's cock disappeared into Silver from behind. He plumped her bottom, one cheek in each hand. He could watch their joining all day. In, out, in. He savored the leisurely bliss of it rolling through his body, knowing her own sensations were a twin to his. Bent over the tiny counter, she clutched the edges and moaned against her hand. Her position on the hard surface brought her to climax faster than any other. And she was almost there. Forsaking his erotic visual, he leaned forward, trapping her, containing her like she so loved.

Over the past two days, they'd tried every position. They'd fucked on the bed, on the chair, on the floor, in the lake, on the snow-littered shore. He'd claimed his mate hungrily and possessively in every way, and then she did the same to him. It was never enough.

They both knew she used their mating as a distraction from training.

They both knew they had unfinished business and this wouldn't last.

But they did it anyway.

Her body was his addiction, his weakness. He'd caught glimpses of memories in her blood, but pretended her secrets didn't exist, pushing them to some far recess in his selfish mind, giving his darkness food to gorge on. He didn't want to lose her but was powerless to find a way to keep her, so he used this time together to make her addicted to him. The stubborn little fee-lion shivered at the very whisper of what he planned for her next.

Her pitched, eager moans increased in crescendo, encouraging him to go faster. He praised her for her part. This was their symphony but, like all, it had an end. With a sense of foreboding, he pressed his forehead against the back of her head. At her cry and arch back into him, he pulled apart her thighs to drive deeper. Her eager sounds drove him to madness until they rocked the counter and climaxed with a simultaneous cry of abandon.

*Music to my ears.*

For a blissful moment, he slumped against her back. He only moved after feeling the evidence of their lovemaking slide down their legs. Over the past days, he'd covered her in so much of his scent, no other fae would mistake her as unmated. It made him proud how she'd taken it all with nothing but a demand for more.

She laid face first, breathless on the counter while he cleaned her. He rinsed the cloth in the washbowl and wiped her again, taking special care to be gentle where he'd been. Through it all, he noticed her darkness had remained firmly in her chest. While she'd used his body to avoid her training, her gift had surprisingly not come out once. That simple fact was more telling than she realized.

With a secret smile to himself, he reverently kissed along her spine and then swiped her sweaty hair from her face.

"Are you hungry?" he asked. They'd only just awoken, and he'd found himself inside her before they could talk, his mating urges strong and demanding.

"Mm," she replied with a lazy smile. "Not anymore."

He gathered her into his arms and carried her back to the bed. He'd done this every time. At first, she put up a fight, but soon submitted to his need to care for her.

"I'll get you anything," he promised.

The haunted look in her eyes only made the affection down their bond more tragic. He could feel her pulling away from him, even as he rested beside her and held her close.

"We need to talk," she said.

"Don't say it."

"You're making me the villain, but you know this won't work between us. This has to end."

"Why?"

"You know why. I'm not going to stop trying to free my people from fae oppression. You're not going to stop protecting this land. We want different things. Actually, we want the same thing, but in different ways."

He traced circles over her flat stomach. "You know my answer to that."

She huffed and captured his intrepid hand as it moved down.

"Shade," she clipped. "Wanting me isn't going to make you give up everything you've ever known. Me wanting you won't make me forget my loyalty to my people. I'll never want to live here in

Elphyne because that's a betrayal to them. You'll never live in Crystal City cut off from the Well."

"You'll come here, eventually."

"Why?" she shot back. "Because you're so damn good looking I can't stop myself?"

"It's hard to deny the truth."

She slapped him on the chest. "I'm serious."

"So am I, which is why I think you'll eventually stay with me. Besides, you wouldn't have kept your fae name otherwise."

She had nothing to say because she knew Shade was right. In her time, she was known by another name—Anika. She'd picked Silver upon waking in this time and decided to assimilate with the fae. When she went back to the humans, she could have reverted to being the other woman.

They both stared in silence at the canopy above their heads. Shade would do it. He would stay here and avoid the world if that's what would keep her with him, but he knew it wouldn't work, just as he knew she was keeping secrets. He should drink more of her blood, but after that first night licking her hand, he couldn't bring himself to do it. Blood held memories, yes. But her blood nourished him for weeks. If he drank now, it would be for one reason only—to abuse her trust.

Then there was that dark, selfish part of him that would do anything to keep her, even betray his own. And he wasn't ready to face those demons.

"How would a life between us even work?" she mumbled, drew his hand up to her ribs and bade him to hold her tight. "You're a Guardian. You'll never stop being one. It's not like you can erase the teardrop beneath your eye."

"I could cut it out. But it would probably grow back." That she'd contemplated a future with him was enough. "We'll figure it out."

"Why do men always say that?" She chopped her hand through the air, irritated. "It's always, 'It will work out.' It's never, 'Don't worry, babe. I have a plan.'"

"Babe? I thought you didn't want to be treated like a child."

"Don't mince my words." She scowled. "It's just a term of endearment we used in our time."

Term of endearment? His brows lowered. "Who said that to you?"

"No one." She blinked rapidly. "Sid. The guy whose hand you broke."

Shade paused. He exhaled. "Is he your lover?"

"Not anymore."

"Why?"

She shrugged and gestured down her front. "I guess he's not a fan of this."

"Then he's a fool," he said. She tried to laugh it off, but he was serious. A flush of good feelings flowed into Shade from Silver, and he wanted to say the words again to make her feel more joy. "It will work, Silver, because Clarke told me you're mine. She's never been wrong. I believe her."

She turned away from him, and the temperature dropped. "Clarke doesn't know everything."

It was one thing for Shade to avoid rifling through her memories for her secrets, but to hear them on the tip of her tongue and deliberately held back. Alarm bells went off in his head.

"What aren't you telling me?"

"Nothing. Forget it."

Simmering doubt floundered in his heart. If she deceived him, he would find a way to get her back. But if anyone else was hurt because of his selfishness, he would never forgive himself.

While the Well-blessed humans from the old world had grated on him at first, he'd grown to care about them as much as his own vampire brothers in the cadre. Even the rest, if he was pressed.

"Silver." A burst of helplessness wrapped in guilt hit Shade. It came from his mate. "Silver, what aren't you telling me?"

She didn't answer, and when he pulled her face to his, he knew why. Silent tears spilled down her cheeks. Her bottom lip trembled, and he didn't know what to do. Where was his fierce kitten? His warrior?

"Why can't everyone just get along?" she blurted. "Why can't we all share?"

"Darling." He swiped the tears from her face with his thumb. "You know why. We're trying to protect the planet from its final destruction. Humans are trying to undo it."

"But we're not."

"You're not. But your leader is."

She shoved his hand away with a defensive scowl. "He's just trying to protect his people."

Shock hit Shade. Did she not know who her leader was? The despicable things he'd done.

"Silver," he sputtered incredulously. "Your leader is the same man who set off the bombs that destroyed your old world."

"What?" she laughed. "That's ridiculous."

"Why?"

"Because he's..." She blinked. Her face paled. She shook her head as though clearing it, or trying to grasp a thought that wouldn't come. Her next words lost their gusto. "He grew up here. I've seen the evidence."

"Have you?"

"Well, I..." she frowned. "I guess I've never been invited into Sky Tower. He's kept me separate and down at the docks."

"Clarke and Laurel knew him in your time. They knew Bones. Bones tortured Laurel at Nero's behest to force Clarke to reveal a secret number they needed for the—"

"The launch codes," she gasped and sat up.

He shrugged. "All I know is—"

"But that can't be true! He's been in Crystal City for years. He's been the president since before I arrived. Everyone knows that!" Her expression hardened. "It doesn't matter. I still believe metal has its uses. People are still starving. We shouldn't be punished for that."

"He doesn't give a shit about metal. He wants to rule everyone, and he wants to pervert mana for his own gain."

"He's... oh my God." Her face paled further. "When we first thawed, there was a woman sent from Crystal City for us. He would have sent her, but he never mentioned it to me. He knew about my darkness, and yet he never sought to throw me out, only to help me hide it. I thought that meant he was a forgiving man, or he didn't recognize me, but Rory gave me the metal armor and told me to use my darkness if I needed it. She's his daughter. Of course they know about me."

Shade squeezed her thigh. "They sound like they've known who you are the whole time. They had you building weapons for them."

"I can't believe he knew. I thought my lie about who I was worked. I said I'd thawed out alone and days before I turned up at their gates. For a man his supposed age, he should look older than he does, but he's always blamed his youthful appearance on his treatments. It just doesn't make sense."

Shade scoffed. "His treatments are drinking stolen mana."

Her eyes locked with his. "What?"

"He steals mana from fae, takes their immortality, leaving them to age and die. He drinks it to keep himself young. The thing is, drinking mana, or manabeeze, only brings madness. It brings the memories of the animal it came from. Silver, do you understand what I'm saying? Your president is insane." The worst part came to him in a sickening realization. "If he's from your time, he probably has a gift. Perhaps that's how he's managed to stay president for so long."

"But... but... the Well wouldn't give someone like that a gift, would they?"

Shade shrugged. "Every human I'd met from your time has awoken Well-blessed. Bones never disclosed a gift, but if that was true, then why did Maebh use him to create a new type of fae? Think about it. How else can you explain your president turning up in our time and suddenly becoming the human leader?"

Silver lurched forward in the bed and placed her head in her hands. "I'm going to be sick."

He rubbed her back. "I would have told you earlier if I thought you didn't know."

She shrugged him off and glared. "You honestly believed I'd put my lot in with the man who destroyed the world?"

He hadn't cared if she did. That might make him a self-centered bastard, but he just wanted her to be his. When she saw the truth on his face, she launched off the bed, found clothes beneath all the mess they'd made and hastily dressed. She ran outside and into the snow.

*Shit.* He planted his feet on the cold floor and let the temperature ground him. She wasn't running away. She wouldn't do that now. Nevertheless, his heart lurched in his chest, forcing him to hasten as he redressed in his Guardian uniform. The time for hiding was over. The sooner he got Silver to the Order, the better.

He knew something was wrong the moment his palm touched the door.

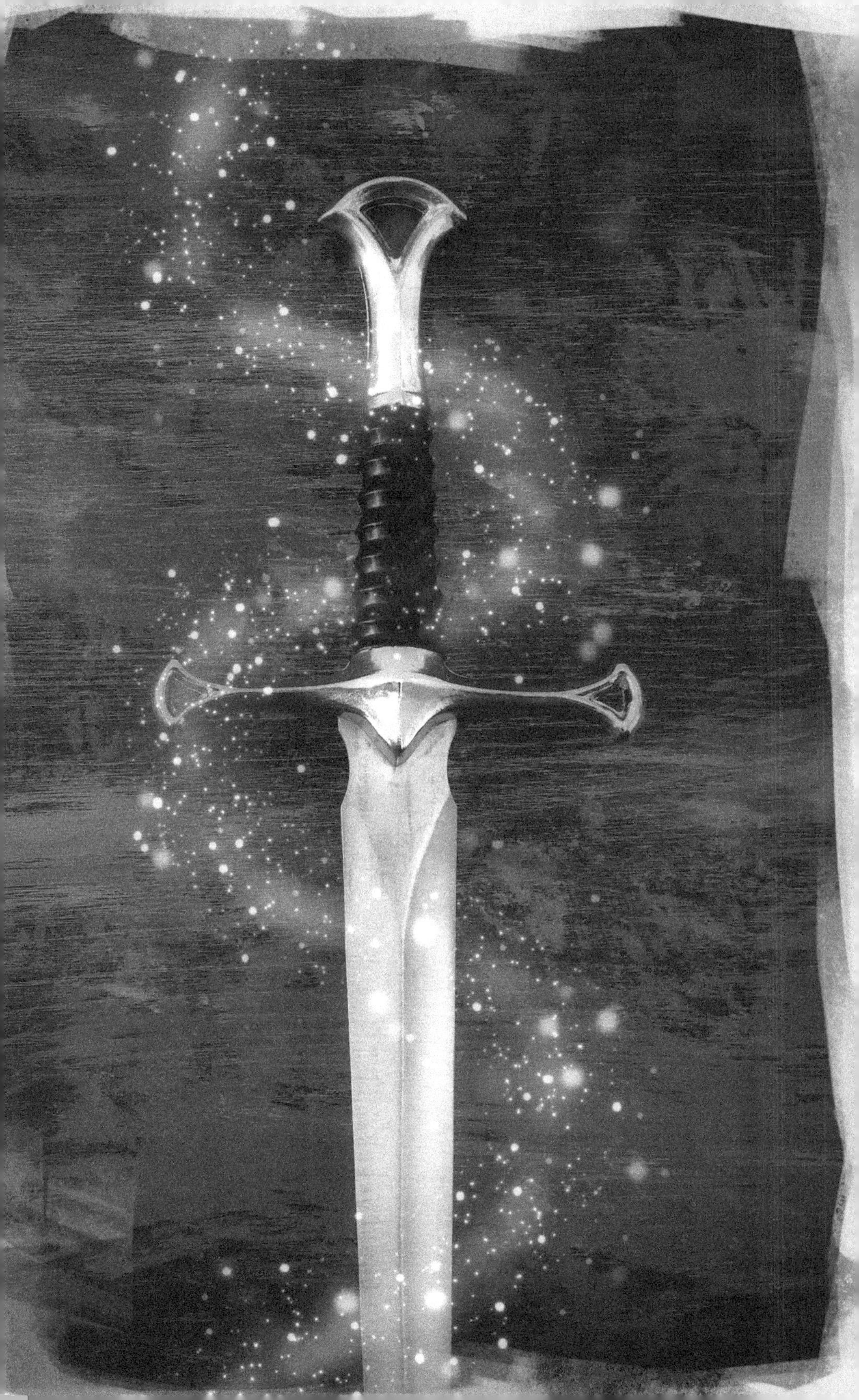

# Chapter
# Twenty-Five

Shade walked outside to a scene from his nightmares.

Silver kneeled by the shore, facing the forest. A scourge of dark smoke poured from her chest across the expanse, reaching for two visitors stepping through a portal. *Intruders.* With an aggressive roar, Shade stepped through the shadows and landed in Silver's darkness, simultaneously displacing the stream and facing the danger with his sword ready. Silver's black smoke danced around his body and coaxed his shadows out of hiding.

"I can't stop it, Shade." Silver's voice was tight with panic.

"Remember what I said about conjuring the feeling opposite to chaos," he reminded her. "Think about something that makes you feel like all is right in the world."

But her eyes darted about, and she tried to lie on her stomach to halt the deadly poison leaking out.

"Do it, Silver. Think of that thing, even if you don't want to."

He turned to the portal and swung Mercy as the first travelers came through. The blade halted an inch from a tanned neck. It hadn't been Shade who'd stopped it, but solidified air. *Mana.*

Leaf, the gilded Elven leader of the Cadre of Twelve, calmly glanced down at the blade with an exasperated sigh. His lips pursed, he put two fingers on Mercy, and pushed her aside before glaring at Shade.

"Really?" he drawled.

Behind him, a second figure walked through and then paused, eyes wide and lips flat. Bronzed and freckled from the sun, Forrest swiped his long auburn hair nervously before putting his palms up.

"What did we just walk into?" he asked.

Two Elven Guardians from the Cadre of Twelve. Leaf had brought backup which meant whatever he had to say to Shade wouldn't be welcome. With a snarl of frustration, Shade dismissed them and went to Silver. He rolled her to face the sky. Her eyes were closed and her arms were crossed against her chest like a corpse in a coffin.

"Darling," he said gently and handed her Mercy. "Hold that."

She peeled open one eye, saw what he offered, and latched onto it with two hands. Shade could have used his shadow to contain her poison until she calmed, but he wasn't sure if it would work on her as it did with the plant. They should have been training over the past few days. He was wrong to let their mating go for so long.

"The rumors are true," Leaf said, eyebrow raised. "And so the ladies of Elphyne weep. This should be fun."

Shade gave Silver a comforting squeeze on her arm. He glared at the blond elf before getting to his feet. Forrest gave Silver an awkward wave. He then folded his arms and assumed the same hard expression as Leaf.

Shade's jaw tightened as dread crawled over his skin. "Why are you here?"

"Playtime is over. You're needed back at the Order," Leaf clipped. "We've let you indulge long enough. Frankly, this vampire mating business is throwing our team's efficacy into chaos. Even the wolves weren't as bad as you."

"And I suppose elves are better?"

"In everything."

As if he sensed the fight brewing between the two, Forrest stepped forward. It was enough for Shade to stifle his rivalry.

"Clarke foretold that each in the Cadre of Twelve will find a Well-blessed mate," Shade reminded Leaf. "Don't think you'll escape this fate."

Leaf's blue eyes flashed, and he gave a pointed look at Shade's mate, who listened to the exchange attentively as she clutched Mercy with white knuckles. In other words, don't speak about fae things in front of the human.

"She's my mate," Shade said, loudly enough for Silver to hear. "I keep no secrets from her."

Forrest's gaze softened in a way that made Shade think he felt pity. A wrong feeling circled in Shade's gut.

"For Crimson's sake," he snapped. "What's happened?"

Forrest and Leaf shared a look.

"Your childhood home has been... devastated."

Shade narrowed his eyes and spoke cautiously. "I already know. I was there two days ago."

Forrest's expression grew grim. "I'm afraid the demogorgon returned. This time..."

"There were deaths," Leaf finished.

"Who?" Shade's blood roared in his ears. He grabbed Leaf by the collar and shoved him. "Who was it?"

Leaf allowed Shade to put his hands on him, which meant only one thing. It was someone Shade cared about. Aravela was dead.

⚖

SHADE STEPPED out of his shadows with Silver by his side. They landed before the gates of his childhood home. Once majestic, they were now torn off their hinges and crumbled into pieces. Even from the street, Shade could smell the old blood. Two cracked pillars made of jade and marble were on either side of the entry. Above each pillar sat a stone gargoyle. Each should have a rosebud stem in his mouth. One gargoyle was missing its head. The other, its jaw.

As a young boy, Shade had spent many hours sitting beside each of them, his wings out, hoping to become invisible, but his shadow gift had been premature.

"What are you doing?" Aravela hovered in front of the child.

"I'm waiting." He knew what she'd say, and he didn't give a flying warada's tail. His mother was lost or had just forgotten, but she'd be back to claim him. She would.

He stubbornly ignored the mistress and played with some rosebud stems, prying open the leaves of the bud to get to the pretty petals.

Aravela sighed, but he didn't give a Well-damn. He was sitting his ass right here on this fence, next to the gargoyles, practicing being invisible, so that when his mother walked by, he wouldn't frighten her off. He'd wait until she was inches from the gates, and then he would pop out of his shadows and yell, Surprise!

She would be so proud that he'd waited for her.

*The sound of wings flapping behind him startled him. Aravela flew up to the fence and sat next to him, dangling her dainty legs over the edge.*

"You shouldn't sit here," he said, pouting. "My shadows aren't strong enough to cover you. She'll see you and keep walking."

"Honey," Aravela murmured softly, putting her arm around him. "It's been over a year. She's not coming back."

"She is!"

"Darling—"

"She's coming back for me." He threw his rosebud in her face and flew off the fence, shouting over his shoulder, "I hate you!"

## CHAPTER
# TWENTY-SIX

Silver seemed to walk outside her body as Shade took her to the place he grew up. What was once a majestic, jewel encrusted, wooden and quartz multi-story mansion, was now half rubble and covered in gore. Sticky blood on the cobblestone street glistened under the setting sun. Crumbled gates. Something lumpy clogged the path of a rivulet of blood as it ran in the cracks between the stone. Brain matter.

It was beyond nightmarish.

Entrails, decapitated bodies, butterflied rib cages—hearts missing. Female fae of all races. All dressed in beautiful, rich clothing and gems that were obscenely at odds with their fate. Within five seconds of exiting Shade's shadows, Silver lurched to a broken wall and vomited in a trampled garden bed. The smell... decay, sour, death. She retched again.

She thought she'd seen it all, but this was different. The lingering ghosts of these people seemed to thicken the air.

"No," Shade whispered somewhere behind her. The anguish in his voice was unbearable.

His devastation and heartache weighed her down. The chaos of the moment reached into her chest and tried to pull out her chaos. Panicking, she found her transceiver in her pocket. Thank God she'd gone back into the cabin and found her old pants under the bed before they'd left. The last thing she wanted to do right now was ask Shade to give her his sword again. He might need it.

Swallowing, she looked around to see if anyone noticed her reaching into her pocket, but the two Guardians who'd just arrived via portal were more concerned with the crowd of Unseelie gathering and sending angry glares their way. More specifically, at the Guardians in uniform.

A cloven footed fae with broken ram's horns picked up a rock and hurled it at the Guardians. Silver would remember the look on his face forever. She'd seen it on the families of soldiers returning from raids. Or rather, not returning. It had been on Carla's and Jimmy's face when their father didn't come back. The mixture of heartache, anger, and denial stole all the air in her lungs. The thrown rock glanced off the russet haired elf's cheek, drawing blood.

"You're supposed to protect us from monsters," the ram bellowed, pain in his eyes. "It killed my son!"

His voice broke along with Silver's heart.

This creature might be fae, but wasn't she planning to bring the same devastation down on these people? The dead bodies and destruction could very well be caused by cannons. She looked around the street, taking in every fae with despair in their eyes. Her enemy had faces. They had sons and daughters. Everything grew cold.

Leaf and Forrest faced the wrath as more fae started hurling insults. Leaf tossed up a windy barrier that pushed back the horde, allowing Shade time to process the scene, but it only incensed them further. The gathered fae grew in size and fury, shouting obscenities about how this devastation was brought on by them—the Order of the Well. Their war with the queen.

Wiping her mouth, Silver turned to Shade. He noticed none of the unrest.

"Aravela!" he bellowed and picked through the bodies and debris to get into the only part of the mansion still standing. "*Aravela!*"

Silver kept her hand in her pocket, clutched around the radio transceiver, and jogged after Shade as he entered the building. A chunk of quartz dropped from above. She dodged and almost slipped on bloody tiles. Rose petals were everywhere.

*Where was he?*

She surveyed the interior—what was left of it. A parlor with a twining wooden staircase was at the back. One side was perfectly intact with lush red carpet, the other side was charred and broken. Wilted and ripe flowers in cracked vases added to the sickly stench. She slapped her free hand over her mouth and tried not to breathe. Voices beyond an open door at ground level drew her in. *Shade.*

She didn't think her heart could break anymore, but when she entered the room, it crumbled to pieces. Shade kneeled by a small circular table for two, his broad shoulders shuddering with sadness. He clutched the legs of a female slumped in a seat; a chipped teacup still clutched in pale fingers, now stiff from rigor mortis. Blood spattered her luxurious robe, and when Silver stepped closer, she knew where it had come from. The female's chest was cracked open, her rips splayed like the corpses outside. Her heart was gone. Her wrinkled face was tilted to the ceiling, horror frozen on her features. Fangs in her mouth had snapped off as though she'd tried to bite her way to freedom. Pointed ears. Vampire.

Silver put her hand on Shade's back.

He took a deep breath and exhaled a slow, shuddering breath. "She raised me after my mother left me." He closed the female's eyes reverently, then touched her age spotted cheek before finding a tea cloth and placing it over her face. "I saw her two days ago. She shouldn't look this aged."

Silver thought of what he'd told her about Nero. Was this his doing? Had he stolen mana and used it for one of his treatments? But Shade's expression darkened to something she'd never seen before.

"This is Maebh's doing," he snarled. "This is a message. For me."

"You mean it's the same creature that attacked us?" But this was so much worse.

"I had no idea it was capable of this."

Silver thought back to how the creature had held back from fully attacking, how it screeched in frustration at him, and how it tried to take Shade away. The taste they'd had of its power was only small. This was—she stared at the ribcage and its eviscerated cavity—this was something else.

"Shade?" The tremulous voice captured their attention.

A female elf wearing a bathrobe entered the room from a side jewel encrusted door. Water dribbled from her wet hair, running down a rosebud tattoo gracefully arched along one side of her neck.

Her pale skin had been scrubbed raw as though she'd tried to scrape away evidence of the attack but couldn't get deep enough. Bloodshot blue eyes darted to Aravela's corpse. Her chin quivered, and then she ran into Shade's arms.

Silver's chest ached as more female fae slowly showed their faces through the same doorway. That part of the building was still standing and intact. Survivors. One by one, they slipped into the room on silent feet. Some were dressed in robes, freshly showered. Some were in opulent gowns, as though they'd come straight from a ball. Maybe they had. Maybe they'd been working somewhere else when this happened.

"I don't know what to do," the female in Shade's arms sobbed. "What do we do?"

Shade stroked her damp hair and glanced at Silver, his brows lifting in the middle, before cooing softly and whispering something to the female that made her stop crying.

"This monster was after me," he confessed. "This is my fault."

The females didn't shout at him or blame him for what had happened. The elf's pretty face hardened with resolve.

"This was Maebh's creature, wasn't it?" she asked.

Shade gave a curt nod.

"That bitch," another blurted from the doorway. Agreeable murmurs rippled across the group.

"She holds a grudge for you leaving her," said the elf, "but I didn't think she'd stoop so low as to attack *us*."

Shouts from outside the mansion grew louder as Forrest jogged in, his eyes alert and bright. He located Shade and then said, "Leaf can't hold them back for much longer. They're blaming the Order for the attack."

The tendon in Shade's jaw popped, and he looked at the courtesans. "I'm sincerely sorry for this. Let me organize the clean-up and pay for damages. Accept my debt. Let me find protection. There are Guardians who'll come and—"

"No," the elf said, stepping away from him. "We don't want your pity, or your debt. This was not your doing, D'arn Shade. Even though you left us decades ago, you'll always be one of us." She looked at the females. "We all came here with baggage. For years, you protected us, and you never asked for a single thing. No matter how much water flows under the bridge, the bridge still stands. We will always be together."

Anguish rocked Shade's handsome features, crumpling them. "Please, let me help, Larelle."

"People already blame the Guardians. If you claim a debt for this, then it's as good as saying you were the monster. Until Queen Maebh's war with the Order is over, there's nothing you can do."

Leaf strolled in, his blond hair spattered with some kind of liquid. Probably spit, or worse. He glared at Shade and grabbed his arm.

"We need to go now."

Shade wrenched his arm back. "I'm not leaving."

"Go," Larelle said, lifting her chin. "They will leave us alone after you go."

Silver gasped as Shade's tsunami of grief washed over her. Leaving would go against every protective bone in his body.

Larelle kissed Silver once on each cheek. "May the water flow again next time we meet. We're all eager to spend time with the one who obtained the unobtainable."

Silver was numb with shock as Shade took her arm and

expanded the night. The moment their feet landed on soft, dewy grass under the moon, he yanked her against his chest and burrowed his face into her neck. Somewhere to their side, the electric sound of a portal ripping through space activated with the smell of ozone. Forrest and Leaf walked through, and then the distant shouting cut off as the portal closed with a whoosh.

Silence descended. Crickets chirped. Their hearts beat together, reminding Silver of the music they shared.

Before he left, Leaf stopped near them to say, "Meeting in the council chambers in twenty."

Shade waited until they were alone before pulling back from Silver's neck. The helpless look in his eyes suffocated her. She touched his stubbled cheek.

"We'll figure it out," she promised.

He captured her hand and held it against his face.

"I'm going to make this right," he promised. "Even if I have to kill the queen herself."

A rush of respect hit her squarely in the chest. "I know you will, and I'll be there with you."

If Silver could boil down the meaning of life into one look, it would be the one Shade gave her in that instant. No words explained the depth of their connection. It was as though she stood with him in the epicenter of a hurricane, in the eye of the storm, untouched while wind whirled around them. All was right in the world, despite the chaos. She glanced down at her chest. Her black heart had stayed silent from the moment they'd landed on this training field of the Order campus.

A melancholy smile touched his lips as he took her hand. "Come on inside. I'll introduce you to everyone."

# CHAPTER
# TWENTY-SEVEN

Silver followed Shade into the Cadre of Twelve's house with trepidation. She was finally here, at the destination of her mission, and yet she felt no closer to finishing it than she had at the start.

She was about to see Violet and Peaches. And they would learn that Silver had done the opposite of assimilating in Elphyne.

With her stomach bundled into knots, she shuffled behind Shade as he gave a half-hearted tour. He tossed explanations left and right. Empty sitting room at the front. Staircase leading up to the sleeping quarters. Kitchen to the left. He tugged her straight there, citing her lack of breakfast as the cause.

Voices greeted them as they turned the kitchen corner. Sitting on the central butcher's block was a petite female with fur-tipped ears, a black tipped wolfish nose, and dark shoulder length hair tied with a leather cord. Her tail swished at her side as she flattened an enormous Guardian's sub sandwich with her hand, laughing as she tried to hold all the contents in.

"No, no, no, Anise," the giant muskox shifter said, his voice deep and full of bass. He was so big that he took up the space on his side of the butcher's block. Enormous muscles stretched the seams of his Guardian jacket, and those curved horns looked brutal. He scowled. "You're ruining it."

"Am not." Anise put her sauce-soaked finger into her mouth and licked. "It needed a slice of goat cheese, or it's not a—" She caught the newcomers and slid off the block. "Oh, hi." She slapped the horned Guardian on the chest. "Car, honey, look up."

He still glowered at the sub but lifted his heavy-browed gaze. The moment he recognized Shade, he grinned and made a big-bellied sound of joy, to which Shade returned a wary glance.

"Caraway," Shade greeted. "You're here again?"

Caraway's cheeks pinked. "Get used to it. I'm Jasper's replacement."

Silver had no idea what was going on. Shade must have sensed it because he leaned in and explained. "Jasper was one of the Twelve. He's the Seelie High King now."

"Right."

They gave each other a masculine sort of clap on the back. Anise smirked in a mischievous way and gave a pointed look at Shade's and Silver's matching marked arms. "I guess congrats are in order for you two. When is the party?"

The temperature dropped and Shade walked out of the room. Anise's eyes widened. "What did I say?"

"Uh... his childhood home was just destroyed."

"*Crimson*, save us," Caraway cursed and followed Shade out of the room.

Starving now that she smelled food, Silver stood there awkwardly.

"I'm Anise," said the wolfish lady with a sheepish look on her face. "I put my foot in it, didn't I?"

"You weren't to know." Silver stuck her hand out. "I'm Silver. I guess... Shade's mate."

This was the first time she'd said it aloud to anyone other than Shade. The gravity of the moment blanked her mind. Anise grinned. Wolfish fangs poked into her bottom lip. Silver couldn't help feeling instantly drawn to her. Her entire demeanor was welcoming.

Shade stormed back into the room with an apologetic look on his face, presumably for rushing off and leaving her behind. He pointed out the way he'd come with his thumb. "The girls are out the back."

Nerves prickled Silver's forehead. Peaches and Violet? Panic threatened to take hold of her, squeezing her lungs and throat, but then Shade stole the discarded sub Caraway had left and handed it to Silver.

"Eat that," he decreed, and then beckoned for her to follow him.

Before Silver could reply, a high-pitched scream pierced the kitchen walls. Heavy footsteps on the wooden floor thundered through the house. More squealing. More screaming. Then a white-haired tornado shot into the kitchen and made a running leap for Silver. She dropped the sub a split second before a little pointed-eared girl landed in her arms.

"Aunty Silver!" she squealed and snarled viciously, gnashing little fangs. "I've been practicing my scary face like you told me."

*Aunty Silver?*

Suddenly, the air left the room. Silver had trouble breathing. Who was this girl? She couldn't be more than five or six. And she'd called Silver aunty... exactly the way Polly had.

A band constricted around Silver's chest, and when the little girl held her folded hand for a fist bump, Silver thought she'd pass out.

"Um." She gingerly tapped her knuckles to the girl, who squealed like it was all a big game.

Hot on her heels was a strong, broad-shouldered, silver-haired shifter. He thundered into the room on powerful legs. His short hair was swooped back at the top and tied off to reveal fur-tipped shifter ears. He gave Silver a hasty hand-sign of apology and offered to take the child.

"My sister's not always like this," he said, eyes sorry.

"Yes she is, Thorne." Anise laughed and pinched the girl's nose. "Aren't you the little alpha in training, Willow?"

"I haven't taught her anything," Silver promised. "I swear."

"Yes, you did. Yesterday," Willow insisted.

"She gets her tomorrows and yesterdays mixed up," Thorne explained. "She's probably seen you in her dreams or something."

"Oh," Silver replied. As if that explained it. Then it hit her. This was Willow. Clarke's daughter. The psychic.

Thorne's pointed ears flattened, and he gestured at the girl, still gnashing her teeth playfully at Silver. "What has your mom told you about using your fae form too much? You need to swap sides to human sometimes, or you'll forget how to be one."

Willow gave him a sullen look, and then suddenly her pointed ears and fangs disappeared. She became an average, rosy cheeked human girl who blurted. "I'm just practicing for when I ran out yesterday. You're always on my case!"

Thorne glanced at Silver. "You've caught us in the witching hour. She needs to have a bath and go to sleep but she won't listen. And her mom is..." His voice trailed off with a concerned frown. "And my mate is in another city with her friend's newborn. I was supposed to join her this morning but with what's happened to Clarke, I thought I should stick around and help but..."

Flustered, he shook his head.

"I got it," came a steady voice from behind Thorne. "You go and check on Clarke and Rush."

Thorne didn't wait for an excuse. He smiled gratefully at whoever it was and left as she entered. Tall, dark hair, severe, smart eyes. The woman in strapped leather was a hit to Silver's memory. The squirming kid in her arms felt heavy and Silver suddenly remembered the horrible situation going on inside her chest. She all but dropped the girl in a panic, but when she checked, thankfully, there were no curls of poison latching onto the child—none whatsoever. She placed Willow down, just in case, and made sure she thought about how Shade made her feel—all was right in the world, her eye of the storm. The darkness stayed down. She flexed her fingers at her side and met the newcomer's eyes.

"Violet?" she breathed.

Violet smiled with genuine warmth she'd not carried last time they met. She checked Silver all over, her astute gaze lingering on Silver's ragged, human styled clothes. A flicker of something—maybe displeasure—crossed her expression, but then she returned her smile to Silver. "It's good to see you."

"I…" She was at a loss for words. Too many things were happening one after the other. "Is Clarke okay?"

It sounded serious.

"Oh, she's fine. She's just been in one of her fugue states for longer than normal, fading in and out of sleep."

"Fugue state?"

"Sometimes her psychic gift overwhelms her, and she's out. It's either a confusing dream, or less likely, but not good. It's something painful to watch. She'll come out of it though. She always does."

With that last sentence, silence filled the room. Silver rubbed her sternum, suddenly wishing for the comfort of her corset, but she'd left it back at the cabin. It had been over six years since she'd seen this woman. They'd been haggard and tired and three fish out of water in a fae land, terrified of what came next. They'd just killed the vampires who'd brutally fed on them and were running for their lives. A single night together in a room, and clinging to each other for comfort, and all with their own part to play in the apocalypse, they forged a bond.

None of them knew each other had gifts then. But from the Well-blessed mating mark on Violet's hand, she was connected to the Well. Silver wondered what her power was.

"I have a lot to share," Violet said, matter of fact. God, she even sounded the same as Silver's memories. "And from what Shade just told Indi, I'm sure you have a story to tell, too. Come out the back. Peaches and Haze are with the boys. Although, I must warn you. Haze just fed, so he's a little out of sorts. But you know what that's like."

Willow tugged Silver's shirt playfully.

"Come and chase me," she said and then squealed as she ran out of the kitchen like a bat out of hell, slipping over the fallen bread, lettuce, and cheese. She face-planted on the floor but didn't cry. She just sang a song, "Pick yourself up. Dust yourself off. Start all over again."

It was the type of song a parent sang to a child. Willow got up, shot Silver a daring look from over her shoulder, and then squealed off with her hands in the air.

Violet sighed. "I suppose I did say I'd take care of her. I'm not really a kid kinda person. Maybe I'll get Peaches to help. She needs the practice with one on the way."

"Don't worry," Anise said as Silver tried to pick up the mess. "I'll fix this before the house brownies catch wind of it. I'll make you another one, too, if you like?"

Relief washed down Silver like warm water. "Thank—"

"Nope!" Anise held up her finger to halt Silver's words. "Don't forget you're in Elphyne now."

"Of course." She knew that. *Stupid*. It was a moment of disorientation she couldn't afford. She hand-signed her gratitude instead.

She followed Violet and the child who was her mission. The same child who'd just called her aunty.

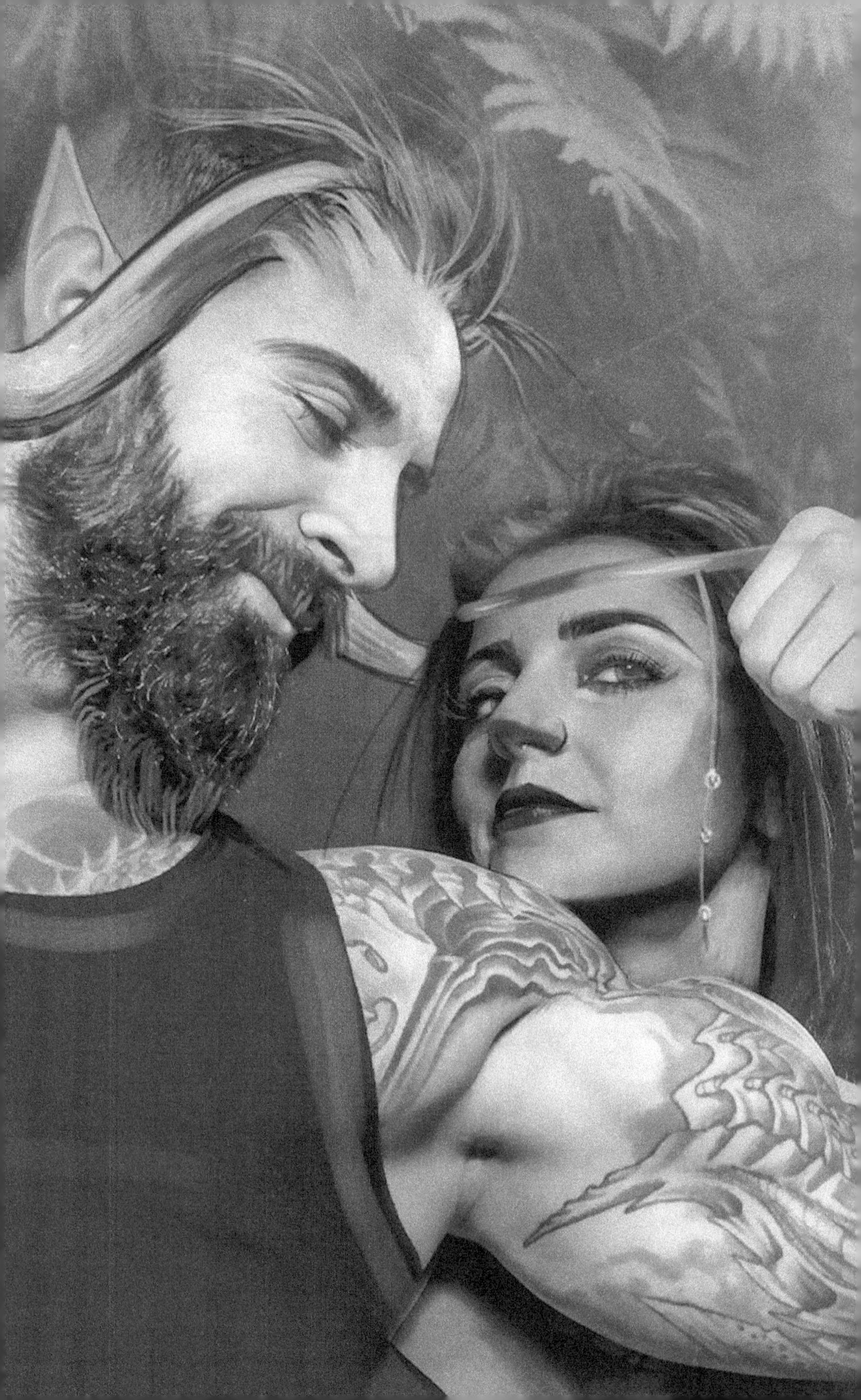

# CHAPTER
# TWENTY-EIGHT

A group of fae sat around a table outside. At the edge of the patio, two fire pits burned with fire and held the cool night air at bay. At least it wasn't snowing here. Beyond was a lawn painted gray in the night. From the flickering shadows further out, Silver guessed the gardens included a fountain and manicured bushes and trees. Fireflies, or perhaps sprites, buzzed about the water fountain. It looked homey, despite knowing this house was a refuge for ruthless warriors.

This was where they came to relax.

*They* being the people at the long wooden table. Silver cast her eye over them. Shade stood speaking with two vampires sprawled on wooden armchairs. They had the same look about them as Shade. Olive skin, pointed ears free from fur. One had a mischievous glint in his eyes, the other was as big as the muskox shifter she'd met in the kitchen. This vampire had a shaved head, tattoos, and piercings. His lashes drooped drunkenly, and he clutched the petite pregnant woman sitting on his lap.

*Peaches.*

Pregnant. Six or so months, by the look of it. The dark-haired woman smiled widely as Silver walked in. She tried to get off the big vampire's lap, but he pulled her back with a scowl and then went back to talking to Shade.

Shade suddenly realized Silver had entered and, in a blink, his shadows brought him to Silver's side. He wrapped his arms around her and glared at the other males sitting at the table. One was an athletic-looking elf with long brown, braided hair and curious eyes. Next to him was a heavily tattooed man with blue-black hair. If Silver had thought the first vampire had a cheeky look, he had nothing on this one. Silver had the sense she needed to watch herself around him. The moment she'd turn her back, the world would crumble, and he'd probably laugh.

She sank into Shade's reassuring arms and checked her chest, just to make sure, but she had her gift under control. Shade gave her a comforting squeeze.

"Silver, these are Guardians in the Twelve. Indigo and Haze over there." He pointed to the vampires, and then to their mates. "You know Violet and Peaches. You'll have a better chance to talk with them after the council meeting." He glared at the unmated Guardians as though they'd leap from their seats and steal her away. "The elf is Aeron. The crow is River. And"—he pointed somewhere out in the darkness—"Now that night has fallen, one of the Six is out there snooping. Don't go out there."

Everyone swiveled in their seats to peer into the darkness as if Shade had dropped a bombshell. If Silver squinted hard, she glimpsed a pale, angelic face with short, messy hair. The tall, lithe Guardian was also dressed in Guardian leather. His glimmering blue teardrop winked in the shadows. Dark eyes seemed to crinkle, as though amused.

All the mated males stood cautiously and urged their women behind them, as if this snooping Guardian was dangerous to them. Shouldn't they be on the same side?

"Who is it?" Silver mumbled to Shade. And who were the Six?

Two things happened at once. Shade replied, "Not sure yet. This one is new." And a luxurious, masculine voice whispered in her head, *My name is Fox.*

"He's been out there every night for the past week," Violet murmured thoughtfully. "I don't know what they're up to, but Legion's got another thing coming if he believes he can send his team to spy on us."

River stormed across the yard. "Just join us, you creep."

Fox winked at Silver and then flickered away. He actually flickered like some kind of old warped VHS tape horror character skipping frames. She could have sworn he had wings, but they weren't like Shade's. They were more sinister and beautiful at once. River pivoted back to them, shaking his head as he sat down.

"I swear one of those creeps is going to wink at the wrong fae," River mumbled, then turned to Aeron, eyes wide. "You ever seen one of them feed?"

Aeron shrugged. "I've heard about it, though. The thing that happens to their mouth."

"Yeah, it's like—" River paused when his gaze flicked to Silver, or more specifically, the vampire holding her. "Shade. He's gone now, buddy. You can calm your farm."

Shade's arms were stone around Silver.

"Who was that?" she asked, because he surely wasn't a fae she recognized.

"He's a Sluagh," Shade ground out. "Don't ever talk to them. Don't go near them. Don't dream of them in case you unwittingly call them in your sleep."

A Sluagh, in the flesh. The boogeymen fae warned about. Silver tried to dredge up tales she'd heard while living among the fae. The saying went something about never leaving a west-facing window open at night, or the soul stealer will be your plight. She'd always thought they were monsters, but that figure out there had looked like an attractive boy next door type—in leather. Of course, she'd have to forget about the flickering impression of a skull she'd glimpsed instead of his face moments before he'd left.

Shade made a feral sound in the back of his throat as he glared into the darkness. It felt more like he held her to stop himself from going out there rather than to comfort her.

Violet let out an exasperated sigh and gave Silver a sympathetic look. "The possessive alpha shit wears off a little, I promise."

"Hey!" Indigo playfully slapped her. "Speak for yourself."

They shared a loving smile that made Silver's heart squeeze. She was so happy Violet had found love. As if their exchange sparked an idea, River's eyes lit up, and he lifted out of his chair to offer a hand in greeting to Silver. "This is what the humans do, right? I'm River. Nice to meet you."

Aeron tugged him back to his seat and mumbled something about stupid crows, to which River complained about him being no fun. Shade turned the full force of his snarl on the crow shifter.

Silver saw it all and felt extremely out of place. These fae were treating her like one of their own. Even the one they'd scared off.

*Fox...* the voice whispered in her mind again, and she straightened. It sounded further away this time.

"Silver?" Shade tightened his hold on her. "What is it?"

"He spoke to me in my mind. Said his name is Fox." She bit her lip at the tension she'd just caused with her words. It was enough to light a match with the heat. They all gaped at her. "What, doesn't he normally do that?"

"Fucker." Indigo's eyes narrowed. "That's how they start. The next thing you know, they're—"

Violet covered his mouth with her hand. "Silver just got here, Indi. She doesn't need to be frightened away."

"For Crimson's sake," Haze grumbled. "Let's get inside, Sweetness. They're acting out of character tonight."

"We have to get to the council meeting," Shade announced.

Silver had only a moment to grasp hands with Violet and Peaches before Shade stole her and stepped through the shadows. She caught the whispered "We'll talk soon" on the wind but couldn't tell who it was from.

Thank God they were the first to arrive in the darkened, stone columned temple chamber, because Silver landed hard on her knees with nausea rolling in her gut. The second she could take a breath, she snapped at Shade, "Maybe ask me if I want to travel that way *before* you take me."

"Forgive me." Her overprotective mate lifted her to her feet and then pressed his forehead to hers. "I needed you away from there. Those menaces are bolder in their interest with our females."

She arched her brow at him. "All he did was wink at me and tell me his name."

"I know, but..." His lashes fluttered in what Silver thought might be shame. "Their team leader, Legion, traded his blood for a memory of Indigo's. We needed the blood to avoid detection by other Sluagh on a mission, but ended up being in more trouble than when we started. They tricked us. We assumed Indigo fulfilled the bargain, but I also drank from Legion. I'm not sure if they'll try to claim the same payment from me."

"A memory doesn't sound too bad."

"Not if it's a memory that hasn't happened yet. And trust me, while I've had my night in the exhibitionist box, the memory they'll pick won't be one you're comfortable sharing." His expression took a grim turn, and Silver was sure there was something she wasn't quite understanding about the situation and promised herself to ask Violet about it later.

Later, when she'd gathered her composure and processed everything that had happened since she'd woken up this evening. The entire day had passed while she'd slept in Shade's arms, tangled in the cabin bed sheets. Were the stars and moon her new sun now that she was mated to a nocturnal fae?

Mated. Mated. *Mated*. She kept saying that word like she meant it, like it *was* her new normal.

"Just promise me you'll stay away from them," Shade said, touching her cheek gently.

"I don't even know them. And look, next time we need to go somewhere, please ask me how I want to get there first."

"A bargain to enforce the rule, then." He went to place his palm on her, no doubt to seal the agreement with mana, but she slapped his hand away.

"It's an agreement between two adults," she grumbled and almost rolled her eyes, but the roguish glint in Shade's eyes stopped her. For a dangerous while, she'd forgotten she was mated to an Unseelie vampire and not a human—he'd rarely had his wings out over the past few days. There would always be a sense of the unknown with him, of a debt owed, or a cost. He loved the challenges between them most of all. She knew this about him as much as she knew it about herself.

She smiled and couldn't help but lean in to kiss him. Their lips touched only for a glorious second before they were interrupted by the arrival of what she assumed was the Council of the Order of the Well.

# CHAPTER
# TWENTY-NINE

Shade wanted to embrace his mate for longer but kept his hands at his sides as the councilors entered the room. He whispered their names to Silver as they arrived. He doubted they'd stop to introduce themselves. Each had an expression like hardened rock, and an aura of barely contained discontent.

Dawn was the psychic with the bow in her hair. Colt was the pixie Mage with prismatic dragonfly wings. Barrow, the weathered Mage, had a tangled white beard with a leaf stuck in it. Of the three Guardians on the council, other than Shade, there were Leaf and Cloud. Both were unmated. Shade's instincts urged him to step before Silver, to keep her to himself, but he retained his footing.

Something had happened to him after seeing Aravela's cold, dead eyes. The fear of losing Silver was an itch across his skin, tightening and tickling, constantly reminding him that she wasn't truly his despite the bond linking them. She'd not proclaimed her love or her desire to remain with him. In fact, the last words they'd spoken about their relationship were about how it wouldn't work between them long term.

Instead of reaching for her, he scrubbed his hand through his hair until he thought he might have pulled out every single strand.

The demogorgon had destroyed Aravela. Not just killed her, but —*wrinkled skin, eviscerated chest, horror in her dead eyes*—he hated how that was the last memory he'd have of her. It would forever push its way into his mind like a disease, festering and multiplying any time he wanted to recall better times.

Shade forced himself to breathe, to lower his hand. The days spent at the cabin had only intensified his possessive instincts. He wanted to steal Silver away through his shadows, never come out, and hold her close. Let the world crumble around them. As long as she was in his arms, he wouldn't care.

That dark, selfish heart of his would drive him to shameful extremes to protect her. It was an irrational urge, but it was there, all the same. Denying it would be to court danger.

*Nothing good comes from denying the Well, or one's natural urges,* Aravela had told him. She was a wise woman, but she also knew the dangers of indulging in them.

The Prime landed on the terrace outside the council chambers in a flurry of white feathered wings. The ageless but ancient owl shifter immediately looked at him with disapproving oval eyes. White-tipped lashes swooped down on a slow blink. Dispensing with proprietary, she stalked toward Shade. Brown taloned toes flashed beneath the blue dress as she strode, clicking on the tiles.

"D'arn Shade," she clipped. "You have explaining to do."

The Prime's presence was a palpable thing. It filled the room with potency. The flowers in the pots shuddered. The veins in the marble writhed in the moonlight as though trying to snake themselves away. Once upon a time, Shade had stared into the Prime's fathomless eyes and remained unflinching. He knew now it had been because he hadn't cared about anyone but himself. The woman stiffening beside him represented everything he wanted, everything fragile and worth fighting for. When Shade's answer was to casually wrap his arm around his mate's shoulder, the Prime's aura grew stifling.

"I've been patient with the Well-blessed matings," she intoned. "Clarke seems to think we need them for the coming war and Dawn doesn't disagree. But you've taken my goodwill to a whole new level. You've spent months away from the Order, and now this. You are, not only one of the Twelve, D'arn Shade, but a councilor." White ringlets bounced as she cocked her head like the bird she shifted into. "What do you have to say for yourself?"

"Give him a break," Silver blurted. "We came straight from seeing his childhood home destroyed."

"Silver," Shade chastised. She didn't need the Prime's wrath directed at her.

But his mate had never been cowed in all his experience of knowing her. Silver's gray eyes flared. The urge to say more played out over her expression, but she held her tongue. The Prime grunted and then pivoted toward Leaf.

"Report."

Leaf launched into an explanation of what the demogorgon had done to the Rosebud Courtesans, how the chest cavities were ripped open, the hearts removed, and the bodies aged. What Shade hadn't known before was that witnesses claimed no manabeeze floated out of the corpses. Leaf surmised the demogorgon was ingesting it like the Sluagh—but where the Sluagh kept the souls they ate in a pocket dimension accessed to summon the Wild Hunt, this new creature simply ended life. No manabeeze drifted to rejoin the Cosmic Well. No afterlife existed as trapped souls in a wraith's army. Nothing.

Voices became white noise as Shade realized the awfulness of Aravela's demise. The fae believed everyone returned to the Well at some point. This circle of life gave them a sense of peace, of being connected and having a purpose. But Aravela would be no more. All that made her special had winked out of existence, consumed by Maebh's ugly creature. All in the name of... what... to capture Shade and bring him back to her? Was she that mad? That obsessed? If he went to her, would it appease Maebh enough to call off her creature? Or was she beyond that point now?

He'd once seen Maebh raze an entire village because the people had refused to pay her tax. She could have sent a message with just one of them, but she'd taken them all.

What worried Shade most of all was that he'd once believed in Maebh. She'd had her moments, but she always had the prosperity of the fae at her heart. His mind drifted to the abandoned nursery in her chambers.

Maebh had lost a child she'd conceived with Mithras. There was something about that child, or that union, that eventuated in Mithras being able to take half of Elphyne from Maebh. It was her weakness. Her truth. For a while after she'd lost the baby, she'd been quiet in her Obsidian Palace, and that was when Shade had entered her life. He'd filled a gap in her heart. He'd brought sense to a senseless world.

Then he'd left her, and Maebh had lost her sense.

The Prime listened to Leaf's report. Her lips pursed, her posture stiff. Not even the wind dared to ruffle her white feathers. When Leaf was done, she returned to assess Silver with unimpressed eyes. Low simmering anger started to boil inside Shade and his feeling of loss amplified. Like he had been to Maebh, Silver was Shade's sense in a senseless world. He tugged her protectively into his side.

"And so, you're the latest human acquisition," the Prime noted dryly.

"Excuse me?" Silver's brows lifted.

"You're the reason my Guardian wasn't here doing his job. You're the reason this beast has remained unchecked for so long."

"Careful, Prime," Shade warned. "You're showing your colors."

"You can't honestly blame Shade for this." Silver glowered at the ancient owl shifter. "Don't you have an army of Guardians to fight this beast?"

"Dawn says you can't be trusted," the Prime continued. "Your future isn't set in stone, and until it is, we can't have you privy to our plans. Explain yourself and then leave."

"Don't talk to my mate like that." The scourge of Shade's shadows unfurled and moonlight leaked from the room.

"Enough." The Prime waved her hand and pushed Shade back by conjured wind. A hurricane surrounded him, and he hit the wall hard. He stayed pinned like an insect. He could retaliate. Every instinct in his body was raw for it. He had the might of Silver's shared mana at his disposal, but the Prime's limits were unknown. And she was his leader.

She was the Prime of the Order of the Well.

She wasn't threatening Silver. This questioning was her trying to figure out what in Crimson's name had happened. Every other

Well-blessed human who'd arrived at the Order had also been interrogated. The Prime had to protect Elphyne from a mad queen's might while keeping it safe from invasion and keeping the Well from drying.

Shade gave a nod of respect, and the Prime was about to back off. He could see it in her eyes, but Silver snarled and stepped between the two of them, taking on the powerful windy prison. Air parted around Silver as though she held metal. The realization hit Shade solidly between the ribs.

She *was* holding metal.

"Let him go," his little fee-lion growled.

The Prime wasn't a Guardian. If she directed her magic at Silver and it failed, she'd know Silver was holding contraband. Shade broke free of the wind and yanked his mate back to him by the hips. Something bulky in her pocket hit him—that was it—he stole the small round object and put it in his.

Mistake. Immediately, Silver's darkness unfurled from her chest and reached for the Prime.

"Silver, calm yourself," Shade murmured.

His mate gave no acknowledgement that she'd heard, or even that he'd removed her metal object—her safety net. The Prime's eyes widened slightly at Silver's threat, but then returned to her usual calculating expression.

"Interesting," she said and stepped back, allowing her wind to die with a dramatic flourish of her hand.

Before Silver moved away, Shade slid her object back into her pocket. He hid his movements with shadow. Her darkness abruptly ended. Did she know what she'd done? Part of him enjoyed his mate protecting him without hesitation, but another part was terrified.

The Prime tolerated much from her Cadre of Twelve, but she could also eviscerate them without a second thought.

Silver's gray eyes had become two raging storms. He lowered his lips to whisper calming words. She held his gaze, and he felt a wave of her restraint naturally through their bond. Her panic turned to peace. He knew then that even if he hadn't put that object back into her pocket, she would have controlled her gift. Her breathing slowed until she nodded.

Everyone in the room eyed her chest warily.

The Prime turned to the Seer. "I've not seen this physical manifestation of the inky side of the Well in generations. This is the darkness you saw linked to her in your visions?"

"What is the inky side of the Well?" Silver blurted to anyone.

When no one responded, she turned to Shade for an explanation but must have seen the fear in his own eyes because she paled and looked away. The inky side of the Well? As in, the part all fae were cautioned never to touch. The part curses were drawn from. The part that made a person go mad.

Dawn looked thoughtful as she assessed Silver. "I will have to meditate on it. When I had visions of this one, much was blocked like the Void has been for both Clarke and myself. Mayhap it was the gift inside her. Mayhap it was something else. I will consult the Well."

Silver's brows puckered.

"The Void is the name we call your supreme leader," he said.

"You mean Nero?"

Conflicting emotions twisted through their Well-blessed connection. Uncertainty hit him as she straightened her spine and set her jaw. She'd not agreed to stay with him yet. He always had the feeling she would come around, but now, looking at that determined steely expression, he wasn't so sure.

She'd kept that metal object because she didn't trust him to help her. And while he could still access her through the bond because of his Guardian status, he wondered if she was able to do the same in return. Or was she cut off from the Well right now?

Did she not care? Did it not hurt her simply to exist without it?

He'd told her what horrors her leader had caused, and yet she still protected him. She still clung to that lump of contraband as though a life raft. He needed time alone with his mate to get her side of the story.

"We didn't come here for an inquest," Shade said to the Prime through clenched teeth. "We need to discuss how we're going to stop Maebh's new pet."

"Now you care." Sarcasm oozed from Cloud's tone.

Wow. That was the first peep out of his usually opinionated mouth. Cloud mumbled something about Shade being a part-time Guardian. Shade let it wash off his back. But Silver didn't. She stepped forward.

"We were attacked *twice* by that thing," she snapped, her impatience pointing at Cloud like an arrow. "Of course he cares."

*Fuck.* Wrong person to pick a fight with. Cloud's dark brows raised so high they disappeared under the loose black curls dusting his forehead. The Prime held up a staying hand toward the rogue crow shifter and cocked her head at Silver.

"What do you mean, you were attacked twice?" The Prime glanced at Shade for confirmation. When he gave a curt nod, she snapped, "Why am I only hearing about this now?"

"We've been busy."

Cloud scoffed, "I'm sure you have."

Shade shook with the effort to hold his response back. The truth was, Cloud had every right to be angry. Shade had neglected his duties, so he deserved shit thrown his way. But Silver had no part in his choice.

The Prime stepped toward Shade. "You mean to tell us that you've had firsthand experience *twice* with this creature? You've *both escaped*, and didn't think to share how you managed to do this?"

"It didn't want to hurt me," Shade confessed.

"We assumed it had something to do with you, but I want to hear your reasoning," the Prime said.

"Each time it attacked, it aimed to disarm and kidnap me. It can't be a coincidence that it went back to hurt the people I care about. It's a message."

"She is uninjured." The Prime's sharp gaze raked Silver from head to toe and then she locked eyes with Shade. "We've lost two Guardians in battle with this monstrous thing. How did you evade it?"

"My shadows helped us escape," he said. "Being linked to my mate, I had a plentiful supply of mana. I don't believe it could track us. Silver also used her gift once. It seemed to injure the demogorgon for a brief while. Enough that we could escape."

"You say it couldn't track you, but it did. Twice."

"Maybe a tracking spell?" Barrow asked, rubbing his beard.

"I'm not sure," Shade replied, frowning as he remembered the way the creature had suddenly been there. "I can't imagine it casting one as we do. Maybe."

Barrow and Colt discussed amongst themselves before offering various tracking methods a magical creature could use, but before they'd finished with their list, Silver answered for Shade.

"It could have been through his blood. Both times it appeared were within seconds of Shade being cut."

The Prime glanced at Silver's chest, where the black smoke was safely trapped, then lifted her white-lashed gaze. "You may go, Silver, but remain on campus until we can have your affinities tested and can safely assess your gift. D'arn Shade, you will remain until we come up with a plan to contain this monster."

Silver opened her mouth to say something, then shut it.

The Prime was right. If Silver's gift was, indeed, pulled from the inky side of the Well, then it had to be monitored. It was better she retire to the Twelve's house and wait for him there. This night could drag on.

"I will return her—" he started.

"No," the Prime said. "You stay. Silver can find her own way back. It's not a strenuous journey. A walk through our vibrant campus might be good for her."

In other words, the Prime wanted Silver to see what rewards the Well gave when they followed its rules. Bristling from her dismissal, in both posture and emotions down their bond, Silver smiled tightly at the Prime and said, "It was a pleasure to finally meet you."

"Darling," Shade murmured. "Perhaps it is time you catch up with your friends. This is Order business now."

She glared at him as though she didn't know him. Although her expression outwardly never changed, he felt her walls slam up. But he couldn't coddle her or belittle her independence. He also understood why the Prime was sending her away. Silver still relied on the metal object in her pocket, even though he'd explained to her there was another way. She'd avoided training, and he had the sense there was more to it than what met the eye.

Suspicion was a dagger entering his chest. He couldn't help thinking the reason Silver avoided her training was because she was going to return to the human city and wouldn't need it. There was plenty of metal there to block her darkness.

She still protected her leader. She wasn't fae.

Shade would have given anything in that moment to be able to reach into her mind like one of the Sluagh, and to tell her he was on her side. But there was only one evil he could fight at a time, and it couldn't be Silver's reluctance to share. Or her leader's long term invasion plans. Right now, it had to be Maebh and the monster she'd wrought, seemingly for the sole purpose of retrieving Shade. He rid himself of emotion and hardened his jaw.

He touched his mate's shoulder. "Turn right at the base of the temple steps and follow the path, straight past the Six's house, until you get to the Twelve's before the smaller barrack's training field. Violet will show you to my room. I'll find you there when we're done."

# CHAPTER
# THIRTY

Silver walked down the temple steps, unable to believe she'd been dismissed. Well, actually, she could believe it. Who was she to sit in on a council meeting for the Order of the Well? She was more pissed off that—she stopped halfway down. Why *was* she pissed off?

Had she expected to be included? Not really. She knew who she was to them.

Was she upset Shade hadn't left with her? The affection in his eyes had suddenly shuttered at the end. He'd found the metal transceiver in her pocket, and then separated himself from her. She shoved her hand in and touched the cold, bumpy object. He'd kept her secret in that room full of people who could eviscerate her without breaking a sweat. But for how long?

Eventually, that powerful leader of his would force him to fall in line.

She already had.

Or maybe Silver was angry at herself. She'd allowed Shade to get close to her, but she hardly knew him. She hardly knew his people, how they worked, or anything. They could turn on her the first chance they got, and eventually Shade could too, or worse—she touched the transceiver—*she* could turn on *him*.

She surveyed the campus. It smelled of freshly cut lawn and a heady floral perfume. Water trickled down culverts at the sides of the steps, adding to the peaceful, starry night.

This place was an oasis compared to her wasteland home. Everywhere she looked was abundance and bright, bustling fae full of life. No sad, saggy faces. No diesel fumes. No stench of desperation or cold concrete walls. No barbed wire nets covering the city for one purpose only—to butcher birds and winged fae. The more that she thought about it, the more she realized Nero wasn't a president, like he claimed. Those people didn't know what a real president was. Nero gave all the orders from a sky tower that only the elite were permitted to enter.

Silver wasn't one of the elite. She was a Reaper, a grunt. She'd never been up there in all her years living in Crystal City. Instead, she'd shuttered her aspirations and distanced herself from joining Rory's ranks.

Crystal City history told of kings and queens who used to reign from the tower. Some of the dock hands had spoken about the old monarchy protecting artifacts and knowledge of the old world. How they would come down from the tower and parade through the streets. That was before Nero had come along. He only came down now to grandstand.

He wasn't a leader who walked among his people. Apart from

the rare brief performances by him, his daughter Rory and a few other dignitaries were the face of his rule.

Maybe the truth had been staring Silver in the face all this time. Maybe they had plenty of supplies in that tower, and they only kept them for themselves.

She scowled to herself.

If Shade and the Prime were to be believed, and Nero was the man who'd set off the bombs, that he somehow found his way to this time like her... then... Shade was right. Nero wasn't to be trusted about anything. He would be stealing mana to stay young. He could also be using it to manipulate and control humans without them even knowing. The leader Silver had fought for was a lie.

Rory made portals to ferry raiders in and out of Elphyne. These portals utilized mana, and Nero had always claimed the Well's rule about metal not working with mana was wrong. It's funny how a small piece of misinformation can spread like wildfire until it became the norm. Silver had never seen a Guardian involved in the portal creation, but after seeing firsthand how this mana versus metal relationship worked, she knew one had to be involved somehow. There were too many things that didn't add up.

Silver didn't know her own mind anymore. All she knew was that she wasn't ready to head back to the Twelve's house, or to face Violet's scrutiny.

The night was young. She wanted to explore the campus. She might not get another chance.

The main Guardian training field was a large rectangle of lawn surrounded by box hedges. A large infirmary loomed behind it, and a smaller billowing forge next to it. The smell of burned air and molten metal filtered on a soft breeze over the field where nocturnal Guardians sparred with each other. She stayed to watch, caught up in the dance between the virile soldiers. How could she not? Grown, half-naked males wrestling was a magnetic sight, no matter what race. One was a vampire—leathery bat wings extended from his back. The other appeared human at first, but then she glimpsed elven ears as he dodged a blade coming for his neck.

Smoke and embers suddenly billowed from the chimney of the forge, the only sanctioned place in Elphyne that worked with metal. The blacksmiths must be Guardians to be allowed to work with the substance. Silver wondered if they'd ever attempted to build a firearm before and had the sudden urge to investigate.

Surely, if Guardians carried swords and iron-tipped arrows, they could use a pistol. They could even operate a cannon without losing their connection to the Well. There were a myriad of weapons they could use to help them keep the peace against magical creatures. There might even be a weapon she could help engineer to work against the demogorgon.

She stood on the outskirts of the field, watching the forge from afar. She'd based a lot of her principals on the fact metal was outlawed, and so many human advancements from her time would be lost—including her vocation. But she'd forgotten Guardians were sanctioned to carry metal—and plastic. In her mind, it had been a small thing, but perhaps the potential was bigger. What if metal could be used in other ways? What if she, or anyone else, could create advancements like medical equipment, communications technology, or a simple compass to guide the way when lost?

She wasn't sure what that meant in her grand scheme of beliefs, but knew it changed things. Maybe this was the reason she'd survived all these years. Maybe she could bring humans and fae together in a way that benefited both factions. Anyone could become a Guardian. All they needed to do was pass the test.

Sighing, and with her mind exploding from all her unanswered questions, she returned to the sparring match. There might never be satisfying answers. That was life, then and now.

The elf was winning through an invisible power he used to hold the vampire still.

She sighed again, this time savoring the crisp, sweet air. Insects and birds chirped. Water trickled somewhere—the sound was everywhere in this place. Probably intentional as a constant reminder of the Well.

Silver plucked a few leaves from the hedge and continued to walk west from the training field. A tall dome in the distance had grabbed her attention. She assumed the grand, mosaic structure was the academy and the library. While she walked there, she tore up the hedge leaves in her fingers, running through different scenarios in her mind, trying to work out a solution to her problem: she wasn't ready to leave Shade, and she wasn't ready to give up on her people—so where did that leave her?

The more Silver walked, the more deflated she felt, and the surer she was that returning to Crystal City together with Shade was not an option. Nero couldn't be trusted. And even if Silver returned to the city to set things in motion—maybe to spread the truth about their leader, or maybe just to get people like Carla the right kind of help—her life was changing.

And then there was the ruthless choice she'd been sent here to make. There were expectations she couldn't keep, but had no alternative in place.

An owl hooted, and suddenly Silver realized she had no idea where she was. She should have gone left to get to the academy, but with her daydreaming, she'd walked past the turnoff. The night seemed darker, the trees taller and bereft of leaves.

She pivoted on the gravelly footpath, the sound so loud it reminded her of fingernails down a chalkboard. A tickle at the back of her neck sent every hair on her body standing to attention. She whirled around and came face to face with a Sluagh—one of the Six.

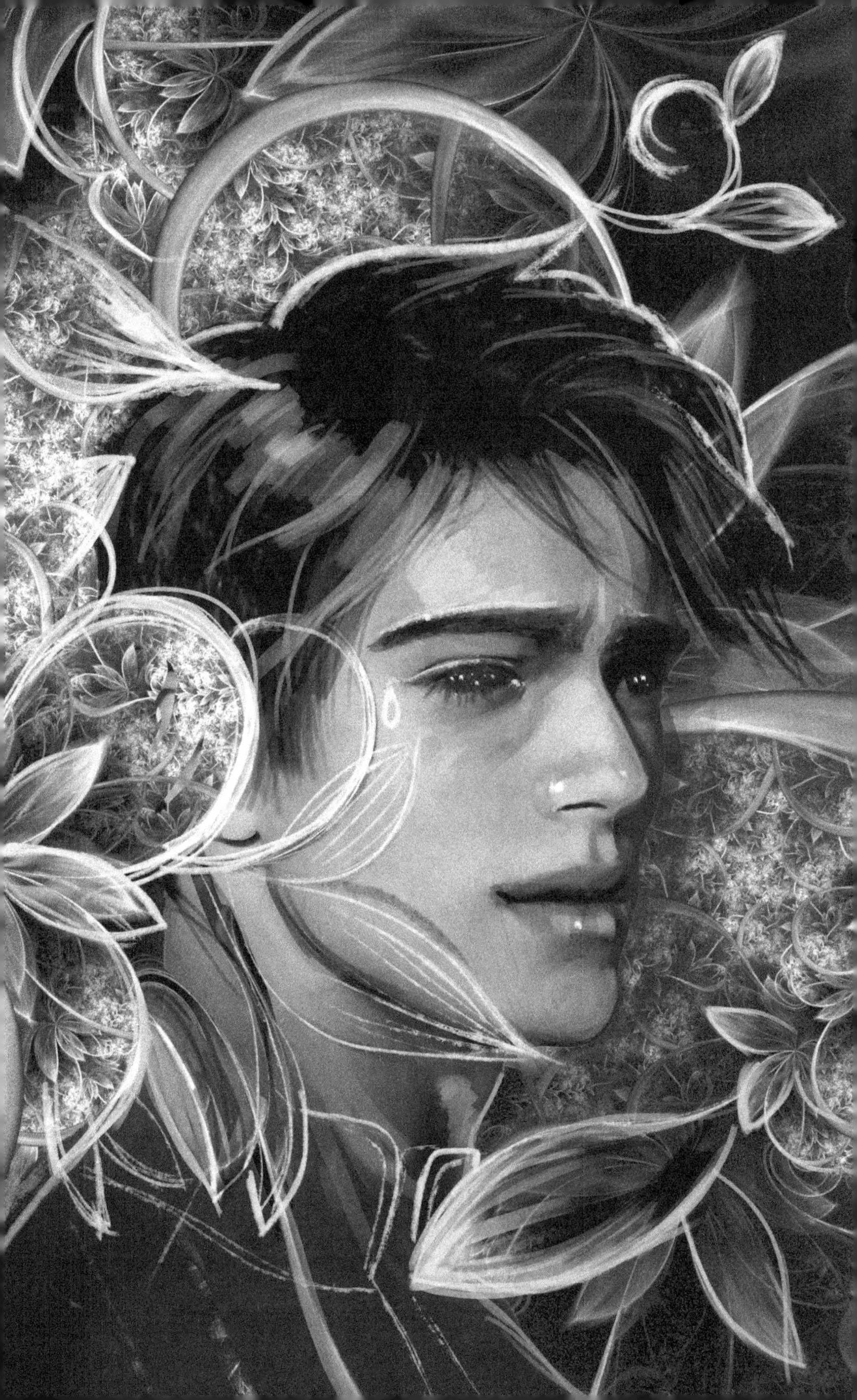

# CHAPTER
# THIRTY-ONE

If there was such a thing as a honey trap, Silver would have bet her soul it looked like the Sluagh named Fox. Tall, agile, and covered in black leather from neck to toe. It was the same Guardian uniform Shade wore, but on Fox, it seemed to swallow the light, much like the demonic wings draping from his shoulders like torn satin sheets. Short, black hair rustled in a wind she couldn't feel. The galaxy glimmered in the depths of his angelic eyes, so innocent at first glance. But the closer she bravely looked, the more she realized it was the sad souls he'd eaten.

Silver felt their screams from the cage of his body as he stared at her, long lashes blinking innocently as she studied him.

She tried to recall the lessons and rumors she'd learned about these dark fae. Unseelie. Malevolent. They only came out at night. They ate souls and trapped them in some kind of purgatory until called upon to fight in a ghostly army called the Wild Hunt. They were hard to defeat with human weapons—she knew the Sluagh were the reason humans lost their war against the fae centuries ago. The losing side never forgets why they lost. Stories of the Sluagh were the warnings whispered from parent to child to keep them from wandering out of the Crystal City gates and into the wild.

*You won't see them coming.* Silver had overheard a mother shaking her finger at her ten-year-old son in the street. *All you'll feel is the wind on your neck, and then you freeze like a statue, locked in your own body while they feed on you.*

The very air vibrated with ominous intentions as Fox titled his head and considered Silver, no doubt listening in on the memory she'd just recalled. She should have heeded Shade's instructions to head straight home.

At first, his lithe body and innocent face appeared youthful and inexperienced, but the more she studied him, the more she realized it was part of the seductive trap this creature of the night exuded. Broad shoulders flexed in the leather. Strong hands at his side. Sharp black talons or nails at the tips of his fingers.

*Come near me, pretty thing. I won't hurt you,* he seemed to say. Silver couldn't tell if it was her imagination or his actual words in her head.

"Fox, is it?" Silver greeted. Interesting name. She wondered why he'd picked it.

*You ever seen a fox in a henhouse?* His answer slid into her mind like a purr as he continued to prowl around her with predatory attention, or curiosity. She couldn't decide.

Would her darkness hurt this fae as it had the demogorgon?

*No,* Fox answered bluntly.

God, was he *in* her mind? Her brows slammed down, and she mentally recited her old favorite Beach Boys song, *Kokomo*. There was only one thing she and her mother had agreed on. It was that Tom Cruise in *Cocktail* was the best Tom movie ever. Her mother liked it for Tom. Silver liked it because that was the only song they both knew the lyrics to.

But there was none of that now—no movies, no Tom. Because of Nero.

Fox stepped closer. That skull impression flickered beneath his skin and she had no idea what it meant... until the sensation of phantom hands wrapped around her body, caressing and examining, unapologetically poking and prodding while his expression remained one of rapt awe.

"What are you doing?" he asked, eyes searching her face as though it was a puzzle.

It was the first time she'd heard his voice aloud. He sounded surprisingly normal, like any male. It erased some of her fear. Some. She moved onto the next chorus in her head. He asked again, a little more insistent this time.

"Standing here, shitting myself," she blurted. "What do you think?"

His lip twitched at the corner. A dimple popped, and he cocked his head, again looking at her like a Rubik's cube. "I meant in your head."

"Haven't you heard singing before?"

"Not like that."

"Because it's in my head?"

"The type of song."

The Beach Boys? She stopped.

He pouted. "Do it again."

"No."

Dark, demonic wings vibrated with agitation. That skull impression grew stronger until it seemed like his skin melted away, turning his eyes to black holes. The phantom touch circling her body tightened. Within seconds, she was immobilized, stuck as though encased in glass. If she could scream, she would.

"Hey!"

Bright light flashed behind Silver and the Sluagh hissed, baring teeth and shielding his eyes. He stepped back and whatever hold he had on Silver was released. Haunted betrayal replaced the skull impression on his face. He glanced over Silver's shoulder, once again the epitome of the anti-cupid.

"You messed with my friend." Violet's fingers glowed as though lit from within as she clutched a collection of books. "That's not cool."

Something unsaid passed between Fox and Violet, and then he returned his contrite but curious gaze to Silver.

*Varen sent me to give you a message.* His voice in her mind held a note of tension. *Follow the crow to be in the know.*

Silver got her chance to see those demonic wings in action. Fox vibrated from head to toe, his dark wings fluttered out, buzzing like a bee, and then he became airborne. Silver watched him fly away until she couldn't make out his pale face from the stars.

"I'm sorry about that," Violet said. "They don't socialize much. If I knew you were on your own, I'd have walked with you."

"It's fine," Silver said. "I think he was just inquisitive."

"What did he want?" Violet asked.

Silver locked eyes with her friend. The bright light that had saved Silver came from her.

*Light.*

Bright, shining light while Silver had death and darkness. Yet another sign that she didn't fit in here. And another reminder that she might never escape the cowardice of her past.

"Nothing," she said, dismissing the Sluagh and his message. She didn't even know who Varen was, let alone if he was to be trusted. "He was just curious."

Violet was a smart woman—a nuclear physicist in their time. From the way her gaze lingered on Silver, she didn't believe a word that was said.

"What are you doing out at night on your own?" Violet asked. "It's not safe."

"You're out on your own."

"I've had training."

Silver pointed at the books in Violet's hands. "Doing some reading?"

"I've been taking night classes at the academy. Peaches is creating mana stones and learning to hone her gift for mining purposes."

"And what about the starving humans?" Silver blurted, her anger simmering beneath her skin.

Visibly taken aback, Violet stared at Silver. "Have you got something to say to me?"

"I..." Silver didn't know why she'd said that. Maybe it was a preemptive strike. "I don't know."

Violet's eyes softened, and she nodded back in the direction Silver had come from. "Walk with me to the academy library. Peaches is already there."

Silver took a few books to help Violet's load. They walked in silence for a few steps. Silver's secrets felt heavy between them. Surely Violet knew about Silver's shameful lies, about her return to Crystal City despite insisting none of them sought refuge there. With every step, and every heartbeat, an ache bloomed between Silver's ribs.

"I'm sorry," she said softly into the night. Trickling water swallowed her voice. The space between words continued. She didn't think Violet had heard her.

The domed academy building came into view. Other similarly designed, less impressive buildings sat on either side. A tiered water fountain was in the middle of the quad separating the academy from a bustling hall. The smell of cooked garlic in butter wafted through the air, and both Guardians and Mages could be seen entering and exiting the building.

Two blue-robed Mages sat on the other side of the fountain, but when Violet and Silver arrived, they quickly hurried away.

A puff of air escaped Violet. "Don't mind them. They do that."

"Run away?"

Violet nodded. "I've been here for six months, and they still treat us Well-blessed humans like freaks. Although, Clarke mentioned when she'd first arrived that they'd thrown rocks at her, so I guess this is an improvement."

Still feeling awkward, Silver bit her lip and nodded.

"Why are you sorry?" Violet asked, proving she had heard Silver, after all.

"Because I lied to you. I deliberately told you that going back to the humans was wrong. I did this because I wanted a backup. I wanted to know that if I failed living in Elphyne, I had an escape plan, and I didn't want the three of us living in the same place."

Violet's brow rose. "Smart. I might have done the same thing myself if I'd thought of it."

"You would have?"

"Don't look so surprised. You've seen me in action. It took me a long time to let go of my self-hate and guilt. I'm not proud of who I was at the start of my life here in Elphyne, but I'm working on it."

Silver remembered the way Violet had stabbed the vampires who'd attacked them, and how she'd kept stabbing them long after manabeeze had drifted from their corpses.

"I also said we should separate," Violet admitted. "If anyone needs an apology, it's Peaches. She was kept prisoner as a blood slave for much of the past six years."

"Blood slave doesn't sound good."

"Because our blood tastes so good to vampires, she was captured and kept. Some Autumn Court fae bottled her blood and sold it as an elite drug, but Queen Maebh kept Peaches as her personal source." She gave Silver a slow, cautious look. "We were right. Maebh had been trying to get all three of us. She only had Peaches because she thought she would eventually find the rest of us."

Anger simmered in Silver's blood. "How can you side with these creatures? They're no better than us."

Violet said through clenched teeth, "I'm siding with Indigo and my friends. I'm not against humans. I'm against the bad man leading them."

"You have all this power, Violet. But what are you doing to help our race?"

"Well, I'm not killing innocent fae anymore. That's for one." She gave Silver a pointed glare.

"Touché." Silver sighed; she'd been doing a lot of that lately—sighing. It felt good, like she was releasing the built-up energy creating chaos in her soul. She reached out and let the fountain water trickle over her fingers. The sound reminded her of the rushing water she'd pushed Shade into, hoping he'd die. "I tried to kill Shade, multiple times."

To her surprise, Violet put a steadying hand on Silver's shoulder and squeezed. "Join the club. I tried to kill Indigo. These vampires have a way of pushing our buttons."

"Tell me about it," she laughed. "I don't know how someone can be so infuriating and seductive at the same time."

"Don't forget obsessively possessive."

"And loyal," Silver mumbled, thinking of how Shade had kept her secret from the council.

She felt the weight of attention before Violet spoke. "They're good people, Silver. All of them. It doesn't meld with my logical brain how they put so much blind faith in something like the Well, but I'm finding my own way to understand and to fit in. I'm learning so much every day. Preceptor Barrow is even allowing me full access to his lab now and—" Her eyes lit up with passion. "But you don't need to hear me talk about that boring stuff. Tell me about your gift. Indi said you stayed here in Elphyne until you couldn't control it. Is it that bad?"

"How did he know that?"

"The vampires tell each other everything. They're very close."

"I admit," Silver said, "I tried to stay here for a year before I lost control. I guess my power was slow to manifest, but when it did—it shot out of me and latched on to..." she trailed off, not wanting to continue, but Violet waited patiently, so she blurted the rest out. "It latched on to a man who was just trying to take me on a date. I killed him by accident."

"What are the parameters of your gift?" Violet asked. She reminded Silver of a doctor sometimes, and the clinical confident manner of hers felt like coming home. It brought a tightening to Silver's throat.

"Black smoke comes out of my chest and decays anything it touches. Anything alive, that is, including plants."

"Fascinating." Violet's eyes lit up. "I've never heard of anything like it. What do you mean by decay? Does the subject go moldy, or turn to ash, or... never mind. I'm sure we'll have plenty of time to talk about it after you get tested, assuming you're not already?"

She shrugged. "Assuming I stay."

"You don't mean they'll kick you out, do you? I find that hard to believe. Clarke will too. She's seen you're integral to our future."

"Well, I've never met Clarke."

"You will. Once she wakes from her psychic sleep."

"I just..." Silver stumbled over her words. "I just don't know if I should stay. I've killed so many fae. Willingly."

"I killed them too. Indigo has forgiven me. That's the only opinion I care about."

"This is different."

"How? Because from where I'm standing, we're not so different."

"Except we are. You've given up on saving the humans. I'm still fighting for them."

Violet's knuckles whitened around the books. "How dare you think that? I'm fighting for *all* life. I want peace."

"But you know that's not possible. People don't just give up wars. One side wins, or a treaty is signed."

"Silver, the Void has lied and manipulated and somehow infiltrated his way into the human city. He's a madman with power. A megalomaniac in disguise as a hero. Surely you can see that you're fighting on the wrong side."

"His name is Nero."

"Why am I not surprised he has the same name as a Roman Emperor rumored to have set fire to his own city?"

Silver hadn't known that, but of course Violet would. It set Silver on the back foot. She hated feeling inferior to other people, especially when she'd already put herself down.

"Are you sure what they're saying is true? I mean... do you have evidence to support him being the one who set off the bombs? I remember the news reports claiming some terrorist cell linked around the world."

"It's him," Violet said grimly. "You know in your heart, it's him. Clarke and Laurel both met the man in our time, and in this one. He tried to kidnap Clarke and tortured her because he'd killed his own psychic and needed a replacement."

And now she knew why Nero wanted Willow. A stone sank in Silver's stomach. She'd known the psychic was dead, but not that Nero had killed her. Too many pieces added up, confirming his guilt.

"How is this even possible? How could he be here?"

Violet shrugged. "I'm a scientist, Silver. One day I have faith I'll come close to explaining how, but I'll never know why, which I think is your real question. The answer to that, like so many other philosophical subjects, will always be a mystery. All we can do is focus on what's in front of us."

Something twanged in Silver's chest, and she looked away. Dread. Disquiet. Wrong. She itched to hold the transceiver in her pocket but knew Violet's sharp eyes would pick up the movement.

How could all these people be wrong?

Nero must be the cruel man they claimed he was, despite being the benevolent leader he projected. That meant Silver had been duped and used, as had all the people in Crystal City.

"What's his end game?" she whispered. "To destroy the world? Nobody can be that cruel."

Violet searched the stars. "I wonder that myself. But I don't think he wants to end the world. I think he had psychics back in our time. Clarke was one of them. She admitted it. I think one of them somehow connected him with this future, and he realized that a smaller world was easier to rule. I think it came down to how easy he could dominate the world. But now that he's here, he's learned that dominating these people is a lot harder than he planned. Whatever gave him power in the past isn't working in Elphyne."

The humans of Crystal City needed Silver's help more than ever.

But what laid on the other end of the transceiver was not the way to do it. Handing Willow over to Rory was *not* the way to do it. Just like that, Silver's mission became defunct. She didn't know what her place was in this new world, but she knew she didn't want to go the way she'd been headed, and she knew she wanted to stay with Shade—wherever that may be.

"You know," Violet said. "When we three first met, we saw something in each other. I want you to know that no matter what happens, we're here for you, just as we were on that first day. Nothing has changed."

"Everything has changed."

# CHAPTER THIRTY-TWO

Predawn light warmed Shade's wings as he landed in the yard before the Twelve's house. The council meeting had taken all night and sleep tugged at the corners of his mind, but he needed to find Silver.

Contrary to his intentions to stay focused on the demogorgon problem, Silver had occupied his mind with a frequency bordering on obsession. While the Prime and other councilors discussed strategy against Maebh, Shade battled his own war inside his head.

Half of him wanted to prove to Silver he was on her side, that he and she were one, no matter what tried to tear them apart. During the meeting, he'd imagined a thousand ways he would show her, and all of them involved his bed. A few involved that lovely rope of hair.

The other half of him was insane, wondering why she carried the metal object in her pocket. There should be no secrets between them by now. He wanted to coax the answer out of her, to seek the truth once and for all. She was his weakness; he could see that now. Instead of concentrating on the council meeting, he'd been thinking of her. He would do anything to keep her safe, even become complicit in hiding forbidden materials, it seemed.

It made him fear what else he'd sacrifice if she asked him.

Doubt had played with his sanity for hours on end. He'd barely paid attention as the councilors came up with a plan to use Shade as bait for the demogorgon. Other Guardians dropped in as required to hash out the details. He wasn't sure what he'd agreed to by the end of the night. But he would deal with that tomorrow.

The rest of this short night was for Silver. Shifting his wings away, he pushed into the quiet house and headed straight up the stairs to his room. He paused with his hand over the doorknob and held his breath. He sent his awareness down his bond and searched for her presence in his room. A flicker of doubt washed through him. Would she be in there waiting for him? He pictured how she looked as she left the meeting. Angry. Tense. Confused.

But her life-force pulsed like an echo of his own. Even the glowing marks on his hand seemed to pulse in unison, excited that his mate was here. He opened the door to find it dark except for a faint light escaping the window. Her curvy silhouette was a welcome sight on his bed—*asleep*—facing the window as if she watched for his return.

She hadn't left. He let the gravity of the moment sink in. She was *here*.

When he stepped into the room, her freshly washed scent invaded his reason and all doubt evaporated from his mind, making way for the other obsession. Need. Want.

He was hard before he tossed her covers off, intending to wake her. She was naked except for panties and a small scrap of fabric across her breasts. The metal corset wounds were healing nicely and almost gone. His mouth watered at the sight of her smooth, bronze skin begging for his lips. Her thick silver braid trailed behind her carelessly. She stirred as he took her chin gently between his thumb and forefinger and angled her sleeping face to his.

"Darling," he said, voice husky and rough. "I need to be inside you."

"Shade?"

"I need to feel you surrounding me." He needed to know she was his. That even though he'd lost so much tonight, she was here, flesh and blood. Everything else could wait.

Maybe she felt the ache in his soul, or maybe it was that she too needed the solace only a mate could give, because she straightened and woke herself.

Primal hunger pounded into him so profoundly, his breath stuttered. He lost all restraint and lifted her roughly by the chin until their lips clashed. Her arms wrapped around him willingly.

Their kiss was brutal and honest, saying everything they held back. It was the kind of kiss that devoured and consumed. His fangs clashed with her teeth. Their tongues dueled. *Blood.* His and hers mixed. He groaned inwardly at the taste. Like a lit fuse blazing through their systems, that little drop of blood was enough to set their bodies on fire. With her kneeling and him standing, her arching and him slouching, they mated with their mouths, hungry and demanding.

He wound his hand around her braid, still damp from a recent bath, and broke from her lips to bring it to his nose. She smelled sweet, like rose perfume. He recognized the scent from his own personal collection. It was a gift from the courtesans a while back. His mating instincts swelled at how she'd helped herself to his things, but his pride was short lived as he pictured those he'd lost. Aravela. Silver's braid cut into his fist as his mind switched to what she'd hidden from him in her pocket. She'd lied to him. He always knew it, but his tolerance was fading. He became desperate to have her. All of her.

"Don't think about whatever is putting that frown on your face," she muttered, and undid the buttons on his breeches with hurried fingers. "Think about being inside me instead."

She had no idea how much her words affected him. It was the only reminder he needed before he blocked everything else out of his mind.

"On your back." His curt demand came from a darker, unmerciful place, but he was powerless to stop himself now. He pushed her onto the bed.

She landed with a bounce and watched him with heated eyes.

"Undress," he ordered as he divested himself of his jacket.

She made a little moan of anticipation and removed her underwear.

"Open your thighs to me," he growled impatiently. "Pleasure yourself. I want you ready and wet by the time I'm naked."

Her knees dropped open to bare the sweetest blushing folds made just for him. While he continued to remove his clothes, she did exactly as he asked. She reached down and played with herself, moving her fingers in hypnotic swirls that almost made him forget to remove his pants and boots. And then her fingers entered herself and she groaned. Within seconds, he was naked.

He climbed on the bed and nudged her hand away so he could

take over. He rubbed knuckles over her folds, spreading her glistening desire before inserting two fingers to test her readiness. She gasped as he filled her. Tight, slick, welcoming. The same as it had always been. But not. That dark, chaotic doubt peppered his actions, urging him to be impatient and greedy. They locked eyes while he worked her persistently. Perhaps a little roughly. A little needy.

He used their emotional connection to preempt her needs and had her soaking, squirming, and begging for him in a matter of seconds. Her eyes fluttered to lock with his and a sudden surge of her melancholy washed over him like a wave.

He stopped.

He kneeled back on his haunches while she laid splayed before him, panting and sweating, gripping his sheets like a lifeline. His little fee-lion scowled at his pause, and he wanted to move, but couldn't. His breath came in ragged. It felt like he'd run a marathon through holding his restraint. Immediately, she knew something was wrong. He probably telegraphed it so badly she could not only feel it through their link, but see it in every part from his eyes to the tension drawing skin tight over muscle.

"Shade?"

"Are you leaving?" He searched her face for signs of a lie.

She sat up on her elbows. "I'm here."

That wasn't an answer. His brows lowered, and he asked his question again.

"Why would you think that?" she asked.

"You were sad just then. Why? Why now when you should be feeling anything but sad?"

Her lips flattened, and she looked away. Was that *shame* she felt?

When she couldn't answer, couldn't refute his doubts, his gaze slid to the side, and he feared the worst.

"No," she said quietly. "I'm not leaving."

He was on her in a heartbeat, flattening her with his body, looking deeply into her eyes.

"This is the last time I'll ask. Are you lying to me, little fee-lion?"

"No," she whispered. "Not anymore."

"Why the sadness? Why now?"

"I felt sad because I realized I'm so invested in being with you that I'll never see the inside of Crystal City again."

He wanted to believe her.

"Why did you have the metal object in your pocket? Why did I hide it for you?"

*Tell me.*

There was no way to describe how she looked at him. Outwardly, it was nothing. A frozen face. A hard stare. An empty expression. But it acted as a guard to her secrets, and he couldn't handle it anymore. Just as his mind started to walk a dark path, about to snap, she confessed.

"It's a radio transceiver," she said.

"What is that?"

"It allows me to talk to someone over a long distance. I was supposed to contact my team when I arrived here."

Cold ice spread through his veins, freezing him from head to toe. He couldn't breathe, couldn't see straight, couldn't think. She was going to betray him, betray all of them. Like a puppet on a string, his instincts moved his fingers to her throat. His thumb hovered over the soft spot, so warm and clammy from the desire he'd evoked earlier in her, a desire now waning and empty.

"Why?" he snarled, hardly able to believe her.

She bravely held his stare. "They want Willow."

Vampiric talons distended from his fingertips. It hurt to recall them, barely stopping them from ripping into her soft flesh before they retracted. *I was supposed to contact my team when I arrived here,* she'd said. *Was.* She'd changed her mind. She might have started her journey into Elphyne with the intention of kidnapping Willow, but it wasn't her desire now.

"But you won't give Willow to them," he confirmed, the words slow and cautious.

She shook her head. "I can't."

"Why?"

Her scowl floored him. She planted her palms on his chest and shoved. "Why do you think, jackass?"

A slow, crooked smile formed on his lips and he pushed against her palms, letting her feel his heavy heart thudding in his chest.

"Oh, don't be so smug," she scoffed. "It's not just because of you."

"My little fee-lion is such a liar," he purred. "You love me." His gaze drifted down the tight curves of her body, lingered on her nipples pebbling under his attention, the goosebumps rippling across her hardened breasts. "Admit it."

His comment didn't have the desired effect he hoped for. Instead of smiling and telling him he was her world, her expression shuttered, and her emotions pulled away like the ebbing tide on the fall of the moon.

"Darling," he said in all seriousness. With a finger to her chin, he brought her eyes to his so she could see the truth in his next words. "I will give up the world to be with you."

Her chin jutted stubbornly. "I'm not giving up saving my people. I just won't sacrifice an innocent girl and there's no way you can live in Crystal City so here I am. I was sad before because I realized how difficult that was going to be with the way I feel about you."

His gaze softened. His smile returned. "I love you too."

"Show me," she demanded, all spitfire and passion. She widened her legs and bucked against him.

Need roared back with a vengeance, filling him until he ached. He found her still slick, so pushed in with a single, hard thrust that had them both shuddering with relief. The respite of their joining didn't last. Every cell in his body craved more. She arched into him, her fingernails scraping down his spine.

"Make me believe it," she urged.

"Then I need you on top." He impatiently moved them against the bed headboard. She straddled his lap and sank down until he was balls deep inside her. He tossed his head back, stared at the wooden beams holding up the ceiling and thanked the goddess. This woman had a way of giving him wings. He guided her hands to the headboard. "Now I need you to hold on."

He smoothed hands over her hips, savored her tight, velvety internal texture for a blissful moment, and then lifted her off his cock to the tip before thrusting them back together. He claimed her, hard and deep, ensuring she knew exactly how he felt.

The change came over her with the rising sun. Light illuminated the room, accentuating the flush rising in her body. She became edgy, fretful, and soon slapped his hands from her hips as though they hindered her pleasure. He returned her feverish glance of apology with a comforting smile of his own. She wanted to use him, and he was down with that. Always would be if it made her feel good. He leaned back and enjoyed his mate sliding up and down his length, rolling and rocking her hips, moaning and mewling as she saw to her carnal whims.

But still she kept chasing. Kept searching. A sheen of sweat dappled her brow. Stormy eyes hit his with panic.

"Shade," she begged. "I need..."

"I know what you need, darling." Containment. Safety. He pushed off the headboard, sat forward, and slid his hands up her waist to encapsulate her ribs. Her pupils dilated, but he didn't press, not yet. No... he needed something too. He slid his arms around her in a vice like embrace and buried his face in her neck. Suddenly constricted, their rocking became gentle, subtle. Close. Intimate.

Their lovemaking became a promise between savage hearts now beating in their own symphony. No matter what war raged, who was fighting, in the future or the past, they would be together on the same side, creating music of their own.

Shade squeezed tighter, pushed their bodies together, driving his aching cock as deep as he could until she cried out with release. The sound of her joy was the button on his own climax. Wave after wave of pleasure crashed through him, and he savored every second as though it was his last... because although she wasn't leaving, he eventually would.

There would be no Silver and Shade if Maebh wasn't dealt with, and he was the only one who could do it.

# CHAPTER THIRTY-THREE

Silver's head rested on Shade's chest, listening to his steady heartbeat beneath his smooth skin. She idly traced patterns down his front, using the valleys and hills of his muscles as a guide. He toyed with the end of her braid, wrapping it around his wrist, then letting it unravel before doing it again.

"Never cut this," he murmured against her head.

She snorted. "Or what?"

He tugged on her hair until her neck craned back and she could look into his smoking hot eyes. "Do you enjoy poking the beast?"

"Someone thinks highly of themselves."

He growled. "Answer the question."

She tried to hold her smile but failed. "Maybe."

"Maybe?"

"Maybe tell me why you don't want me to cut it."

"Because you're made for me," he said, frowning. "From that sweet tasting pussy to the long rope of your hair. It all fits me perfectly, and if you cut it, darling, then I'll make you grow it back until we fit together again."

She grinned against his chest. "I suppose that's an answer."

"I have many plans for this." To punctuate his point, he pulled the length of her braid around her face and slotted it across her open mouth. Like a man with a mission, he moved her wrists over her head and then looped the rest of her braid around them before resting her against the pillow.

He grazed his knuckles over her lips.

"For when you poke too much," he explained with a cocky arch to his brow.

She would have teased him somehow, would have maybe seen how far she could push him, but he kissed her neck, and everything unraveled.

"Instead of enjoying the moment," he finished.

He kissed down her decolletage and latched onto her breast. His tongue rolled and tweaked her nipple until it hardened in his mouth. She fell into the moment he created. Her vampire warrior worshipped his way down her body until he nuzzled between her legs, making them fall open to him, and then he gave her a quivering orgasm with nothing but his demanding tongue.

When it was over, and she was gasping for air and wondering what the hell had just happened, he unbound her wrists and tucked her into his side. He settled behind her with one hand splayed on her stomach, the other fisting the rope of her hair like a silken security blanket.

"Okay, fine," she mumbled. "I'll keep it."

She wasn't sure if Shade heard her. He'd fallen asleep within seconds. She tried to doze alongside him, but found herself wide awake. She'd already rested for hours before he'd arrived, and now it seemed her body was sated. With a little effort, she untangled herself from her mate. Even in his sleep, he was unwilling to let her go. But the longer she laid there, the more she wanted to have this transceiver business done.

She needed to destroy it, but she needed to talk to Rory first. Rory deserved to know the truth about her father.

Dressing as quietly as she could, Silver pocketed the transceiver and braced herself for the sensation of being cut from the Well. The more she did it, the more she felt the sense of loss, and the more she understood why the fae wanted to protect this connection. Losing it was the epitome of sadness. It was the moments after sunset.

Silver slipped outside of Shade's room and closed the door quietly behind her. The house was quiet. Early morning had most people asleep. Keeping her feet as light as she could, she tiptoed through the house. As she passed the landing, a little voice stopped her.

"Pssst."

Silver stopped and looked around. The door of the last room was partly open, and a little pale hand with claws at her fingertips scratched the ground through the gap, marking up little math equations on the wood.

"Willow?" Silver whispered. "Shouldn't you be asleep?"

The hand disappeared, and a shadowed little face squished to the gap. "I'm bored. Can I come with you, Aunty?"

"Um..."

"Mama is still asleep, and Daddy says I'm not allowed to leave the room unless Thorne goes with me, but he's sleeping, too."

"I don't think it's a good idea, honey."

"But I'll stay close, I promise." Willow edged out the door an inch, her big blue eyes begging Silver. "You can teach me the Bish Boys to make me not scared."

Only through the hand of God did Silver stop herself from bursting out laughing at Willow's mispronunciation. She didn't even worry about how the little girl knew about the Beach Boys, or that it was something Silver did to keep herself from getting scared sometimes. Silver touched the transceiver. She was only going to the roof to get a better signal. It wasn't like she was heading outside the Order grounds.

But no. *Too dangerous.*

"I'm sorry, Willow. You need to stay here."

"No," she whined loudly. Too loudly. Silver hushed her and walked abruptly away, hoping it would be enough to dissuade her. The last thing she needed was to deal with chasing a child around a campus she knew little about. And the child reminded her too much of Polly.

Silver frowned as she crept through the house. She opened the front door and entered the fresh, early morning air. Before she shut it, Willow came running out. Silver grabbed her by the arm before she escaped. Two blue eyes burning with defiance flashed at her.

Silver wanted to smile, but the girl would think it was permission.

"Willow," she said. "Please go back."

"No, Aunty. I won't."

She crouched low and asked, "How many aunties do you have, Willow?"

Her little face brightened. "I have lots of aunties. Aunty you,

Aunty Laurel, Aunty Ada, Aunty Melody, Aunty Flory, Aunty Soopy—"

"Aunty Soupy?"

"Yeah, sure. She's friends with Aunty Rory—"

"What?" Silver straightened. "Did you say Rory?"

"Yes, but she's my aunty from tomorrow. The others are my aunties from yesterday."

An unsettled feeling rolled through Silver. How could Rory be one of Willow's aunties, unless... unless they succeeded in taking her.

"Willow, I mean it. I want you to stay in the house, okay?"

"*Noo*," Willow whined. "But I've practiced my angry face *as well as* my scary face like you asked."

"Okay, now you're confusing me. When did I ask that?" Silver scratched her head.

She blinked up at Silver as though that was the dumbest question, but her reaction didn't change the dark premonition tugging on Silver's instincts.

"No," she clipped. She figured if this girl called her aunty, she had a right to reprimand her. "Go back inside until your big brother wakes up, okay? I have something important to do."

Willow scowled. Silver latched onto her defiance and used it to her advantage.

"Okay, I'll take you out later on one condition," she said.

"Practice my scary face?"

"You got it. Pretend you're the biggest, baddest person in the house, and you'll see, people will think twice about messing with you. Show me what you got."

Willow bared her fae fangs and snarled.

"Okay, but with more growling this time."

Willow repeated it, this time adding claws like a monster.

"Good. Go inside, shut the door behind you, and keep practicing until I get back."

"But..."

"When I get back in a few minutes, I'll teach you the Beach Boys."

Willow's eyes lit up, and she nodded vehemently. "Teach me now 'cos you won't have time later."

"Oh my God, fine. Here goes..." Silver launched into a hasty rendition of the song. She repeated the first verse, and Willow joined in, giggling and laughing.

*I so don't have time for this.*

"On the floorda keys..." Willow sang.

"Okay, looks like you got it. Time to go inside, got it?"

"Got it."

"Good girl."

Willow slinked back inside and closed the door. Somewhere inside, the muffled sounds of little girl growls could be heard. Exasperated, Silver shook her head. This kid was exhausting. She didn't know how Clarke and Rush did it.

The picture of Violet and Thorne jumping in to help babysit came to mind. They did it through the help of their friends, that was how.

Finding a trellis on the side of the house, Silver climbed up the two levels until she crested the top. Made of terracotta tiles, the roof sloped in multiple places, but also had a flat spot running across from side to side. Curiously, in the middle of the strip, she found some discarded drinking bottles. This might be one of the winged fae's quiet place.

Taking a deep breath of the restorative morning air, she settled on her rear and dangled her feet over the edge. A quick check in the field's direction gave her confidence no one could see her. Even the Sluagh would be hidden away now that the sun was out. Feeling mollified, Silver pulled out her transceiver and turned it over in her fingers, watching the metallic surface catch the sun.

This was it. Her last chance to back out, do what she'd originally set out to do, help Carla, Polly and Jimmy, and the hundreds more like them. She could return to Crystal City a hero, like Nero had claimed. But even if Nero wasn't the person they said he was, even if killing fae wasn't the answer to living peacefully between the races, she knew that the time for blindly following orders was done.

The cowardice in her heart, the guilt, it had all been because she'd ignored her instincts long ago. She'd run away instead of facing the danger, and she was okay with that. Like Shade had said, she needed to learn to love herself, for all her twisted darkness. She realized another side of his meaning—not *including* her darkness, but *for* her darkness. So, in order to control it, she had to love herself, warts and all.

Mistakes were only something to be ashamed of if she didn't learn from them.

Before she lost her nerve, she flipped open the transceiver lid. The round object looked like a compass on the outside. She pulled out an antenna and wound up the clockwork cogs, starting the tiny motor that would create the electrical charge to fill the battery. She'd practiced this many times, but her fingers still trembled as she hit the talk button.

"This is Reaper Nine to base. Do you copy?"

Crackling static was her answer. She waited a few moments and then tried again. On the fourth go, she got her answer.

*"This is Reaper One."* Rory's voice sounded hollow and distant, but it was unmistakably her. *"What's your status?"*

Her status. She froze. It was funny, Silver had plunged her blade into the hearts of fae, but the very thought of telling her first friend in Crystal City that she was not completing the mission, was more than she could handle. Rory never used to be so stringent and cold. Once, Silver had caught the woman stroking a black feather, staring vacantly into space as though trying to capture a memory floating away. When Silver had questioned it, Rory pretended she didn't know what Silver was talking about, and she would launch into instructions on the next Reaper mission or raid. Rory never mentioned the feather again.

It was Rory Silver worried about leaving the most. She had no other friends. Nothing else but her father's purpose for her. The purpose of a megalomaniac so adept at making people follow him, Silver had fallen for it too.

*"Reaper Nine?"*

"I'm here."

*"Are you ready for extraction?"*

A little girl's squeal down on the field captured Silver's attention. *What the unholy fuck of all fucks?* Panic speared Silver. She jumped up, almost slipped, and looked down. Willow was running around in the grass training field before the house. She'd found a fluffy rabbit with antlers and wings and chased it around.

"What the hell are you doing, Willow?" she shouted, muffling the transceiver. "Get back inside."

"I'm showing Tinker my scary face!" she shouted back.

*"Reaper Nine? Are you ready for extraction?"*

"Negative," Silver replied, uncovering the device. "I'm not going to need one at all."

Crackling and static.

*"Can you please repeat?"*

"I'm not coming back, Rory."

*"Why the hell not?"* Another pause. *"Have they got to you? Are you compromised?"*

Silver's eyes tracked Willow, making sure she didn't go anywhere else but the field. She tried to hurry her words.

"Only in the sense that I'm finally seeing the truth. I know this is going to be hard to hear, Rory. But your father is someone like me. He's from my time, and he's the one who set off the bombs that destroyed our world."

Static crackling, then: *"You're wrong."*

"I'm not. I've heard it from multiple sources here."

*"Silver. He married my mother, who was queen here before he changed everything and brought back hope for these people. His family has been in Crystal City for generations. There are paintings on the wall in the ballroom. It's impossible he's who you say he is. I don't know what they've done to make you believe that, but it's not true. Now, where are you?"*

Silver clamped her lips shut. Willow squealed again and shouted up something exciting to her aunty. Silver slapped her hand over the transceiver and winced. Static and crackling filtered in and out. It was almost as if someone else was speaking, but their voice wasn't quite loud enough to carry over the radio waves. Who was there? Goosebumps erupted over Silver's flesh. She had to cut this call now.

Her fingers gripped around the transceiver, and she lowered her voice to make one last valiant, maybe stupid effort in this mess. "I'm not coming back, Rory, but I'm going to continue to fight for peace. If you're open to it, I want to set up a meeting between you and representatives from here. Maybe we can negotiate a trade treaty. Get food and supplies in and out of Crystal City."

"*Frankly, I'm disappointed in you, Silver. I thought you were smarter than this,*" Nero said, his voice deep and cutting.

Silver's stomach dropped. She forced the next words out. "This is me being smart. For too long I let my fear of my gift get in the way of listening to my instincts."

"*You're a traitor. A coward. You're probably not even at the Order and this is just you running away.*"

Silver shut down the connection just as a portal ripped open at the end of the field. No! How?

*Willow's voice.*

It must have traveled through the connection and Rory, or Nero, had put two and two together. Alarm ripped through Silver and she skidded down the roof, grabbing hold of a broken tile just before she fell over the edge.

"Willow!" she shouted. "Get inside *now.*"

Willow's sharp eyes lifted to Silver. She dropped the winged rabbit and jumped to her feet and pivoted, only to freeze, mesmerized as the glowing hole grew larger.

Silver judged the distance to the ground. *Too far.* Twenty feet, maybe more. She might break both her legs, but the closer she got to

Willow, the easier she would be to protect. Silver leaped off the roof, trying to clear the bushes at the edge of the house. She connected with the ground. Her legs folded beneath her. One of them made a cracking sound, but she felt no pain. She tucked her shoulder and rolled and rolled, and rolled. Halfway through, the pain hit, searing through her body like napalm. The transceiver fell from her fingers. Her mind screamed. She grasped her left knee and refused to look at it.

Instead, she searched for Willow. She oriented.

*There.*

She was in the middle of the field, running toward Silver. Away from the bright rip in space buzzing with electricity.

"Aunty?"

"*Run*, Willow."

Behind her, the portal fully opened and a team of Reapers walked onto the field. Each looked fearsome in full tactical gear—Rory in the lead. Sid, Martin, and a third Reaper, whose identity was covered by a full-face aspirator. In his hands was a device she would bet carried poison, or sleeping gas, or something equally abhorrent. The rest had pistols, rifles, and knives. A fourth, final Reaper walked through. What he had in his hands made Silver's blood run cold—an automatic mini Gatling gun that weighed more than Willow. He could barely walk with it. Hundreds of ammunition rounds trailed behind him on a belt. It took another person to hold the train. Jimmy, Silver realized. Her heart lurched as the boy lifted his gaze and somehow locked onto Silver as the motor whirred, winding up. The mini gun operator lumbered onto the field, hoisted, and aimed.

Time slowed. People moved as though underwater. Sounds warbled. The air thickened. And then everything happened at once. The howl of a furious wolf rattled the earth. Shade burst through shadow at Silver's side. Dressed only in leather breeches, he reached for her, but she refused.

"Willow!" she pointed. The child had turned to the intruders and snarled, facing danger with a heart of steel. Silver tried to get to her feet, but the pain in her leg blinded her. It drew Shade's attention, only for a second, but it was all Rory needed to lift her pistol and shout, "Fire at will."

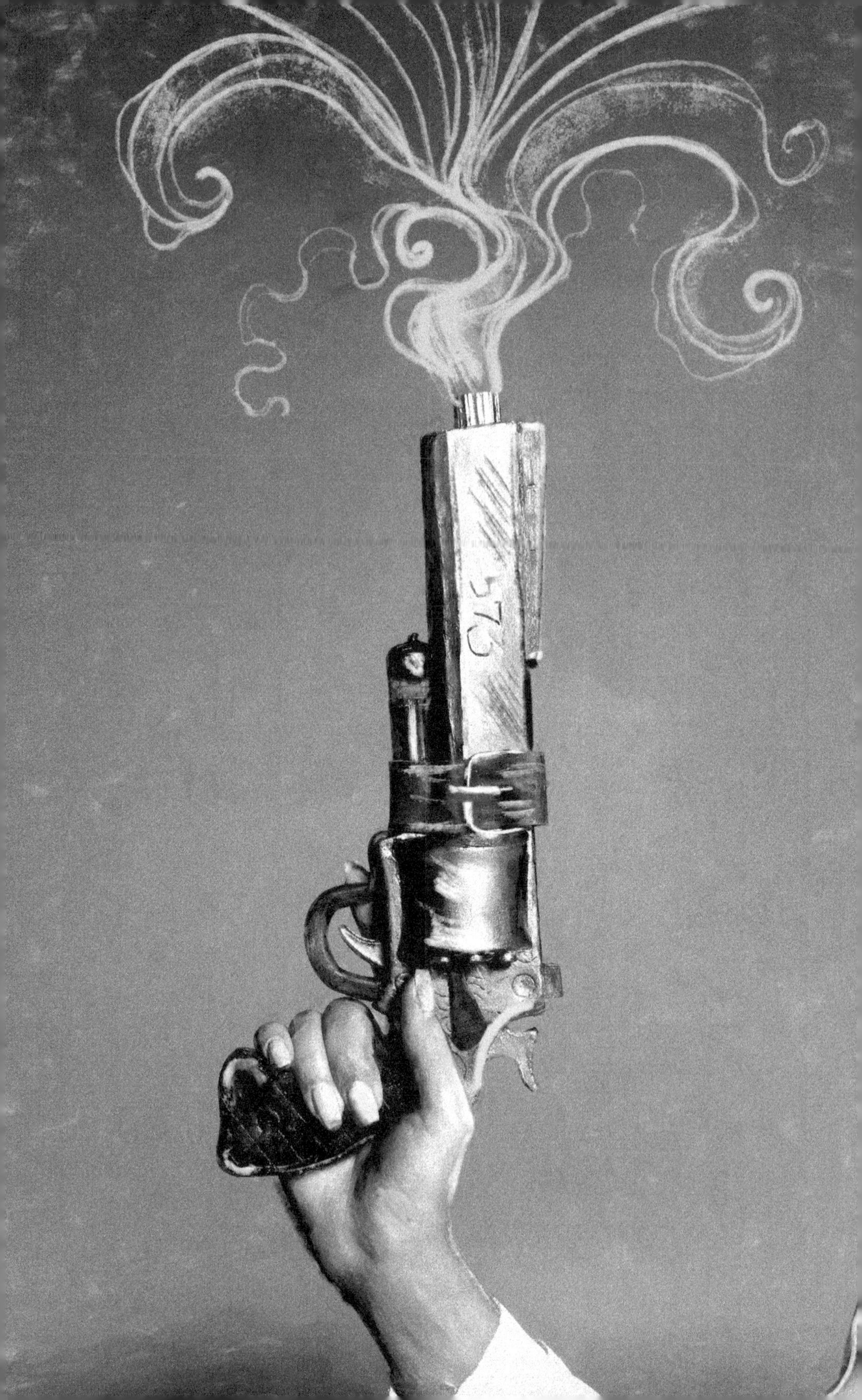

# CHAPTER
# THIRTY-FOUR

A bullet ripped into Shade's shoulder. He staggered in pain as the lead embedded, cutting him from the Well. The humans corrected their aim toward others—to Silver and the Guardians running out of the house, to Rush and Thorne transforming into wolves, tearing through their clothes. Another shot rang out, and another. Any Guardian who had the sense to think, threw up shields of solidified air, but with hundreds of bullets spraying, a few slipped through. Shade covered his mate, taking a hit to his chest. Or so he thought. Silver went down behind him.

No. He was hit, not her. Blood poured from holes in his body. He lost all sense of place and time as his vision started to tunnel. The furious roars and howls of Guardians exploded—no, some*thing* exploded. Wind? Air? Fae retaliation?

Dust and grass blew up. Shade's ears were ringing. He flattened himself over his mate again until the explosion settled. What was happening?

"Silver?" He patted her face.

She blinked. *Alive*. In shock, maybe. Her face was so pale. He had to get her out of there. He tore into his bullet wounds with a roar of determination, digging until he found lead. He tossed the offensive substance with a snarl of impatience. Another bullet had gone straight through. *Lucky*. Clear, and reconnected to the Well. He reached for Silver, but she shook her head.

"I'm fine. Get to Willow," Silver gasped, tapping his shoulder before clamping her hand over her thigh, staunching the bleeding of a flesh wound.

He wrenched his gaze from her to search through the dust. No Willow. But there, lying inconspicuously on the dirt mere feet away, was a familiar small, metal object that filled Shade with dread. Hadn't Silver said she was going to destroy that? Hadn't she also said it was for communicating with the humans? The same humans who were here and now wanted Willow?

Nausea rolled. His skin went hot and prickly. Had his mate betrayed them?

He picked up the round object. "What did you do?"

"I'll explain later," Silver shouted, her eyes pleading. "Get to Willow before they take her. Trust me."

Her words snapped sense into him. Of course she hadn't betrayed him. She was his *mate*. This was something else. He used his pain to ground himself, shifted his wings out, and then shifted them away to complete his healing. He searched for the child. *There*. Through the fighting, dirt, and dust. Human soldiers dragged her toward the portal, kicking and screaming. Heart in his throat, he summoned his shadows until day became night.

Everyone looked up. Everyone feared the darkness he wrought as he blackened the sun. It wasn't enough, so he drew more mana from his reserves, from Silver's. The darker he could make it, the more advantageous to the vampires—a screeching demogorgon broke through his shadow, maw wide with spittle spraying, wings splayed as it landed on top of Shade and pierced with its talons. *His blood.* Silver had been right, and it tracked him through spilled blood. Before the beast could take a hold of Shade, he stepped through his shadows.

He landed somewhere to the right, just far enough to catch Aeron and River charging toward the monster. Both were half-dressed like him. Both were disrupted from sleep. Aeron had the sense to bring his bow. He aimed and loosed arrow after arrow, targeting the monster's eyes, his long brown hair flying as he walked toward it. But the beast's flesh pulled apart and evaded the metal before reforming like liquid.

A glint was the only sign River threw daggers. None of them hit. Every single one sailed straight through the demogorgon as its flesh moved to make way. The monster located Shade with a preternatural sense, tracking him like a vampire tracked his prey.

To get here so quickly, it must teleport. It made sense if the queen created it from a myriad of other creatures. He was so stupid to not think of that earlier. But even if he had, he'd still have shielded Silver. Dread sank in his stomach. The creature was here for Shade. Anything that happened from here on would be his responsibility, his fault. *Butterflied rib cages and missing hearts.* He shook his head to dispel the images. He had to keep Silver safe—he had to keep them all safe.

The scene was mayhem. Shouts. Cries. Power unleashing. Guns firing. The demogorgon plundered, stealing attention that should have been helping Rush and Thorne as they tore into humans in a valiant effort to get to their kin. Clarke must still be in her psychic sleep, or she would be here.

Suddenly, the ground rumbled. Shoots of vines burst forth from overturned earth and wrapped around the demogorgon's scaled legs. Peaches stood on the porch of the house, one hand out and pointed at the beast, the other supported her swollen belly. Haze's shadow peeled away from him and made for the portal while he stayed to protect his mate and unborn child, cleverly remaining as far as he could from the Well-cutting metal.

Peaches' attack on the demogorgon incensed it further. It screeched so loudly that a silent sonic boom blew air and dirt outward, like the unseen force of an explosion. Windows shattered. Glass burst. Eardrums pierced. Only a yard away from the beast, Aeron went flying backward and landed, unresponsive in the dirt.

Taking advantage of the confusion, the humans launched another attack. Gun spray peppered the sky. Haze, only moments earlier virile and potent, covered Peaches with his body and took hit after hit. A shot to Shade's arm cut his mana flow again, and he fell from his shadows mid step. He landed hard somewhere between Silver and the portal, winded and stunned.

With ringing in his ears, he staggered to his feet just in time to see Cloud descend from the sky, lightning in his eyes like an avenging angel, raining bolts at any human he could see, but with the demogorgon wreaking havoc, the humans were slipping away. And they were taking Willow with them.

Only Shade could level the playing field.

With a panicked glance between his mate on the floor, alive, then at the humans dragging Willow toward their portal, and then the demogorgon—he knew what to do.

There was no time to explain. Blood oozed from his wounds. Wincing in pain, he limped and jogged as best as he could and he offered himself up to the beast. No words were needed. It knew exactly what Shade intended... or it didn't care because he was the prey all along.

Unforgiving talons dug into Shade's shoulders, and they took to the sky. The last thing Shade saw as the ground grew distant was the portal closing, and every survivor encroaching on his mate... as if she was the prey, as if she was the enemy.

# CHAPTER
# THIRTY-FIVE

Silver wished she could laugh at the irony. The one thing she'd claimed so vital to her existence—metal—was now the one thing keeping her from protecting the child. It stripped her of all power, both magical and physical. The hopelessness of her situation was too much. She almost gave up.

Shade had just limped toward the beast, and she'd known what he was about to do. The look he'd sent her moments before he started running was the same haunted look she'd glimpsed when they had arrived at his old childhood home.

She couldn't stop him. But she could try to reason with Rory, who stood guard at the portal, barking orders at her soldiers. Nero was nowhere to be found. He rarely was in the thick of the battle. Silver had always thought herself a coward, but after seeing Nero's absence, she knew she was anything but.

Too afraid to check her wounds, she crawled on hands and wounded knees toward the portal as chaos reigned around her. It called to the thing dancing around her black heart. Although she couldn't access the Well, she still felt phantom echoes of that urge, wanting release. *Needing it.*

She hated this feeling; being inconsequential, ineffective, useless. A disappointment.

The electric crackle of the portal drowned out her voice as she shouted for Rory to stop. Ozone mixed with blood and dirt. A child's screams—her panicked rendition of *Kokomo*—and her father's growls. A tattooed, winged Guardian landed like a meteor between Silver and the portal, knocking her backward. Cloud.

"Rory!" Silver shouted, trying to get to her feet. The pain blinded her. She cried out and collapsed. Her next shout was rough and choked. "Don't do this."

"Don't bother coming back," Rory shouted at Silver as a Reaper tossed Willow into her arms. Wind gusted, clanking the copper beads in her hair. She clutched Willow to her side, but looked at Rory. "You're dead to us."

Cloud's eyes lit up like he'd just been plugged in. Electricity flickered in his newly white gaze like a thunderous storm. He was within reach of the portal, within reach of grabbing Willow as she kicked and screamed in Rory's strong hand, but the Guardian hesitated.

He and Rory stared at each other as though each had seen a ghost. A human princess and a fae warrior.

Then the portal shut down, taking Rory and Willow with it. Silver glanced over her shoulder in the direction Shade had gone, and found him not on the ground, but dangling from the talons of a monster as they flew into the sun.

He was gone.

Willow was gone.

The howl of wolves filled the air with a haunting note that wouldn't end. It went on and on and on until Silver was sure there was no place left on earth it didn't reach. Until it finally died. Everything went silent, and every person alive on the field turned to Silver with vengeance and despair in their eyes. She deserved every ounce of that hate. *My fault.* Rory had tracked Silver here, probably through the transceiver, and she'd stupidly given away everything in that one conversation.

Cloud still stared at the scorched earth where the portal had been. Fallen were everywhere. Some Guardians were on the ground. Some were unresponsive—the elf, Aeron. Was he dead? Violet was running toward Silver with a look of such sheer panic in her eyes that it confused the heck out of her. Why was she looking like that?

A wet, guttural growl behind Silver made her almost lose control of her bladder. She swallowed and turned. Two enormous white wolves spattered with blood prowled closer.

*Fuck.*

Willow's father and brother. Silver was about to die, and she would never see Shade again.

"STOP!" a woman shouted. Petite, freckled, long red hair. Agony on her face—tears streaming from her eyes. She tripped on her night gown and stumbled down the porch to land hard on her knees. She held her hand out, eyes begging as she shouted again for them to stop.

Red hair.

*Willow's mother.*

For a moment, Silver thought Clarke was speaking to her, but then she saw her gaze locked firmly over Silver's shoulder, at her mate, Rush. The large wolf growled so deep and guttural that Silver forgot to breathe. He took a step toward Silver, his intentions clear.

"No," Clarke said, shaking her head for emphasis. "If we want Willow back, we need her alive."

The golden eyed wolf whined and trotted to Clarke. She grabbed hold of his bloodied fur and buried her face in him. The blue-eyed wolf continued to watch Silver with a snarl.

Everyone else was shell-shocked as Mages ran onto the field to heal the fallen. There were no words Silver could give to alleviate their pain. She'd fucked up. Her own regret and guilt compounded like death drums beating down her door.

*"One of these days you'll see, you'll be a bigger disappointment than me."*

The memory of her mother's insidious voice echoed as two Guardians lifted her roughly, uncaring of her wounds, and carried her away.

---

Silver was shoved into a holding cell at the back of the barracks. She wanted to be tough. She wanted to hold her head high and pretend that Shade's and Willow's loss didn't affect her. But the moment her feet hit the ground, searing pain lanced through her wounded legs, and she cried out in agony. Everything hurt, from her toes to the throbbing headache threatening to claim her consciousness.

She collapsed onto the piss-smelling dirt and curled into herself, vaguely registering the clang of metal doors grinding closed and then locking. Of course the Guardians would have a metal cage. This was probably their interrogation room.

And what would they ask when they finally came for her? Silver didn't know the answer to the question she'd been asking herself since setting foot in Elphyne.

Who was she fighting for?

All she knew was that her ache for Shade was so desolate that she wanted to burrow into the ground and never come out. She wanted her black heart to swallow her whole, to decay her flesh so she could become dust.

Silver wasn't sure how long she lied there, tormented by her own company, until the sun set and she started to shiver. No one brought food, no one brought a blanket or jacket and, certainly, no one saw to her injuries. The blue light on her arm mocked her. It gave no solace with lead bullets still in her body. Every time she moved, pain lashed like a whip, causing her to shudder and gasp and thank God no arteries had been hit. Maybe once she was brave enough to dig them out, but she was too much of a coward.

Always had been, despite pretending to be fearsome.

*Disappointing.*

It wasn't the wolves who would be her end, but the substance she'd placed her staunch beliefs on. Lead bullets. Delirium took hold as infection set in. Silver's mind played tricks on her. She saw Shade not running toward the demogorgon, but into the queen's arms. In her imagination, the queen looked like Rory. Proud, tall, invincible. Hard. Unbending.

They picked up their suitcase together and walked through an open door, into blinding light.

"Don't leave me!" she shouted.

*"You'll always be trash."*

"No!"

*"He left because you can't be helped."*

"Come back!"

The cawing of crows turned to mocking laughter. She drifted in and out of sleep, cold and shivering, and yet hot with fever. Time blurred until she wasn't sure if she was alive or dead.

"You can't leave her like that," said a clipped, no-nonsense voice. She sounded terrifying. A goddess in command. "It's cruel and counterintuitive."

A male grumbled.

"Clarke said we need her alive to save Willow." This was a smaller, gentle voice.

More grumbling rumbled like thunder. And then everything went dark.

---

"Wake up."

The sting of a hand hit Silver's cheek. She roused with wide eyes and glanced around. Where was she?

Cold. Dark. Smelled like urine. *Still inside the cell.* She inhaled and almost cried from the sharp pain stabbing her ribs. Throbbing in her legs and head echoed each other like a macabre masterpiece. Even though the air was brittle and cold, her mouth was arid and as dry as a desert.

After wiping hair from her fevered face, the crowded cell came into focus.

Violet stood next to Indigo, glaring down at Silver with a mixture of anger and concern. Peaches was in the corner beneath the big arm of her vampire Guardian. Clarke stood next to a long, silver-haired shifter with hard, golden eyes. He must be Rush—the wolf who'd wanted to kill Silver. Both parents looked haggard and exhausted.

Next to Rush stood Thorne, Leaf, Cloud, and the Prime. It was her voice and hand that had awoken Silver.

The Prime of the Order of the Well crouched until her pristine blue dress dragged on the soiled cell floor. She grabbed Silver's chin and forced her eyes up.

"Did you do it?" she asked, straight and to the point. "And before you consider lying, please know we have a powerful psychic adept in truth seeking standing here."

Silver's eyes slid to Clarke. The woman's passive face gave away nothing except that she hadn't slept. She'd stopped Rush from killing Silver, but it didn't mean they were allies. Otherwise, why was Silver still in this cell?

"If you're so powerful, how could you not see this happening?" Silver cried, flinging her regret and guilt onto the woman. "How could you have sent Shade to find me in the first place?"

Clarke's chin wobbled. The whisper that fell out of her was almost inaudible. "I saw," she said. "I saw, and I tried to find a way out. It's why I was asleep for so long. But I couldn't find a solution. I don't' see everything. And the alternative was worse if Shade never met you."

All eyes snapped to Clarke, as if this was the first they'd heard of it.

She paled as she explained. "If Shade never met Silver, he was going to flip into a blood rage so deadly that he killed half the house, including Willow... or he was going back to Maebh, and then all of Elphyne suffered."

Shit.

Rush's lip curled, flashing sharp canine fangs at Silver. "Answer the original question before I rip it from you. Did you do it?"

For some stupid reason, in that moment, she remembered being in the boat under Shade's wing. He was so sure that to control her gift, she had to accept the parts of her life she wasn't proud of—the dark, twisted cowardice. Conjuring his memory, his scent, his sure words, sometimes cocky and infuriating, she felt herself become sure too. She'd been fighting for so long that she didn't know when to stop. There was no point lying. No point passing blame. This was all on Silver.

"I admit," she said, "that I set foot in Elphyne with the intention of doing exactly what happened. I was to infiltrate the Order, hunt Willow down, and call for extraction. I'll own that. But I didn't call them here. Not intentionally, anyway."

The Prime let go of her chin and straightened.

"She's telling the truth," Violet clipped. "Indigo heard her on the roof, telling them she'd changed her mind."

Indigo scowled and nodded at his mate. "I was half asleep, but now that we've pieced together what happened, I know what I overheard wasn't a dream. Silver's suffering has gone on long enough. Shade would be furious to know his mate is being treated like this."

"Regardless of intention, she is the reason my daughter is missing," Rush growled. "She suffers for as long as I say she suffers."

The shadow snake tattooed on Indigo's neck slithered along his skin, as though it had taken offense to Rush's words. But the vampire himself stayed staunch.

"She's lucky we don't tear her limb from limb," Thorne sneered, eyes flaring with anger.

"The bullets stay in her until we're sure she can be trusted," the Prime confirmed.

Silver hoped her insides didn't pack it in by then.

"I get that," she said, her voice small. "I wouldn't trust me either."

It was a wonder Shade pursued her or cared for her at all. Silver still had no idea where she fit in this world, on his side, or somewhere between. Shade had willingly walked toward the queen's creature, and Silver's fever dreams made sure to taunt her with doubt. She wanted to believe, with all her black heart, that Shade wasn't going to abandon her for the sake of appeasing a mad queen, but he was fae. He was centuries old. What if this sort of thing was normal?

What if their mating bond meant nothing when the most powerful female in the land wanted him? Who was Silver to compete? She was a nobody. Someone who couldn't be trusted. And didn't Clarke just say she'd seen a future where he went back to her?

Only if he never met Silver.

"What do they want with Willow?" Rush asked, golden eyes pinning Silver to the ground.

"Nero lost his psychic years ago. Willow's her replacement."

"I was right," Clarke gasped. "This is my fault."

"It's not your fault, princess." Rush cupped her face. His brows joined in the middle.

But Clarke was having none of it. "We brought a child into this world before it was safe. We knew the Void had it in for me. *We knew!* She was always going to be a target, even if she didn't have my psychic ability. Which she does."

"We didn't plan for Willow," he admitted. "But we will never regret having her."

She blubbered her agreement. He pressed Clarke's face to his chest. She hugged him. Their pain was too much for Silver to bear.

"Willow will be alive," Silver said. As if it mattered. They wouldn't believe her, anyway. "She'll be safe. Nero won't lose this advantage."

Rory would look after the child. She'd train her like her own—even Willow had said she'd end up calling her Aunty. They had time to stage a rescue.

"She's not an advantage," Thorne snarled. "She's a fucking child."

"I know that!" Silver snapped back, tears spilling from her eyes. "From the moment I met Willow, I knew I couldn't hand her over. She called me aunty, for Christ's sake. It's the same name another little, malnourished human girl calls me. I'd never met Willow, and she *ran* into my arms, telling me she practiced her scary face like I'd told her, wanting to learn a fucking Beach Boy song no one else knew I sang. I mean, who does that?"

"Willow does," Rush said, his eyes grave.

Clarke's glistening eyes stared at Silver, long and hard. No one said a word.

"Then why did you contact them?" Violet tossed the transceiver onto the floor before Silver. "This is what you used, isn't it? Why tell them you changed your mind? Couldn't you have just left it?"

Silver sank into herself. There was no way this would look good for her, but she confessed everything anyway. "I don't know. Maybe it was a moment of hopeless optimism. I thought if I told them I wasn't going to go through with it, that maybe we could come up with another solution to the food shortages and the starving children and families in Crystal City. I hoped they would see if I changed my mind—me, of all people—then we could find a way to work together. But they must have tracked me."

They must never have trusted Silver.

"How do they move metal through a portal?" Leaf stepped forward, hijacking the interrogation. "Do they have a Guardian working for them?"

"I don't know."

"Liar," Cloud spat. "You're nothing but a filthy liar."

"You don't have the right to an opinion," Violet shot back. "You stood there in front of the portal, within reach of Willow, and you did nothing. So, unless you're going to fill the class in on why, I suggest you keep your judgements to yourself."

The tension in the room ramped up to sizzling. Cloud's stifling aura suffocated them as his eyes and tattoos filled with electricity. Silver truly thought he'd attack, and he did. But not a person. He punched the wall, let loose a bolt of lightning, and then stepped out.

Multiple exasperated sighs rippled across the group.

"I don't know how they do it," Silver repeated. She raised her hand and gestured. "Scout's honor, I have no idea how they create portals. I never see fae behind the Crystal City gates. All I can say is that Nero has found ways around your rules, and I'm not privy to them. I'm a grunt. A Reaper. I live with the other starving and malnourished humans on diesel-soaked ground. I do what he says when he says it. I build cannons for airships, and I use my knowledge of old school weapons to give us an advantage in this war."

"*Us*," Violet said quietly. "You're still putting yourself in the same lot as them."

"I told you, Violet. I haven't given up on wanting to save the humans."

Silver could have wept at the slow understanding in her eyes as Violet voiced her opinion. "You have to wonder what life would be like without Nero in the world."

Another Guardian entered and spoke quietly to the Prime. Her expression deadpanned, then she motioned for everyone to leave.

"There is nothing else we need from Silver now. I will send in a healer, but Silver will remain locked in this cell until I decide otherwise."

They all filed out of the cell. Peaches and Violet were the only two who glanced at Silver before they left.

"What about Shade?" she blurted. "Is anyone going to find him?"

The Prime was the last to leave. She faced Silver with cold eyes. "The situation D'arn Shade has found himself in has nothing to do with the Order, or the Well. It is a political maneuver made by the queen, caused by his reluctance to face the consequences of his actions. His negligence has brought death to members of our organization multiple times over. We are perilously understaffed. As such, it will not be a battle fought by the Order of the Well. We do not concern ourselves with everyday politics. As long as Maebh's creature remains in check, we have other, more pressing business."

"You're just going to abandon him?" Silver shouted, and tried to get to her feet. Pain thundered through her body, and she collapsed, vomiting up bile. She retched until she saw stars. Heat flushed her cheeks, making her prickly all over. The fever was back.

With no energy to spare, Silver submitted to the pounding in her head and passed out, holding onto the tiny kernel of hope the Prime had left her. She was sending someone to heal Silver's wounds. The moment that happened, she would unleash her black heart and find a way to escape.

There were plenty of things Silver didn't know, but one thing she knew with all certainty. She would not abandon Shade.

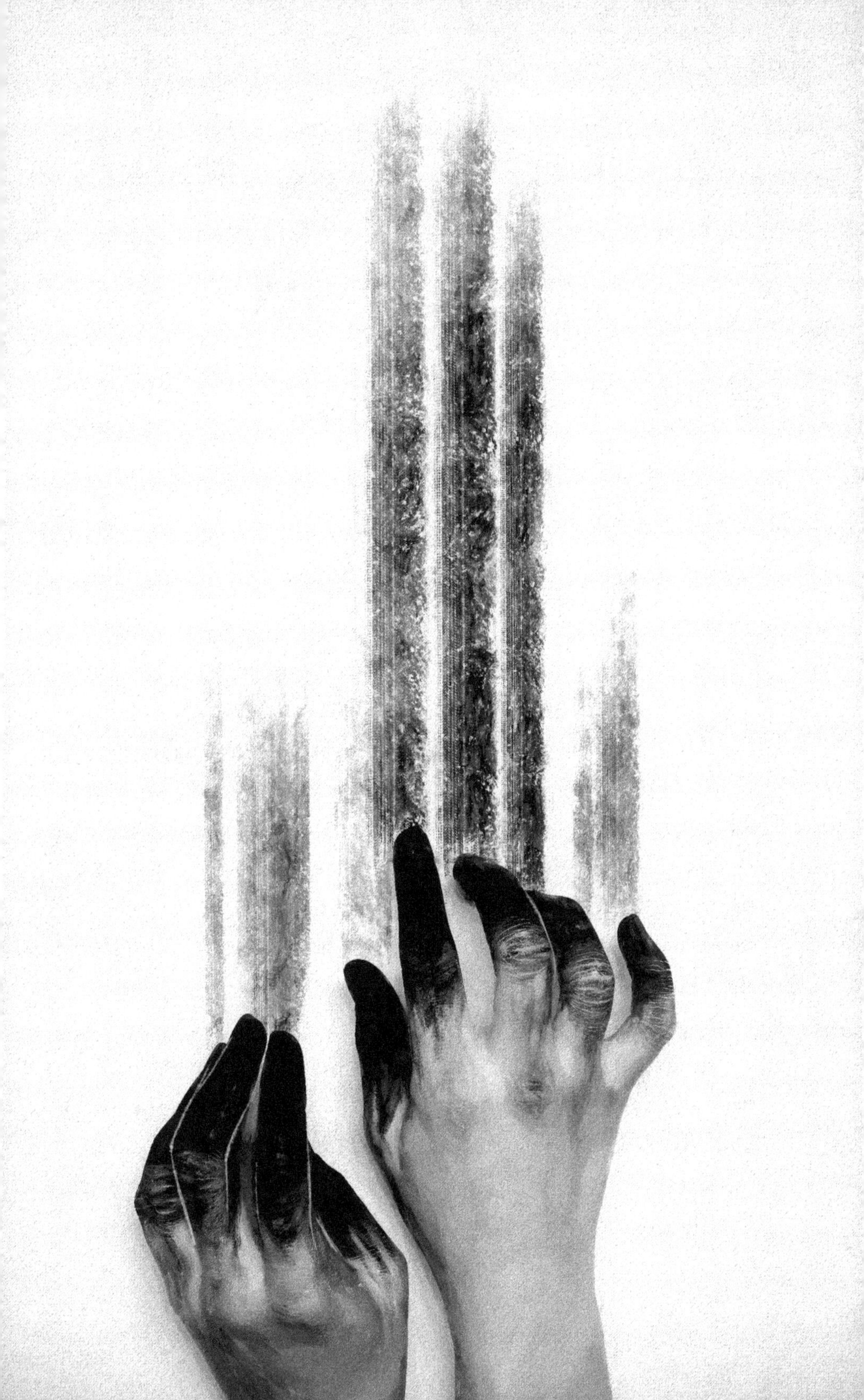

# CHAPTER
# THIRTY-SIX

The demogorgon tossed Shade on the queen's private terrace high up in the Obsidian Palace. He knew the spot well. He'd sat on the black stone on many nights, gazing up at the stars with a queen who was his whole world... for a time. As he landed, the lead pellets in his body dug deeper, tearing into flesh and muscle. He stared at the cold floor catching his reflection, breathing hard through the pain, refusing to move an inch and reveal his weakness to the female gliding toward him like a shark through black water.

*No weakness.*

He refused to think of his mate, of the fae he thought had his back stalking toward her on four paws. They would see the metal object he'd left. They would blame her, as he had almost done.

There was nothing he could do about that now. He had to trust that the others would see the truth, especially his vampire brothers and their mates. Right now, his focus needed to be here, on this present danger—one he'd neglected for too long.

Each slide of Maebh's slippered feet drew her closer, and knowing the bullets blocked his mana, he wrenched himself upright. Her dark afro had been pulled back from her face in rolls that spilled into tiny braids down her back. She wore a black dress so shiny it melted into the polished obsidian around her like camouflage. On her head sat her crown of antlers, roses, and thorns, as if she'd known this was the day he'd come and had dressed to strike with the power of her queendom.

Black stained lips. Black stained fingertips. Black, soulless eyes that had always been there, hiding behind the warmth. She looked ill, and not in a natural way. It struck Shade as odd that she didn't, or couldn't, cover this affliction up with a glamor.

The warm trickle of blood down his torso was nothing compared to the injured look in her eyes as she took him in. The look was beyond hurt, beyond betrayal, and had tipped into something far more frightening—vengeance tainted with madness.

Still, he lifted his chin. He'd reached her once, he could do it again.

*No weakness.*

"I'm here to negotiate," he said.

She blinked, stunned. Then she tossed her head back and laughed. Her crown almost fell off. She straightened it but kept laughing. Her cackle peeled off into the wind where it seemed to hiss and echo over the frozen bay. The demogorgon clicked and cooed deep in its throat, as though it mocked Shade, too. Two royal guards behind Maebh—one of them Indigo's wayward brother Demeter—smirked as though they knew something Shade didn't.

Okay. Not the reaction he'd hoped for.

Shade slowly covered the leaking bullet wound in his arm. If he could get the lead out, he was two steps closer to accessing his mana. But the moment his fingers twitched, the queen snapped her fingers. Perhaps something mana related was supposed to happen, but the metal inside him blocked it from reaching into him. Her brows puckered and she gestured irately for her guards to take him.

"Wait," he said. "You wanted me, and here I am. Let's talk about this."

"Talk about it?" Maebh snarled as her soldiers secured his hands behind his back. Agony screamed through his body as the lead moved internally. Her gaze dropped to the blue glowing Well-blessed marks winding up his arm, still flickering with a promise that the Well would one day reunite him with Silver. But the same hope to him was anathema to the queen. Her lips moved with a cruel and insidious curve. "You've had decades to talk about it with me. No, my *amaro*. You've made me look weak for too long. It is time you learn what happens to bats who fly the coop." She turned to her soldiers. "Put him in a cell and keep the bullets in him. We don't want him disappearing on us. Not before the final act."

"The final act?" He bucked as they tried to hold him down.

"Yes," she said. "There is only room for one ruler in this world, and it's not the Mithras spawn, that Order bitch, or the filthy Untouched who stole my legacy. My new pet and I will reunite Elphyne, as the way it used to be. We will create a new legacy. One ruler, as it always should have been. Me."

# CHAPTER
# THIRTY-SEVEN

Not long after the Prime left, a Mage with skin like pale Ash wood bustled into Silver's cell. As the guard let him in, the Mage tutted and clicked his tongue in disapproval over the conditions. He called for fresh water and food, a cot and chamber pot, then he swished his blue robes out of the way with a flourish and set down his basket to see to her wounds.

"My name is Melwyn," he announced. "I'm here to see to your wellbeing. Please, if I may, I'd like to tend to your wounds."

Silver blinked at him for too long to remain polite. His skin didn't just *look* like Ash wood. It *was* wood. Darker striations ran down his cheeks and curved around bone structure. His eyebrows sprouted dark twigs, not hair. A small, glowing blue teardrop was on his bottom lip like all Mages.

She'd never seen a Mage up close, and certainly not one made of wood. There were so many fae out there she'd never known existed, even after spending a year living amongst them. That time had been fraught with fear, for both her safety and her out-of-control gift.

"Finished looking?" he said, but with humor in his eyes.

"Yes, I'm sorr—"

He took her hand and put it over her chest, then made her do the hand-sign for apology. "You're going to live among us now. You need to start acting like us."

Live among them.

*Don't bother coming back... You're dead to us now.*

She nodded, a little embarrassed at her state, but also so exhausted, cold, and sore enough that she didn't care. Melwyn worked methodically from her head to toe, limb to limb, using his gift to sense where she needed healing, and to locate where the bullets were. There were two. He couldn't start the healing process until he removed them.

While he worked, Silver's mind traveled to dark places. Jimmy had been one of the soldiers with Rory. He was right there, fighting, putting his young life at risk for an evil madman. It made Silver sick to think about. She had to find a way to get him and his family out of there. She had to help all of them, Willow especially.

Her only solace was that she knew, without a doubt, that Rory would protect Willow. She might be cold, but she wasn't like her father. And if Willow called her aunty, then hopefully that meant they had a good relationship.

"I'm an Oak Man," Melwyn said, answering the unsaid question earlier. "You don't see many of us around. We prefer to keep to ourselves and stick to the forests we make our homes in. But a handful of us are imbued with the gift of a plentiful internal well. We come here to learn how to harness our gifts. Few of us stay."

With that, he started pulling out supplies from his basket. A bone blade. A vial of something. Some cloth. The Mage was going to perform surgery on her in this dirty cell.

She didn't have the energy to worry. He must know what he was doing. She downed the bitter liquid he gave her and submitted to his expertise. If she wanted to find Shade, she needed to be well. Within minutes, she drifted, her mind clouding. When she woke, she found herself in virtually no pain and only the aftereffects of whatever tonic he'd given her. It had all happened so fast. Her clothes were a mess of blood and grime, but her cell now had a rickety cot, water, bread, and a chamber pot. She drank greedily and relieved herself. When she lifted her shirt, she found even her old metal corset wounds were gone. She rubbed her skin. Shade's attention had almost completely healed them, but Melwyn had taken it the rest of the way. Only a phantom ache existed when her fingers bumped over her scars. Such was the power of the Well.

The urge to find another corset rolled through Silver. Now that Shade was gone, the sense of needing containment was fast returning.

She fell back on the cot with a sigh. She'd never been so injured before when she'd lived in Elphyne, and even though she was a Reaper, she'd been lucky to survive those experiences with minor scrapes and scars. These recent bullet wounds should have killed her, but through the power of the Well, she'd been saved. Carla's fingers wouldn't need medicine or supplies. She would be able to just have them fixed on the spot by a healer.

There was nothing more uncomfortable than having stalwart beliefs rocked.

She managed to keep some bread down and fell back asleep,

exhausted. The second time she woke, it was because she had company. Violet and Peaches were allowed into the cell. Each carried a bundle of what smelled like food. Haze loomed outside, giving Silver the side-eye in case she tried anything that might harm his mate and unborn child. That's when it hit Silver. Using her gift to escape would mean she had to hurt someone, and she'd already hurt these people enough.

She eased off the cot and went to the bars.

"Have you heard from Shade?" she asked.

The two women shared a look that meant they hadn't. Even the big vampire warrior looked concerned. Peaches handed Silver a bundle of clothes.

"We brought you some clean things to wear," she said.

"And some proper food." Violet unwrapped her bundle to reveal mouthwatering sandwiches filled with healthy salad.

"Thank you." She swallowed the lump in her throat. "I don't deserve this."

Violet handed over the unwrapped sandwich. Silver set to work devouring it immediately as Violet spoke.

"I can honestly say we would have much rather you filled us in on your problem so we could help you. But we understand why it's hard to trust. We've both been there. It's not easy having your world turned upside down."

"So, no one's heard from Shade?" she asked through a mouthful. "Or news on Willow?"

"No. On both accounts." Peaches bit her lip and rubbed her belly. "We thought maybe you'd be able to confirm whether Shade's... you know."

"Alive," Violet finished for her.

"You mean through the bond?"

"Yes. Now that your metal has been removed, if you concentrate, you should be able to feel him connected to you. Sometimes you can feel emotions across the distance. But it all depends on how far away you are."

"I think I can feel the connection. I mean, it's still there. I would imagine feeling nothing if he was dead." The thought made her shudder. Finished eating, Silver wiped her mouth with the back of her hand. "Is there a plan to get him? Has the queen released any demands?"

Haze, who'd been trying not to look like he was eavesdropping, finally gave up, ducked to get under the beam holding up the doorway, and joined them in the cell. His massive shoulders barely fit through the gap. If his wings were out, they'd fill up the entire space.

Hard eyes met Silver's as he lowered his voice to speak in a deep rumble. "Indi and I are working on a plan, but since the Prime's resources are stretched thin, it's taking time."

"Stretched thin?"

Haze's scowl deepened. "Order business. Plus, Maebh has launched an attack on the Seelie, and half the Cadre are working on getting Willow back."

Violet blinked at the barrage of information and tried to work out which piece to address first. "Willow will be okay. I'll help get her back as soon as we get Shade. They shouldn't launch an attack on Crystal City until I can consult."

The last thing Silver wanted was more bloodshed. There had to be a way to get in quietly and return with Willow before anyone found out.

"Well," Haze replied dryly. "You don't need to worry about that. They're handling it."

Violet's lips flattened at Haze's dismissal of Silver, and in that moment, Silver knew she had an ally in her. And when she spoke, she knew Violet had always been on her side.

"So why isn't the Prime helping get Shade? Hasn't he worked here for decades? He's one of her own. I know there's a war happening, but she's always stretched thin."

Haze nodded. "Laurel's drive to get more recruits doesn't seem to be working. Fae are still afraid of being judged. At this stage, the Prime is going to call for tributes for the ceremonial Well."

Silver narrowed her eyes. From memory, tributes were one of the taxes the Order demanded. But instead of money, it was fae required to join the Guardians. The only thing was, they had to survive a grueling initiation at the ceremonial lake among the Well Worms. The success rate was less than thirty percent.

Haze's fingers bumped over eyebrow piercings as he scrubbed his face. "The simple fact of the matter is we don't have enough Guardians. Without them, the Order is powerless to hold their standing. The queen is kicking our asses, ruining our reputation, and we can't do anything about it."

"So, what does that mean for Shade?" Silver asked nervously.

No one answered her. Did that mean they had no way of getting to him?

"Release me," Silver said. "Please. I'll go on my own. I'll bring him back."

"It's not that we don't believe you," Violet said.

Her next sentence was interrupted by a clanging sound from the entrance of the holding cells.

"Time's up!" the guard shouted.

Death danced on Haze's face and he boomed back, "It's up when I say it's up, rookie."

Silver was sure she heard a squeak of fear. No other reply came, but Haze looked Silver in the eyes and said, "We need to go."

"There's a mana stone in that bundle," Peaches said, pointing. "It's like dry shampoo. You can use it to wash without water."

"We'll be back," Violet promised.

Silver hand-signed her gratitude.

After they left, Silver cleaned and dressed herself. She occupied her mind by running through escape plans, trying to come up with a scenario that didn't involve hurting someone who was just doing their job. It all came down to control of her gift, and Shade had been right. Silver had to accept her own tumultuous emotions first.

Looking around the cell, she thought she was finally ready to do that. Maybe she already had been. For much of the time she'd been with Shade, her gift had stayed dormant in her chest. Even now, she realized, she was calling it her gift, not a curse. She could see that, while killing people was never a good thing, her power could also be used to protect.

She didn't think she'd ever lose the need to feel constrained by a garment, but she was okay with that—and that feeling, that being okay with her flaws and weirdness, it was exactly what Shade was talking about. No shame. No guilt. Just be her, in all her twisted darkness.

But now that she was okay with herself, she had to remember how to feel the chaos to trigger her gift. For the next hour, she did only that. It was harder than it looked. She had to suddenly shift her emotions one way, then another. Exhaustion returned, and she took a nap. When she woke, she got up and paced in the cell. She accessed her gift, pulling it out of her chest and then sinking it back in.

The work was slow going, but she doggedly applied herself, knowing the longer she took, the more danger Shade would be in, and the more time would pass for Nero to groom Willow into being the deadly psychic he wanted.

Another day passed. Silver was fed. She cleaned herself, relieved herself, and she trained. She trained her body, she trained her mind, and she trained her gift. Each time she let the poisonous black smoke out, she worked at controlling the direction the darkness moved. If she could target its trajectory, then she could increase its efficacy.

She wanted to be ready when the time came.

Sometime after midday the next morning, Silver heard muffled voices at the entrance, just out of view. When no one came inside to get her, her heart sank. She paced and practiced until the sun went down, and then some more. When midnight rolled around, she worried no one would ever come. They would leave her locked up forever.

Another two days passed. She drifted to sleep on the second night, but awoke at the sound of tapping. *Who's here?* Her heart leaped into her throat, and her dark gift activated. It defended her at the first thought of trouble, but upon seeing a Guardian sitting against the bars, *inside* her cell, she relaxed. Then, when she caught the murder in his electric blue eyes, she wondered if she'd made a mistake.

Cloud.

He deftly flipped a butterfly knife and then tapped it idly against the metal bars. His worn and patched leather uniform had seen more battles than the queen's army and hugged his athletic physique like a second skin. When he flicked the blade, moonlight caught his flexing neck tendon, shimmering the prismatic oil slick tattoo. If his black wings were out, she had the sense she wouldn't even see them in the shadows. He looked like he was born to live in the dark. From beneath a mop of curls, his glare followed the path of black smoke oozing back into her chest.

She wouldn't be surprised if her gift retracted from fear of him.

"You're lucky I've been practicing," she said. "A few days ago it would have shot out and turned you to ash, no matter who you are."

His lips curved on one side, but the smile didn't reach his eyes. There was nothing in his expression that revealed he gave a damn about anything she said.

"What do you want?" she asked. Because she wasn't in the mood for defending herself again. Too much time had passed since the battle, and no one had given her word of Shade. As far as she could tell, he was alive, but for how long?

"Tell me the woman's name," he said.

"You're going to have to be a little more specific, sunshine."

"Don't be cute." He stopped flicking the knife and leaned forward. "You know the one. She stole the kid."

"Rory?"

"Is that her full name?"

"Uh..." Silver tried to think. It's possible Rory's father had called her by another name once. "I think it's Aurora."

Pure liquid hate washed over him. It was so intense that Silver shuffled backward on her cot. She had to consciously conjure the feeling of Shade's safety to temper her chaos. Her breathing quickened. Her eyes squeezed shut, and she wished for a corset. Any of them. Even the leather one Shade had gifted her at the cabin. While she'd made headway controlling her gift, she hadn't tested it like this, and she sensed that if she had that feeling of containment, it would take her the rest of the way to complete control. Wheezing, she got to her feet and pulled the sheet from the cot.

"I'd get out of here, if I were you," she burst out, her voice trembling.

Cloud stood and eyed the black smoke oozing from her chest. "What does it do?"

"Give me something living, and I'll show you." She ripped a strip off the sheet, but it was so resistant, it made her hand bleed. "Something not human," she blurted, shaking her hand. *Goddammit*, she wasn't going to be responsible for the death of an unsuspecting soul. She could just imagine Cloud being the type to drag in the rookie guard.

Exhaling with a slow controlled breath, she wound the strip around her middle, cinching it tight, feeling better already. *Calm. Control.*

"What are you doing?"

*Panic.*

*Chaos.*

"Don't you have any sense of self-preservation? Get out unless you want to die a slow, horrible death where your body decays before your eyes."

He pointed at her with the knife, opened his mouth to say something, then clamped his jaw shut. "And that—thing you're tying helps you?"

"I used to have a metal corset blocking it. That is now lost. I know it sounds dumb, but Shade brought me a leather corset and it still helped. This helps. Now, let me calm myself." She exhaled and inhaled slowly. *Think of Shade... think...* but thinking of Shade meant her mind wandered to why she hadn't heard back about him. Then her thoughts wandered to Willow. Then the chaos and panic came back.

"I'll find you one," he announced, strolling to the cell door as if he wasn't about to be choked by death. "And then I'll help you get Shade back."

Hope surged. "What?"

"On one condition." He dragged the cell door closed and then locked it. He faced her through the bars.

"Anything," she said, hating every second of it.

"You'll owe me a favor."

A favor could mean anything. It could mean he asked her to kill an army. It could mean he wanted her to prance around naked in front of the entire congregation of the Order. It could mean *anything*.

*Follow the crow to be in the know.*

That's what Fox had said. But could she trust Fox? She scrutinized Cloud. He gave her nothing except an unreadable face.

"Deal." She held out her hand.

He looked at her like she'd grown demogorgon scales. "Think about it before you agree."

"I don't need to. He's my mate."

He rolled his eyes. "You sound as bad as Shade did, and that was before he'd even met you. I'll tell you what I told him. There's no dick, or pussy, in the world worth dying for. Now tell me, are you sure?"

So, he'd basically admitted whatever favor she owed him would put her life at risk. Still... she was sure. If he'd said that to Shade before they'd met, and Shade still hunted her down, then who was she to deny these feelings?

Shade made everything right in the world.

"I'm in," she said.

"When I get back, be ready."

# CHAPTER THIRTY-EIGHT

Two guards hauled Shade across the queen's chambers. His feet dragged over the carpet, leaving a trail of blood and mud. They burst through the terrace doors and dropped him on the cold, glossy surface reflecting a sunset.

A few days had passed since he left Silver. Since then, he'd enjoyed a regular dose of beatings by guards. Then they'd tied his hands and returned him to the old nursery chamber where they left him to rot with bullets still inside his body, festering and digging in deeper. Surrounded in signs of Maebh's misery, and alone, all he had done was stew over Silver's fate. But this particular day felt different.

His puffy eyes peeled open to see Queen Maebh overlooking her lands, still wearing the same dress as the first day he'd arrived. It was like time had stood still. She had no crown this time, but severed heads by her feet. Their identities ranged from High Lords and Ladies to random animals and monsters—all of them Seelie.

Shade could tell from either their clothing or identifying features, which put them as residents of Jasper's kingdom.

With every muscle and bone aching, Shade pushed to his feet and shuffled closer. He was lucky he could stand. His fae biology was probably the only thing keeping him alive. That, and maybe Silver's nutritious blood. But he wouldn't be cowed into submission. He'd have risen to his feet by the last scrap of his will, even if it killed him.

"Ah," Maebh said to him, oblivious to his bloody state, and pointed at the twilight sky over the arctic Aconite Sea. "Just in time. We're about to have another delivery."

A dark silhouette with tentacle wings flew closer. It had something in its talons. Below on the ground before the palace, Maebh's army moved into formation, preparing to march—presumably on the Seelie, the humans, or the Order. Maybe all. The sounds of their assembly liquified Shade's bowels. Hundreds of Unseelie fae... maybe thousands. And that would only be a fraction of her army.

She was going to war, and she would probably win. Jasper might be older than Shade, and more powerful, but he was a new king. He'd just had his first child. He would not be ready to defend his kingdom against a mad queen with centuries of amassed power and a seemingly immortal creature. The demogorgon only needed to enter the human city, and it would devour them all. Unlike Shade, bullets would fly straight through it.

"What happened to you, Maebh?" Shade asked. "What happened to the adventures in far-off lands we talked about rediscovering? We would sit right here and read about them."

Her sitting parlor was crowded with ancient books preserved by mana. One of them had been something called an atlas and mapped out every landmass that used to exist. Even in the nursery, while he'd been fading in and out of consciousness, he caught sight of some ancient nursery rhyme books.

Empty eyes slid to him. "*You* happened, Shade."

"No," he replied curtly. "You were gone before I was here. You were gone the moment that cradle in your chambers started collecting dust. I was just a temporary distraction, a replacement for your affection, and you know it. So don't blame me for all this." He surveyed the murder at their feet. "You've become heedlessly cruel."

Once, in the early days of their relationship, his words would have evoked a rage so blinding that Maebh would have crushed the closest guard's windpipe or fucked Shade in front of him as punishment until he couldn't walk. But she never went to these extremes. Now, he could barely rouse an insult from her. The only thing sparking any kind of life in her eyes were the severed heads on the floor.

She returned to gaze across the sea, to her creature flapping and flickering closer.

Shade walked his fingers to his thigh wound and started digging for the bullet. The pain was unimaginable. He'd partly healed and had to reopen the wound. His vision tried to close in agony, but he made himself focus on the black shape flying closer. *Think of Silver.* She needed him. The sooner he removed the bullets, the sooner he could shift and heal.

If he kept talking, Maebh might not notice his work.

"You wanted a legacy to be proud of," he reminded her. "But it won't be glory or industry like you'd hoped. It won't even be how your Sluagh turned the tide of the first war against the humans. It will be this—" He nodded down at the heads, using the action to hide his wince as the bullet evaded his fingers. "It will be madness and fear."

She ignored him and remained facing the sea. Shade checked over his shoulder. The guards had retreated and stood somewhere inside by the entrance to her chambers. Good. He tried again for the bullet.

"And what is the purpose of this new legacy?" he asked. "Who are you handing it to? A broken people who couldn't care less about you. They're only in your army because they're afraid of the alternative." He paused for effect. "It's not too late for you to find meaning," he said, his thigh screaming as he plunged a finger inside. "To make new kin worthy of your crown."

*Success.* He dug out the bullet and clenched it in his fist. Maebh whipped around and snarled at him, her fangs flashing, her braids swishing. His heartbeat sped up.

"Make new kin," she blurted, eyes raging. "Who would want to lie with me now?"

Confused, he looked for the fault she so dramatically proclaimed, but only found her stained fingers and lips. What had made them turn black? They almost reminded Shade of the way Silver's gift decayed living things. A dark thought whispered in the back of his mind... was this the source of Maebh's madness? Her dipping into the inky side of the Well? Or had she been ingesting manabeeze like Nero had?

Nevertheless, he said with as much calm as he could muster, "You look perfect. As you always have."

She studied him a moment, and then her glamor dropped. No longer was she the young female with rosy brown skin, but an old lady. Wrinkles sagged her jowls. Age spots colored her cheeks. Her eyes were almost colorless.

"Who would lie with me now?" she repeated, her expression darkening.

He gaped at her shocking appearance. He'd known Maebh for decades—centuries—and she'd always looked the same. "What happened?"

"This was the sacrifice I made," she snarled. "I gave everything to create my new legacy. I even gave up my precious Sluagh." She sneered. "Apart from the traitors who joined the Order, they're all gone, and those left won't be long for this world without a queen to hold them together. Soon, my pet will be the most powerful fae in this land. He has no limits, and he answers only to me. If I die, he will be unleashed on this world with no master."

"Maebh—"

"My queen!" she reminded.

"My queen, this desire of yours to rule Elphyne is consuming you. Perhaps it's time for you to stand down," Shade suggested. He may as well go all in. "You fought for Elphyne for millennia. Let someone else take over. Don't let this senseless war take the last you have to give."

"Who would take over? You?" She laughed at his flinch. "No. Once I thought you were worthy of being my consort, but my *amaro*, you are not fit to rule. The people wouldn't have you, anyway. You have too much compassion, just as your Guardian king has. You won't do what needs to be done to save your people. The Unseelie know this. The Seelie know this. They might not like me, but they understand I'm vital for their survival. Elphyne is all I have left. It is *mine* to reclaim under one queendom."

"The humans want us to kill each other off so they can swoop in and take everything you've built. Don't give them what they want."

"They won't defeat my pet."

Her pride was devastating. She was using up every ounce of compassion left in his heart, and he knew he should just forget about saving her. She was probably past redemption. But a part of him hated the way this was ending for her. Did he owe her anything? She'd given him decades of entertainment and affection. Some of it good, some bad, but for a time, they'd almost become their own family unit. Then he remembered she'd taken Aravela from him and all compassion evaporated.

The demogorgon screeched as it flew over. With a sickening wet thud, another severed head hit the terrace. Shade didn't want to look. What if it was someone he knew? What if that was why Maebh had him dragged out there?

"Who have you brought for me this time, my precious?" Maebh's dress trailed through the old blood and dust as she went to collect the head. "Ooh. A Spring Court dignitary. At least—" She trailed her finger over the insignia on the collar still miraculously attached to its neck. "I think it's Spring Court. That could also be an Autumn leaf. Hard to tell with all the blood. What do you think?"

"Maebh," Shade growled. "Why am I here?"

Serious eyes met his. "You're going to witness the fall of everything you've loved. And then your head will join these. I'll put them on my wall as trophies. Won't that be grand? You will finally have a purpose—to serve as a reminder of my failings."

"This is your way of torturing me." He wanted to dig the bullet out of his shoulder, but it would be harder to go unnoticed. "This is your way of punishing me for leaving."

"If I wanted to punish you, I'd kill your mate before your eyes." She giggled maniacally. "I suppose I did ask my pet to kill her, but he brought you instead."

"My mate isn't easy to kill, unlike Aravela. I'll never forgive you for what your beast did to her."

She said nothing after that. Shade's eyes narrowed and for long moments he thought of nothing but driving his hand through her chest and pulling out her beating heart. Then he glanced through the doors into her chambers and glimpsed an oil painting she'd taken out of storage. It was a portrait of her and her baby. He must be stupid, because his vengeance melted a little. Or maybe it was the fact that he now knew the potential for loss. First Aravela, and then the sight of Silver in danger. If his cadre hurt her, he would find a way to kill them all himself. Severed heads would be the least of the destruction.

He shifted his eyes back to Maebh. There was a heart still beating in her chest. It had survived millennia. Perhaps the way out of this was to convince her to surrender. Failing that, he would end her.

His mind drifted back to his mate, to the bond he still shared with her. The metal might have cut his access to the Well, but the marks were still active on his arm, waiting for that connection to strike again. That meant Silver was alive. He clung to that knowledge.

The queen's pet scrambled on the slippery obsidian terrace. It ambled to her and bowed in reverence. Shade couldn't believe she'd sacrificed so much to create a single monster. For that act alone, there should be consequences. She'd blatantly used contraband, and she'd admitted to perverting the nature of the Well for her own gain. The only reason she hadn't been forced to atone for her crimes was that she was stronger than the Order.

The Prime knew it. It was probably why she had allowed members of the Cadre of Twelve—like Shade—to deviate and claim their Well-blessed mates. So far, all of them had returned to the Order and brought with them powerful women. In Violet, they'd gained a weapon against the previously undefeatable Sluagh. But what use was that advantage now? Maebh had just admitted to killing them all in order to create the demogorgon. The only remaining Sluagh in Elphyne, the Six, were already working with the Order. They were notoriously recluse, and now Shade knew why. Maebh said they were dying without her to hold them together.

Every time the Order came up with a weapon to use against her, she'd found a way to come out on top. It was almost as if Maebh, like the Void, had been one step ahead of the Order.

"MAEBH," a male voice boomed from deep in the queen's chambers, hunting her.

Tentacle wings flung up to cover Maebh from attack. Jasper—the Seelie High King—strode out of her chambers and onto the terrace, looking like fury personified. Laurel, Thorne's Well-blessed mate, followed him. The king's Well-blessed marks glimmered through his fine linen shirt as he tugged the hem of his sun-embroidered tunic. No glass crown on his dark hair. The ex-Guardian's fur-tipped ears angled backward in a sign of aggression. No weapons or armor, but there was no mistaking he was ready for battle.

Flames danced up Laurel's arms, licking the cap shoulders of her black shirt, but somehow not burning them. Leather straps crisscrossed over her front. On her bottom half, she wore pants made for conflict—reinforced leather and strapped with weapons.

Laurel would have chosen their outfits for a purpose. She was the king's and the Order's brand ambassador, a role she'd claimed was common in her time. Shade still had trouble understanding what she did. Jasper's outfit was unassuming—a king without a crown, willing to parlay. Hers was a show of strength, a reminder to accept the parlay, or there would be consequences.

Jasper must have portaled them in.

At the sounds of intruders, guards came running. Laurel twisted, her short black bob fanned out, and she released the flames gathered around her wrists. Fire shot from her fingers like dragon's breath, igniting the guards where they stood. They ran about the room, arms flailing. Eventually, their cries died, and they fell to the floor. Their queen did nothing to help.

Probably because she couldn't, Shade realized. She'd sacrificed her ability to carry mana for the demogorgon. She was conserving every ounce she had left.

"Come to surrender so soon?" Maebh stepped out from behind the shelter of her beast, her youthful glamor intact once again.

"Brave words for a dead queen walking," Jasper snarled.

"You won't kill me." She wore her smug expression like second nature. "You can't."

Gold flashed in Jasper's eyes. "You have no idea what I'm capable of."

"What you're capable of has nothing to do with it." Maebh scratched her pet under the chin. "You can't kill me, because then you'll unleash this beautiful creature into the world without a master."

"I'll kill it first."

Maebh's lips curved wickedly. "I'd like to see you try."

While they went tit for tat, Shade dug his fingers into the wound at his shoulder, not even hiding his pain or movements. This might be his only chance.

"Maebh..." Jasper's voice softened, incredulous. "Are you really doing this? Are you waging war against half the fae people?" He gestured at the demogorgon. "All I need to do is portal inside that beast with metal, and then I'll do the same to each one of your Sluagh."

"Can't," she giggled, her hand covered her lips in a parody of modest remorse. "My pet ate all the Sluagh. How else did you think he gained the ability to eat souls, only, you see, there's one difference. My precious doesn't just take the essence. He eats the heart too. That's where the good stuff is, isn't it my darling?"

It cooed as she tickled and scratched it beneath the scales until its left leg thumped like a dog.

"You fed your Sluagh to it?" Jasper's eyes widened.

She waved him off. "Since the Six broke the hive, they were dying anyway."

Jasper shook his head, shocked. He glared at the demogorgon and tensed.

"She's telling the truth," Shade announced. He yanked the last bullet from his flesh. The glory of the Well rush back into him like a tsunami. To temper his reaction, he tossed the slug at the beast. They all watched as its flesh pulled apart to make way for the tiny lump of lead, allowing it to sail right through and bounce off the painting of Maebh with her baby.

Jasper's wide eyes turned to Shade. "There has to be a way to kill it."

"There is." Shade shifted his wings out, stretched them, and then shifted them away to heal. He rolled his shoulders, feeling the new flesh was strong. "And we'll find out what it is. My mate's gift can hurt it, can't it Maebh?"

She flinched as Shade's wings disappeared. Each weighed each other in a silent battle of wills. Maebh's dark eyes tried to hide her fear, but he saw it in there. He knew her tells. She didn't know Silver's gift had hurt the beast. Shade couldn't decide if that was a good thing or bad, because if she had no idea, then the beast had healed fast.

But why she was afraid, he couldn't understand. She'd beaten Shade. Treated him like trash. He studied the bloody tiles, thinking hard, wondering. If anyone could decipher Maebh, it was him. She'd kept him here, but she'd not done any of the torturing herself. And, when he really thought about it, she could have done worse to him.

His gaze snapped back to hers. Was she afraid he'd leave her? Was she afraid of being alone, just as he'd been? Was that her true weakness?

Shade tensed with the sudden realization that he felt the presence of his mate down their bond getting stronger. She must be here in Aconite City, perhaps even in the palace.

Maebh whispered something to her pet, it spread its wings and took off. Within two flaps of those tentacled wings, it flickered out of existence just like the way a Sluagh could move. *Crimson, save him.* That's how it had moved so fast to hunt Shade. It had all the power of a Sluagh, but without the weakness of the sun.

Now they couldn't kill her unless they wanted to unleash

unprecedented destruction on the land—at least until they managed to hunt the thing down.

The self-satisfied smile on her face made Shade's stomach churn. Jasper's jaw clenched, and he pointed at her as he, too, came to the same conclusion.

"This is far from over, Maebh. You'll have your war. In fact—here's my first move."

Jasper took hold of Laurel's arm and portaled them out.

Maebh's brows lifted in mock surprise. "His move is to run away with his tail between his legs? Can't say I expected anything else from a cowardly mutt."

Jasper returned with two people. Shade's heart lurched in his chest as Silver came into being. She smiled tentatively at Shade before her eyes tracked all over his body, assessing for injury. He wanted to shout at her to leave, for Jasper to take her away to safety, but the king only gave Maebh a mock salute and disappeared.

Next to Silver, decked out in Guardian gear, Cloud's hands hovered over knives strapped to his legs. With his wings shifted away, and reckless danger in his eyes, he was ready for battle. It was a shift in the current of air, a lick of lightning before the storm.

Shade paused a little too long to return Silver's assessment. The sounds of boots jogging, leather shifting, and weapons drawing filled the room as soldiers entered under Demeter's command. The captain of her royal guard glared at Shade, as if he was the source of the world's problems.

"Maebh," Cloud greeted casually as he circled her. "Long time."

She narrowed her eyes, but said nothing in return. Instead, she turned her cold stare to the one person in the room Shade would lay down his life for. In a blink, he was by her side, his ribbons of shadow still settling as he stood before her, shielding her from Maebh's coiled wrath.

Cloud inched closer to Shade and Silver and whispered something. His words rocked Shade to the core. He had to ask Cloud to repeat himself, and even then, he was frozen solid with the implications.

"Are you sure?" he asked Cloud.

Irritation swam over Cloud's features. "Did I stutter?"

"Kill them," Maebh ordered her soldiers.

Each guard looked nervous. They knew who they had in their midst. Two Guardians and a woman leaking a power they'd likely never seen before. Silver flourished her hand and then pointed at the closest guard. Her darkness shot out. The moment it hit him, she called her stream back to her chest.

Shade gaped at her, not even caring that a guard was falling to pieces behind him, writhing in agony as he decayed into crumbling ash.

"Darling, you did it." Shade stared into his love's eyes with awe.

Soldiers around them swore and cursed, shuffling back, afraid. Even Cloud stood back warily, conceding the floor to Silver.

Silver tried to stifle her grin, but he felt the pride through their connection. They had much to talk about.

"What are you doing?" Maebh screamed at her guards. She pointed at Shade and Silver. "Attack them. Attack!"

Silver's expression hardened, and she allowed her darkness to bloom. She focused on the queen, who stood back, her eyes wide. Maebh stumbled over a head and almost fell. Her weakness only gave Silver the ammunition to intensify her gift.

As bittersweet as it made him feel, Maebh deserved to die for the destruction she'd caused. The lives she'd taken. The fae she'd hurt, including him. He used to believe power was all one needed in this world, and he'd been wrong. Being with Silver taught him that. And she was here, alive and healthy. They would have a life together. Maebh had no one.

"Wait," he said, even though it physically hurt to do.

Silver gasped and cut off her darkness. She looked at him with a question in her eyes... so Cloud hadn't told her? He glanced at the queen, then to Cloud, wondering why the news he'd come here to bring was for Shade's ears only. The atmosphere was a string pulled taut on a bow, ready to either snap or shoot. Silver frowned at him, waiting for explanation before she unleashed her gift. Cloud had given Shade the power to decide which way this could go.

Why? What game was he playing, because Shade had never believed Cloud was altruistic. But this was the only solution Shade could think of that didn't end in fae kind killing each other. Cloud knew it, and he didn't want to claim responsibility.

So be it.

"You can't kill her," Shade explained to Silver. "It will unleash the demogorgon without a master. But..." He met Maebh's dark eyes. "There's something you should know before we leave."

Shade deliberately went to the fallen oil painting and looked at the child depicted in a young Maebh's arms. He touched the child's face. As if sensing what his words might be, Maebh pushed around her guards, her eyes wide and agonized.

"No," she gasped. "This is a trick."

She clutched at Shade's shoulders, begging him with her eyes not to hurt her. Silver stepped forward. And he loved her for it, but he silently prayed she'd halt. She took one look into Shade's eyes and knew something was going on, so stepped back.

"Everyone knows the story of how you lost your baby, Maebh," he started. "Most think she died. But a few of us know that wasn't the case. You handed her to the humans as a changeling, hoping that one day she would grow and remember who she was, and she would dismantle the city from within. But that wasn't what happened, was it?"

"Shut up," Maebh cried. "Shut your ugly face up."

"You talk about your sacrifices, but you keep the true cost hidden from so many."

"I said shut up!" The defiance ebbed from her voice. She clung to him in agony. Her legs buckled, but he held her up.

"For your grievous crimes, I should keep this information, but I don't want my legacy to be like yours. I want this pain to end."

She whimpered and whispered, "Don't say it."

"Maebh, you misunderstand. Cloud has brought good news, not bad."

His words triggered a torrent of tears. Maebh's face crumpled. "No," she whispered. "You lie."

A few hundred years ago, a little mischievous crow shifter decided to scale the high walls of the human city. He'd never planned on being captured. Everyone thought he had died until one day he returned to Elphyne, missing his feathers and scarred all over. He jumped in the ceremonial lake, vowing to himself to do anything to make himself stronger, to never be weak again. He emerged as the Guardian standing beside Shade. Those tattoos not only enhanced his power, but hid the dark terrible things done to him in the name of humanity's survival.

Demeter snapped out of his stupor. He stormed over, sword held high, "Harm my queen, and I'll—"

Maebh stopped him with a glare. She gathered herself and stood unhindered. "Let him speak."

"Your legacy is alive," Shade said to Maebh. "And she's living in Crystal City."

Maebh's chin trembled, and she swallowed hard. The look she gave Shade cut his soul deep. It begged, *Don't break what's left of my heart. There will be nothing left.* It spoke to the sentimental trust they used to share. That was why Cloud gave the news to Shade to deliver. For this to work, Maebh needed to believe it.

Shade took Maebh's chin in a way that made his chest contract. So familiar, this pose, but so different now. He held her still, so they locked eyes. If what Shade said next didn't move her, then there was no hope of saving Maebh. They would kill her monster, and then her, but there would be blood shed among the fae, and then the humans won. He hated to think it, but the demogorgon was the only defense against the machines Silver said were coming to destroy Elphyne.

"Call off your pet," Shade demanded. "Agree to only use it in defense of the fae people, and not against them. Call off your war, and we will tell you who she is. We will bring her back to you. And when we do, you must step down from your queendom, Maebh. You must pay for your crimes against the Well. For your people, for your legacy. It's time."

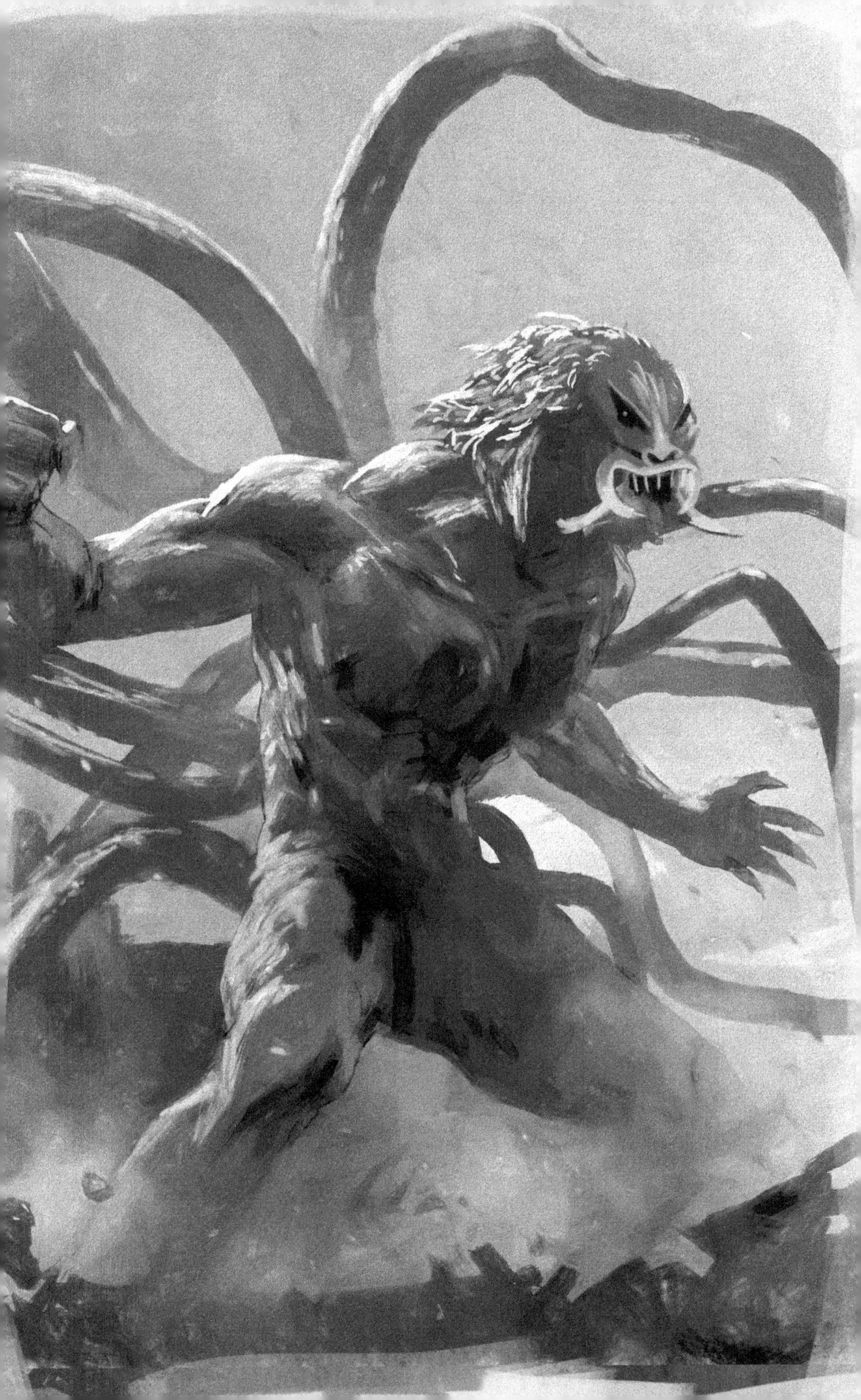

# CHAPTER
# THIRTY-NINE

Forrest leaned forward in the old velvet armchair sitting at the end of Aeron's bed. His knee bounced beneath his elbow as he watched the third set of healers pack up and leave the room. The last healer was an elf from Delphinium City. They were meant to be the best. Her flowing pants billowed as she walked. Her belt of glass tinctures and elixirs tinkled, taking with her the crushed hopes of Aeron's full recovery.

She gave Forrest a pitiful look before rubbing her fist over her heart in a clockwise motion and left the Guardian's dim room. Aeron lay on the bed, facing away from Forrest, staring out the window, looking at the pink-leafed tree behind the cadre's house move with the wind. For all intents and purposes, he was as strong and healthy as he had been before the battle with the demogorgon. His long brown hair was washed and brushed by the healers. His linen tunic and buckskin breeches were clean. He looked ready to head out to the markets to procure his latest curiosity. But Aeron hadn't moved since he'd been brought here after the demogorgon had screamed in his face, bursting his eardrums.

Apart from the healers, Forrest was the only one allowed into the room.

He put his hand on Aeron's shoulder. The elf jolted, then turned with a scowl. Forrest made the hand sign for an apology. He didn't mean to startle. He should have walked into Aeron's view first to catch his attention.

"They're back from the council meeting," Forrest said. "Silver and Shade are also back. I'm going to head downstairs. Do you want to come?"

Aeron's scowl deepened as his eyes dipped to Forrest's moving lips. Exasperated, he gestured to his ears and shrugged before lying back down and staring out the window.

Forrest felt useless. He searched the Guardian's pristine room. Unlike the others, Aeron's was filled with books, gadgets, and manabee-related inventions. He'd always filled his time away from missions with scholarly pursuits. The elf was relentless with his study and self-improvement. There wasn't a fae Forrest knew who had more knowledge locked away in his head than Aeron did, and yet, he couldn't help himself.

That was probably what hurt the most.

The evidence of passion unrelated to a Guardian wore on Forrest. Aeron was only at the Order because he'd followed Forrest out of misplaced loyalty.

Forrest's birthright was being the Autumn Court tribute to the Well, and Aeron's was being an Autumn King's bastard. They were half-brothers and longtime friends. Forrest was seven when Aeron's mother dumped him on the steps of the court, claiming the king was responsible for his welfare. Aeron had been three. Unable to deny the connection in a public forum, the king took in Aeron as his ward, but made sure the mother paid for her humiliation. He executed her.

After that, the king did his best to forget Aeron, but the rest of his legitimate heirs did not. They teased, beat, and bullied Aeron for his mother having the gumption to claim blooded status. As an unwanted child himself, Forrest shielded him from as much animosity as he could. The two grew close, and they grew up together.

When the time came for Forrest to be sacrificed to the Well Worms in the ceremonial lake, no one expected him to survive. No one from the Autumn Court family had ever survived. That's why they'd come up with the system to sacrifice one purposefully born child, so they never had to worry about fulfilling that responsibility again.

They filtered all the riches, learning, and opportunities into the first six born children, but the seventh, Forrest, was trained in nothing. He'd been invisible.

Forrest didn't die when jumping into the ceremonial lake. And neither did Aeron when he followed Forrest. They both emerged as Guardians—the first in the history of the Autumn Court royal family.

And now Aeron was deaf.

Guilt stabbed Forrest. He pushed through it and found paper and ink. He scrawled his message and then stepped in front of Aeron to show him. Reluctantly, the elf read. It changed nothing. He'd lost interest in Order issues. Every healer had said to give him time, that his hearing might never come back, but there was a small chance it would. He had hope.

Forrest worried about Aeron's state of mind.

If he didn't find a way to carry on, he'd be demoted from the Cadre of Twelve, and Forrest knew Aeron. Being in the Cadre, along with Forrest, was all he cared about in life. None of these gadgets or books fulfilled him. They distracted him.

"I'm going, then," Forrest mumbled.

He touched his half-brother on the leg as he rounded the bed and made his way downstairs to where most of the Twelve and their mates had collected in the crowded living room. Some Guardians were notably absent. Ash and River, the crow shifters weren't there, but at quick glance, the rest were. No Prime. Half the gathered looked poised to give Cloud a piece of their mind about helping Silver escape. Even covered in grime and blood, Shade cut an imposing figure next to his equally proud mate and steered the conversation toward a plan to extract Willow.

Forrest was late. He almost wished he'd brought his sword. Tension was thick and palpable between Rush and Shade, who'd just returned with Silver and Cloud. Forrest took up position nearby Leaf, who glanced at Forrest with a noticeably concerned face. But apart from that, he gave away nothing as to what had transpired at the council meeting. Leaf folded his arms and allowed Shade to take the floor, which was a miracle.

*This should be interesting.*

"We've brokered a peace with Maebh for the time being," Shade announced. He held up his hand to halt the questions already firing from mouths. "We did this through intel Cloud and Silver provided about a particular female within the human ranks we've now identified as Maebh's granddaughter. And before you all tell me it's impossible because of the time difference, we've seen evidence that their leader, Nero, has used mana to stay young. Somehow, Maebh's granddaughter has also retained her youth. Cloud recognized her as the female who took Willow."

"Cloud hasn't been in the human city for over a century," Rush barked.

"It's her," Cloud shot back, his eyes burning coals of hate. "I'd stake my life on it."

"Your memory is foggy," Rush returned. "I've been to that city, too."

"I know that bitch's face like the back of my hand." The hate in Cloud's eyes flared, as if this female was the source.

"What does this mean?" Rush asked. "If that's her, then will she help us get Willow?"

Leaf replied, "It means that for now, Maebh is calling off her war."

"And Maebh just gets away with everything she's done?" Forrest couldn't help asking.

"She'll get away with nothing," Shade replied. "When we retrieve Willow, we will also retrieve Maebh's granddaughter. And when this happens, Maebh will abdicate and hand herself over to face punishment for her crimes against the Well. By putting this caveat in place for her conditional surrender, we've ensured the Prime will allocate resources to help us with our mission into Crystal City to extract the child."

*Clever*, Forrest thought. Shade had managed to solve their resource issue by involving the queen and the Order at once.

Leather uniforms creaked as bodies shifted in the room.

Murmurs rose as Guardians voiced their concerns. But Leaf stepped forward, hushing everyone.

"I feel this is the right time to let you all know there will be another issue occupying Guardian time for the foreseeable future." He stepped forward and sent a glare to Shade as a reminder who was boss, before sweeping his glance around the room, ensuring each of his team paid attention. The dramatics made Forrest straighten with foreboding. Leaf continued, "It's clear now that Maebh drew too much from the inky side of the Well to create her monster. As a result, the poison has infected the usable portion of the Well. We've already had reported incidents where mana isn't acting the same as it should. The Prime and I have been investigating this and working on purifying the source. But this infection has never happened before. This is new for us."

Grim looks passed around. The Well was infected?

"What are you saying?" Caraway scratched his head.

"I'm saying that if we can't separate the taint from the Well, then it may not be safe to use. Your spell casting will be unpredictable."

"Forever?" Forrest asked.

Leaf didn't respond, but his lips set in a firm line.

"And what about Jasper?" Cloud asked.

"What about him?"

Cloud glanced at Shade. "While we were there, he declared war against the queen who'd sent her pet to kill Seelie high fae. As far as he's concerned, they're at war."

Shade rubbed his chin. "I'm sure we can work on him."

Thorne shook his head. "I don't know if we can. Laurel said he's obsessed with protecting his newborn and mate."

Rush stood up. His aura sucked the air out of the room and all voices hushed. His voice was deep and gravelly as he brought the subject back to his interest. "What about mine? What's the plan to get Willow back?"

He looked directly at Silver, and to her credit, she didn't balk. She stepped forward and looked the wolf in the eye.

"I'm going to do everything I can to help."

"They don't want you back, traitorous human," Rush replied. "We all heard her say that. So how are you going to help?"

Shade hissed at Rush's insult to his mate. "Be careful, wolf. Your mate wasn't exactly squeaky clean when she came here. Give mine a chance."

"We've come up with a plan," Silver continued, unaffected by Rush's imposing personality.

Forrest's opinion of her went up a notch, and he couldn't help wondering what kind of mate he'd end up with. A strong woman, a broken one, or a soft one with a sense of humor? He'd never fancied himself with a partner—being the royal family's invisible son had that effect. And then when he joined the Order, matings were frowned upon. He'd saved himself some trouble and just stayed away from females altogether. He wasn't even sure he'd know what to do if a mate did turn up, as Clarke had predicted. Realizing he'd drifted, he tuned back into Silver's talk.

"... and I know all the secret entrances in and out of the city. I know places Rory and Nero don't know. They lived in Sky Tower, insulated from the worst of the hunger and desperation, but I lived among the people. I know what they want, and it's not more war or death. We thought war would bring us prosperity, and we were brainwashed into believing you were the enemy. Those that haven't bought into the hype just want to live. I'm going to smuggle supplies and resources in, and in return, I'll gain their trust. Eventually, we will be able to send in soldiers disguised as humans to track Willow and Rory down and then extract them through the secret entrances I've located."

Rush snorted. "How are you going to disguise fae? Glamor won't hold in there. We've all got distinguishing features and tattoos or markings that can't be covered. And as Leaf pointed out, we can't draw from the inky side of the Well to cast a curse to make someone invisible. *Crimson*, there can't be drawing from the Well at all." He glanced around at the mated females and pointed to their glowing arms. "Mated females and males are out." He pointed at Haze and Cloud. "Those tattoos are too obvious. They're out."

"We can go anyway," Thorn growled. "We can cover up."

Clarke's eyes flashed white, and she stepped forward. "I don't think you can."

"She's right," Silver confirmed. "Covering up is a last resort. They complete nude body checks upon first time entry into the city. If I can't get you through the tunnels, then we prepare a team to go in through the front. They'll need to look as human as possible to pass the checks."

"We've considered who should go," Shade said. "There are only three Guardians who fit the requirements. Leaf, Ash, and Forrest have no tattoos and no mating bond."

Forrest jolted at his name, but then slowly understood. He had no tattoos, and apart from his teardrop and ears, he looked relatively human. Leaf immediately said he couldn't go, citing the mess with the Well as his responsibility. Rush flung accusations about cowardice at him. Arguments erupted.

"Peaches and I passed as mutilated fae," Violet said loudly, interrupting them. "There's no reason why fae can't pass as human if we cut ears or identifying fae features and heal them. Ash will be easy to disguise, but Forrest will have to change."

Unbidden, Forrest's fingers went to his pointed ears. They wanted him to cut them off. He wasn't vain by any means, but it was the only feature that distinguished him as fae. Cutting his ears would be like removing his identity.

"What about the Guardian Well mark beneath the eye?" he asked. That was the most obvious of all.

Shade answered, "We think it can be cut out too. If not, an eye patch could work."

"What about sending soldiers who aren't Guardian?" Caraway suggested.

"No," Rush replied. "This is my daughter we're talking about. I refuse to lose Willow for decades like I lost Thorne."

Silver took her mate's hand, and together they faced Rush and Clarke. "Asking for forgiveness is not what you need, but I'll ask, anyway. I'm deeply sorry for the pain I've caused through my actions, and I'm going to prove to you that I can be trusted. I promise we'll get your daughter back in one piece, healthy and just as vibrant as she was the day I met her."

Rush said nothing, but Clarke walked over to the woman, and they stood face to face. Silver had just announced in a very public space that she owed this family a debt. It was within Rush's and Clarke's right to claim it in any way they saw fit.

"Nero is a very bad man," Clarke said, a frown marring her brow. "I can't see into the future where he is directly related. He steals my vision like a black hole absorbs the light. But I'm here, looking into your eyes, appealing to you, woman to woman. Willow is our life. Please don't make promises you don't intend to keep."

Silver's gray eyes held Clarke's. "I'm going to use every weapon in my arsenal to bring her back. I won't stop trying until she's back with you."

"I'll be right there with her," Shade promised.

One by one, every Guardian in the room stood up and offered their help. It brought tears to Clarke's eyes.

Forrest stepped forward and said, "I'll go. You can cut my ears and my Guardian mark. Whatever you need, I'll do it."

Clarke ran into his arms and hugged him. She blubbered something into his chest. Forrest smiled awkwardly and hovered his hands above her head, not knowing what to do with it. Should he stroke her hair or pat her like a fee-lion? Females always made him nervous. Give him a kuturi or a horse, and he could tell you what it was thinking. But a woman?

"There's another reason I think I should go," he added quietly.

Not many people knew about Aeron and Forrest's familial relationship, but it would allow them to communicate through water.

"My connection with Aeron will allow us to communicate if I can find somewhere in there to access the Well," he said more loudly, finally voicing his relationship to the elf.

If Aeron was here, he'd hate it. He was an elf who loved his privacy, but Forrest wanted assurances Aeron would be looked after while he was gone.

Silver's eyes lit up with recognition. "I think there is a spot. It's a small garden in the center of the city. Nero has adhered to the fae rules to keep it protected and vibrant. The garden is locked, so only a select few can access it, but Rory is one of them. Now that I know she has fae blood, it makes sense he's kept it."

"That's probably how she remained young all these years," Cloud added.

Silence descended as everyone ruminated over their conversations and plans. Rush stood up suddenly, his face hard and staunch as he looked at Silver. "I won't have you staying here. I don't care what you've promised. Even if we get Willow back, I'll never forgive you for the trauma you've brought on this family."

Shade looked at Clarke. She went to her mate and slipped an arm around him, but she said nothing. His gaze circled the room. "Is this how everyone feels?"

Thorne was the only one who voiced his agreement to Rush's proclamation, but apart from the vampires and their mates, who voiced their support for Silver and Shade, no one else said a word. Including Forrest. He didn't know how he felt.

Shade slid his arm around his mate. "I go where she goes. We'll base our operations out of Rush's cabin. It's closer to the human city. Anyone wishing to join us can meet us there tomorrow at dawn. There's no time to waste, and we'll begin plans then."

Shadow wrapped around the couple, but before they stepped through them and left, Shade turned to Cloud and said, "You're wrong."

"No, I'm not," Cloud answered abruptly. Then frowned. "About what?"

Shade glanced at Silver before locking eyes again with Cloud. "You know what."

And then they were gone.

Cloud swiped a vase off a table, cursed loudly as it broke, and then stormed outside.

Everyone else started leaving, too. Feeling a headache coming on, an affliction that had followed him since his youth, Forrest returned to Aeron's room to let him know what was happening. He had the feeling this was only the beginning of the end, but for whom, he wasn't sure.

Maybe everyone.

# CHAPTER FORTY

Silver stepped out of Shade's shadows and into the log cabin by the lake. Before she had a chance to speak, he pushed her against the wall and slammed his lips against hers. Stunned, it took her a full three seconds before she kissed back. It was long, hard, and full of everything she'd needed over the past days without him. He gave her confidence, connection, and a pledge of the heart.

Since Jasper had taken them to Maebh's, they'd been surrounded by people. This was their first private moment after days apart, and her feelings were no less dulled.

"You didn't abandon me," he murmured, voice croaking.

"Never," she returned. She speared fingers into his hair and clenched tight, pulling until his pupils dilated. "You defended me. You—"

Her words died in her throat. Shade had given up living at the Order to be with her. Everything he'd loved had been there. Those soulful eyes softened on her, making her feel better than a queen. And she was, she realized. To him, she was better than anything. He'd stood before Maebh, and still he had her back. There was never a doubt when she was there of what the two of them shared.

"Darling," he said, trailing his touch along her jaw. "You are my world. I will follow you anywhere, even into Crystal City." He swallowed. "Don't think you'll be going in there without me."

"But you'll be powerless," she gasped. "You'll have to cut your ears and under your eye, and—"

He silenced her with a kiss so hot it melted her insides.

When she'd arrived in the queen's chambers and saw the blood on him, she was ready to unleash every dark and violent part of herself. She knew Shade would survive her black heart, and in that moment, when she'd thought the demogorgon would take her love away from her, she was okay with everyone suffering too. If it meant she'd save him, she would poison the world. Did that make her a villain? She rubbed her hand over his chest, suddenly needing to feel the heat of his skin, to make sure he was whole and healthy.

He watched her attentively as she unbuttoned his torn and battered jacket.

"Are you sure you're okay?" she asked with a frown, exploring his warm skin.

"I should be asking you that."

"I'm fine. They kept me in a cage and—never mind."

Shadows filled the room. He held his breath. Paused. "*What* did they do?"

The softness in his eyes dissipated. Silver slid his jacket down his shoulders and used it to hold his arms before he disappeared and wreaked vengeance on those that hurt her. She shouldn't enjoy seeing that fire in his eyes, but it made her feel strangely grounded. No one else put that look in his eyes, but her. If she was a villain for his love, then he was one back.

Perhaps the Well was right to give her a dark, poisonous gift. A part of her would always be cold and merciless and sometimes cowardly. She could accept that now, because the Well had also given her Shade. And he showed her there was a part of her that was warm, giving, and brave. It was okay to be both.

"I'm fine, Shade. It was nothing I didn't deserve."

Her words only incensed him further, and he started disrobing her and casting his own obsessive inspection. "Who laid a hand on you?"

"No one," she insisted.

"Was it Rush?"

"Shade... let it go."

"Thorne? The Prime? What happened to put that pain in your eyes?"

She ground her teeth, knowing he wouldn't let this go unless she confessed.

"They left me for a few days in a dirty cell. They also left the bullets in my body so I couldn't call on the Well. But then they healed me and brought me food. I'm surprised Rush didn't tear my throat out the moment we appeared at the Order tonight, but I think they know Clarke was right. They need me. They need us. And I wasn't lying when I said I was sorry for my part. I meant it."

The vampire warrior looked back at her, but there was no one home. Shade's mind had gone to a dark and terrible place where revenge and violence lived.

"Shade," she whispered, and ran her finger along his jaw. "I'm fine. You're fine. We're together and we have a plan."

He searched her face. "It means a lot to you to do this, doesn't it?"

She nodded. "To bring Willow home, and to bring humanity some kind of relief. I used to think fighting for Nero was the way, but now I see I'm the right person to start a resistance. At the very least, I want to smuggle in food and medicine. I want to give those people a chance at a life."

"I believe you can do it. You might be the only person who can."

She hoped so. She gave him a small smile. His thumb brushed her lip. His next kiss was soft and loving. But soon, their passion became hard, dueling tongues, and hands exploring bodies, tugging closer and removing clothes. He was down to his breeches before he started on her corset, but then stopped. His expression darkened. He met her eyes with a challenge. "Who gave you this corset, my little fee-lion?"

"Cloud found it for me. I needed it when you were gone to help me contain—"

"*Cloud* gave you a gift?" Darkness flashed in his expression. "That replaced my gift?"

"I asked for it." She scowled right back at him. "And it didn't replace your gift. He couldn't exactly shadow walk himself here to collect it, though, could he? He had to find me a new one."

"And would you like it if another female gave me a gift that smelled of her?" His lashes lowered to shroud smoldering eyes. "And I wore it all over my body?"

Revulsion pulsed through Silver so sharply, she had to force herself to exhale. She shook her head. "No. I would *not* like it. I barely contained myself when you took the queen's jaw in your fingers."

She shuddered.

"So, take it off," he demanded. "And if I ever see you in a corset not from me, I'll—"

"Spank me?" she teased with a wink. There was nothing she liked doing more than riling this vampire up.

"Careful, darling, I bite." He gnashed his fangs and reached for her.

"Promise?"

Their humor died, and his gaze steadied when he asked, "What did Cloud ask for in return?"

She glanced away. "Nothing."

"Silver, look me in the eye and say that."

But she couldn't. She shook her head.

"Tell me," he demanded.

"I owe him a favor."

When Shade didn't reply, Silver looked up to see death in his eyes.

"I'll kill him," he said calmly, his eyes darting to and fro as he made plans in his head. "I'll come upon him while he's asleep and kill him."

"If it wasn't for Cloud, you'd probably be dead. And Maebh's pet will still be killing fae, and we'd have no help infiltrating Crystal City to save Willow and the others." She touched his cheek gently. "Even if he did none of that, which was never part of the deal, I'd still have agreed to the favor because I'll burn the world to ash if it brought us together. If that makes me a villain, then I don't give a fuck."

Shade growled, "It makes you *mine*."

Before she could take another breath, Shade's mouth was in the crook of her neck. Razor sharp fangs followed, and then heat and sex scorched into her veins. Her knees buckled. He caught her with a strong hand at her waist and another behind her head. He fed from her ravenously, breathing hard through his nose, raging against her skin with his need. Once, she would have been afraid of this. But now, she saw what this loss of control meant—trust.

She trusted him to care for her, and he trusted that she knew that.

Silver gave herself over to the sensations. It was more than feeling needed. It was safety. It was trust. It was the thrill of an unknown future together.

Feeling drowsy and completely aroused, she whimpered and tugged at the opening in his pants. She didn't care if he was dirty. The male sweat and filth only made her more attracted to him. Her skin was on fire. She ached to feel him inside her, every last manly inch.

He carried her to the bed and dropped her on her back, then ripped the corset laces with his fangs. With an impatient growl beneath his breath, he yanked the ruined leather from her body and tossed it into the fire. The sprites squeaked, but he paid them no attention. He was too busy removing her top and drawing her nipple into his mouth, coaxing new cries and pleas from her.

"Shade," she begged, tugging at his hair. "Slow down."

"You don't get to decide that," he growled around her breast. "All I thought about was you while I was gone. And this. This is mine, and I'll take it however I want."

Oh, God. Why did that make her wetter? Shade yanked her

pants down and spread her legs. His mouth landed between her thighs, his tongue inside her, his fingers following. He made indulgent sounds as he feasted, murmuring into her sex that it belonged to him too. He licked and nipped her sensitive bud until sensation exploded. Fireworks burst in her vision as she came, pulsing against his relentless tongue.

Gasping at the ceiling covered in leaves, she pulled him up her body by the hair, yanking roughly, showing him that she had every right to make demands as well. She wrapped her legs around his hips as he pulled his heavy erection free from his pants. He fit himself to her core and slid in. They both whimpered at the joining. They made love with an urgency that defied logic, hard and rampant thrusts, knocking the bed against the wall.

When the position wasn't enough for Shade, he pulled her up, flipped her over, and lifted her to her hands and knees before entering her from behind. He pistoned into her like a machine, keeping pace until he wrapped his hand around her braid, brought her head back and kissed her fiercely. With a grunt and stutter, he pulled out and slid his cock between her bottom cheeks. He pumped twice and then came over her back.

Silver collapsed face first onto the bed, only vaguely aware of Shade's ragged breaths disappearing for a moment before he returned. As he cleaned her with a cool, wet cloth, he promised her they would to do that again, multiple times overnight. They had lost time to make up for.

Despite the fervor in his words, they both slumped lazily on the bed. His histamines were running their course through her blood, and her blood was doing the same to him. He drunkenly slung his hand over her back and traced patterns down her spine.

A deep, self-satisfied feeling fell over Silver. She'd never felt so content in her life, so at home and welcome, and it didn't make sense. The world was still burning around them.

"Do you think my plan will work?" she mumbled through her haze. "Do you think we have what it takes to make a difference?"

*To find Willow?*

Shade was quiet for a long time. He twirled the end of her long braid around his fingers. She startled when he eventually spoke.

"War isn't pretty, Silver. But I suspect you know that. It's dirty. It's stabbing your friends in the back while they sleep. It's senseless and stubborn and it's coming for us from multiple directions."

"I don't want to fight friends anymore," she sighed.

"For your plan to work, you'll have to. But you'll make new friends too. I can promise you that. Fae understand loyalty. They value family more."

"Will Forrest turn up tomorrow?"

"If he doesn't, Rush will find a way to get into the city, be damned with the risk."

"It won't come to that."

"I know."

"How?"

"Because I know you. You don't give up on people you care about."

She rested her head against her mate's chest, listened to the lullaby of his heart near hers. Finding solutions to her problems wouldn't be easy, and it wouldn't be quick, but if they had each other's backs, then they'd find a way to make it work.

As her eyelids drifted closed, she caught sight of the plant in the corner of the cabin, still with Shade's shadow halting the effects of her dark gift. He'd once said she might be able to reverse her curse. Without thinking, she reached out and, with all the peace and contentment he gave her, she called her chaos back.

Slowly, inch by inch, her black heart returned to its home, and she smiled.

"What did you do?" Shade whispered. "How did you learn to control your gift?"

"You," she said and patted his chest.

"Because I taught you?"

"You said that to bring it back to me, I had to learn to love myself, for all my twisted darkness. And, Shade, knowing you love me, and knowing I feel the same about you... it makes everything right in the world, no matter the chaotic reality."

He tugged her close and slurred something sweet into her ear before relaxing. As she drifted asleep herself, she returned her gaze to the plant, now with a second chance at life despite its decayed parts.

And she smiled.

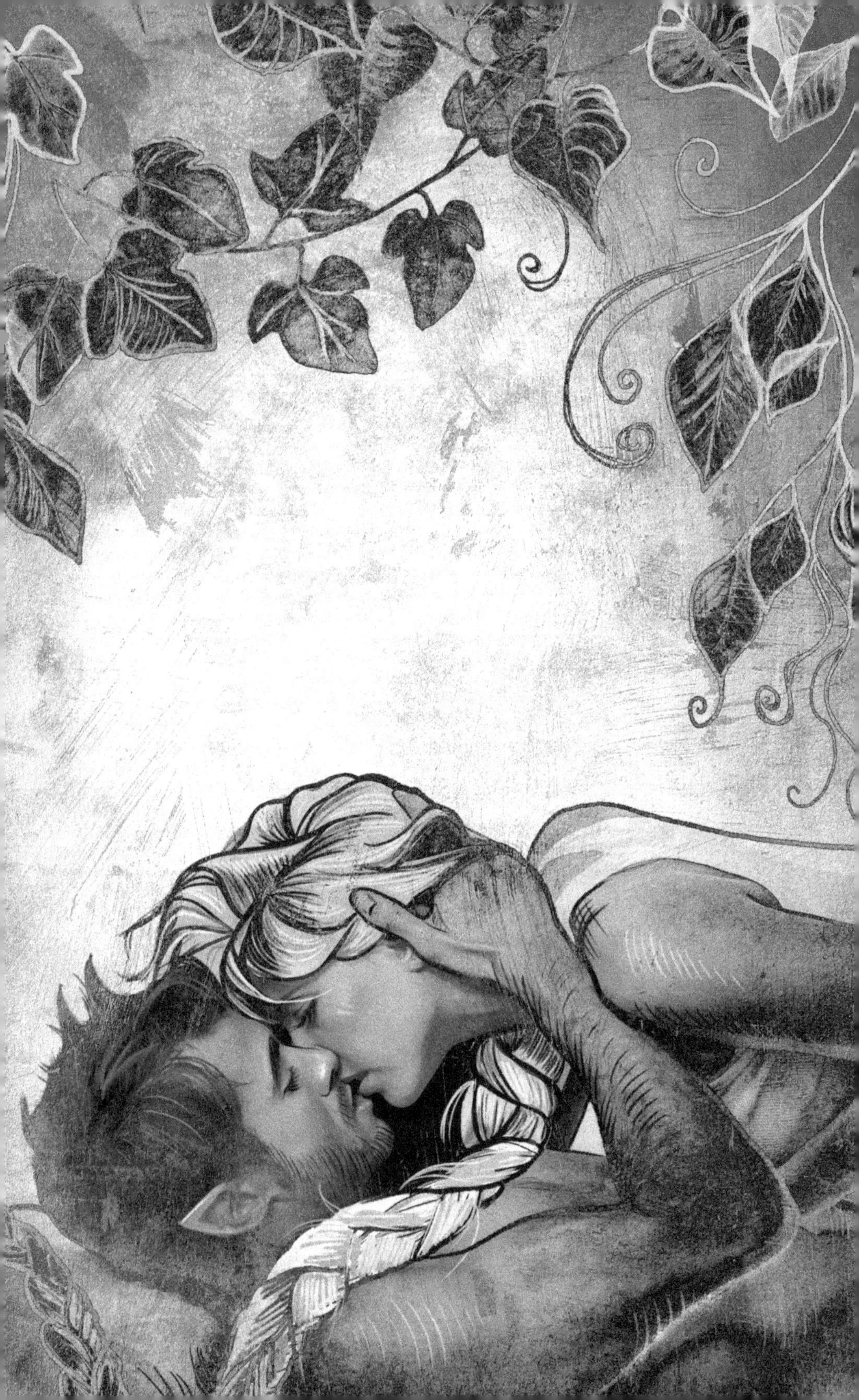

# EPILOGUE

Rory stormed into her father's greenhouse, and right up to his tinkering table, where he inspected maps through magnifying glasses. The whimpering white haired fae girl trailed behind her, one hand on Rory's belt loop, refusing to let go. She kept calling Rory aunty, and for the life of her, she couldn't refuse.

"Well?" she said to her father. "Aren't we going to do something? Silver has betrayed us. We should launch our campaign now before she gives away all our secrets."

She couldn't understand why this treachery hurt so much. It wasn't like she and Silver braided each other's hair and had sleepovers. They trained. They killed. They fought side by side.

"She probably already has." Unconcerned, Nero didn't even lift his eyes from his maps. "Besides, we don't interrupt our enemy when they're in the process of destroying themselves. We continue with our plans." He finally lifted his black gaze to stare at the child, and Rory couldn't help but step across to block his view. Nero straightened and hardened his tone. "We continue with our plans, Rory. Especially now that they are falling into place."

**The End.**

Of the Season of the Vampire... but more is yet to come.

*Next up is Season of the Elf.*

**Never miss a sale, giveaway, or book news.**
*Subscribe.LanaPecherczyk.com*

# Need to talk to other readers?

Join Lana's Angels Facebook Group for fun chats, giveaways, and exclusive content. https://www.facebook.com/groups/lanasangels

# ALSO BY LANA PECHERCZYK

**The Deadly Seven**

*(Paranormal/Sci-Fi Romance)*

The Deadly Seven Box Set Books 1-3

Sinner

Envy

Greed

Wrath

Sloth

Gluttony

Lust

Pride

Despair

**Fae Guardians**

*(Fantasy/Paranormal Romance)*

Season of the Wolf Trilogy

The Longing of Lone Wolves

The Solace of Sharp Claws

Of Kisses & Wishes Novella (free for subscribers)

The Dreams of Broken Kings

Season of the Vampire Trilogy

The Secrets in Shadow and Blood

A Labyrinth of Fangs and Thorns

A Symphony of Savage Hearts

**Game of Gods**

*(Romantic Urban Fantasy )*

Soul Thing

The Devil Inside

Playing God

Game Over

Game of Gods Box Set

# ABOUT THE AUTHOR

**OMG! How do you say my name?**

**Lana** (straight forward enough - Lah-nah) **Pecherczyk** (this is where it gets tricky - Pe-her-chick).

I've been called Lana Price-Check, Lana Pera-Chickywack, Lana Pressed-Chicken, Lana Pech...*that girl!* You name it, they said it. So if it's so hard to spell, why on earth would I use this name instead of an easy pen name?

To put it simply, it belonged to my mother. And she was my dream champion.

For most of my life, I've been good at one thing – art. The world around me saw my work, and said I should do more of it, so I did.

But, when at the age of eight, I said I wanted to write stories, and even though we were poor, my mother came home with a blank notebook and a pencil saying I should follow my dreams, no matter where they take me for they will make me happy. I wasn't very good at it, but it didn't matter because I had her support and I liked it.

She died when I was thirteen, and left her four daughters orphaned. Suddenly, I had lost my dream champion, I was split from my youngest two sisters and had no one to talk to about the challenge of life.

So, I wrote in secret. I poured my heart out daily to a diary and sometimes imagined that she would listen. At the end of the day, even if she couldn't hear, writing kept that dream alive.

Eventually, after having my own children (two firecrackers in the guise of little boys) and ignoring my inner voice for too long, I decided to lead by example. How could I teach my children to follow their dreams if I wasn't? I became my own dream champion and the rest is history, here I am.

When I'm not writing the next great action-packed romantic novel, or wrangling the rug rats, or rescuing GI Joe from the jaws of my Kelpie, I fight evil by moonlight, win love by daylight and never run from a real fight.

I live in Australia, but I'm up for a chat anytime online. Come and find me.

*Subscribe & Follow*

subscribe.lanapecherczyk.com

lp@lanapecherczyk.com

- facebook.com/lanapecherczykauthor
- instagram.com/lana_p_author
- amazon.com/-/e/B00V2TP0HG
- bookbub.com/profile/lana-pecherczyk
- tiktok.com/@lanapauthor
- goodreads.com/lana_p_author